I0761744

THE BLACKSMITH OF DACHAU

ELAINE HUME PEAKE

DON KEITH

Severn River Publishing
www.SevernRiverBooks.com

ISBN: 978-1-64875-666-5 (Paperback)

ALSO BY THE AUTHORS

A Call to War Series

The Kaboom Boys

The Blacksmith of Dachau

Goodnight from Berlin

Also by Don Keith

The Hunter Killer Series

The Tides of War Series

To find out more about the authors and their books, visit

severnriverbooks.com

From Elaine:

For Michelle Perotte Desrues, aka Hélène LeRiche — a true friend to my father, Captain Edward Hume, during six weeks in the summer of 1944, and then with me eighty years later. You will never be forgotten for your insatiable curiosity, contagious laugh, loving words, and authentic wisdom. In your 100th year, your loving family and friends lost you, but your memory lives on. I will never forget your disgust over the world's many injustices, inhumanity, and the world's senseless conflicts. You overcame more than you should have ever faced, surviving with a positive attitude, infectious smile, and wonderful heart. Thank you for the vivid memories of my father during a heartbreaking time. I hope we captured what he knew: your robust spirit, powerful courage, the quest for knowledge, and the inspiring choices you were forced to make, resulting in a fully lived life. You defined a generation of brave young people across France and around the world during WWII when resilience was the only path forward.

World War II will not truly be over for at least another three hundred years. An estimated ten percent of Axis and Allied bombs that were dropped during that conflict did not explode. Many will not become inert until well into the twenty-fourth century. Such devices are regularly discovered today across Asia, Oceania, North Africa, the United Kingdom and continental Europe. Rendering them safe often requires uprooting residents and disrupting travel and commerce.

Though the war officially ended in 1945, anyone injured or killed by such unexploded ordnance officially becomes a casualty of World War II.

Under a spreading chestnut-tree
The village smithy stands;
The smith, a mighty man is he,
With large and sinewy hands,
And the muscles of his brawny arms
Are strong as iron bands.

His hair is crisp, and black, and long;
His face is like the tan;
His brow is wet with honest sweat,
He earns whate'er he can,
And looks the whole world in the face,
For he owes not any man.

From "The Village Blacksmith" by Henry Wadsworth Longfellow

"I didn't write. I just wandered about. I followed the war wherever I could reach it."

—WWII journalist Martha Gellhorn

PROLOGUE

Cigarette smoke encircles her head like a wispy tiara as she furiously types away. Then, frustrated, she stops mid-sentence, drops what remains of the cigarette from her lips onto the marble floor, and ferociously grinds out the butt with a bare heel.

"Why bother?" she asks herself as she abruptly stands and walks over to the hotel room window. She slips through the blackout curtains onto the little balcony and gazes down on the darkened streets of Naples. Arms crossed, she tosses her blonde curls and answers her own question in a whisper. "Because I'm either blessed or cursed to have to report what I see of this damn war. That's why."

Cursed or blessed. Maybe both.

She hopes she can persevere, but her firsthand account of the biggest story of World War II so far, the massive Allied landing on the beaches of Normandy, has been edited down to a single page and buried deeply in the D-Day edition of Collier's *magazine. This while her husband's article on the assault is featured on the cover of the same publication with the bold words* Voyage to Victory by Ernest Hemingway.

Now, in the still, chill Italian night, she hears distant rattling of machine gun fire and the almost continuous buzzing of feisty Spitfire sorties as they depart from the newly established Royal Air Force base at nearby Capodichino. War, she knows, is a pot of stirred stew made up of many powerful human stories. And she sees it as her mission to share generous portions with readers. She lights another cigarette as she steps back through the curtain. There, on the desk, is the July 22, 1944, issue of Collier's.

She pauses to read for the umpteenth time some of her sparse bit of surviving prose:

"Everyone was violently busy on that crowded, dangerous shore. The pebbles were the size of apples and feet deep, and we stumbled up a road that a huge road shovel was scooping out. We walked with the utmost care between the narrowly placed white tape lines that marked the mine-cleared path and headed for a tent marked with a red cross. Everyone agreed that the beach was a stinker, and that it would be a great pleasure to get the hell out of here sometime. Whatever life might be it could not take away death."

She flips to Ernest's article and reads aloud the prologue, attempting to imitate her famous spouse's blustery cadence:

"Real war is never like paper war, nor do accounts of it read much like the way it looks. But if you want to know how it was in an LCV(P) on D-Day when we took Fox Green beach and Easy Red beach on the sixth of June 1944, then this is as near as I can come to it."

She drops the magazine on the floor. Martha Gellhorn is not jealous of her husband.

At least not jealous of his fame or his brilliant way of describing things in the minimal number of words necessary. After all, once the editors named him Collier's *lead war correspondent—with Ernest claiming Gellhorn's credentials and assignment in the process—it was she who arranged for him to fly comfortably from Cuba to Britain, traveling with other journalists. There was even a movie star or two aboard the plane. She ultimately had to make the trip on a Norwegian freighter with cargo that consisted mostly of dynamite.*

No, she is simply frustrated that she and the few other female war reporters have been denied press credentials—merely for the crime of being female—to cover history's greatest military invasion. So, as usual, she took matters into her own hands. She stowed away on a hospital ship the evening of June 5, 1944, hiding in a lavatory for the whole transit. Then she waded ashore, interviewing soldiers, medics, and nurses while she helped carry stretchers, tended to the horribly wounded, and ducked German bullets and shells. That made her the only female journalist to cover in person the D-Day landing.

Also on the hotel room desk, next to the typewriter, is an overseas telegram from her editor, urging her to consider finding a safe route to Paris upon the city's imminent liberation. He knows she has now been denied correspondent credentials by the US military as punishment for her subterfuge on the Channel crossing. Yet he is confident she will find a way. The City of Lights may well be under Allied control by the end of August, a timeframe both Eisenhower and Patton are pushing. They know the symbolic and strategic value of the city's liberation, including the message it sends to Herr Hitler.

But Collier's *readers will want to know if any of the Parisian culture and charm, its fashion and cuisine, have survived Nazi occupation. A female perspective is required. And the missive pointedly mentions that Ernest will be there, too, arriving along with and as part of the liberation forces, French and American. As if that bit of news might offer additional incentive to her to find her way there.*

She takes a deep draw on the cigarette, steps to the bedside table, and flicks on the radio. Music might bolster her mood. But as she twists the dial, she finds instead a familiar, rabid voice, overriding the static and the screeching heterodynes of competing signals.

Der Führer. *Hitler.*

"Shit!" she spits. "The bastard's still alive." Sources have shared with her the rumors of another assassination attempt on Hitler. She has been actively scouring for confirmation. Such a thing could abruptly end the war in Europe without requiring the deaths and suffering of so many more.

She knows enough German to discern the madman's message: "The great cause which I serve will be brought through its present perils and...everything can be brought to a good end."

As she angrily reaches to switch off the radio, another voice spills from the speaker. A smooth tone, speaking in unaccented English.

"And with those hopeful and encouraging words from our Fuehrer, *we end tonight's broadcast schedule. Good night from Berlin!"*

She drops the cigarette from her lips onto the marble floor, looks at it for a moment, and then grinds it out with her bare, calloused heel.

There will be so many more stories to tell. Tales of seemingly ordinary people caught in extraordinary situations who do remarkable things, emerging fundamentally changed, whether for better or worse.

She renews her resolve to do what she believes she has been put on this planet to do regardless of the pushbacks and challenges.

"I have no intention of being a footnote in someone else's life," she tells herself.

No, she will continue to find and transcribe those stories as an eyewitness to the unleashed chaos of war. She will be a witness blessed with enough agility in the arrangement of words on a page to precisely and powerfully describe to others exactly what she sees.

♠

"Uh-oh!"

"Sir, 'uh-oh' isn't something a BD captain oughta be saying when neutering one of these bad boys. Should I start praying?"

"'Uh-oh' counts officially as my reaction, Corporal. Prayers are always appreciated but keep 'em silent, please."

"Sir, we ought not blow up any more of the countryside around here. The locals are mad at us already. Even if we did chase away them nasty Krauts for them."

"'Uh-oh' still applies."

The captain and his temporary right-hand man on one of the hottest days in late July 1944 would present an odd sight had someone else been watching them. Instead of kneeling as expected in a church, the commanding officer is lying on his back, most of his body beneath the credence table adjacent to the altar at the front of the Church of Notre-Dame de Saint-Lô. The corporal lies next to him, but on his stomach. After relentless Allied bombings and heavy ground combat, this house of worship is one of the very few structures still standing in this historic town in France's Normandy region. With most everything else around flattened, the main spire still reaches prayerfully skyward.

The table holds what appears to be undisturbed pewter chalices and containers for bread and the other necessities for Holy Communion. The Germans—or maybe even desperate locals or Allied liberators—have snatched up the original gold vessels used by priests here for centuries. Even so, the table setting could be a still-life painting with the glimmer of light shining through the cracked vaulted ceiling. Surviving stained glass windows reflect a kaleidoscope of color.

Only a sharp, well-trained eye would have noticed the hair-thin wire running from beneath one of the replacement wine cups, along a seam in the white tablecloth, and then disappearing behind the tabletop.

"'Uh-oh' because this evil bit of booby trap was specifically meant for you and me, Corporal."

It is the thirteenth explosive device they have found in the church so far. The others have already been rendered safe, their remnants now in a canvas bag lying next to them. Judging by their locations and triggering mechanisms, it is likely these were placed by the Germans to kill or maim anyone, especially Allied soldiers looking for souvenirs and specifically BD—bomb disposal—men.

"Or anyone who came in here to say a prayer, sir."

"That, too."

"What makes you think that somebody's going to that much trouble just to kill you and me?" Curious, the corporal, still on his belly, scoots farther beneath the table alongside his captain. He angles his camera to get photos of what must be some unusual aspect of this device. Their superiors will want precise details on such calculated evil.

"Notice that wire? It snakes up under the wine cup on the table and goes directly to the battery taped here. See it?" The captain speaks precisely and points so the corporal can get photos. "And that charge over there, attached to the table leg, would only be spotted by someone crazy like us and willing to crawl under here." Touching a wire, the captain is deciding whether to just pull the detonator out of the end of the main charge and walk off with it or keep cutting wires one at a time until he finds the main one that goes to the detonator. "Our orders are not to blow up this church any more than it already is. So, a careless BD guy could come along and clip that wire to the battery figuring he could safely grab the charge and be out of here for supper. He would end up prematurely shaking hands with St. Pete instead. If you look at that seam there in the wood, you'll see another wire from the charge." The captain needs to talk through everything. It helps him think more clearly. "I'd bet a dollar to a doughnut it goes to a second battery that's also part of the circuit."

"Crafty, sick fellows, those Nazis."

"That they are. Whoever rigged this might as well have put our names on it, they wanted so bad for you and me to find it. And right here where the body and blood of our Lord Jesus Christ is."

"Sons of bitches," the corporal mutters. "You know the word booby trap *comes from* bobo, *the Spanish word for* idiot *or better yet—"*

"Save it! You can give me the whole song and dance once we're in Berlin sitting around Hitler's gravestone, drinking schnapps, toasting his demise."

"Hell, Captain, at the rate we're going, we'll still be defuzing bombs here in Normandy 'til General Patton's president of the USA and—"

"Huh?" the captain abruptly interrupts.

"'Huh' is about as scary as 'uh-oh,' you know."

"You notice anything else odd under here?" The captain points toward the underside of the credence table. The corporal now sees it, too. Someone has scratched out some words there, probably using one of the calcified communion wafers—the Body of Christ—from the dish on the tabletop. A message intended for a US Army explosive ordnance demolition tech to see just before he clips the wrong wire to the explosive charge.

The captain aims his flashlight at the scribbling.

Bis zum bitteren ende, *it reads.*

"What's it say, sir? I can't quite see."

The captain shines his flashlight on the words. He knows just enough German to translate.

"It says, 'To the bitter end.'"

1

Except for a few distinctive markings, it would have been impossible to distinguish the two military vehicles from any of the hundred or so others stalled in the midday traffic jam in the narrow main street of Pontorson, France. They were mired amid the chaos of bellowing horns, the loud cursing from soldiers crammed into trucks like livestock on the way to slaughter, and the constant growl of military aircraft zooming above them, but low enough to kick up smothering clouds of dust from long-neglected fields. Dull-eyed refugees with their ox- and horse-drawn carts only added to the tangle.

It was a common scene throughout France's Normandy region since D-Day, June 6, 1944, and the massive Allied invasion. Traffic clogged not only main arteries but less-traveled country lanes as well, routes more accustomed to horse-drawn carriages and oxcarts but now clotted with heavy vehicles of war. They carried the insignias and flags of Great Britain, Canada, the United States and other nations as they strained to maintain momentum, intent on pushing Hitler's occupying army eastward. Or supplying the invaders with the necessities to continue shoving the enemy all the way back to Deutschland.

The odd pair of vehicles smack-dab in the middle of the parade, though, were a generic jeep and a Dodge "weapons hauler" three-quarter-ton truck. Both sported the US Army's usual dull green paint job, just like many of the others. However, these two vehicles' fenders were colored a bold red, and the white letters "BDS" appeared in various other spots on their bodies. These were the distinctive markings of vehicles assigned to the relatively new US Army Air Force's bomb demolition squads. They mimicked the paint scheme of their counterparts in Britain's Royal Air Force. There was one difference. In the lower corner of the passenger-side windshields of both these vehicles, there was a sign that identified them as belonging to "THE KABOOM BOYS."

The jeep's driver, Corporal Henry "Hank" Anderson, joined the orchestra of frustration, futilely depressing with the heel of his hand his own horn button at the center of the steering wheel, tapping out over and over and over the Morse code letters for "GO."

"Goddammit, it's been an hour already! Who's running this circus?" His wire-rimmed spectacles were fogged and his face reddened by stifling heat and peaking annoyance. But he only added to the din with no effect on anyone's progress on the quaint, narrow street through the twelfth-century burgh. There was not even room to turn around and look for an alternate route.

"Jesus, Hank! Give it a rest!" the captain sitting in the passenger seat next to him ordered. "If honking worked, we'd be to that UXB and have it castrated by now."

A "UXB" was an unexploded bomb. This one could be armed and ticking, nose down in the ground or inside a building somewhere, threatening to abruptly become an "XB," an "exploded bomb." And it was the squad's next mission to defuze it. (To emulate the Royal Air Force's way of doing bomb demolition, the Americans even used the Brits' spelling of "defuze" as opposed to "defuse.")

Captain Edward Hume removed his helmet and ran his fingers through his longer-than-regulation chestnut hair, then idly scratched the patch of stubble on his chin. He did not like noise. That was an odd quirk for someone who dealt most days with stuff that was created to make an abundance of it. He also despised not being able to move about freely. That was one of the few perks of being in a BD squad. He valued getting ahead of challenges, dealing with the lethal stuff his team was assigned before more of this beautiful bocage country was reduced to yet another pile of ugly rubble. Or before somebody else died when a bomb randomly exploded hours, days, or even weeks after having been dropped from the sky.

"Probably some farmer tipped over his oxcart and spilled a load of turnips," Anderson offered, guessing a possible cause for this gridlock. But Hume was now distracted by something else, a scene playing out at the street corner ahead. An animated discussion between a US Army soldier and a strikingly attractive young woman straddling a bicycle.

"Hey, I know that MP over there," Hume told Hank as he put his helmet back on and jumped from the jeep. "Maybe he can tell us what's going on and shoo us ahead." Edward cupped his hands and called back to the truck where the other four squad members sat, impatiently watching. "I'm trying to square-up this circle as quick as I can, guys!"

They waved a bored acknowledgment.

The military policeman was Captain Mickey Berg, a recent acquaintance of Hume's. They had met at an officers' club poker game at the headquarters near where they were now stalled. He was a good guy, Brooklyn as a bagel, and he was deeply involved in conversation with the pretty young lady. She looked to be near tears, eyes wide, trying to understand what this American soldier was asking her, not in French or English, but in broken German.

"Might've known you were the one puttin' a kink in the main drag!" Edward called out to the MP. Berg's head snapped around, his dark eyes intense and his hand hovering over the pistol holstered at his side. "Whoa, buddy!" Edward put up his hands as if to surrender. "Don't shoot!"

Mickey relaxed and his face broke into a sideways grin. "No sneaking up on me like that! Damn, I could've shot you, Hume!"

"I didn't mean to interrupt your interrogation. You got a Nazi spy here?"

"Not sure yet," Berg growled with a nod at the flustered young bicyclist. She did not appear to be a German spy at all. Nineteen or twenty, long, blonde hair tied back in a tattered blue, red and white scarf, she was dressed attractively enough considering what she had likely been through already in this war. Her brown cloth skirt and tan, homemade knitted sweater had clearly seen some wear and tear and needed considerable mending. Probably much like her young life.

"English, sir! Speak English, yes! I understand!" she pleaded, but with a strong French accent. "Then I will know what you are asking me, sir." She stamped her foot for emphasis. "German, I do not know. I refuse to know German!"

Hume studied her face curiously. Something besides her natural beauty struck him. Then it hit him. "I know you, don't I?"

"On the causeway from Mont Saint Michel last week," she answered with a nod and smile and in a rush of words. "My friend, Pierre Devereaux, and I. We, us. *Nous vous avons alors parlé. Non*, I mean, we spoke with you then. I thanked you for all that you and your men did for the village. *Le village du Mont Saint Michel.* You remember? For offering hope for so many. My name, I am Hélène LeRiche. My mother and I, we are...how you say? Refugees. From Cherbourg. A village near there. Équeurdreville. We now live here in Pontorson. My English, not good, but I study every day to be more like you Americans."

"That's it. I remember you." She would have been hard to forget, as would her heartfelt expression of appreciation that day for what Hume and his men had just accomplished at iconic Mont Saint Michel. Twelve bombs had been jettisoned into the waters near the island by US Army Air Forces on the way back from an aborted mission. A dozen problem UXBs the Kaboom Boys successfully detonated as Hume and his squad braved weather, maritime mines, quicksand, and the dangerous tidal waters that were poised to race back into the bay. Not to mention the lethal risk from the fickle bombs themselves. All of that to head off a major dust-up between the Free French and Eisenhower's Army. And in a place so very special to Edward Hume, a symbol since his boyhood of the adventurous, colorful life he craved beyond the coal mines and dreary winters of Mahanoy City in northeast Pennsylvania.

"Pierre and I, we watched you from the abbey as you dealt with *bombes*, courageously out there in the bay and—" She stopped. There were tears in her eyes.

"Please don't say any more," Hume told her. Berg looked at them, not sure what to make of all this. "That's all top secret, that mission. Never talk of it," Edward sternly instructed. Then he smiled and pointed to Mickey Berg. "Especially to this guy here."

"But it was you. I saw you. You, *Capitaine*, saved so many lives while risking yours. *C'était spectaculaire*!"

"That, my dear, is our job. But it'll remain our little secret, *oui*?"

Captain Berg was unsure why his friend Edward would keep anything from him. But this mysterious secret between him and the girl only made the MP more intrigued with her.

"Well, Hume, since you and 'Bicycle Girl' here are such fast friends, I suppose you'd like to vouch for her? Should I lock her up or let her go?"

Edward looked at Hélène sideways. She turned her head and gave him a glorious smile. It was as if the sun had suddenly broken through the high loft of clouds overhead.

"Nah, I don't think she's a spy at all. But I do have a question for you, Mickey. Can you tell me why we've been sitting here in a traffic jam for the past hour holding up the war while you harass this nice lady? Me and my boys got a pretty big appointment just up the road a bit and we need to get there."

"Yeah, well, here's the thing," Berg replied. "One of the 101st guys was gettin' himself a real personal thank-you from a grateful local gal last night when they realized they were screwin'—" Berg stopped, glanced at Hélène LeRiche, and blushed blood-red. She grinned at his obvious embarrassment. Both officers noticed how good the smile looked on her. "Uh, excuse my French," Berg said.

Edward laughed. Hélène giggled. "*Relations sexuelles*. I heard about this."

"Anyway, turns out they were doin' it up against an unexploded Luftwaffe bomb that had come down in the bushes next to the main road. A bunch of people will get hurt, and the main street'll be cut if that thing blows up now. So, that's why you and your gang of misfits are here, right?"

"No, no. Not at all," Edward responded sarcastically and with a dismissive wave of his hand. But he simultaneously nodded a "yes." "Wouldn't want our Nazi spy here to know what us BD boys are up to."

There was now a mock frown on Hélène's face. She winked at Berg.

"Let me see if we can route you around this mess, then," the MP offered. "And Miss Hélène LeRiche, you are free to go."

But the young woman had a sudden thought. "Please! I can help you.

See that alleyway?" She pointed down an even narrower street up ahead, between the Hotel Montgomery and a row of apartments. "You can get to the other side that way." She had another thought. "I would like to thank you by receiving you both for dinner."

Hume and Berg were surprised by the offer. "I don't know if that would be...way we work and all..." Edward said.

"It will be a typical French meal that my mother, Marcelline, and I will prepare at the home of our friends, the Devereaux family. My friend, Pierre Devereaux, you met that day on the causeway at Mont Saint Michel?" The two soldiers looked at each other. If they had time away from the war for poker, then surely they could accept a dinner invitation. "They live only a short distance from your headquarters. We will be chaperoned, so it will be okay, *oui*?"

Hume and Berg looked at one another again. Berg shrugged. "We got restrictions on fraternizing with the locals. But if we bring along Captain Lowe, we should be okay." Russell Lowe was a chaplain who also happened to be a deceptively ruthless poker player.

"Sure, and judging from his belly, he likes to eat, too," Edward agreed. "We'd have something besides K-rations or mess hall chow. And much prettier scenery."

"*Vendredi*...Friday, then? 6 Rue Couesnon. Chaperoned. All will be okay. *Au revoir*!"

She peddled away as both men jotted down the address in their leather-bound pocket notebooks and Hume marked it in the calendar he always carried. She was halfway up a sliver of a side lane when she stopped, turned, and waved a fetchingly girlish goodbye. They waved back. Edward noticed the look on the MP's face.

"You're married, right?" Edward bluntly asked Berg. Edward knew his friend well enough already to recognize that he was smitten with the young French woman. A married guy with a two-year-old son back home in Carroll Gardens, Brooklyn. "Married in the US, married in France, right?"

"Jeez, it's just dinner, Ed. With momma there. The chaplain. And half the neighborhood. Heavily chaperoned. I'm pretty darn sure nothing will happen, you know. And don't we Army guys need to build rapport with the locals after the hell they've been through?" Berg quickly changed the subject. "Wanna play some poker tonight? I'm off duty at 1800 hours."

Hume glanced at his watch. "This job'll keep us busy 'til dark. Longer than usual 'cause we'll have to try to defuze it, not just detonate it, so we don't lose the street and a bunch of houses."

"And some precious French souls, too, right?"

"No. First thing we'd do, unless the thing decides to blow up on its own schedule, which could happen if we don't get over there soon, is evacuate most of a square mile. Any MPs up there to help keep people back?"

"I'll radio ahead and let them know."

"Good. Nice to know people like you in high places."

"Glad to be of service." Berg began waving some of the vehicles to the side so Edward's squad could squeeze past and into the even tighter confines of the alley. That set off a renewed cascade of protests.

"But tell me, Ed, couldn't you let one of your guys do that job while you get rested up? I see you around here all the time, runnin' yourself ragged. It's gotta wear on a guy."

"Not an option. BD rule number one: Only the captain handles the defuzing phase of BD. That's thanks to our friends at the RAF who gave all of us on-the-job training. They set that peckin' order and about everything else us Americans do in bomb disposal."

"Must've trained you all real damn good. You're still in one piece."

"BD squads still have about a ten-week life expectancy. Ten weeks. We're beating the odds so far, but—"

A farmer with his ox and a cart was stuck crosswise of the roadway, stalling traffic. That forced Berg to maneuver into the middle of the road to direct a clog of jeeps, trucks and now, a mixed herd of cows and sheep lazily crossing the thoroughfare. He waved to Hank Anderson.

"You guys go now! Go! Go! Go!"

The red-fendered jeep lurched toward the shortcut the girl had shown them. Berg stopped blowing his whistle in short shrill spurts long enough to say, "Just remember, Eddie, old pal. You and me, we got us a dinner date with a fine-looking French gal that'll make us forget all this shit for a minute or two, right?"

"Got that!" Edward responded. "The French know how to cook and us sons of coalminers know how to eat."

As the jeep eased on past Mickey Berg, the MP's face grew serious. "Godspeed, Ed." He rapped the front red fender with his knuckles. "I mean that, pal. Godspeed."

"Not too sure even He would crawl in a hole with us and a UXB, but thanks for the good wishes!" Hume leaned out the side of the vehicle to look back and add, "Same to you, Mick! But watch out for them young, pretty German spies!"

That was something else Edward was learning. In war, it was difficult to know who to trust, and since spies came in all shapes and sizes, figuring this out could be the difference between life and death.

2

Józef Steiner knew well why he had survived his long imprisonment while so many of his fellow inmates had not. How he managed to wake up alive every day in a shared cell while others abruptly and permanently disappeared. Everywhere Steiner looked he saw impending or recent death: bone thin men and women with hollow eyes, searching each other for the lice that fed on their blood. The stench of rotting flesh everywhere. Maggots feasting on those who succumbed but whose bodies remained in their cells for days. Steiner vowed to avoid their fate but to never cross the line and become complicit with his captors in order to do so. He willed himself to live. It was his only way to rebel.

No, the reason he remained alive—or maintained some semblance of living—was because of his unique skills. The ones that made him valuable to the Nazis, attracting the attention of his SS jailers when he first arrived. He was barely eighteen years old when the Germans took Poland. Or rather, "Liberated Poland from the communists and trade unionists," according to the Nazis' justification to the rest of Europe and the world for their brutal invasion.

Józef Steiner was not political, only a lukewarm member of a Polish group that wanted to remain independent from Germany. He was out on his own already, a working blacksmith looking for other sources of income, accustomed to self-reliance after growing up in an orphanage run by German nuns. And despite being Jewish. The orphanage was where he learned to speak fluent German and even a bit of English along with his native Polish. His political activities were driven by passion, not for his country but for a young woman who had shown hints of interest in a relationship. Józef had long since forgotten her name, but she was the reason he attended enough group meetings to land his name on a list when the Germans came in September 1939. Being on that list earned him an eventual ride to the concentration camp at Dachau, near Munich, and a cot in a cramped cell with five others there for the crime of being Jewish. The place had been built on the site of a former munitions factory permanently made dormant by the Treaty of Versailles. That had ended the Great War, later dubbed World War I. That treaty severely limited Germany's military might. By its terms, the nation was supposed to never be allowed to build another munitions factory. Or a military force, for that matter. The camp was initially intended to intern Adolf Hitler's political opponents, as well as communists, social democrats, clergy, homosexuals, other so-called "dissidents," and anyone else the madman considered inferior, useless subhumans.

Being a Jew with a yellow star pinned to his prison uniform did not help Józef's situation, and he was certain his eventual fate matched that of so many others. That is, until his specialized talents caused his luck to abruptly change.

One of the SS guards learned Józef had been a blacksmith in Poland. A favorite horse belonging to the concentration camp commandant had a nasty hoof infection from a stone trapped beneath a shoe. Józef easily remedied the issue, but also noticed that a large, ornate clock in the stable vestibule was not working. He offered to fix it.

Steiner was confident in his ability to repair anything. It was a transferable skill he hoped he might trade upon in tough times in the camp, a way to survive, and potentially receive less harsh treatment in his quest to stay alive until his nightmare ended, one way or the other. He saw others who lost all hope and gave up, flinging themselves onto electrified wire fences. Or begged the SS guards to shoot them, to end their hell on earth. Or simply willed themselves to die. But Józef remained determined to live.

When he slept, his dreams both blessed and tormented him, not with the horrendous things he saw every day. Instead, they put him in a time and place in which he was free again, walking in a field of wildflowers, eating an apple, sometimes being with a woman, her face never fully detailed in his dreams, but with a calming breeze blowing, often near a cool-flowing river, far from the claustrophobic stench and perpetual death of Dachau. Then, when he woke up, his reality would be even more unbearable. But the dreams still gave him a reason to survive.

Before being rounded up and thrown into this abominable stockade, in addition to smithing, he had repaired clocks, radios, bicycles, automobiles, and anything else that ticked or moved mechanically. At the Catholic orphanage where he grew up, the caretaker took him under his wing and taught him the basics of plumbing, electrical wiring and carpentry. Later Józef decided to open his own mechanic shop and do less blacksmithing. He rented a basement space below the family-run restaurant in Poznan, three hours west of Warsaw, not far from the German border. He knew he could always fall back on farrier work if times got tough.

"*Schmied*, wake up!"

Schmied. "Blacksmith." This predawn ritual typically meant a day of hard labor. This morning, though, Józef was escorted by two heavily armed SS guards to a large building in a corner of the camp he had never before visited. There he noticed dozens of buildings labeled with signs declaring them to be scientific laboratories, most with closed doors. There were chained prisoners being forced into or dragged out of the structures.

Józef Steiner already knew what was going on here. There were multiple experiments underway. One of his cellmates had shared rumors of studies using humans as guinea pigs.

"They want to know how long a Luftwaffe pilot can survive when shot down over a body of cold water, like the North Sea on an approach to England," the prisoner whispered. He knew. He had been forced to assist in some of those tests.

"What exactly do they do?" asked Józef. He wanted to remember details so he might one day—should he be lucky enough to survive—testify to the atrocities that took place at Dachau.

"The doctor made me help put the prisoner in a large vat of sea water.

They forced him to stand there in frigid water to just below his chin. He screamed but nobody helped him. He died. They warned me if I told anyone else of this, I would be the next one into the vat."

Now, with a different itinerary for this morning, Steiner was certain he was being marched off to just such a terrible experiment. The guards shoved him through a door. At the end of a long dark corridor, a rifle butt nudged him into what appeared to be a workshop. Or maybe one of the interrogation rooms he had heard about.

There was a man there in a lab coat with what Steiner assumed was a permanent scowl on his pasty face. Józef soon learned the man was assistant director of the laboratory, Dr. Ernst Alwin. Truly one of Hitler's "mad scientists," men who delivered to the Führer more clever ways to kill people.

"So, this is the *schmied* I have heard so much about." Alwin dismissively looked him up and down. He paused briefly, considering the yellow Star of David badge on Steiner's filthy, striped prison uniform.

"Yes, sir," the lead guard confirmed. "He has been here since shortly after the camp opened. A quite helpful prisoner, in fact."

"I understand you are very clever with your hands," Alwin said. Józef did not respond. Alwin turned and took from a briefcase on his desk—an expensive-looking brown leather bag with a gold imprint of the initials E. A. on its top—a small device, maybe made of brass. He held it up between his thumb and index finger for Steiner to see. "What can you tell me about this?" He placed the device on the table and pushed it across to Steiner. "Take it!"

The guard jabbed the muzzle of his rifle into Józef's spine, between his bony shoulder blades. Steiner picked up the brass piece and studied it from all angles. It occurred to him then that this device might be his ticket to better treatment, to increase his chances of surviving hell. He glanced at a workbench that ran along the back wall and politely asked to borrow a screwdriver.

Alwin nodded. Józef picked up the tool, worked a bit, and pulled off the object's cover.

"Some type of switch. A condenser, I believe. If charged with alternating electrical currents, it would slowly discharge and activate a switch, closing or opening a circuit. Perhaps to turn on a delayed light or close a timed lock after a specified period." He placed the object back onto the table precisely where Alwin had slid it. "That is all I can determine without seeing it in use or inspecting anything that might normally be attached to it."

The German scientist stared at the prisoner for a tense, silent moment. Józef could hear cries and shouts of pain and misery coming from other rooms. Alwin seemed oblivious to it.

He reached into a desk drawer and pulled out a small hand mirror.

"Have you seen yourself lately, Herr Steiner?"

Before he could look away, Józef caught a glimpse of the pitiful image of his face in the mirror. His hair had once been long and black, as much a source of pride as the strong, sinewy muscles of his arms. Now the hair was mostly shaved away, the skin on his head and face scaly, and what little of his former mane that remained had gone gray. His arms were skinny and weak, the muscles diminished.

"I will speak with the commandant about you doing important work for this department," Alwin finally said. He snatched the metal device off the desktop and threw it back into his briefcase. "If you are as helpful as you appear to be capable, you will spend more time away from the camp. You will receive more and better food. We will allow you to grow your hair out. Fresh air and exercise will greatly improve your appearance, your health, your outlook on life, blacksmith. And you will be able to assist us in shortening this war and saving innocent lives."

Unlikely, Steiner thought. But his curiosity was piqued.

"At the same time, you can shorten your sentence considerably. We might be able to overlook your misguided politics and disloyalty to the Reich if your abilities can be put to such use." Even more unlikely, Steiner knew. Alwin picked up his briefcase and stepped to the door. The scowl still claimed his face. "You must not mention this department or your new duties to anyone, including other prisoners, or you will be removed from this mission and harshly punished. Do you agree to such a work assignment, *Schmied*?"

As if on cue another awful scream reverberated down the hallway. Józef Steiner knew he had no option. He simply nodded.

This was how he found himself at first assisting in manufacturing more reliable fuzes for Luftwaffe bombs, then soon clearing and detonating unexploded bombs and other devices. A Jew fixing a Nazi problem. In his first job, he soon figured out ways to sabotage the weapons to actually save some lives. And maybe, in his own little way, he would help end the insanity of this war.

He knew if he was caught sabotaging fuzes he would be thrown back into that ghastly cell and left to rot away. Or, more likely, hanged alive from a pole in front of his fellow prisoners as an example, then left there so the ravens could peck out his eyes. Even so, and though it increased the risk, he felt compelled to etch with a jeweler's drill a tiny Star of David on the metal rims of sabotaged devices. It was Józef Steiner's dangerously personal statement against Hitler, the Third Reich, and the Nazi Party.

But then Steiner was shifted into *bombenentschärfung*. Bomb disposal. Defuzing unexploded ordnance dropped from Allied bombers. That made him a part of the newly formed group that dubbed themselves the "Dachau One Hundred." The other ninety-nine prisoners were also ordered to perform the risky work, but with practically no training on how to make such devices safe. Few had the skills of Józef Steiner. Many died horribly. New prisoners would be promptly conscripted to take their places.

The "Blacksmith of Dachau," as the guards had named Steiner, soon came to a startling realization. Though he could no longer sabotage the fuzes of Luftwaffe bombs, he was now able to do good. Neutering unexploded bombs would save lives, not claim them. That gave him yet another reason to live, to exist.

Besides, Steiner now suspected something else was imminent. The war was not going well for Hitler. The guards were edgy. Some had even disappeared, deserted. Thousands of prisoners had been marched away, deeper into Germany, south to Austria. He overheard talk—some frightened, some hopeful—when he was working outside the gates. Could the Allies be coming? There was talk that there had been a major Allied invasion into France. Could they soon bring an end to the war and rescue all those walking skeletons inside the electrified, barbed-wire fences of Dachau? Or find the bodies in the mass graves providing fertilizer for the edelweiss the young girls gave to departing soldiers for good luck?

He prayed he was not being delusional, that his desperate hopes did not exceed reality.

Meantime, he also prayed that one of the live bombs on which he worked would not detonate in his face.

After all, if freedom was near, that was yet one more reason to do all he could to survive hell.

3

If only the clamor of horns and sirens would stop! The cacophony of the passing traffic was stunting Captain Edward Hume's concentration as he set to work on the menacing roadside UXB. Mickey Berg's MPs had kept all the hosed-up convoys, staff cars, and the locals' wagons and carts a good distance from where the German bomb was half-buried in dirt, lavender, rosemary, and boxwoods, but that just made everyone angrier and louder.

The Normandy bocage of thick hedges and bushes bordered a tangled network of sunken roads and small fields. And the cylindrical bomb was buried beneath dirt and four years of undergrowth. Edward recognized it at once, a 2,200-pound *Sprengbombe Cylindrisch 1000*. For some reason jettisoned by a Luftwaffe bomber pilot, maybe while returning from the "Blitz" or an aborted flight. The Blitzkrieg, or "lightning war," was the sustained aerial bombing attacks on British towns and cities carried out by the German Air Force from September 1940 until May 1941, so this relic had likely been here for a while.

That made it no less lethal.

Several locals wandered over to see what was going on. Edward learned from them that children from Pontorson had been playing on the above-ground part of the bomb carcass, using it as a fortress. That created great distress for their parents and annoyance for town leaders. They all knew the device could be dangerous, but the German occupiers seemed unconcerned. The SC 1000—nicknamed "*Die Hermann*" by German pilots after their portly commander, Hermann Göring—had come down next to the cobblestone main street, much too close to several residences where people had stubbornly continued to live. They had now been evacuated in case it exploded during the attempt by the Americans to finally make it safe.

"Okay, guys! Get your axes and hatchets. We gotta cut through this jungle," Edward ordered. The men groaned. It was grueling work hacking their way to the device in the late afternoon heat and humidity.

After clearing the bomb for Edward and Hank to work, the rest of the squad—four of them—found a nearby spot in an apple orchard where they quickly dug a deep hole. Then they sat waiting, smoking, talking, eating apples, and swatting swarming bees that craved the rotting fruit on the ground.

"I can't handle all these bees," Private Carl Kostas proclaimed. "I'm gonna go wait in the truck." There, he could not resist honking back at the drivers stuck in traffic, shouting suggestions for an alternative route out of the mess. Another way to Avranches. To Mont Saint Michel. To Saint Malo. To Hell.

Then came the corker.

"Jesus," Captain Hume whispered as a drop of sweat slid down his nose and dripped onto the steel-cased weapon three inches from his face. "Get this on your film, quick, then put the roll in the canister and walk it to the jeep. Put it in my satchel, and hurry back. We wanna be sure our guys have a photo in case this thing..." The captain's voice trailed off tellingly.

Hank Anderson grunted. He had only been Hume's temporary number two for three weeks. Only since the death of his fellow squad member and good friend Sergeant Ace Taft, who was killed in the explosion of an ammo dump near a field hospital at Saint-Lô. The men had complained to the captain that they sorely needed a replacement for Ace with all the work they needed to do. Hank was a good alternative, but Edward knew he needed a BD man trained at APG—the Army Air Forces Ordnance Demolition School back at Aberdeen Proving Ground, Maryland—someone who could possibly become a squad captain. When pressed by the men, Edward explained he had been writing headquarters, pleading for help, but with no promises made.

"Captain, just tell me you know what you're looking at and exactly how to fix it," Anderson pleaded in reaction to Hume's whispered, "Jesus."

Both soldiers were on their bellies in the muddy hole the squad had shoveled out around the bomb. The sun had now sunk below the horizon, back toward the sea and the Channel Islands. Hume and Anderson had to use their flashlights to try to figure out what they were looking at and how to deal with it.

This weapon, which had landed nose first, was nine feet tall and more than two feet in diameter. It was painted a cheery sky blue with a yellow stripe around its tail cone. The bomb jutted up above ground but was still mostly hidden from the lane by the hedgerow. There it had been resting until it brought an abrupt end to the copulating couple's tryst and somebody up the command structure saw the need to fix it. It could be mostly safe already, not really a risk to explode since it had not done so on impact or since. It could also be waiting for a jostle or tug to blow. Or some version of an anti-tamper fuze could be lurking, set to activate if bothered.

"I've not seen one exactly like this," Edward admitted. "These used to only come with impact fuzes and could be set to detonate immediately. Or, at most, wait about twenty seconds after hitting the ground or a ship. They use these SC 1000s a lot to attack ships. They wanted them to blow quick. Now we're starting to see these anti-tamper mercury switches. I'd say our friends in the lab in Dachau are getting more creative. And damn deadly, the sons of bitches."

There had been many notes sent down from Colonel Thomas Kane—the "Father" of unexploded-ordnance disposal—and his APG staff about a cadre of the Third Reich's top scientists working in their lab near the German town of Dachau. Major General Henry Sayler, Eisenhower's Chief Ordnance Officer for the European Theater, had sent similar intel that made it down to the squad level. They described a facility full of men whose mission it was to find more innovative ways to blow things up and kill people. And now, there was new emphasis by the Germans on slaughtering those who were charged with safely cleaning up UXBs and UXOs, unexploded bombs and undischarged ordnance. Men like Edward Hume and his Kaboom Boys.

"Deadly and downright wordy," Anderson added, nodding toward a spot at which he now aimed his flashlight beam. There were some German words scrawled and scratched into the bomb's steel carcass. They had spotted the same phrase a few days before beneath a communion table in a church not far away while clearing booby traps. "But I gotta say, not very original."

"*Bis zum bitteren ende.*"

Those four simple words. Sadist Adolf Hitler used the phrase to command a fight to the death in the name of the Reich, a continued butchery, if necessary, to keep the Allied invaders from reclaiming Paris. From marching on to the Rhine River and then crossing into the Fatherland. And to do so no matter the cost. A few years before, Hitler vowed to bring back Germany's wealth, end civil strife, communism and socialism, halt strikes and demonstrations, eliminate Jewish financiers, and make Deutschland again a world power.

"To the bitter end."

"Those damn Krauts are obedient unto death. I just gotta figure out how best to keep this steel bastard from causing you and me to have a bitter end, Hank."

"Trust your training, Captain. That's what Colonel Kane told you, right?"

Intense field exercises at Aberdeen Proving Grounds under the colonel himself followed by on-the-job instruction with the Royal Air Force in Great Britain. It was there, since war was declared on September 3, 1939, the Brits had developed the art and science of bomb demolition on the fly and out of desperate necessity. But the German scientists were just as dedicated in developing new means of dispensing instant death, whether for French citizens, passing Allied troop convoys, or BD technicians.

"If they really want to turn us into blood-red vapor, they will," Hume quietly said as he studied what he could see of the earlier German bomb's fuse mechanism. Edward's job had recently become an even more lethal game of chess.

"Captain, did I ever tell you how much I miss being back home in

Denver at Perkin's Service Station, giving rich women oil changes, if you know what I mean—"

"Damn," whispered Hume, not really listening to Anderson, fully focused on figuring out the wires leading to the fuze.

"Okay, I'll hush." The rest of that story would have to wait for another time. Hank leaned in as closely as he could and, with his ever-present Leica camera, snapped a couple of photos of the hole in the bomb's skin where the fuze assembly was located.

"Double damn! God, these guys are clever," the captain murmured, squinting to better see the fuze. "Oh, wow! I heard about this deal here. You remember our RAF friend, Captain Duncan Smythe, don't you?" Edward stretched and leaned in closer to the detonator, his nose almost inside the chamber. "He told me about these German exploders just after the first ones started showing up in peat pits all over England. I've seen a couple of these detonators in SC 2000s but they're all different." Hume was thinking out loud. "Can't use neutralizing fluid or freezing snow on 'em." He was talking about a liquid similar to auto radiator anti-freeze, typically employed to deliberately short-out a bomb's electric circuits. "I'll have to trace every wire and switch to make sure it goes where I think it goes. This is probably one of the early ZUS-40 anti-withdrawal devices we're seeing nowadays on the long-delayed fuzes. If I can't bypass it or neutralize it, we may still have to blow the thing up right here and make a mess. Damn diabolical bastards!"

"Captain, how long-delayed you reckon that long-delayed fuze is?"

"That I have no way of knowing," Hume answered matter-of-factly. "It blows when it blows. And we'll likely notice it if it does."

"Thanks, sir. I feel much better now." As Hume diligently studied sketches in his notebook, tapping his chin with the eraser end of his pencil, the corporal rolled over onto his back, trying to ease aching muscles. "My dad was dead set on me being a dentist like him. All that schooling to learn how to yank molars? No thanks. I broke his and Mom's hearts and quit school in the tenth grade." Anderson gazed up at the bomb and frowned. "Besides, I didn't want to have my hands in other people's spit all day. Now, I love spit!"

The captain did as he usually did. He ignored Anderson. The late

Sergeant Ace Taft did not talk nearly so much. After considering his notes, and adding some quick sketches to the notebook pages, Hume went to work. Even the slightest mistake could end both their lives in sudden and violent fashion.

"One thing, Hank," the captain advised. "Hone your analytical skills. I like how you develop alternatives when the stock one doesn't work. Ya gotta be born with it. Those without patience don't last. Hank, I think you got it. Youse would make a damn good BD officer, doing what I'm doing. And we need all we can get these days. I'm gonna make recommendations we don't always stick so stubbornly to the RAF way and see if we can get you promoted."

"Thanks, Captain," Anderson responded. "But maybe I'd have to think about it, okay? I kinda dream of being a writer. A journalist. Typewriters don't go kaboom in your face."

"Sure. Likely won't be able to change things anytime soon anyway. So, get some pictures of this thing."

While maintaining his concentration as best he could, Edward found himself thinking of the young woman at the side of that Pontorson lane being confronted by Mickey Berg. Even though he knew it was not smart to lose any modicum of focus, he could not help himself.

What had life been like for her for the past four or five years? She had mentioned a mother but no father. Who knew what happened to him? With his flashlight gripped firmly between his front teeth and fighting to overcome the numbness in his muddy fingers as he probed, Edward came to a basic conclusion. At that dinner he and Berg planned to attend with the girl and her mother, he would ask those very questions. He wanted to better understand what had been happening here and to these people. Somehow, it might help him justify the risks he took to help them. To help real people trapped in something over which they had no control. And that now included the onslaught of Allies traipsing through their country.

Edward did not need any more incentive to do dangerous work for God and the US Army and the good people of Occupied France. But sometimes it helped to solidify his own resolve when he found cause for their mission here. He looked forward to hearing about what these folks had suffered. This pretty girl and her mother would provide just that.

When Anderson returned from taking a roll of film to safety, the captain asked, "Corporal, how about handing me my green-handled pliers and let's see if I can yank the backbone out of this thing without unleashing holy hell?"

That was another trait of the captain's that Hank Anderson had noticed. He never avoided saying out loud and in vibrant detail exactly what might happen if something went wrong. Never avoided the subject of their imminent demise. Even making jokes or finding colorful ways to describe such an unthinkable and grisly outcome. No tiptoeing around the obvious. The rest of the squad had soon adopted the same grim habit. It seemed to help, even if it did earn them some puzzled looks from those they met along the way who were not quite so cavalier about violent death.

Thankfully the vehicles awaiting safe passage past the UXB had quit honking and yelling by now. Many of the troop transports had found detours to squeeze through. Others had simply pulled over to bivouac in that spot for the night. The refugees had tied up their animals and bedded down beneath their carts, full of their possessions. But just as Hank handed his captain the tool he requested, a lone truck up the way somewhere let loose a long, shrill blast that sounded like a wolf baying at the newly risen sliver of a moon.

Hume jerked, fumbling the pair of pliers, dropping them with a splat into the goo at the bottom of the hole.

"Uh-oh," he said, reaching for them, finding them in the mire, wiping them as clean as he could on his pants leg.

"With all due respect, sir, didn't I beg you to never say 'uh-oh' again?"

"Can't make that promise, Corporal." Hume assumed an awkward body angle so he might gain better access to the compartment that held the bomb's fuze circuitry. "But it's all a matter of timing. Long as I'm still intact enough to say it and you're still around to hear it, then I'd say all is well in the exciting world of ordnance demolition."

"Damn good point, sir. Damn good point."

CLICK!

It was a tiny sound, but it was mightily amplified by the tenseness of the situation. It was only the lens opening and shutting on Anderson's Leica as he snapped another picture of the "bitter end" message. But that was not what startled Hume. A shrew darted out of its hole and scampered across the bomb. Edward lost his grip on the pliers as well as the screwdriver he held in his other hand. Both tools disappeared into the soupy sludge that covered the captain's boots.

Both men chuckled. But their laughs lacked humor.

Edward and Hank were exhausted when they finally carried the canvas bag full of the bomb's exploder remains back to where the squad waited.

"Uh-oh! Not there!" Hume whispered so only Anderson could hear him.

"What?" Hank could see that the pit they had dug was beneath a massive fruit-bearing apple tree.

"Guys!" Edward shouted, then started jogging their way. Hank tried to keep up.

Private Pete Ronzini nudged Private Morty Schwartz, the man sitting next to him at the small campfire, and pointed to their CO running their way.

"Now what? A problem with the bomb guts?"

"Jeez!" growled Morty. "I thought we were almost done for the day."

It was a third soldier, Corporal Gene Wozinski, who responded to the boss. "What's up, Captain?"

"I dearly love the nice hole in the ground you boys dug but we can't blow up this shit so close to that tree!"

The men looked at each other in the deepening darkness. "But why, sir?" inquired Private Carl Kostas, the fourth member of the squad.

"Look, the people who live around here rely on these trees for food. Especially nowadays. If they're anything like the fishermen at Mont Saint Michel, they won't appreciate our blowing up a food source, and especially one of their precious apple trees. Not when the war has taken down so many of 'em already."

The men looked at each other. Captain Hume often surprised them. The guy had risked his life to remove bombs jettisoned into a bay in part so superstitious fishermen could row past the spot and resume their trade. Now he was worried about a lone apple tree when so many other orchards in the area had already been flattened.

"So, we'll dig a new hole," Wozinski said, looking mournfully through his thick, black-rimmed spectacles at the perfectly good one beneath the heavily laden tree. "In the dark. It all pays the same, I guess."

"Way the hell over there. Next to that manure pile. I'll help dig!" the captain offered.

A half hour later, they dropped the remains of the bomb guts into the new hole, covered them over, ran a fuze line a safe distance away, and blew it all up.

The result was a spectacular, noisy, smoky fireworks display, briefly blotting out the rim of the new moon and most of the stars that were dusted across a deep-black Normandy night sky. How many more such ugly bombs would they have to confront here in one of the most beautiful but devastated parts of the world?

She rarely sleeps anymore. Even when she is exhausted from helping her husband run Pops' Bar, babysitting her only grandson—now fatherless—and still dutifully keeping house and caring for herself and Pops. It is hard to find rest. Sometimes in the early hours, she awakens, wanders the house, and often ends up sitting on the bed. She opens Eddie's closet door and studies the clothes that hang neatly there. The clothes her older son left when he joined the US Army and went off to war. It's as if she's browsing a scrapbook or photo album.

But sometimes it's Eddie's younger brother's room and his closet where she settles down. It holds a few of Tommy's clothes from high school and when he worked in the coal mine, before he married, moved to his own place, and became a father. They, too, are washed and ironed and ready, hanging where he left them. She wrings her frail hands. Tommy will never wear them again. That became certain the night the deer ran in front of his truck, he swerved, and her younger boy went to be with Jesus.

Odd that the son who stayed home is the one who has gone to heaven now. Yet the boy who voluntarily went off to the horrors of war to work around bombs—BOMBS, for God's sake!—is the one who might one day come back and wear those washed-and-ironed shirts and carefully creased trousers hanging in the closet.

Nothing makes sense anymore.

She has letters from Eddie that she bundles with rubber bands and keeps in a shoebox in a drawer next to her Bible. Not as many lately since he completed training and was shipped overseas, so she reads and rereads those she does have. There is still an occasional bit of cash-money inserted in the envelopes with his letters. And he always promises his mother that he is taking good care of himself and the boys he commands. They are his priority, he assures her. Men not much younger than he, the bomb disposal captain. He tells her they call themselves "The Kaboom Boys," a befuddling name. And he assures her he will write again soon and send more money when he can. Those letters—although some sentences are blacked out by the censors—help her feel closer to him, even if he is more than three thousand miles to the east, across the Atlantic Ocean in a foreign land. His job, he tells her, is part of some special, new squad created by the Army to wrangle unexploded bombs. A scary-awful assignment!

Pops told her to write his son, "If it's gonna blow, run away as fast as if you stole it!" She knows that made Eddie smile.

She still does not understand, though, why Eddie decided to use the war and the army to go off in search of something bigger, someplace new, better, different, and dangerously exciting. To her, only family mattered. And, when Eddie received a 4-F deferment from the draft, she assumed he would always be there in Mahanoy City. He had a solid job offer to become a night manager down at the shirt factory working for his girlfriend's father, the owner. He would not have had to go to the coal mines like Pops and Tommy did. He also had a day job as a congressional aide to Doc Fenton. Working for an actual US congressman in a clean, safe office with a ceiling fan.

At other times when sleep will not come, she opens the bottom bureau drawer in Eddie's room and pulls out some of the things he kept there. Among them is a yellowed newspaper and a thick magazine with a catchy colored cover. Turning on a lamp, she sits on her boy's bed and studies those items, as if they might hold some answers to her questions.

The newspaper. The Allentown Morning Call *from more than a year ago—though it felt more like a century before—it's headline shouting:* "World in Misery to Serve One Man's Senseless Ambition," *and a picture of the leader of the Third Reich, that man with the wild eyes, odd mustache, and suppressed smile. She wonders what the writer means by the words* "malignant narcissist" *in a smaller headline beneath the big one.*

The magazine. An edition of Collier's *from the same month as the newspaper. The color picture on its cover of an odd-looking island, buildings clinging to every inch of a rock rising almost straight up from the sea, and the towering spire of an abbey at the top. It is identified as Mont Saint Michel in the Normandy region of France, wherever that was. Eddie has more pictures of that same place set about or hanging on the walls of his tiny bedroom. Pictures of Paris, too. His infatuation with France and this place called "Mont Saint Michel" is yet another mystery for her to ponder in the predawn darkness.*

There are no pictures of her or Pops on his bedroom walls. She sometimes feels she is in competition for her son's attention with a church on an island in France and that tall tower on the river in Paris. One of his recent letters mentioned he had finally been to Mont Saint Michel. However, he has still not shared details about his visit. Or, if he has, the censors have blacked it out, keeping it a mystery for her.

She hopes now that he has been across the ocean, he will be satisfied, that he will be ready to settle down back home in Mahanoy City and marry that lovely Rachel Levine—even if she is not a Lutheran but a wonderful Jewish girl—and then Eddie's future Mrs. Hume would give her more grandchildren.

Now that the big invasion they call "D-Day" has happened, why can't he put in a request for a discharge? Won't the war soon be over as the other mothers of soldiers are saying?

The radio does say the Allies are sweeping across France, nearing Paris, driving toward Germany. There was even word of a failed attempt on Hitler's life by some of his own generals. Was that a signal that the end was near?

Deep down inside, she knows that Eddie returning home anytime soon is no more likely than Tommy climbing out of his grave and bounding up the front steps of her row house, looking for a pancake breakfast and a catch-up chat.

She tries not to cry. She knows how much it upsets Pops to hear her sniffling in the middle of the night. He still has bad dreams about his own time away at war, in the same part of the world where their older boy is now. The Great War. The War to End All Wars.

As the sun rises behind the coal mine towers down at the far end of Centre Street, she tucks away all these thoughts and goes to the kitchen to make Pops's lunch. It's the same meal most days: buttered bread, thinly sliced ham, gherkins made from cucumbers that she and Eddie—in happier times—nurtured in the tiny courtyard garden out back. There is little sunlight for the cucumbers and the thorny red rose bushes to fight for. And they often must defy a late frost or a too-

wet spring. Still, they managed to coax the plants to grow so they could put up pickles in mason jars and provide fresh roses for the altar at church.

She pries open her final mason jar of pickles. She plans to grow cucumbers next spring. Surely Eddie will be home by then and will help her put up a new batch.

She smiles at the idea. It makes her feel remarkably better, ready to carry on, prepared to face a new day.

4

That statistic about the ten-week life expectancy of a bomb demolition man had been a taunting shadow following Captain Edward Hume. Ever since Colonel Kane wrote it out like a dare on the blackboard that first day of training at Aberdeen Proving Ground, it became one of the things that kept Edward awake at night. He had purchased a pocket calendar at the post exchange before he shipped out for England. He wanted to keep up with how he stacked up against the average bomb squad member's survival rate. And hopefully he and his men could skew that death stat upward.

When he returned from the post exchange to the barracks that day, he wrote on the little notebook's back page—well past what he felt would be the ten-week page—a Mark Twain quote he recalled from high school. "I do not fear death. I had been dead for billions and billions of years before I was born and had not suffered the slightest inconvenience from it." Somehow, those words made him more optimistic about his chances of surviving this high-risk duty he had voluntarily undertaken.

He had considered writing another phrase but never did. It was original, one he came up with, and it became his mantra: *"The closer to death I am, the more alive I feel."*

That phrase had come to him when he was half-drunk, and his testosterone was in abundant supply. And while he was trying to impress a woman in a bar just off base at Aberdeen Proving Ground. He decided adding the quote to the calendar was a bit egotistical, that it might tempt fate, so he never did.

But it was true. True and beyond explanation. Winding his way through the military system to become a BD squad captain, Edward Hume had determined he was not the only one who felt that way. Many of the other explosive ordnance demolition men—those who had decided to fight this war by stopping thunder—held that same incongruous outlook.

Such men were most alive when they were just a tick away from death. Even as they heard and saw other BD men—US Army and British RAF—killed or maimed. The death rate was daunting yet remained oddly stimulating.

Edward's biggest fear in life: being ordinary. He needed more than most to make him feel alive. Staying back home, playing it safe, relying on his initial 4-F deferment, meant he would have forsaken the opportunity to live an original life. That, to him, was a fate worse than death.

There was no emergency mission on Friday night for the Sixth Ordnance Bomb Squad, Ninth US Army Air Forces, though their captain had fully expected there to be. At least nothing that could not wait until reveille Saturday morning. He had no excuse to avoid going to the French girl's home for dinner. Hume gave his squad permission to leave their cramped barracks in Pontorson and go to a local restaurant. The spot had recently reopened to the public and Allied soldiers now that the Germans had fled, most of the fighting shifting eastward.

The three captains—Edward, Army chaplain Russell Lowe, and Military Policeman Mickey Berg—had planned earlier in the week to arrive on their own and meet at the location of their dinner after completing daytime duties. There, at the centuries-old house owned by the Devereaux family, Hélène LeRiche and her mother were to welcome them for the first home-cooked meal the officers had had since leaving America many months before. It had also been years since such a happy occasion for their hosts.

Conveniently, the home was only a few blocks from Allied headquarters at the Hotel Montgomery. That was the same place where the German Army had their own HQ from the first days of occupation in June of 1940 until they were chased away by the invasion force on August 1, 1944. Now high-ranking American officers stayed there. Others worked, drank at the bar, and ate and played cards when they could.

The Devereaux house was in a pleasant enough neighborhood of similarly weathered gray and beige stone homes, undisturbed by battle, across the street from and north of Pontorson's train station. Edward felt a chill as he walked briskly past the big, darkened, vacant building. It was the same feeling he had often experienced when passing the entrance to the Hall and Pitt Coal Company back home. A place where accidents regularly occurred, injuring or killing miners. That included good friends of Edward's. And where his younger brother and father had risked their own lives to bring up coal from inside the mountain. Similar as well to the sensation he had around the ominous Bore Hole, the old quarry near Mahanoy City where he and his buddies often swam, ignoring the "DANGER" signs and Hume's inability to swim. That was where he had once witnessed the deaths of two twelve-year-old boys who jumped into the murky, cold water and were impaled on submerged junk. The first time he had been witness to sudden, brutal death.

Now, he had no idea what it was about the railway station that caused him to shiver. He hurried on to a pleasant evening with newly acquired friends.

Then Edward noticed another invitee up ahead. Captain Russell Lowe, wearing his ministerial collar, making the sign of the cross as he walked past the train station. Russ, a young man of the Lutheran faith, appeared out of sorts, as if something was bothering him. Maybe that same aura of lingering evil, a cold wind stirring like a premonition.

"Hey, Russ! Wait up!" Edward shouted as he jogged to join the chaplain. "Jeez! I dunno, but for some reason that place gives me the creeps. Like walking past a cemetery at night."

"Don't you know it. Whenever I feel something like that, I say a prayer," Lowe said as he waited for Hume. Happy to change the subject, he held up a box. "I hope this is okay, but I brought some chocolates. Can't attend a dinner party without a gift, right?"

Edward laughed and raised his own box of Hershey bars he had just retrieved from HQ.

"Spooky place," Russ said as Edward caught up, nodding toward the station.

"Yeah, kind of eerie. But I didn't think guys like you got spooked?"

"Oh, yeah. Chaplains like a good ghost story every now and then." They walked on toward the Devereaux house. "But not the kind I heard about today. About my German Lutheran pastor brethren. Jews, too. Hundreds of them. All rounded up and interned in places they call work camps. I say they're more like *death* camps from what I'm hearing others say. Many were taken away from this town, placed on train cars and forever disappeared through places like this, probably even this very train station."

"My God," gasped Edward. "And they say Germany is a Christian nation."

"I thought so, too. But Hitler's changed all that. Christianity's a threat to his power and his Nazi ideals." Russell Lowe appeared to wipe something from his eye. A tear? "He wants the German people to only idolize him, not Jesus."

Edward put a hand on Russ's shoulder. "You still want to do this tonight?"

"I need to. My spirit needs it."

They reached the designated address, and after a brisk knock on the front door, they entered another world, that of "Chez Devereaux."

They were warmly welcomed by the man and the woman of the house, Madame Séverine Devereaux and her husband, Monsieur Jacques Devereaux. Neither spoke English. The two captains each presented their boxes of sweets to Séverine.

"Oh, *merci. Chocolat. Merci beaucoup*."

Holding a lantern—there appeared to be no electricity in the house—Jacques gestured for the two officers to follow him toward the dining room. Just then, fifteen-year-old Pierre Devereaux bounded into the foyer.

"Howdy, cowboys!" the teenager said with a chuckle. "Welcome to our home!" Pierre liked to speak English whenever he could. It was not perfect but nobody else's in these parts was. And he assumed all Americans were cowboys, like in the western movies. "Welcome to our ranch!"

An elegant woman of about fifty, her brown hair with strands of gray in an updo, in a blue dress and a white apron, greeted them next. It was

Marcelline LeRiche, Hélène's mother. Behind her stood Hélène, looking radiant in a frilly light-green dress. She would later reveal it was the only suitable dinner outfit she still had. The other women would make similar admissions. They had been all day preparing a special meal for their guests, picking fresh ingredients from the modest garden out back and hard-to-get items only recently available from industrious shopkeepers.

As they exchanged pleasantries in broken English and French, they made their way to the expansive yet sparsely decorated dining room. The oil lamps set about gave the home an Old-World charm. There was a vase with wildflowers at the center of the table as well as some worn but ironed blue linen napkins, a variety of utensils from different sets, and simple blue-and-white porcelain plates the Germans had not taken time to steal. The Devereaux family had survived the occupation better than most of their neighbors, but they had obviously lost much. During the evening, they apologized several times for not having this or that, for being unable to properly and fully receive their guests in the typical hospitable French way. Over the four years of occupation, the Germans made off with the Devereaux family's valuables including heirloom furniture, china, linens, silverware, crystal glassware, and jewelry. Even the table around which they sat had been recently crafted by Mr. Devereaux using a discarded sienna door he retrieved from a nearby bombed-out building. It replaced a family heirloom table the Germans had taken.

Thankfully, as the evening progressed, the dreadful topic of death was not on the menu. There was concern that the third guest, Captain Berg, had not yet arrived but Edward assured everyone he would be along shortly, that he had been looking forward to the evening. Jacques Devereaux urged everyone to have a glass of wine and then begin serving dinner before it got cold or overcooked. Even if they did have to use glass jars for the wine instead of long-since-swiped crystal tumblers.

Marcelline left the room and then reentered with the first course. The aroma of butter and garlic captured Edward and Russ's attention while Hélène described the appetizers in proud detail. It was a delicacy she had helped to catch that very morning.

"*Des anguilles!* Eels, fresh from the river. Pierre and I gathered them from the Couesnon."

Edward and Russ only nodded and smiled politely. Then Edward said, "Eels? Okay! My favorite!" He had never had them before, but he did not want to offend.

Hélène chattered away, maintaining an animated running commentary, sometimes getting her verbs and nouns mixed up or lapsing into the wrong tense or pulling up the wrong vocabulary word. But she took cues from their guests' faces and backtracked, making sure she was understood. Hélène was even prettier than Edward remembered from their two earlier chance encounters. And her spontaneity and enthusiasm made her even more attractive.

"Bon appétit," Jacques announced, raising his wineglass, nodding for everyone to begin eating.

"Greatest night in France by far!" Edward said, truly enjoying the buttered eels in their tasty garlic sauce. Hélène translated for the others. This course was the only one she and her mother had been worried about, the girl admitted to her guests.

They had just begun the soup course, ahead of the evening's featured dish, braised salt marsh lamb shanks, when there was a knock at the door. Jacques rose to answer it and returned with Captain Mickey Berg in tow. He was apologizing to Mr. Devereaux, who did not understand a word of the military policeman's broken French.

Hume and Lowe looked at each other and grinned. Berg smelled of black-market cologne. When he removed his cap, his longish dark hair was heavy with tonic and combed straight back behind his ears. He made a dashing first appearance, late or not, as he offered his own gift to their hosts. A box of a dozen Hershey chocolate bars from HQ.

"Captain Berg!" Hélène jumped excitedly from her seat, took his hand, and escorted him to the chair next to hers. "I did not think you would come."

"I apologize. There was some last-minute paperwork. But something smells wonderful!" He later admitted to Edward and Russ that he was late because he had taken time to write a letter to his wife, Ruth, telling her he was attending a dinner with a lovely French family and that he would write to her later to tell her how it went. He knew she would be jealous, even though she did not know the primary reason for his going was not the braised lamb or the apple tart. Or even the welcoming company of these strangers. It was the beautiful young woman sitting next to him. But with the letter now on top of the "OUTGOING" stack at HQ, Berg's conscience was clear. And he was delighted the young woman seemed just as excited to see him as he was her.

Edward had already decided not to ask all the questions he had about this group's experiences in the war. This evening was to forget such, not dwell on it.

At the conclusion of the meal, Edward stood and raised his glass. "On behalf of the three of us, I cannot thank you enough for this wonderful dinner and most pleasant company. And I sincerely tell you this is by far my greatest night in France."

Hélène translated. Everyone smiled and nodded. Obviously, it had been a special evening for the hosts as well. But that was when Edward—maybe a bit tipsy from all the wine—had to go and ruin it as he sat back down.

"Hélène, you mentioned your father several times tonight. Have you heard from him?"

He immediately wished he had not asked the question when he saw the wounded looks on the faces of both Hélène and her mother. *Un grand faux pas.*

Hélène carefully placed her fork back onto her plate, hesitating as she tried to fight back tears. "The Nazis forced Papa to work at the hospital in Cherbourg. Procurement. He is an expert, a job he did before the war. They made him stay there, day and night, not allowed to come home even though he was very close to our apartment in Équeurdreville. We have not seen him in over three years, but we are more fortunate than some. At least we have reason to believe he is alive." She cleared her throat, summoning strength. "Many men were, how you say, conscripted. Forced to build fortifications, barracks and aerodromes, sent to labor camps, shipped away in boxcars from the railway station. That was the situation with my brother. Some joined the Resistance. Few have returned. Many will never." Hélène breathed deeply. "We do not know where my brother is. I am sure he is alive. He *must* be."

"I understand," Edward started. "We don't have to—"

"Two days before the Allies invaded, German officers took Papa from

Cherbourg to where we do not know. The constant bombing, the crude German soldiers with their nasty words. We heard they took pills to make themselves even more fierce. But often they were not human. Mama and I ran from Cherbourg, and we have been refugees two times now, carrying only what we could manage, relying on friends for a place to live."

The young woman stopped to take a sip of her wine, hoping her mother did not understand enough English to know what she was saying. But the look on Marcelline's face indicated she got the gist.

Hélène suddenly smiled at the three captains and its effect was the same as always. A bright sun in a dark sky.

"But now, we are here in Pontorson, enjoying a wonderful meal with our liberators from faraway America. Perhaps life will soon be normal once again."

"*Je suis vraiment désolé*," Edward responded, inadvertently using French, saying the words he had used in so many situations since arriving in France. "I am so very sorry." Words offered when he had to blow up some-one's bomb-raped home or booby-trapped church or school or business. A devastating decision but necessary to save lives from lethal ordnance.

Marcelline suddenly rose, picked up several empty plates, and departed the table for the kitchen. There were tears on her cheeks. Mme. and M. Devereaux, with Pierre in tow, assisted in clearing the table.

"Each of you are very far from your own homes and families, your parents, wives, children," Hélène said. Mickey Berg winced without real-izing it. "In a foreign country, fighting a foreign enemy, *non*?"

"We are," Mickey whispered. Russ Lowe nodded.

"...and always in so much danger."

"Yes, we are," interrupted Edward. "But, Hélène, we are here to fight for you, your mama, your papa, your brother, the Devereaux family." Edward looked into her eyes. "Yes, to lessen the chance that the war will spread across the Atlantic to our own country. But we want to stop Hitler here and now. My squad does what we do so unexploded bombs don't kill or injure our soldiers, yes, but innocent people like you, too. And even in the years to come. We fight the Nazis and win the war by preventing death, not causing death."

"God willing," added Chaplain Lowe, nodding solemnly, chewing on the last of his apple tart.

But Mickey Berg was gazing at Hélène LeRiche, his feelings for her already well past a simple crush on a pretty girl while a long, long way from home and hearth.

She turned, looked at him, gave him a dazzling smile.

Then she did the same to Captain Hume.

5

A couple of the Kaboom Boys were about to come to blows. But then, before fists flew, the scuffle was inadvertently broken up by an old friend.

"Not all Germans are Nazis. Y'all know that, right?" Private Carl "Hollywood" Kostas announced. "They say most of them are perfectly nice folks. Pretty as a pup, too, the *fräuleins*." The five young soldiers who made up the seven-man Sixth Ordnance Bomb Squad—with two of the original members missing this evening—were picking at each other as they normally did. The one who typically kept everyone in check died in the explosion of an overflowing ammo dump several weeks before. The other, their commanding officer, Captain Edward Hume, was dining with a French family this evening.

"Jesus H. Christ!" seethed Morty Schwartz as the others, bellies full and mostly mellow from the wine, ambled back toward their quarters. They had devoured a typical Normand meal and three bottles of wine from a limited menu at a newly reopened restaurant in the heart of Pontorson. As they passed shuttered businesses, they had kicked around the idea of finding a bar, maybe even meeting some local women, but they were bushed after a long day of wrestling with UXBs and clearing a monstrous minefield two and a half hours eastward, just outside of Caen. There was a limited number of BD crews in the region to cover a wide area.

But when Carl made his remarks about the nice folks of Deutschland, Morty exploded. The only Jewish member of the squad, a rage had been building up inside him, a delayed-action time bomb, an anger festering since the day he landed at Normandy and saw evidence of what he had been hearing from many sources.

"Deal with your bad facts, Hollywood. Loyal Nazis or not, them 'nice folks' sure to God turned a blind eye and let Hitler and his gang of bastards do whatever they wanted to my people!" Schwartz shot back. "You cannot ignore that fact. They're complicit, if you know the meaning of that word, ya Greek hillbilly. Jeez, why am I even tryin'?" Morty had heard other squad members talk nice about the Germans, too. Not the SS or the Nazis. Germans in general. They all knew people of German heritage back home. They seemed nice enough. A lot of their fellow soldiers were Germans, too. Some had parents and grandparents who came to America relatively recently. How did it feel to them to come shoot at what could easily be some of their kin?

After a few steps, Schwartz stopped walking and squared off in front of Kostas. "I got relatives over here ain't been heard from since the Nazis locked them in what they call ghettoes and put 'em in boxcars and hauled 'em off to labor camps. But nobody gives a shit. My folks get letters, though. They know better what's going on than we do and we're in the middle of it." Morty took a step closer to Carl, fists clenched. "You better stop chappin' my ass, Hollywood. I'm not gonna put up with your shit, you get me?"

Kostas had earned his "Hollywood" nickname from his time in California, working as a carpenter on movie sets, but had originally emigrated from Greece to Birmingham, Alabama. Now he stared back at Schwartz. Over the past few weeks, Morty had gradually become more and more agitated about newspaper clippings sent to him from home, articles buried deep in the newspapers' back pages. But that news was prominent in the Hebrew one-sheets distributed in the Lower East Side, Williamsburg, and other Jewish enclaves of New York City. He had been needling Captain Hume to urge the brass to do something. Anything. Morty had even put in for a transfer to the infantry so he could be closer to where those family members might be held in labor camps. BD had him stuck well behind the lines so far, unable to do anything about what was happening. The captain buried the New Yorker's transfer request.

"Morty, the best thing you and me can do for Jews, Gentiles, and stone-cold atheists is defuze ticking bombs and nullify ordnance," had been Captain Hume's retort. "And clear the way so the Allies can get to them and help them. Got that?"

That response only added to the private's growing frustration. And, from Hume's point of view, caused distractions for the squad. That he could not tolerate.

Now, stopped at the side of the narrow street, Carl looked at his squad mate and held up both hands. "Easy, pal. Nazi bastards ran all over my homeland, too. I was born in Greece before my family moved us to Alabama and on to California. Now the Greek resistance is doing all they can to push 'em out of there."

"Hollywood's right," Hank Anderson interrupted. "Not all Germans are on board with old Adolfus."

"Yeah," was all Morty could come up with for a response, but his fists were still balled up, ready.

"Germans thought he was going to bring 'em back from the bad times they had after the Great War. That's all." Hank was easily the most well-read member of the squad, always devouring a book, magazines, newspapers, comics, any reading matter he could beg, borrow, or steal. He saw himself more and more as a peacekeeper, too. Filling the late Ace Taft's role. "Anyway, they'll all pay the price soon enough when Patton and Stalin and everybody marches through the Brandenburg Gate and right down Adolf Hitler Plaza."

"Yeah," Carl agreed. He didn't want to have to fight Morty. It was getting late. Reveille was at 0500 the next morning.

"But who knows what my people, my relatives, are suffering?" Fatigue had erased much of Private Morty Schwartz's ire. He dropped his head and started to slowly walk again. Private Pete Ronzini sidled up to his fellow New Yorker and put a consoling arm around his shoulders. It was an unusual gesture. Hard to do for Ronzini, too, because he was so short he had barely met the minimum height for induction into the Army. And despite having New York City as their common hometown, the two were more likely to feud over minor differences than agree.

"We'll get our chance to help 'em, your people. Maybe even find some of the missing ones. You'll see. When we head east toward Germany, buddy." Ronzini was trying to show, in his own way, that he cared. "You know us New Yawkers. We don't get mad. We get even."

Schwartz did not respond. He frowned, nodded, shrugged off the arm on his shoulder, and walked on. Finally Corporal Gene Wozinski fell into step with Morty, reached over, and patted him on the back.

Schwartz spun and cocked a fist, again ready to fight. "Dammit, Woz! Don't touch me! Ain't I told ya not to touch me? And what do you guys know about it? Gettin' spit at on the way to synagogue. Bein' called a 'kike' on the playground? You guys have no clue what it's like to—"

Then, unexpectedly, there was a long, shrill blast of a vehicle horn just to the left of the squad. And a booming voice yelled, "As I live and breathe! If it ain't the goddam Kaboom Boys!"

Despite the late hour, the archaic street was bustling with passing military vehicles and truck convoys loaded with troops. There was even an occasional rumbling clump of battle tanks. With no sidewalks, groups of soldiers walked alongside the tangle of traffic, too, and had to duck and dodge to keep from getting sideswiped or to allow other pedestrians—all in combat fatigues—to squeeze past. There were no locals to be seen.

The BD boys spun around to see who was causing the hullabaloo. It was a captain in the passenger seat of a red-fendered jeep, well-marked as "BDS." A captain who was a dead ringer for the actor Clark Gable. There was a sign in the corner of the windshield announcing the vehicle belonged to "The Bomb Merchants." It was Captain Hedley Bennett, tossing an informal salute as he motioned for his driver to pull over next to the squad.

"Where's your dogie rustler of a CO, boys?" Bennett was commander of his own BD squad, had undergone training in Maryland and then England alongside Edward Hume, and was one of the captain's good friends. "Bet he's out trying to lasso himself a heifer, right? Man's got to bang something warmer than a bomb sometimes, I reckon."

Bennett was from Washington, DC, but had spent time with the Civilian Conservation Corps in Texas during the Great Depression. There he adopted the vernacular of the cowboy and often wore a broad-brimmed Stetson on his head and a scarlet bandanna around his neck while defuzing bombs.

Hank Anderson stepped over and shook Bennett's offered hand, then that of his driver and number two, Sergeant Fifth Grade Tony Gabler. Hank also waved to the self-dubbed "Bomb Merchants" in the truck that had followed the jeep to the side of the street. "Yes, sir, he's having dinner with somebody he met back at Mont Saint Michel."

"Filly, I betcha."

"Yes, sir. And her momma."

"Might've known that, too." Bennett winked conspiratorially and glanced at Hume's squad. They had stepped over to the truck to exchange hellos with the other BD men. They had gotten to know each other through previous encounters. "I count five of you, Corporal. Six with the head buckaroo. You're still down a man."

"Yes, sir. A BD-qualified number two. They tell us they got some guys just finishing up in England and they'll send us a replacement soon as they can. I told the captain I could be his number two, but..."

Several trucks, trying to squeeze around Bennett's vehicles, were blowing their horns, yelling obscenities. The captain glanced back, acknowledging for the first time the long line of trucks and jeeps tangled up behind them. The captain waved for both his drivers to pull as far as they could up onto the slim curb.

"It can take some time backfilling BD men. I know from experience. Don't worry. Old Hume's gonna take good care of you, Corporal. He likes you," Bennett offered. "By the way, remind him the bet's still on. You know about our bet, right?"

It was a wager made between the two squads in the afterglow of the harried but successful mission at Mont Saint Michel. The payoff was a bottle of Jägermeister liqueur. "Yes, sir. The first BD squad to the Eiffel Tower wins. But the way we're going, we'll still be sweeping churches and defuzing bombs right here 'til the war's over, sir."

"We were on the fast track to Paree for a minute, tryin' to stay the hell outta Patton's way, but looks like now they want us to head on up north. They're thinking Hitler's gonna try to take back a seaport somewhere up there. And whatever's left of the Luftwaffe, they've been shittin' dud bombs all over the place on Belgium and Scandahoovia. We'll have to put on our wooden shoes and go give 'em some help, I reckon."

Hank glanced at the backed-up vehicles, now making even more noise. "You got yourself a traffic jam, sir. I'll be sure to tell the captain we ran into you."

"Do that very thing, Corporal." And then Hedley Bennett colorfully laid out a prediction. "Tell my friend I don't forget a wager. The Bomb Merchants will be there waitin' at the Eiffel Tower with a baguette and a chunk of stinky cheese when you cowpunchers come stragglin' in, right behind the USO Camp Show with all them Hollywood types, you know, like Bing Crosby, Mickey Rooney, Judy Garland, and even that dame, Marlene Dietrich. You'll be a day late and a dollar short as per usual. But you better come equipped with a bottle of Jägermeister to pay up."

"Haven't you heard, Captain Bennett?" Anderson asked with a grin. "The Nazis chopped down the Eiffel Tower and melted it down to make ammo. Guy from the 101st told us about it the other day."

The captain snorted. "Don't believe any of the scuttlebutt you hear and half what you see. Truth is, the Germans ain't messed with anything major in Paris so far. I reckon that'll change if the Parisians are forced to evacuate. Now, I call that 'job security' for the likes of us, though, pardner. Clearing booby traps out of vacant whorehouses might be our fate once we get there."

"We'll just have to do our duty," Hank said, grinning.

Bennett again noticed the impatient drivers trying to squeeze past. "We're kinda in a hurry now 'cause we got a half dozen RAF exploders lined up in a row we got to deal with. They got dropped alongside the main road into Le Mans, near the start of the racecourse they got over there."

"Some RAF hotshot pilot messed up." It was Sergeant Gabler, Bennett's number two, jumping in. "Now it's our problem. Right now, sir."

"Yeah, we better get this posse moving. We may have to steam 'em out and blow up the others on site. Just don't know until we get there and crack 'em open."

"I'll give Captain Hume your message, sir," Hank promised.

With a wink and a wave of a hand, Bennett and the Bomb Merchants pulled away, again leading the parade through the streets of Pontorson.

"I kinda like that guy," Gene Wozinski said. "You know, his swagger. Like a real cowboy."

"Wouldn't trade him for Captain Hume, though," Hank offered.

"Me neither," Morty agreed. "I got a bad feeling about those guys."

"Funny. I got the same feeling," Hank said.

"You notice how shorthanded they always are? Why's that?" Pete asked.

"Yeah, I noticed it back at Mont Saint Michel but didn't want to say anything." Carl shook his head. "Could be a sore subject, but I think we all know the answer."

"They've had tough times. They even got trapped behind the front lines," Hank said as they walked on. "Captain showed me a dispatch, a warning from the top brass for us BD men to not get too close to the enemy because there already ain't enough of us to do what we do."

"Okay, so why hasn't Captain told us this?"

"He keeps us back. Something awful happened to those guys even before we saw 'em at Mont Saint Michel," Hank noted. "I think the captain's best buddy gets a little reckless."

"You'd never know it by the way he acts," Gene said, sarcasm obvious.

"That's not all. After Mont Saint Michel, they lost two men who were scuffling over a booby-trapped SS helmet." Hank went on. "That could've taken out the whole squad."

"If they get a third strike, they're out," Wozinski said solemnly. "I'm sure he's a good guy to drink a beer with but I wouldn't want him leading us."

They were quiet the rest of the walk back to their makeshift quarters. That night—maybe from the rich food and drink, maybe from the near-fisticuffs, maybe from the discussion about Captain Bennett and the Bomb Merchants—every one of the Kaboom Boys was visited by vivid nightmares.

She has long since stopped staring at the bombed-out bones of buildings, churches, and homes standing naked everywhere. Stopped looking at the bones protruding through the skin of wounded boys, too. Any more than required to do her job, that is. Legs mangled, arms ripped away, ribs crushed, skulls pierced or split.

It is her job to deal with the flesh-and-blood aftermath of war.

Army Nurse Lieutenant Virginia Brown refuses to become emotionally blind to what she sees day in and day out. Other nurses and medics and docs are desensitized after a time. She believes if she stops noticing, stops feeling, stops caring, she will not be able to do what she must do.

After crossing the English Channel on the hospital ship with the invasion force and then going ashore to set up a tent-city field medical facility, the carnage bothered her so much that she considered quitting, running away. But it was a question from a female war correspondent—one who had to stow away on the hospital ship to cover the invasion landing—who asked her the question that made her think about it.

"How can you witness what you do every day and not become either overwhelmed or numb to it all?"

She did not attempt an answer. Now that she has had time to consider it, she knows she must not allow herself to lose her horror and hurt. She does all she can, takes joy for those she helps save, prays for the souls of those she cannot. She will give the correspondent her answer if they ever meet again.

Now she has become more mindful of her mood and takes regular breaks to stand outside a tent and smoke a cigarette. She tries to catch a stray whiff of the salt breeze, all the while aware that sea air could make her even more homesick for Miami Beach, for the peace and quiet and soft whisper of waves kissing the beach instead of the artillery thunder, howling airplanes, and groaning, damaged young men. Now that she and her medical unit have moved farther inland, chasing battles, there is no more salt air. The screams of the wounded cancel out memories of the gleeful cries of the gulls and terns.

For the past hour, Virginia Brown has been assisting, as usual, one of the Army surgeons. Captain Paul Richardson is an arrogant doctor with a hard-to-take attitude. But she knows if she were the kid lying supine on the operating table —this one now before her a teenaged infantryman from Middle Tennessee, barely old enough to shave—Richardson would be the one she would want to do the work. It was not a bullet wound or shrapnel that chopped down this kid. It is a compound fracture of his shinbone. His injury did not come as the private was running toward battle but happened when he accidentally stepped into a hole in a picture-postcard pasture as he and his buddies tossed around a football. The boy played baseball for his high school team back in Nashville. He had serious interest from big-league teams. A bright future. All this Virginia Brown learns while trying to comfort the kid through his agony, between screams into his pillow, and while Dr. Richardson carefully examines his busted leg.

It is swollen five times its normal size, his foot and toes turned a disturbingly purple/black color. Action must be taken and taken fast.

"Acute compartment syndrome," is Dr. Richardson's boastful diagnosis. "Thank the Germans for defining the condition back in the 1880s. Paralysis and contracture develop simultaneously as a result of a stoppage of blood flow to the affected muscles." The doc relishes showing off his knowledge for Nurse Brown. But the injury is now a surgical emergency if amputation is to be avoided. "He's still a kid, really, so his growth plate isn't fully developed, and it severed a main artery. And there's serious muscle damage. Rare, actually." Richardson takes a deep breath, thinking through the possibilities. "But what we've got to do to fix him will cause more damage. Pretty brutal procedure, Ginnie." The surgeon looks at her over the top of his mask. "He plays ball back home, right?"

"That's what he says," Virginia answers. She's holding the kid's hand. The ability to ease pain by a mere touch is one of her talents.

"We could operate but under our conditions here his recovery would be for shit. If this had happened back home and we could have gotten him to Walter Reed in Washington or one of the major hospitals..." The surgeon adjusts his face mask. "Even Vanderbilt, there where he's from. But he's here in West Bumfuck. That kind of surgery here could be fatal." He glances over to catch Lt. Brown's emerald-green eyes welling up. Richardson moves closer to her, maybe so the boy cannot hear. "We have no choice, Virginia. We'll have to take the leg above the knee."

This Army surgeon rarely worries about what effect his decisions might have on a suffering soldier. But this time, Dr. Richardson appears to have real concern. Then he touches Virginia's shoulder, lingering for a moment longer than she appreciates before his hand slides to the small of her back, gently massaging.

He intended all along to amputate. His cocksure diagnosis, his feigned compassion, is all to simply get to her. He is every bit the egotistical cad she has always known him to be.

It is another talent of hers, being able to quickly assay a person and determine his or her true intent. Brown took quick measure of Dr. Paul Richardson and, other than his skill as a surgeon, liked nothing she saw. It was the opposite of her take on the bomb demolition captain from Pennsylvania the day he dropped into her ether-perfumed world outside the surgical tent near Saint-Lô. Yes, as with most males of the species, there was lust in the BD man's eyes, too. But there was so much more. Enough to make him a recurring leading character in her dreams each night, even if it is unlikely they will ever see each other again.

"So, sir, I suggest we get on with it. We got plenty more customers in triage," she says as she not so subtly moves away from his unwanted touch.

"After we filet his leg, we could use maggot therapy."

"What?"

"You know, to keep things clean. Place some fly larvae in the dead tissue, let 'em eat up the infection. They do that all the time in Africa and during the Civil War."

She looks at his bizarrely amused eyes. He is only trying to unnerve her. His odd way of flirting. Not as obvious or repulsive as the times he deliberately touches her breasts in the middle of a procedure. Or insists she come to his tent for a drink after a bloody day. To talk, relax, get to know one another better. Not, though, to talk about his wife and two kids back in Greenwich, Connecticut.

Richardson steps back, reaches for his well-used bone saw. She reluctantly puts the ether sponge to the boy's nose.

"Fix it good, Doc," the groggy boy whispers. "Joe McCarthy. The Yankees. Comin' to see me play soon as I get..."

No, *Lieutenant Virginia Brown tells herself again,* I can't allow myself to become numb to the butchery of war. Or the flaws of man.

Thirty-eight-year-old Ernst Alwin is not comfortable around high-ranking military officers, top Nazi Party leaders, diplomats and important businessmen. Men with their short-cropped hair, officers in impressive well-starched uniforms and civilians in fashionable suits being served canapés and champagne. He feels most comfortable in his white lab coat, horn-rimmed glasses, the uniform of so many of his fellow military ordnance scientists. Ernst prefers the antiseptic confines of his laboratory where he relishes the loyalty of an efficient and obedient

staff who follow his every order, pushing the engineering boundaries of explosives technology to hasten victory for the Reich.

Ernst and his family live in the town of Dachau in the state of Bavaria in Southern Germany where they maintain a tranquil existence, but now with a growing concern for their and the country's future. He has little time or tolerance for such negative thoughts. In his lab on the outer boundaries of the longest operational German concentration camp, he spends long days and nights working. It is where Alwin devises many varieties of bombs, booby traps and other lethal explosives to repel Germany's many enemies. Even figuring out unique delayed-action bombs that stop even the most skilled Allied demolition men.

The lab is a place where he is unquestionably in charge. Not like at a party where he is essentially a nobody. But events such as tonight's reception are required if he is to achieve his and his wife's ambitious goals of rising in the ranks. His aspiration since first hearing Hitler speak at the Berlin Sportpalast *after Alwin's graduation from Humboldt University engineering school in May of 1928. As an "always and forever more" member of the National Socialist Party, Ernst will do what is required, remaining loyal to Germany, to the Party, to Herr Reichskanzler Hitler.*

His wife, Helga, on the other hand, thrives on her status as the daughter of a wealthy businessman and the wife of a very senior scientist and high-ranking military officer. She admonishes him for his negative attitude about functions such as this evening's. Helga understands politics and how to handle social situations much better than her low-born son-of-a-coalminer husband.

But Ernst is a willing supplicant who, unlike his meek coalminer father, will do whatever is necessary to rise and be acknowledged for his contributions to his country. His willingness and ability to create more devices to kill those who would try to stop the Wehrmacht is but one example.

The chancellor himself makes a brief appearance at tonight's event, but he is hastened away by his bodyguards before he gets anywhere near where Alwin and Helga wait. Ernst has heard that their leader is more careful after another failed attempt on his life. He cannot imagine such deadly disloyalty to the man who is bringing Germany—and the rest of Europe—back from the brink. Even God is taking care of the Führer, protecting him from the traitors who stalk him from within his own military.

Alwin's boss, Albert Speer, the Minister of Armaments and War Production, makes it a point to stop by to thank him for his work on new and better bombs. And specifically, the very creative fuze mechanisms and clever booby trap and germ warfare methods he has developed. Speer shares with Alwin that intelligence operatives confirm his creations are having an impact on the war. The Americans find it difficult to recruit bomb demolition technicians in great part because of Alwin's work.

"I am confident you will do even more for the cause in your new position, Herr Alwin," Speer tells him. "And know that we have more willing volunteers from our concentration camps, including there in Dachau, who will gladly assist you in your efforts. Even the Jews."

High praise, *Ernst thinks. Such a lofty Party official hailing the son of a humble coalminer from Essen, recently promoted to* Oberst *(colonel) and chief scientist. But there is something else he hopes to discuss with Speer.*

"Sir, I was hoping while I am in Berlin to have the opportunity to talk with you about the super-bomb project and how I might..." he started, but Speer has already turned to Helga, gallantly kissing her hand and telling her how lovely she is this evening.

"Please thank your father for all he and the loyal workers in his factory are doing," he tells her. "We are aware the bombings have set him back, but we stand ready to assist in any way we can. He, too, is assuring our eventual victory." Then, with a dismissive nod to Ernst, Speer spins away to greet others spurned by Herr Hitler but worthy of attention from some high official of the Party.

Helga notices her husband's frown. "See, Ernst," she tells him. "Allow me to take care of the politics, which I am good at thanks to Papa, and you concentrate on making things that go click-boom."

"Oh, but I could do so much more."

"You worry too much. I know how men like Hitler think. Why do you think my father and his weapons factory are doing so well? My family understands politics and, Ernst, we are on Hitler's good side. Do not do anything to threaten that. Concentrate on what you know. Soon, when this war ends and we are victorious and Herr Kanzler Hitler and Germany oversee a united Europe, we shall be among the most important and admired."

"Yes, my dear, you do know better than I about these things," Ernst says, his words punctuated by a peck on her cheek.

But despite his wife's warnings, Ernst Alwin will secretly plot to personally present his ideas to the Führer. Ideas that could in mere seconds assure total victory for the Third Reich.

6

BD boys did not get weekends off. Indeed, the Kaboom Boys were up early Saturday morning, stopping off for breakfast at the temporary mess hall in a dusty building near the center of Pontorson. They sat in a circle on a patch of grass in front of a monument to the local men lost in the Great War, taking advantage of the early-morning peace and the day's first rays of warm sunlight as they ate.

Hank Anderson was not among them. He quickly grabbed a canteen cup of black coffee and a piece of toast slathered with apple jelly and butter. He then headed straight for the truck, suspecting it was a dirty gasoline filter that had been causing the vehicle to run rough lately. He had a lot of experience as an Army mechanic in England and as a teenaged civilian back home in Denver. Waiting for the motor pool to get around to such a minor issue could take weeks. His fixing it would save time and trouble.

Morty Schwartz, still intent on continuing the previous night's conversation about the fate of his fellow Jews across Europe, grumbled under his breath. He had received another urgent letter from his mother pleading for him to do whatever it took to find missing relatives across the Continent. As if he could simply walk away from his unit and go in search of mistreated Jews.

"Can't even find a synagogue open," he mumbles. "You guys notice that?

All burned down, marked up with graffiti 'n shit. And not a Jew to be found. Like they're hiding or something. It ain't kosher."

"Morty, you heard New York City's not there anymore, right? Nothing left of it but rubble," Carl Kostas told him, his face serious as he again repeated rumors.

Morty's head jerked around, eyes wide. "What? What ya sayin', Hollywood?"

"I was talkin' with a guy at the restaurant last night. His unit's watching over a pigpen full of German POWs. Out of the blue, one of the Krauts asked him if any of New York was left standing," Kostas explained. "He also said they were told the Luftwaffe's been bombing the place every night for the past three months and most of its obliterated north of Staten Island. The guy said that Panzers had captured Bermuda and that's where the bomber base was. That's how the Krauts are keeping these guys fighting, telling them they've almost won the war and all they gotta do is hang on a few more weeks until the Allies surrender."

There was a two-second pause before the whole squad broke into loud laughter.

"I figured I would've heard if them bastards had crapped so much as a grenade on da Big Apple," Schwartz said, but at least his mood had brightened considerably since his near fight with Carl the previous night.

"Yeah, and I got some cousins dat would cut off Adolf's balls demselves if his guys so much as lit a firecracker within ten miles of Flatbush, Brooklyn," Pete added. From previous stories he had shared about his Sicilian immigrant relatives, none of them doubted what he was saying. The private turned toward Edward, who had so far remained silent. "Captain, you hearing anything about when we might move forward. Not that we wanna go back to living in pup tents or sleeping under the truck again, but how long are we gonna be here?"

Hume nibbled on his biscuit for a moment before answering. "You mean you guys are tired of your nice vacation at taxpayer expense in lovely Normandy? I kinda like it here."

"Aw, sir, you know what I mean," Ronzini responded. "We move east, that means the war's moving closer to Hitler and his goons. And that gets my young ass one day closer to back home in Bay Ridge."

"Well, boys, they could keep us in Pontorson for twenty more years and we couldn't make a dent in clearing all the live ordnance laying loosey-goosey around here. Theirs and ours. But I'm thinkin' once we get the most dangerous UXBs handled, we'll be sent eastward for the ones affecting the advance. They'll have us running right alongside Patton and his Third Army, clearing stuff that might slow down 'Ole Blood 'n Guts.'"

Edward downed some reconstituted powdered eggs and savored a sip of hot coffee as he wondered if he should be sharing any of this information with his men. It was classified and came from his commander during the daily predawn briefing at the Hotel Montgomery HQ. He decided to go on. Who were they going to tell? And the Germans knew it all anyway.

"I'm hearing that Patton told Bradley that his guys were ready to break out of Normandy and make a run for Paris. Sorta blitzkrieg in reverse. Patton got the okay, but Bradley wanted to first bomb the hell out of what's left of the German front line to soften 'em up. And they did. Or they tried. They for sure got some Nazis, but they accidentally took out a bunch of our 30th Infantry boys."

"Accidentally? I'm always hearing bomber pilots bragging about how they could drop a one-tonner into a pickle barrel from ten thousand feet," Gene Wozinski said, shaking his head.

"Whatever they do, we'll have plenty of devices to deal with," Edward went on. "And that's whether we're here where it's all bucolic or east of here where the war's some crazy shit. We go that way, there'll be two thousand bombers dropping over three thousand tons of blow-up damn close to us." Edward took a big swallow of coffee. "Don't complain about Pontorson. And for God's sake don't share any of this information with anybody. Especially the locals. A lot of them still think the SS will come storming back here, kill us all, and reoccupy their nice little country. And some still aren't sure yet whose ass to kiss. Got that?"

Everyone replied, "Yes, sir."

"Our boys did hit the Panzer Lehr Division hard, wiping out all their communications, a lot of tanks and Kraut soldiers," Edward told them. "The French Resistance saw hundreds of them throwing down their rifles and running like hell toward the Rhine. Good thing. We already got more POWs than pens to put 'em in."

The men laughed at the images. "Maybe they'll tell the Führer what it was like to have a five-hundred-pounder land in their skivvies," Schwartz said.

"He damn well knows," Edward said with a grin. "We've been bombing Berlin even in the daylight since March and the Luftwaffe is just about kaput. We don't even need to look up anymore to see if a plane overhead is German. We know it's one of ours. Our biggest problem is that the big bomb craters get in the way of the Third. Patton's having duck fits because he can't go faster. He promised Ike he'd take and secure fifty miles a day. The engineers are doing what they can, but they won't touch anything that's ticking or still has a fuze."

"Nothing like job security," Pete Ronzini said.

"Speaking of which, there's a five-hundred-kilogrammer that failed to redecorate a school over in Caen," the captain told them. "I suggest we quit trying to guess our future and go give the kids their classrooms back before the UXB decides to go ahead and level the joint."

"Remember to keep your knees bent, fellas," Carl chimed in as he stood.

"Hollywood, there you go again with that 'knees bent' stuff," Hank said. "What the hell you talking about?"

Kostas grinned. "First thing I tried when I moved from Birmingham to California was to learn to surf. That's where the girls were. The beach. A guy told me when you're on the surfboard and the wave's trying to throw you off and drown your ass, remember to keep your knees bent and ride it out. Forget to and you get your tail dumped. That don't impress the girls one bit, you come up spittin' out seaweed and clam shells. You gotta be ready for anything, so you keep your knees bent." Kostas extended his arms at chest level, palms down and knees bent as if he were riding a wave. Then, with a thoughtful expression, he added, "But you still oughta bend your knees and pray sometimes, too."

Once the squad turned northeast on the main road to Caen, traffic thinned to practically nothing, only an occasional Army staff car, jeep, a few motorcycles—most with occupied sidecars—and long-faced farmers plodding along in their horse-drawn wagons in the hot sun. At a crossroads, they merged with a fast-moving medical convoy marked with red crosses, hauling tents, boxes of medical supplies, and doctors, surgeons, dentists and nurses dressed in utility uniforms. The action had moved eastward for sure. That was where the casualties would be now.

Edward searched faces of the medical personnel to see if he could see that of Lieutenant Virginia Brown, the woman he had met at the surgical hospital near Saint-Lô. Unlikely as it was, when he did not see her, it left him in a foul mood that lingered the balance of the day.

Edward signaled to Hank, who was driving the jeep, and back to Gene, who was driving the truck, to allow the faster-moving medical convoy to pass.

A few miles later, another convoy crossed in front of them from a side road. Fifteen trucks were packed with German prisoners of war standing shoulder to shoulder. Hume assumed they were bound for Cherbourg, to the harbor where a ship was waiting to take them to POW camps in the United States. Some of the Germans grinned at Hume's squad, even giving friendly enough waves, glad to have survived the war and to be out of Hitler's control. Others spat and cursed in the direction of the paused BD squad. Oddly, these Germans were headed to America with a half million others while hundreds of thousands of American soldiers were going the opposite direction, on the way to Germany.

Farther along the road, a jeep full of international war correspondents gave them a wave. A "PRESS" sign was displayed prominently on the front bumper.

"Betcha they're chasing Patton and the real action," Hank observed.

Edward nodded. "Not much news in what we do, I don't suppose. We're sorta like the trash collectors of the Army Air Forces."

"Yeah, like our name. Disposable," Hank said with a laugh.

"But I'd also bet they're more interested in getting to Paris," added Edward. "There'll be plenty of stories there with all the Brits, Americans, Free French and Resistance converging. Regardless of how it goes, even if the Germans blow it up as they leave—especially if they blow it up—that's where the story is now." Edward considered for a moment the image of

Paris in flames but forced a lighter thought. The city and its iconic tower were symbols to him of the richer life he sought. “Jeez! There’ll be lots of hooch and *femmes*, too, and from what I hear, those writer guys thrive on all that.”

Edward decided to get Virginia off his mind by using the time lost to the ride to Caen to start a letter to Mom. It had been weeks since he had had a chance to draft anything, yet it was difficult to come up with any news to tell her that would not upset her. He avoided anything that might make her worry—she had enough on her mind already, trying to cope with the death of his younger brother and helping raise Tommy’s son, her new grandson—and he knew detailed information would not make it past the censors. And black marks canceling out his words only worried her more. She always assumed those redactions hid bad news.

Edward took a different tactic, writing about the weather, the beautiful places he had seen, as if he was on vacation, not at war. Those words served to lessen her anxieties.

But at least Hume could once again assure her he was doing fine, that he was relatively safe, not anywhere near the front lines, something he had promised her before he left home with no assurance he could keep such a vow. That he was taking good care of himself and his boys. His feet, too. She worried a lot about his feet since his dad came home from World War I with a bad case of trench foot. And the usual promise to send her money when he could. He was about to give her some details of the fine dinner he had enjoyed the night before with Hélène and the French families, including the eel appetizer, when his driver interrupted.

“Sir, I’ve been thinking about how many different types of fuzes and bombs you think the Krauts have.” That was how the young Coloradan’s mind worked, always curious. As the unit’s documentarian, Corporal Hank Anderson had studied and absorbed everything the Germans had thrown their way. “So, what type of evil pounders do you think we might have to deal with?”

“Nobody knows,” Edward replied, a bit irritably. “They’re designing new stuff all the time and letting go of whatever doesn’t work. And they abandon devices when they run out of components, chemicals, or key elements. We know there's some crazy-ass guy in a lab coat somewhere in Germany whose only job is to send us BD boys off to meet our Maker."

The corporal stared at the road ahead, deftly steering around a wagon being towed by several haggard refugees. "Just since Ace got killed and I've been your temporary number two, I've seen instant, delayed action, vibratory, magnetic, acoustic, water pressured, and anti-tampering, nose and tail fuzes—inert and not so inert—showing up in incendiary, armor piercing, shrapnel, blast, and poison-gas devices. We'll be seeing plenty more landmines, I suspect, where they've had a chance to plant 'em to slow us down. I've seen Teller anti-tank and anti-personnel mines." A Teller anti-tank mine was plate-shaped, the size of a small human, and could be detonated by as little as ninety-nine pounds of weight. As usual, when he got wound up, Hank sounded like he was reading from an encyclopedia. "An engineer told me they're finding ones made out of Bakelite and even wood so metal detectors miss 'em. How in hell do you find those things before they find you?"

Edward would have preferred to get back to Mom's letter, but Anderson was going to have to be his primary assistant until the Army sent him a new one, somebody trained at APG and with the rank of Sergeant Fifth Grade. And he and Anderson would be clearing together for a bit longer even more minefields and other UXOs. He decided to support the corporal's curiosity.

"Some of the same ways we find the metal ones. The eyeball method." Edward extended his left hand, palm down as if waving it over a field. "You gotta lie down on your stomach and look across the field for any humps or clods that don't match the terrain. Or look for newly planted bushes that seem out of place. Or get on our bellies and crawl, using a bayonet to probe for them. Slow going, that's for sure. As many as twelve thousand mines in a single field have been found up near Lorraine. That'll ruin a BD squad's day. But better than having a Teller cut a kid in half or knock out one of our Shermans."

That disturbing image silenced Anderson the rest of the way to Caen. Then, just as they entered the town, the corporal said, "Maybe we just back up some of those trucks full of Nazi POWs, lower the tailgate, and make them run to the other side of the minefield. They'd find the mines for us."

Edward looked sharply at Anderson. "That sounds like something the SS would do. We're just not that barbaric."

"Yet," Hank responded. "This thing drags on, we might get as evil as we have to."

"That sounds like what Hitler's been doing with those 'revenge bombs.'"

"Say what?"

"Yeah, I'm just now hearing about 'em in briefings. The Brits call them 'Doodlebugs.' Hitler's trying something new just to demoralize the Tommies. They make a nasty droning noise. People on the ground listen for them because when that weird sound stops, it means the engine has cut out and the bomb will drop onto somebody's house in about one long minute."

Anderson shook his head and frowned, then noticed something up ahead. "Look, sir. See those kids?"

Edward and Hank would have no trouble finding the object of their mission, a five-hundred-pounder lodged in what was left of a damaged school a few miles from the coast in the ancient town of Caen. They were welcomed and guided by about two dozen children in tattered clothes, running ahead of the jeep, dancing and singing.

In his improving French, Edward good-naturedly shooed the children away once they reached the site. He then focused on the building, which seemed mostly intact, located in what had once been a quaint residential neighborhood. Much of it was now ruins. They saw no one else around except for the excited and boisterous children.

"Captain! Captain!" Morty called out. He was waving, hanging halfway out the window of the passenger side of the truck. "Sir! You see that house back there. It's all burnt to hell, covered in swastikas!" But the captain was concentrating on the gang of children who were now dangerously dancing around the moving BDS truck.

"Captain can't hear you over all these ankle biters," Gene Wozinski told him.

"That house back there, Jews lived there. You saw that?"

"Okay. It's damned awful," replied Gene, shifting into neutral and applying the hand brake before hitting any of the children. Schwartz, in his obsession with the treatment of Jews in Europe, now openly wore his Star of David necklace outside whatever uniform he had on at the time. Back in England, at the first meeting of the Kaboom Boys, Captain Hume had okayed his wearing the non-military symbol so long as he kept it hidden. Hume had so far not said anything to him about ignoring that directive. His squad mates were convinced Morty was becoming dangerously unhinged.

"We gotta do something, Woz," Morty went on. "So many missing. Where are they?"

"Okay, then, we'll do what we can," Gene announced loudly. "We'll dig the blast pit back there in that big park. Let's go." The hole would become the resting place for the bomb guts—fuze, exploder, other vital parts—once Edward deactivated and carefully removed them. Then the boys could safely blow up the remains. The rest of the bomb would be left in place until engineers arrived with a winch and truck to steam out the rest of the lethal explosive chemicals. Then they would snag and haul away the steel carcass.

Meanwhile, Edward and Hank gathered their tools, checked flashlights and continuity indicators, and started up the front steps of the school toward the entranceway. However, they found it blocked by a woman and a girl of about four that they had not noticed before. Their dirty clothes, unkempt hair, and blank eyes were familiar to Edward by now. The little girl was crying softly, hugging a torn cloth doll. As Hank and Edward drew close, the girl held up her babydoll to show them that one of its arms was missing.

"We stay for a place to live in the school now," the woman said in English. "Our house hit by, how you say? *Canons.* Artillery. You fix so we can sleep inside again. And so maybe we find the rest of Adeline's *puppe*...her doll...*bitte*?"

"Adeline. What a beautiful name. Yes. *Oui.* We will fix," Edward assured her as Hank nodded vigorously. "You need to leave the area now, though. Go!" Edward gestured for her and her little girl to move back. "Two hundred meters or more. We will fix."

The little girl looked back wide-eyed as she walked away with her mother, then held up the doll to again show the missing limb. The expression on her face was heartbreaking.

"Puts pressure on a BD boy, doesn't it, sir?" Hank noted.

"More pressure than two hundred pounds of ammonium nitrate? Yeah, maybe so."

The five-hundred-pound bomb had crashed through the roof and ceiling into what appeared to be an office area. It rested nose-down, the snout buried about a foot deep in the marble floor, its six-and-a-half-foot length resting against the splintered remnants of a desk and bookshelf the weapon had rudely shoved against a rock wall. The reports were that it had been dropped on Wednesday night, a rare occurrence anymore since German aircraft were not seen much in Normandy. But rogue dive bombers did occasionally make an appearance, mostly targeting troop convoys or places where soldiers might be sleeping. There were Germans who still wanted to be heroes for Deutschland. At any rate, that meant the weapon had been ticking away for two and a half days.

"Check that out, over there," Edward said, pointing to an area behind the bomb. There were blankets, a beautiful handmade quilt, a stack of books, a few simple toys, a mattress, several bottles of wine, and what appeared to be a full set of china stacked on the shelves, all miraculously undisturbed and unbroken. "Looks like we—and that damn bomb—found our sweet French friends' temporary bedroom."

"Jeez-us! Lucky for them they weren't here when it came down."

"The thing smacked down hard but still didn't detonate," Edward said, mostly to himself. That was yet another trait Hank—and Ace Taft before him—had noticed. The captain argued out loud with himself to better assess and analyze any particularly knotty situation. "I saw plenty of these back in England. The Germans have dropped thousands of them. This is a model JA, one big chunk of poured, forged steel. Now, if it's a 25B impact fuze, it didn't do its job, or this place would look like the rest of the neighborhood. If it's a Type 17 clockwork delay action fuze, it can be set for up to seventy-two hours and could be ready to wake up any minute and do some hefty damage. And if it's a Type Y, it's anti-tamper, so if we jiggle the thing, it will make lots of noise and smoke and they'll send home what's left of you and me in a pickle jar." Edward could not help noticing the look on Hank Anderson's face. "Sorry, Corporal. That was an expression Colonel Kane used to remind us trainees how important it was to stay focused on the job."

"If it's all the same, I don't need any of that sort of motivation to stay focused, sir." Hank quickly snapped a picture of the weapon as punctuation for his statement as Edward noticed something else. An object snagged between the bomb's backside and the fractured floor. He stepped over and pulled it loose, assuming that it would not create enough agitation to cause the bomb to settle any more.

"This will make Adeline a happy girl," the captain showed the doll's missing arm. He smiled and put it in his pocket.

"Jeez, no wonder they didn't find it. But I'm glad you did."

Edward went to work with tedious caution. Hank, after slapping away plaster pieces and dust from the seat, eased down in a convenient chair to watch. Maybe catch a catnap until needed. Then just as he was about to nod off, Edward made a loud announcement.

"25B fuze, all right. It failed, and I think I know why. You won't believe this, Corporal. And neither will Private Schwartz."

Hume tossed Anderson the detached fuze switch. Hank, a puzzled look on his face, made a one-handed catch, then intently examined the small assembly.

"Sir, it looks like any other German fuze I've been blessed to look at. Other than the fact it didn't activate and unleash holy hell. What's different about this one?"

Edward was busy removing the rest of the firing assembly from the fuze pocket. Removing it more cavalierly than Anderson would have preferred. "Look carefully at the top. Yeah, that end."

Hank saw letters and numbers stamped into the metal of the rim. "A." "Z." "1944." Then, something very small. A symbol. It appeared to have been etched rather than stamped into the brass, maybe with a jeweler's engraving tool.

"Is that what I think it is?"

"Yep. Now we know why this one was a dud. And thank God for that. Morty will appreciate this more than any of the rest of us. The guy who worked on this bomb, certainly a Jew, purposely sabotaged this fuze and even took the time to let us know he was poking his thumb in Chancellor Schicklgruber's eye when he scratched out that tiny little Star of David."

"Who's that, Captain?"

"You didn't know? That's a first. 'Schicklgruber' is Hitler's original family name before his papa changed it."

"Well, sir, it's kinda hard for me to imagine that shithead even having a father, dammit to hell," growled Hank.

He handed the fuze back to Hume but kept the angry scowl on his face.

Adeline was overjoyed to get her doll's arm back. It was likely the first time she had smiled in a very long time. She hugged Edward, thanked him, and cried some more. But her tears were rare, happy ones running down her dust-covered cheeks.

"Captain really knows how to charm the ladies," Pete noted as the squad watched.

The men were gathered around the truck in the shade of a scraggly sweet chestnut tree, its leaves shredded by six weeks of heavy combat.

"My experience is the ladies always want both an arm *and* a leg," Carl deadpanned. "But Captain's really hot for that Pennsylvania gal who sends him all those perfumed letters. And that nurse with the green eyes from the field hospital. Maybe that young one he ate dinner with last night, too."

"Captain's a cocksman," Pete Ronzini deadpanned, nodding.

Edward, his tools repacked and bomb guts handed over to the squad, walked over and only then noticed that there were two American soldiers sitting on motorcycles next to the jeep, idly smoking. The dispatch riders jumped to attention and saluted.

"At ease, boys. I'm Captain Hume. What can I do for you?"

Each man handed him an envelope, asked Edward to sign receipts, casually tossed another salute, hopped on their bikes, and roared off, side by side through the wounded city, job done.

Worn out from neutering the bomb, Edward eased into his regular spot, the jeep's passenger seat. As they moved toward the bomb pit, the men glanced back, watching him open the envelopes. Whatever happened to their CO also happened to them, one way or another. They hoped to discern even from a distance if this was good news or bad news.

Envelope one confirmed a replacement for the late Sergeant Ace Taft had been identified and would be en route soon to join the squad at Pontorson. That impending confirmation had been weighing heavily on Edward's mind. Yes, they needed to fill the gap, but he was pleased with the guys he now had in place and how well they worked together despite some rough patches. Edward Hume was still not comfortable in a position of military authority. He felt he was closer now yet still surprised that the deadly mechanics of BD work came easier to him than managing an eclectic group of willful young men. What concerned him was whether this new sergeant would mesh with the squad. Would he fit with the other pieces of this flesh-and-blood jigsaw puzzle? Or would the new guy cause more problems than he was worth?

The second envelope was an unusually fuzzy set of orders for Hume to attend a proposed but undefined event at a yet-to-be-determined location on an uncertain date. The only specifics were that it would be one or two weeks after the official liberation of Paris, somewhere in that city, and the head of the get-together was a certain US Congressman, Dr. Ivor Fenton. That was the man Edward had worked for back in Pennsylvania, the town doctor who originally certified Hume's 4-F "physically unfit to serve" draft deferment, but then undid it at Edward's pleading request so he could volunteer for bomb demolition command. The doc who also happened to be a very powerful and important man in Washington, DC, a Republican member of the United States House of Representatives from Hume's Schuylkill County district. The orders also directed Edward to select one man from the squad to accompany him to serve as his driver and assistant during the three days he would be away from his typical BD duty. General Patton demanded that no officer drive his own vehicle, that they focus on critical decision-making and not driving.

His hands hurting from the day's intricate disarming operation, head aching from breathing the dust in the demolished school office, dehydrated from the unusual heat, Edward could only read and sigh. He slid the two sets of orders back into their envelopes and placed them in the satchel he kept beneath his jeep seat. He would contemplate both on the ride home. He walked over to where the bomb innards were about to be blown, and, in the process, once more disturb the historic city of Caen.

"C'mon, men, let's light the fuze. We got a minefield, a midsize ammo dump, and some kind of unknown device off the roadway between here and Pontorson before we can goldbrick for the rest of the day." Then Edward remembered something. He nodded to Morty. "Hey, I wanna show you something, Schwartz."

As he pulled the fuze from his vest pocket, he wondered who would be happier: little Adeline with her doll once again whole, or this troubled Jewish soldier from the Lower East Side of Manhattan when he saw the tiny Star of David etched into the metal rim of this sabotaged death trigger. Either reaction was a powerful bit of justification for Hume's volunteering to become a BD man.

Two such reassurances in one day? Even better.

7

Stress. Everybody in the Kaboom Boys had experienced some level or another. Self-imposed or not. Even though he was only twenty-eight, Edward Hume was certain that was what caused the odd strand of gray hair to sprout at his temples of late. No surprise. Stress was a constant companion in his job, and, for some, a professional deal breaker. Bomb disposal men learned to cope or else asked to transfer to do something less lethal. Others who thrived in this line of work possessed split-second life-or-death decision-making skills, mental and physical agility, and more while facing potentially explosive combustibles. Hands-on bomb disposal was a vocational calling to which only a few could respond.

Hume had survived much, born in a year when the Great War raged, then the worldwide Spanish Flu epidemic, a schoolboy during Prohibition, and a teenager during the Great Depression, resident of a town in which the ground sometimes shook from deadly explosions in the coal mines beneath their feet. Now, in his twenties, he was in the middle of another world war. He could see the gray hair clear as day in the little shaving mirror in his leather Dopp Kit. Hume had not analyzed his face or hair in a while, not since the night before D-Day. That was when he and his entire unit had their heads shaved in the Mohawk style by amateur squad barber

Pete Ronzini. That had been an act of solidarity with paratroopers who were about to jump into Normandy during the wee hours of June 6th. Then his gray was pointed out to him right there in front of the whole squad by his corporal, Hank Anderson, who had not been blessed with a tact filter.

Gray hair was not the only evidence of stress. There were the nightmares, too. The ones that caused him to suddenly spring upright on his cot from a dead sleep. Especially the ones that had nothing to do with Ace Taft or the sudden death of his brother, Tommy, or the girl back home, Rachel Levine. Or even ticking bombs. They were the recurring dreams about the Army nurse, Lieutenant Virginia Brown, the woman he had met outside that battlefield surgical tent. A chance encounter as he dealt with a live bomb resting only thirty feet away from her tent. The chief surgeon, Dr. Richardson, refused to evacuate. Everyone remained inside, working away within the blast zone of that UXB.

They had exchanged only a few words that day, but then, within minutes of first meeting him, she initiated a sudden, out-of-nowhere kiss that left them both breathless but wanting more.

Edward and Virginia's paths crossed briefly again a few hours later. That was after Edward had completed his job. Richardson brought her along as he presented Hume with another potential mission, a lethal ammunitions dump nearby, filled to overflowing with live grenades, bullets and other munitions taken off hundreds of wounded and dead soldiers.

That second encounter with Virginia gave her the opportunity to impulsively give Edward her Miami Beach home phone number. For after the war. Just in case neither of them died in the interim. Somehow, without either of them saying so, they knew something mysteriously strong and binding had passed between them right there in the midst of Hell.

Maybe there really was such a phenomenon as love at first sight.

It could have been their shared desire to win the war by saving lives, not taking them. Or Edward thought, maybe it was because Virginia Brown—even in her bloodstained scrubs and with eyes and face lined and strained from the enormity of it all—was easily the most interesting and desirable woman he had ever met. And he first met her while wearing an ugly, bulky anti-blast suit for the first and only time.

Now she was even intruding on his much-needed sleep in vague nightmares filled with generic bad things happening to her.

"Captain, you feeling all right?" It was Hank, looking over the top of the book he was reading while Edward and the rest of the squad gobbled up a quick breakfast.

"Sure, Corporal. Why?"

"You just look distracted, out of sorts, is all."

The other squad members rolled their eyes.

"I got a lot on my mind, Hank. Trying to stay focused. New guy coming. War dragging on. Hitler probably about to make some kind of last-ditch strike to try to save his ass. Command riding my ass to get reports in. The good guys still leaving dud bombs we'll have to deal with for another few hundred years." Edward sighed. "But I'm staying positive. So should you guys. We're winning this thing."

Then, as they were loading the truck, preparing to sweep a minefield south of Mayenne, a messenger from HQ ran up and breathlessly redirected their day. Edward studied his map.

"The US Army is sending us elsewhere, boys," he announced. "There's a thousand-pounder that one of our bomber jockeys left right in the middle of a key intersection east of Argentan. And they're expecting lots of traffic through there in the next little bit."

"Least it's one of ours," Pete noted. "Still, all 'n all, an easy day and lots of pretty scenery."

"And even an old, gray-haired BD captain like ours oughta be able to defuze one of ours," Hank added with a broad wink. "Right, sir?"

"I earned every strand. And if you keep harping about my gray hair, I'll find the closest stockade and give you some free room and board," Hume said with a snort.

"I figure I'm safe to pick on you, Captain, long as we're shorthanded," Hank theorized with an eager smile.

"I'd advise you not to test that theory, Corporal. Now let's get going before our next adventure puts a halt to the whole liberation of France. It's a three-hour trip and there are still some Nazi lingerers who'd love to put some more notches on their gunstocks."

Jinxing the squad with what-ifs was not typically Edward's approach but today he had a bad feeling.

Once through the town of Argentan, an area the US 80th Infantry had liberated only a few weeks before in brutal combat against two SS Panzer divisions, the bomb they sought was easy to locate. HQ said to look for where local farmers had stacked piles of branches and debris in a broad circle around the intersection of two major roadways to keep away children and livestock. As Edward and Hank took a look at the UXB, the rest of the squad backtracked to find an open field accessible through the maze of hedgerows to dig a disposal pit.

"Well, well. What do we have here?" Edward asked himself.

"That's an odd-looking one all right," Hank agreed.

"It's an Azon VB-1. A radio-steered, guided bomb used mostly for railroad tracks and bridges, lines of tanks or troop carriers, and long, narrow buildings." Edward glanced around as he put his stethoscope into his ears. "You see any railroads or bridges around here, Corporal?"

"No, sir, all I see is flat land and a couple cows." Hank did a three-sixty looking for something the bomber might have considered important enough to blow up. "So, you've seen one of these VBs before and know how to spay it? Right, sir?"

"Yeah, that's what I do. Spay it. Make sure it can't reproduce."

Edward had already stuck the cup of the stethoscope to the bomb's steel case. Its nose was impaled two feet deep into the gravel roadway. That was all that kept it standing upright, its odd-looking tail fins pointed toward the cloudless sky and relentless sun.

"I've seen pictures and diagrams and plenty of notes. They really haven't been used much here. The problem is, when a B-24 drops one of these bastards, the pilot can't pull away too fast because the bombardier has to keep it in sight to guide it to the target." Edward tapped the smoke flair container near one of the fins. "That's where it ignites, sparking a flame, and smoke comes out the tail so the bombardier can see it as it falls. I'd guess these guys dropped it, hoping for the best, and pulled away to head back to England." Edward was befuddled by the fact that one of these monsters was here in the middle of nowhere.

"Do you know how to defuze it, though?" Hank was no longer concerned about the why, only the how.

"What makes this bomb different is that it decided not to blow. Typically, we've got seventy-two hours since impact, if we're lucky. No telling when they set that fuze. So, go get your pictures now of the tailfin assembly."

"So, sir, since they don't usually survive getting dropped without exploding, this must be delayed action or a dud."

"Doesn't really matter. Look, radio the squad and tell 'em to go ahead and inform the engineers this one will be ready to haul off in a couple of hours. I'm surprised there's not a traffic jam already, what with the Third Army on the move in these parts."

Hume stripped off his shirt, revealing a farmer's tan, tugged a bright red bandanna from his trousers pocket, and tied it around his neck. He had stolen the idea from his APG buddy, Captain Hedley Bennett, but with no intent to play cowboy. The scarf came in handy, keeping sweat from running down his body, and to wipe his eyes. The bandanna was—he admitted when the guys would kid him—a dashing sartorial accessory, too. But in this instance, it served its utilitarian purpose as he kneeled next to the Army Air Forces' mistake and gave it a long listen.

Then there was a new diversion. An odd one. As he settled into position, he could feel the earth vibrating beneath his knees.

"Corporal, you know all there is to know, right?" Hume asked Anderson.

"Not exactly, sir. You recall that I quit school in the tenth grade. I just claim to know a little bit about a lot."

"Then tell me, do they have earthquakes in France?"

Anderson had read scores of travel guides about the country, one issued by the Army to troops during D-Day, quite a few more that he had swiped from barracks, unmanned desks at various HQs and makeshift offices, latrines, and any other place he found reading materials lying about.

"Earthquakes are very rare here, sir. But there are some dormant volcanoes, not locally but down south."

The vibration became stronger, and the corporal felt it, too, silencing him. The ground was definitely shaking. And there was now an ominous cloud of dust and smoke to the west of the intersection, as if some super-sized, fire-breathing dragon was coming their way.

"Gotta be the Third Army, or a good portion of it," Edward decided with a shout. "And if they cause enough of a stir, this damn bomb may go off and scramble the whole lot of us. We've gotta stop 'em!"

Edward raced down the middle of the road to meet whatever might be charging toward them. Then he spotted the longest line of military vehicles and equipment that he had ever seen, still two miles away. It seemed like the whole Third Armored Division, the "Third Herd," was coming straight at him—jeeps, motorcycles, supply and gasoline trucks, mobile medical units and more. And it was all bearing down on Hume at a steadfast clip.

Shirtless, bandanna waving in the breeze, he waved his arms wildly as the lead vehicles drew closer, daring them to run him over. Hank pulled up behind him in the jeep, red fenders glistening. He scrambled to stand at Edward's side and began waving for them to halt. If the massive convoy of vehicles got any closer to that UXB, it could be disastrous.

The column shuddered to a stop with more than one rifle in the lead vehicles pointed at the two of them and many more aimed into the bocage and bushes, anticipating an ambush.

"Stop! Stop! Bomb demolition!" Edward shouted, waving his arms. Hank joined in. "We got a live bomb over there! Live bomb!"

Nobody in the vehicles said anything. They knew their general would be royally pissed if they stopped—or even slowed—for anything. Anything at all. Then there was an odd sound. An air horn of some kind, blowing a throaty warning. And a siren, screaming. All that menacing racket was coming their direction, the siren changing pitch as it drew closer.

It was a jeep, squeezing past trucks and tanks and finally sliding to a dusty stop five feet from where Edward and Hank had apparently brought to a complete halt a very large portion of the US Third Army. Hume could not believe what he was seeing. It was a distinctively modified Dodge WC-57, with its extra-wide fenders to keep the mud and dirt off its occupants and a .50-caliber machine gun mounted behind the front seats. It carried a metal sign above the radiator, painted red with three silver stars.

The jeep belonged to a lieutenant general. One who clearly did not care if the Nazis could easily identify its passenger as a high-ranking commander, pleading to be shot at. One who felt it was important that his own troops could see their boss was leading from the front.

When the dust settled, both BD men could tell that the general had three stars on his helmet, three more on the shoulders of his jacket, and another three on the collar of his khaki shirt. And there was no doubt who the man in the jeep was.

General George S. Patton. "Old Blood 'n' Guts." The commander of the Third Army.

And he was seething.

"Who the hell's stopping the entire goddam Third Army in its tracks? Where's your CO, soldiers? I wanna know where to deliver your flattened bodies when I run your asses over."

Edward had been in the presence of Patton once before. He and his friends, Captain Michael Berg, and Hélène LeRiche had hitched a ride with a local Pontorson official, traveling in the back of his old pickup truck to Rennes. They had heard Patton was going to give one of his legendary speeches to troops and townspeople. Though most of the locals knew little English, they cheered and applauded in most of the right places, continually holding up and waving two fingers in the "V for victory" sign, as the general stood on the balcony of the town hall. As he spoke, he was surrounded by members of the French Resistance and local officials. Edward was so impressed with the speech that when he got back to his quarters that night, he wrote down a quote from Patton on the back page of his pocket calendar. The page reserved for the most forceful and inspiring passages.

"No bastard ever won a war by dying for his country," the general had observed. "He won it by making the *other* poor dumb bastard die for *his* country." Only later did Edward learn it was a go-to line used in most every speech Patton gave, but it always earned cheers, including that sunny day in Rennes when half the audience did not understand a word of it but cheered and applauded anyway.

"I'm Captain Edward Hume, sir." Edward employed a commanding voice, speaking fearlessly. He knew a man like Patton only respected those who had inner strength. "We're about to defuze a live bomb that came down—"

"Cut the crap, Captain. You can defuze to your heart's content once we get past. Now, though, I'm telling you to move your ass, or we'll move it for you." Patton was standing now, leaning on his jeep-mounted machine gun, waving for them to move aside.

Edward summoned up guts he was not even aware he possessed. As a kid, he had tried to save a couple of drowning boys even though he could not swim. More recently, he had swept manor houses and churches for booby traps, disarmed lethal, ticking bombs of all types, and pushed himself and his squad more than once into unsecured enemy-occupied territory to complete a mission. However, standing his ground in the path of George Patton's jeep required the deepest courage he could muster.

"Sir, that's a thousand-pound VB-1 bomb up ahead, and just the vibrations from all these vehicles will—"

"We'll just drive around it. Now move!"

"Sir, if that bomb explodes, it'll kill you, me, my corporal here, and a whole bunch of your troops." He swallowed hard. "And look, General, I know you're in a hell of a hurry to get to Paris, but—"

"Fuck Paris! I don't give a good goddam about Paris. I'm on my way to Berlin and you, Captain, are slowing me down." Patton, jaw jutted out, studied Edward for a long moment. "All right. Defuze the son of a bitch but do it as quick as you can. Jeep!" Patton turned to his driver, Corporal Francis "Jeep" Sanza. "Tell everybody to cut their motors off and save fuel, have a smoke, eat and take a shit. When we get moving again, we'll need to make up for lost time!"

Working on his first Azon, it took Edward a little longer than usual, just over two hours, to render it safe so it could be moved. He still could not determine why it failed to detonate and crater this strategic Normandy crossroads. Edward and Hank drove to the lead convoy vehicle and gave the "all clear." Then Patton's jeep raced up and stopped next to them.

"Son, I hope you know you just postponed Hitler's surrender by two hours!"

"Sir, blame it on the bomb crew who dropped this sucker in the middle of Nowhere, France," Edward replied with a grin. "Me and my boys won't take a spit of blame."

Patton allowed himself a slight smile of approval. "Point made. Good work by you and your men. God bless you for being willing to do one of the dirtiest jobs of the war for God and country. Be safe, Captain Hume."

And with that, the general's jeep scratched away, followed closely by the bulk of the US Third Army.

♠

"Guys, let's wait 'til the dust settles to blow the guts and then we'll start back," Edward said as he examined the bomb's carcass.

The continual and impressive line of military vehicles raised billows of Normandy dirt, but it also blocked the primary road back toward home for the captain and his squad. The "main route" was little more than a two-lane roadway, and Patton's army was expanding it to three lanes at a time at the expense of hydrangeas, lavender and the occasional hawthorn that grew at the roadside. When they encountered stone fences, three lanes melded back into two or even one. Or they simply allowed the tanks to smash their way over them to make a wider path.

The squad settled under a bit of shade and broke out their field rations and cigarettes while the Patton military spectacle passed in review, shaking the earth substantially more than Edward had anticipated. Nearly an hour later as some of the last vehicles passed, Carl excitedly pointed out something interesting.

"Look at that! Son of a bitch, I never! Colored tank crews!"

Sure enough, the men riding on a passing herd of M24 Chaffee tanks and those who poked their heads from the various openings on the vehicles were indeed men of color. The tanks bore insignias of the 761st Tank Battalion, and other signs depicted a black cat with a banner beneath that read, "Come Out Fighting."

"Hey, I read about those guys in *Stars and Stripes*," Hank informed the squad. "They're the Black Panthers. Patton wasn't sold on Negroes in combat but when he saw them training, he changed his mind and gave 'em a big speech and made sure they were part of his Third Army. The paper said he told 'em, 'I don't care what color you are as long as you go up there and kill a bunch of them Kraut sons of bitches.'"

Everyone laughed. Everyone but Carl. He chewed a moment, a frown on his face. "I don't know much about that. I didn't know many coloreds back in Birmingham, but down south they just don't get important jobs like this."

Then, as if they had heard Kostas's comment, the Black Panthers abruptly ground to a noisy stop right next to the squad. Actually, the entire line had come to a halt while a holdup uncoiled up ahead somewhere.

Captain Hume suddenly jumped to his feet and his eyes went wide.

"Victor! Victor Stapleton! Hey! Hey! Is that you?"

A tall soldier riding on the hip of one of the M24s looked up, startled. Then, rifle in hand, he jumped down, ran toward the BD squad, met Hume halfway, and the two men hugged like long-separated brothers.

"Jesus, it's good to see you, Eddie!" the soldier said, pulling back, looking Hume up and down. "Uh, I mean Captain Hume. Wow! Somebody from home. You lookin' good."

"You, too, Victor. I see you got into the war after all. You takin' care of yourself, right?"

"Daddy said he'd come to France and whup me with a tree limb if I got myself killed," Stapleton said with a deep laugh.

A siren on one of the tanks sounded a short yelp. The column had started back up.

"Tell Calvin you and I met up," Edward said, then grinned. "I'll write to your momma that I saw you. And take care, soldier. That's an order."

Victor stepped back, came to attention, and snapped off a salute. "Yes sir, Captain."

Edward watched him run back to his tank and climb to his resting spot. Stapleton waved and then he and the tank were lost in the dust.

"God, guys. What's the chances of that? Quarter of a million men in the invasion force and I run into a guy from back home on a road in Normandy, France, of all places." Edward settled back down, leaned against a hawthorn tree, and pensively watched the lethal procession go past. "That made my day." Only God knew what those men—or the Germans they stalked—would endure before this war ended.

"So, sir, you...you really know that guy?" Carl asked.

"Yeah, his dad runs the little newsstand. I used to stop in every morning and pick up a newspaper on the way to work. He was all torn up when

Victor enlisted, knowing how tough it would be, not just the war but him being—"

"Colored?" Carl interrupted and started to say something more but thought better of it. The men ate quietly until Hank spoke up.

"You know the black panther is not actually a panther at all. It's really a leopard or a jaguar and—"

The men good-naturedly pelted the know-it-all corporal with the remains of their C-rations.

8

Sometimes, in the darkest part of the night, when sleep became stubbornly elusive and he remained amped up from another day's harrowing activities, Edward would lie there, eyes open, and, like every other soldier, he would think of home. He knew loved ones back there were likely wide awake as well, losing sleep over their sons and daughters who had answered the call to war. Edward constantly relived his decisions as his wristwatch seemed to remain dead still. That started with his decision to abandon the provincial life in search of a more exhilarating existence. To deliberately ride away from home on that smokey old Greyhound bus on a chilly, misty morning while his family and wannabe fiancé grew smaller, dimmer in the distance as they waved goodbye. But this time it was not homesickness that had him lying awake on his cot, listening through the thin canvas to the noises men made as they slept. Nor was it regret over any decision he had made. After all, he was living the adventurous life he had desired since he was a kid.

"The closer to death I am, the more alive I feel."

It was not his nerve-shredding job either. In fact, he would never admit to anyone his secret thrill at the inherent risks. It made his blood race like a lucky streak on a poker night. He had been compared to a surgeon, most of whom were accused of loving to cut flesh. But Edward believed most of them cut because it was necessary to repair damaged tissue, to achieve the best possible outcome for the patient, just as he did in his own hazardous operations.

Maybe tonight's vivid nightmare had been triggered by his running into Victor Stapleton from back home. He had been dreaming of an oddly shaped bomb that exploded while he was working on it, but not in Normandy. In his family's living room.

There were parts of his life, six time zones away, that he missed mightily. One o'clock in the morning in Pontorson would be dinnertime at the row house back in Mahanoy City. But with Pops manning the bar and Tommy now gone, Mom would be eating alone, sitting beside the radio, listening for any news that might affect her boy. Or sometimes she would pack up a basket and go down to join Pops for dinner at the bar. Edward felt guilt about the effect his enlisting had on his parents. Mom was alone now in part because he had signed up to seek adventure. Pops, on the other hand, had no illusions. He knew from his own experience in the Great War what his son was facing. His biggest worry, one he would never utter to his wife, was something a buddy told him: *"Only the dead see the end of war."*

It had been a month since his last perfume-saturated letter from Rachel Levine. In her own cryptic way, she hinted of other love interests. Men who were trying to meet her high-bar standards and had shown interest in her.

And so many of his friends were gone now, off to war or anywhere else where there was no coal mine augured into the earth beneath them. Some had not survived the fighting. Others would not survive the coal mine. His mother kept him updated on all of them.

Even word that his former boss, Congressman "Doc" Fenton, now wanted him to be a part of something taking place in Paris, an event that offered another connection to—and strong memories of—Mahanoy City.

It took none of that to eventually conjure up an image of Virginia Brown, usually just before that son of a bitch with the bugle blew reveille to begin another day of bomb busting.

The German defense forces had been ordered by Hitler to die in place rather than surrender. American pilots from the landing base at Pontorson were ordered to expend their bombs against the medieval fortress city of St.

Malo on the coast rather than waste them at sea or risk landing with them still aboard. A bulwark on the edge of shell-shocked St. Malo was the final German holdout on the Brittany mainland. About thirty miles away, the Kaboom Boys could often hear the air raid sirens, the boom of the ordnance, reminding them there was still a shooting war going on in their part of France.

At least they were based in Pontorson, and the squad could find some relief from the anxieties of war, if not too dog-tired from the day, by going out at night. They could hit a bar, meet locals, girls, and down a drink or three while hanging out with other soldiers from different units or countries, joking, swapping stories, telling lies, and sharing bits of news from home.

Edward had become a regular partner with Chaplain Captain Russell Lowe and Military Police Captain Mickey Berg while visiting with the French girl, her mother and their friends. Hélène LeRiche had become an enthusiastic tour guide now that there was less danger. Edward and Russell assumed the role of chaperone to Mickey and Hélène, trying to ensure that he did not cross the line with her. For Mickey's own good. And hers, too.

Hume often found himself taking the long way back to the barracks on his bicycle, pedaling past the military hospital the Army had set up inside a nunnery. He was hoping to find Virginia Brown there, maybe standing outside an entrance, smoking a cigarette, blood up to her elbows, green eyes as fetching as the day he first met her. Exactly as they appeared in his dreams. But he never saw her. Edward figured she was farther east where more of the bloody action was underway.

Maybe—again as it sometimes happened in his dreams—she could be out there somewhere, looking into the faces of passing soldiers, hoping to catch a glimpse of him.

It was an early morning, almost seventy-five days since Edward and his team had come ashore after D-Day, when he learned at a briefing that the Germans had surrendered Paris. That General Charles de Gaulle, the leader of the Free French Army, was there already, saluted by blue, white and red rockets, and French tanks rolling up to Notre-Dame and adding their sirens to the cheers of the throngs lining the streets. And that the brutal destruction of the historic city had not occurred after all. This despite intelligence confirming that explosives had been planted at practically every iconic site there. The German commander of the city had apparently disregarded Hitler's orders to destroy Paris.

Edward assumed all those demolition charges would require the services of the Kaboom Boys. Likely those of Captain Hedley Bennett's Bomb Merchants, too. He could only hope that bunch of *schnickelfritzes*—Edward's Pennsylvania Dutch word for "mischievous rascals"—would not get to the city ahead of him and his squad. Bragging rights and a bottle of Jägermeister were at stake. Hopefully they would toast one another at the Eiffel Tower, then go defuze whatever volatile device the Germans had left for them there.

Hume's life was abruptly altered three days later. Those previous hazy orders about an impending event once Paris fell to the Allies were replaced by dispatches with pressing classified details. Then, as happened when he received the first two notes at the bombed-out school in Caen, he was tracked down by a dispatch rider and presented with three more messages. All on a day when he and the squad had their hands full clearing a nasty minefield and a couple of UXBs in Avranches. The contents of these latest missives made it difficult for him to concentrate on the minefield. Edward made the decision to turn the squad over to Corporal Wozinski to complete the final details of the routine job so he could retreat to the shade of an apple tree to consider it all and map out his plan.

The orders to Paris were clear. He was to choose a driver from among his squad and proceed in the jeep to a hotel in Paris. There he would report to and serve as an aide to Congressman Ivor Fenton from Mahanoy City. Doc had been a captain in the US Army Medical Corps in Europe in the Great War. Now, he and other dignitaries and politicians were to be in Paris on a congressional junket to see how the city was recovering since its liberation and how American money was being spent. And Doc wanted to hold a special celebration to honor military medical personnel who were unsung heroes of D-Day and the ensuing march to Paris. And they were dead set on doing it in a Paris hotel, where war correspondents would be in abundance and the event would garner the most attention from constituents back home.

"Colonel, I don't know about taking away one of my men from his duties just to escort me to Paris," Edward groused later that evening to his CO, Colonel Tom Arundel, at the bar at HQ in the Hotel Montgomery. "I can aim a jeep about as good as anybody can. And you know I won't be doing any missions or figuring out any bombs along the way. I can drive myself, sir."

"I'm sure you can, Hume," Arundel shot back. "But this here is a Patton reg. He won't allow officers in his army to drive a vehicle. That's that. I just worry about you gettin' boiled as an owl on booze they'll be pouring for you by the barrel over there."

"Not with Doc Fenton," Edward answered. "He's a teetotaler. He even gave me grief for drinking Coca-Cola because he claimed it used to have a touch of cocaine in it."

The second document he received that day was confirmation that the new member of his squad would shortly be en route to join them, dependent on transportation. The US Army was set up to deliver troops to a spot by company, battalion, brigade or division, but not one soldier at a time to a roaming mobile unit. According to the paperwork, Sergeant Jack Morrison was a native of Hebron, Nebraska, had attended one semester at a small religious college in Iowa before enlisting, and had applied to become a chaplain in the Army but was denied for some unstated reason. Morrison then chose bomb demolition and went through training at Aberdeen Proving Ground, Maryland. But he came up just short of making captain, again for unspecified reasons. He had just completed five months of on-the-job training under the supervision of the bomb techs of the Royal Air Force in England. Edward was certainly curious why the new guy had failed twice to become an officer. That was something he kept in the back of his mind and vowed to reach out to his former instructor, RAF BD Captain Duncan Smythe, for more intel.

But one fact on the sheet hit Edward square between the eyes, stunning him. Morrison's birthday. The sergeant had turned twenty-four years old on July 9. That was a date forever seared into Edward's psyche. That was Sergeant Ace Taft's death day. When he disintegrated in a heartbeat. A sudden flash of seething ammo in the middle of a dump next to a huge encampment of American soldiers. Edward was not superstitious but the coincidence of those two dates was unnerving.

Hume looked up at his squad, spread out, joking loudly and profanely with each other as they worked, crawling on hands and knees across a picturesque tableau of fields and hedgerows, probing for landmines. Fields seeded not only with bright sunflowers but also with destructive mortality. Edward again felt a pang of doubt. How would this new guy fit in? Would he disrupt the delicate balance of a bunch of guys who had been facing death together daily for months? Each anointed with his own strong personality? One thing was certain. He would warn the new guy that he might not want to mention the date of his birth to any of the others right away. Especially to Hank Anderson. He had taken Ace Taft's loss hardest of them all.

The third piece of correspondence turned out to be from Captain Duncan Smythe, the legendary figure in the RAF who had trained Edward and, in turn, this newcomer, Jack Morrison, in the fine but potentially terminal art of BD.

"Eddie, old man," he had written in his distinctive script. The lettering even carried an acquired upper crust British accent, inscribed in ink on paper. He could almost hear Smythe's singsong Geordie dialect as he read. An accent he worked hard to mask but it came out whenever he drank too much. The man had only become an aristocrat by saying the words "I do" when marrying Lady Lilly Crimples. In the process, he took a leap well above his social status and his northeastern Great Britain working-class origins.

"Assuming you will not have had a device go north up your nostrils by the time you receive this communication, I've just spent several months training with your newest mate and thought it my duty to apprise. Firstly, he is a talented BD man. He has a strong sense of anticipation, is solidly cautious, not in the least cavalier, a wicked-quick study. Quite adept at finding solutions to problems when first blush observation does not do the trick. In short, he could make you a capital BD number two and is ambitious (and talented) enough to be going after your job if you do not keep an eye on your arse."

Edward grinned, took a deep breath, and, knowing already there was about to be a "but," flipped over the page to continue reading.

"But be aware: YOU need to figure out this arsehole and set him straight or else he could be the death of you or your men. The bloke's limitations juxtapose you and him in sharp relief. We like a laugh, you and I, yet your new man never gets the joke. I wager he has never once on purpose said anything wry or even faintly amusing. From my observation, his idea of a joke is a crass comment, an illiterate insult, a casual act of cruelty, maybe even something just this shy of belittling. To we Brits, a lack of a sense of humor is almost inhuman."

"Holy shit," thought Edward, but read on.

"Then, though not quite so serious, is the overplay on the pious thing. The man is evangelical to a fault. Fine for anyone to be beholden to his Maker, but Sgt. Morrison will quote scripture to a bloody pig. This you can handle. The other thing, you must give thought. No man is stronger in such delicate matters than you, Hume. I mean that."

A compliment from a rascal blessed with copious charisma and charm.

"This war appears to be flagging finally, but it has left the likes of me and you with sweeping up much rubbish in its aftermath. Stay alive and come visit Lilly and me soonest. I miss that odd American accent of yours. I am anxious to introduce you to a new pet, my most extraordinary new friend from India. She's the children's nanny and my lovely Lilly's helpful assistant: Dahlia Dagger."

Edward suspected there was something more intimate with Duncan's relationship with Miss Dagger than he was writing. Otherwise, he never would have mentioned her.

"Now, never clip a wire or fidget with a circuit until you know where the current flows, my friend. Captain Duncan Smythe, in the service of King George VI and his Royal Air Force."

Edward had plenty to ponder as he folded up the letter. Duncan himself was quite the puzzle. His wife was sickly, and Smythe had had many affairs. That risky lifestyle could jeopardize his position in British society and claim to thousands of acres of prime hunting grounds and impressive residences. Dahlia Dagger, a stunningly beautiful Indian immigrant who served as nanny for Smythe's child and sitter for his wife, was likely the latest with whom he was involved. But the man seemed to dodge all guilt, living a charmed existence. His long success in bomb disposal, including during those early times when the RAF learned through blind, deadly experimentation, was a testament to his staying power.

But could he survive Dahlia? *Borrowed time* was a phrase that kept traipsing through Edward's mind when he thought of his friend Duncan. But the man did have keen insight into what made men tick. Especially those whose actions could get him maimed or killed. And he had kindly shared his thoughts with Edward on his new squad member. In the process, though, Smythe had given him yet another knot to attempt to untie.

Surely, Edward could find a way to bolster Jack Morrison's positives and effectively defuze his negatives. Sitting there beneath the shade tree, watching his men crawl across hair-trigger ground, Hume came to a conclusion: He would simply have to.

"Alrighty now, the folks who live in this realm, a once proud royal domain of Newcastle upon Tyne—" are the words being uttered by Royal Air Force BD Captain Duncan Smythe. He gestures broadly toward fresh ruins that were formerly homes at the edge of a town near a decimated field along the North Sea in northeastern England. Smythe is in the middle of an intensive training session with the newly assembled Kaboom Boys. He continues, his thick dialect like a foreign language to the American BD men, but as he carefully lays out the intricacies of bomb disposal, the language differences melt away. "—and those now homeless blokes lost everything during the Newcastle Blitz. They got to be damn near knackered after hundreds of bombs was dropped on their noggins, squashing loads of tosh all about, if ye ask me."

Only a few weeks off the ship from New York, Captain Edward Hume still has trouble understanding the Brits. The place is called England. Why does it not sound like English when they talk? Especially Captain Duncan Smythe. But the Brit RAF bomb demolition officer has a laugh as he tells Edward the same thing about the American captain's own northeastern Pennsylvania accent.

"Everybody is 'youse,' Eddie! What's the nature of a bunch of 'youse guys'?"

The two officers walk together through the narrow streets of the suburban

Newcastle town of Sunderland, trailed by members of Hume's unit. There is obliteration all around from German Luftwaffe bombings. The fishing port was an early target, resulting in hundreds of deaths and injuries and major destruction of industry. Four thousand homes were either damaged or destroyed. There remain plenty of unexploded bombs and devices for BD men to handle. And the Luftwaffe still occasionally seeds the sky with plunging ordnance. They had done so the previous evening. One has struck a building that already has a dud stuck inside. Though the old bomb did not blow up this time either, the fear is it is now unstable. It holds a deadly amount of explosive charge.

"I bloody well know what it's like to lose everything." Smythe sighs as he surveys the rubble. "Me mum and me, we lived in a tenement that burned to the ground when I was a mere tyke. Made smoke and ash out of what little we possessed and made dead a dozen souls less lucky than we." He points to what had been a simple cottage a year before. But on this misty coastal morning it is unrecognizable as such. "You never forget something like this."

Edward knows Smythe well enough by now to intuit what drew the man to bomb disposal, and at a time in the early 1940s when such duty was tantamount to suicide. And at a time when Hitler's panzers rolled through France, confident democracies had little with which to fight and even less will to do so.

Hume seeks drama, action, and risk. Like others in the BD trade that Edward is coming to know, he realizes Captain Duncan Smythe is addicted to the thrill of the ride. Maybe addicted to other vices as well but definitely hooked on living best when closest to death.

They reach their destination, a larger building with the remnants of a fountain and lovely landscaping hardly visible beneath the wreckage out front. Heavily damaged, smoking timbers remain wet and steaming from the efforts of the fire brigade the night before. A small crowd has gathered, looking at what had likely been an important structure to them.

"Okay, let's see what the Devil left for us this time."

Edward has remained mostly quiet, focused on Duncan's words and actions. Edward knows gleaning all he can from Duncan's expertise might save his own life one day.

"What do we do with all these people in the way here?" Hume asks his mentor. "We seem to have this problem on every mission."

"School circle! Pay attention, men. The life you save might be your own,"

shouts Duncan, waving to the squad to come closer. "Rule number one: We always set up a perimeter. If we have it, we string rope around trees or lampposts or whatever. People tend to stay behind a line when they see something official going on. Watch out for the homeowner, though. He has a tendency to want to go inside and retrieve belongings. Or the wife-mate goes back for photographs or to fetch her mother's fine china. That's when we become benevolent diplomats and offer them the opportunity to go inside after the job is done, not prior." Duncan bends down and picks up pieces of shrapnel, maybe parts of a kitchen stove or some bomb guts. "Captain Hume, I think you know this, but it begs mentioning. We've been at BD work for a while now here in England. Early on, even in the first of the Blitz, the bombs were small and simple in design. Now, every device is dodgy as dog shite."

Edward nods his understanding. The squad moves closer. They, too, know that whatever the RAF man says is vital to their average life expectancy, currently about ten weeks. If only they could better understand his turn-of-phrase dialect.

"We're not the only ones who do this," Smythe goes on. He clearly enjoys talking. That makes him a good teacher. "The chaps at the British Army have their version of us. The Royal Navy has bomb disposal experts working on torpedoes and sea mines and the like." Duncan tiptoes his way through rubble, moving closer to where a sizeable, unexploded bomb has been standing near the building's outer foundation, skewering the ground for over a year. He motions for Edward to join him. The squad stays back as they are trained to do. There is an odd-looking metal device just visible beneath a splintered board. It must have blown off upon the latest bomb's hit. "You see that? It's the timing device. Still intact, which almost never happens. Always something new, so stay ready, steady, got that, Freddy?"

"Got that," Edward says. He's heard "stay ready" plenty of times in his few weeks in England.

"Back to our history lesson. Our mates the Royal Engineers, the very blokes who took the brunt of it all in the early days of the Blitz, decided only the squad member who was fully trained should ever touch a bomb. Anybody else will be 'gone for a Burton.'" Smythe notices the puzzled look on Edward's face. "'Pushing his luck,' the way 'youse guys' would translate it."

Sergeant Ace Taft waves his hand like an inquisitive student. As the son of Scottish immigrants to America, Taft comes closest to understanding Smythe's brogue.

"Captain, sir, is there a book, a course or something we can look at?"

Edward knows his sergeant, who had studied at APG but failed to complete training to become a captain, already knows the answer to his question. There are no books or curricula for bomb disposal.

"'Ay, there's the rub,' as our friend Bill Shakespeare once wrote. We received a course for the RAF at the Armament School at Manby and a few other choice spots. They quite cleverly call it 'Unexploded Bombs.' I endured it meself. Damned waste of time, only talking about our own devices since they knew nothing of Hitler's at the time. More amusing than instructive. Mostly just convinced us of the validity of Sod's Law. Whatever can go wrong, will."

"Thank you, sir."

"Captain Smythe, that first UXB job you did must have been a real humdinger," Edward says as he moves a step closer to the stubborn dud they are investigating.

"A who what?"

"Humdinger. Doozy. Impressive. You know, 'something else.'"

Smythe roars with genuine laughter. "They're right, you know. Yanks don't speak English at all. You've butchered our language. But yes, it was, as youse say, a 'humdinger.' So, yes, I come upon two massive holes, and each holds an unexploded mass of Luftwaffe shite, both still ticking, daring me to climb down and mess with them. My commanding officer tells me, 'Smythe, you've had the bomb demolition course at Manby, so just climb down in there and fix up those two straightaway.' Then the CO suddenly remembers he has to see a bloke about something over at another place out of the blast zone and decides to leg it. But my mum taught me to always obey my superiors, so I did just as he ordered, much to his surprise. And, you know, I've been playing around with bombs ever since. And I continue to follow the advice of my instructor at the armament school. 'Well, chaps,' he tells us on the day we complete the course. 'We've just taught you all we know to date. The rest, I'm afraid, you will have to figger out fer yerselves.'"

Duncan Smythe breaks into a fit of unforced laughter, bending at the waist, slapping his knees. The Kaboom Boys look back at him, wondering if the Brit has lost his mind.

But Edward fully understands why the punch line to Smythe's story is so ironically funny. He joins in with his own sincere laugh. For Edward and Duncan, it *is a devil-may-care cackle that follows precisely the kind of dark humor required if they are to get past all that this war—and BD duty—will throw at them.*

"You better be flexible enough to learn as you go," states Duncan. Another valuable lesson Edward can learn from that compendium of hard-won knowledge known as Captain Duncan Smythe of the 5131 Bomb Disposal Squadron, British Royal Air Force.

Hume can only hope every member of his squad is paying proper attention.

9

In late August, Captain Hume received another TWX teletype he had been expecting from Supreme Allied Command, with details of his trip to Paris and his meetup with Dr. Ivor "Doc" Fenton. The legislator would be arriving by military transport the next day as part of a congressional junket to see how American taxpayers' money, funneled through Paris, was being handled. Edward was ordered to assist the congressman in overseeing the details for a special dinner to pay tribute to American military medical personnel.

Every member of the squad had expressed at one time or another an interest in visiting Paris. Edward decided to make the selection in a fair way. He sent Hank into their barracks to find a deck of cards.

"High card wins a free trip to Paris and the pleasure of my company on one hell of a boondoggle," Hume announced as the men gathered around the jeep. He cut the deck, shuffled the cards several times, then fanned them out on the hood, face down. "Okay, guys, you know the drill. High card wins. Tie means those guys draw again."

"So, an ace is high or low?" Carl Kostas asked.

"High!" Edward looked to the men. "Okay, Pete, you go first!"

Ronzini took his time, savoring the dramatic moment. He drew a card, looked at it, frowned, and stepped away, shaking his head.

"Worst poker face in the history of the US Army Air Forces," Morty Schwartz goaded, then picked his own card. He grinned broadly.

"And look at you, bluffin' like a son of a bitch," Ronzini pushed back.

One by one, the rest of the men each selected a card. Everyone else seemed pleased. Especially Hank Anderson.

"All right, who's got what?" the captain asked.

Pete had drawn the two of diamonds. Each of the others had face cards, a jack, a queen, a king. Hank did a jig as he held up his ace of spades so all could see.

"You know, Hank, I always thought the ace of spades was a bad luck card," Gene noted. "Sure was for a bunch of our D-Day paratroopers."

Paratroopers on that fateful day used the spade painted on the side of their helmets as a symbol of good luck. Nearly twenty-five hundred lost their lives in the mission.

"Not unlucky for *moi*!" Hank happily responded as he headed off to pack. "I'm going to *Paree*!"

"Wait a minute, Captain," Pete sniped. "Ain't he the one who went and got that deck of cards? You don't suppose he rigged it somehow, do you?"

"Okay, Pete, let's not say something you might regret later," Edward responded, raising his hand.

"But, sir, Pete has a point there, dontcha think?" Carl still wanted to go to Paris. So did Pete.

"Easy, men. No reason to suspect Hank of any hanky-panky. He won fair 'n' square and as equitable as I could make it. Now, let's get a move on 'cause we got big-ass duds we gotta de-claw between now and supper."

But both men were still frowning, grousing under their breath as they headed for the truck.

Edward's gut was tied up in knots over leaving the squad on their own for three days and two nights. But how much could really go wrong? They were instructed to handle only small ordnance in his absence: hand grenades, landmines, booby traps. No bombs. Mostly just to keep the locals happy, reassuring them that the US Army BD squad was doing their job by placing white flags to indicate danger and where future jobs would be tackled.

All Edward could do was trust them not to disobey his orders while he was away. Even so, Edward had sent Doc Fenton a note, questioning why it was vital for him to be there. Was there not another who could do what was needed for the event? He and his men were finally in a rhythm, helping the cause.

He received no reply and there was no way of knowing if the congressman even got his note. So, he had to move ahead with the plan for the squad in his absence.

"Men, here's the peckin' order 'til Tuesday or if the new sergeant miraculously arrives, and in that case, he'll take over, and you guys will do all you can to help him settle in," Edward told the squad that Thursday night over a mess hall dinner. "If he doesn't show, and until Corporal Anderson and I get back, Corporal Wozinski is in charge."

"Good luck with that, Gene," Pete whispered to Morty, who promptly shushed him.

"But I thought any in-the-field promotions were against BD rules," Carl noted.

"It's not a promotion. All Woz is gonna do is kick ass and take names," the captain explained.

The men did not try to hide their disappointment. They all had assumed the captain's temporary number two—Anderson—would be the one to remain behind and act in Edward's absence. And it would be one of them instead who would enjoy a once-in-a-lifetime euphoric weekend in recently liberated Paris. A time with little else to do but see the sights while the captain was occupied by whatever it was that he was there for. Rumors abounded about food, drink, and giddy, welcoming women. And happily, not a UXB or pick or shovel in sight.

"If and when I do get to Paris, I'm gonna get laid, re-laid, and parlayed," Carl predicted with a laugh. The others cracked up, all with similar thoughts.

"I'm still gonna be in charge, even if I'm 175 miles away, got that?" Hume shot back. "So don't be thinking about staging any kind of coup d'état. I just need one of you to handle any correspondence, make sure basic jobs get done, and alert me via teletype if anything...anything at all...goes haywire. And that's Wozinski."

The men looked at one another. "Yes, sir," they responded, if not enthusiastically.

"So, since I asked Corporal Wozinski to handle the day-to-day, I expect none of you will give him any shit. Got that? Never touch a bomb, even if it's straightforward and one of ours. Like we've discussed, set up perimeters and white flags to keep the locals away until I get back, and then we'll handle the device. Got that, Gene?"

"Yes, sir."

Only the captain saw the odd expression on Wozinski's face. His eyes were nervously wide, cheeks flushed. Even though he and the captain had held an hour's powwow the night before and everything seemed settled, the corporal still looked surprised when it became official and was announced to his squad mates. Now, he swallowed hard and appeared to be having trouble maintaining an appearance of calm.

However, it was time to head out even if Edward was concerned with Gene's apparent discomfort. Maybe it was just from being singled out in front of his squad mates. He was the sensitive type. Edward had heard he was lately spending off-duty time with a French woman, so maybe he was just concerned the extra responsibility would take away from their time together. Of course, that new development had come as something of a surprise since the captain had assumed for a while now—based on close observation—that Woz did not necessarily prefer the female gender when it came to romance.

Driving eastward, Hume and Anderson passed plenty of signs of battle and mayhem. The devastation they saw on their journey was so commonplace that it would have been easy to simply ignore it. It was not lost on Edward and Hank that these piles of ruins were very recently the homes, churches, businesses, schools, hospitals, and other normal edifices of rural French society. Death was everywhere, and for those who had somehow survived, they were still suffering mightily. All those thoughts only added to Edward's lingering guilt about leaving his squad for some silly soiree. Even if it was Doc's deal.

They also noticed hastily erected encampments where Allied troops were briefly resting before the Third Army pushed on. They had to pull over several times to be lapped by convoys of machinery, supplies, and ammo, men hurrying to yet another fight and to hoist the stars-and-stripes on more liberated territory. The two also spotted some unusual tanks, equipped with makeshift metal attachments bolted to their front ends, being used to push holes in the hedgerows so troops and equipment could hustle through. Early on in the invasion, many fields and pastures had become death grounds as Allied troops tried to make their way through those bocage country barriers and were easily cut down by hidden German machine guns, tanks and artillery. The two men saw long lines of German prisoners, too, trudging to POW camps. There were even more convoys made up of truck after truck loaded with thousands more German prisoners. Their war was now over.

The going was frustratingly slow as Edward and Hank were often stopped at checkpoints, their credentials perused, but ultimately waved on toward the Big City. Then, topping a hill, there it was, spread out before them, almost like the City of Oz. Edward had watched *The Wizard of Oz* with Rachel Levine several times at the town theater back home, in a previous life.

Hume had seen this very same vista many times, in magazines, on picture postcards. Like Mont Saint Michel, the iconic images of the sights of Paris had become powerful symbols for Edward, representing his chosen life of adventure and excitement, a Pennsylvania Homer on an odyssey. It was another world far away from coal mines and rural life. When Hank steered the jeep to the side of the road, the Eiffel Tower was clearly visible, and a winding ribbon of water, the River Seine, glistened in the late afternoon sun like a necklace of strung diamonds.

Despite the German occupation, Paris had mostly survived. Once inside the city proper, there were scattered signs of skirmishing, and even a block or two marred by serious damage, but most everything else seemed unbroken. There were French soldiers everywhere, and a few Brits, Canadians, and members of the US Army's 4th Infantry, and that meant still more checkpoints and waiting in line. Troops had to make sure the jeep with the red fenders did not carry escaping Nazi brass or saboteurs still intent on wiping out the Louvre or Notre-Dame Cathedral or taking potshots at General de Gaulle.

Directions to their destination were cryptic, and the streets narrow and confusing, cluttered with happy pedestrians and rushing vehicles of all types. They finally found where they were going. The Hotel Astoria, 133 Avenue des Champs-Élysées, just happened to occupy a strategic corner on what appeared to be the widest thoroughfare in all of France. The Arc de Triomphe was only a block away. The hotel was a remarkable bit of architecture with individual balconies at every window of its six floors. They would later learn the only guests staying in the hotel over the past four years had been Germans, mostly high-ranking officers and civilians in lofty positions within Hitler's government. Ivor Fenton and his invited guests would be among the first non-Germans to sleep there in four years.

Hank stayed with the jeep, hungrily taking in all the sights, sounds, and commotion around him while the captain went inside. It seemed as if there was a giant, endless street party underway, and the mood was intoxicating. The corporal was already making plans to join the celebration, maybe meet someone interesting.

"Hey! Eddie Hume! Eddie Hume!" a familiar voice called out as Edward entered the impressive first-floor lobby. His eyes had not yet adjusted to the dim light inside. "I'm sorry. *Captain* Hume! Over here!"

Congressman Ivor Fenton sat in a huge lounge chair arranged in a grouping of similar pieces of furniture in the *premier étage*, a formal sitting room off to the side of the lobby. He motioned for Edward to come over as he stood to greet him.

"Doc, it's great to see you, and not just because you're somebody else from East Centre Street here in France either!" Then the two men bear-hugged.

"You said 'somebody else'?" Fenton inquired. Edward told him about the chance encounter with Victor Stapleton. "I'll make it a point to tell his folks that you saw him. They've been worried sick. Literally. I've been seeing his momma, making sure she gets something for her nerves."

Then, at Fenton's suggestion, they settled down. Doc nursed a glass of water and offered to order Edward water, coffee, tea, anything nonalcoholic he might want. Hume wished the teetotaler doctor would have an alcoholic drink, especially here in Paris, but took him up on the offer of water.

"Frankly, Doc, I'm a little miffed that youse pulled me off duty for whatever you got going on here. Me and my guys, we're doing good and valuable work. What you've always told me to do."

"I know, I know," Fenton interrupted with a dismissing wave. "But I figured if I could get you away from bombs and mines for a few more days, it might mean a few more days you stay alive out there, Eddie. I have to confess I still feel guilty that I reneged on that 4-F form and allowed you to go off and perform such risky duty."

"Valuable duty. Vital."

Doc nodded, but he clearly remained concerned. "Anyway, this event is important. I need you to help me pull it off and do it right, just like you did for my campaign events, Eddie. I have a special place in my heart for the men and women who've done so much for our young boys just like we medics did back in Ardennes. All those brave docs, surgeons, nurses, stretcher bearers. Heck, even those ambulance drivers and morgue guys. We must honor them. Those that Hemingway wrote so much about."

"Jeez, sir, everywhere I go I hear about that guy."

"Yeah, he's built quite a name and reputation for himself. I recall you always had one of his books with you at the office."

"Yeah, I guess his stories hit a nerve with me. *A Farewell to Arms*. I liked that American ambulance driver, the guy facing danger on the Italian front during the Great War. His romance with that English nurse. I hear Hemingway's here in Paris now."

"Raising hell and working on landing a new wife is the rumor."

"Martha Gellhorn?"

"Nope. Another one. Gellhorn's wife number three, so I'm told, and they're what the gossip columnists call 'estranged.' I suppose it's hard to keep count of all that kind of important gossip when you're fiddling with bombs all the time." Doc laughed. Another personality quirk of the doctor and congressman. He liked good gossip. "Lots of people here, though, like it's Times Square on New Year's Eve."

"I've noticed."

"Anyway, the reason we're here, Eddie," Fenton said, changing the subject. "The first thing I wanted to do in a free Paris was to put on a banquet to honor military field medical personnel. We never got that kind of honor after the last war, so this is my chance to let the voters back home, some of my fellow lawmakers, and members of the press know it is not just the artillerymen and bomber pilots and foot soldiers who are winning this war."

"Maybe you can do an event for the BD guys one day," Edward said with a crooked smile.

"Maybe. But believe you me, right now, the world's attention is on Paris. This is the time and place to get that attention focused on these most deserving people and we'll do it tomorrow night right here."

Edward nodded. He had one particular medical person in mind, but he doubted she would be in Paris to attend some banquet. She would be in a field hospital somewhere patching up wounded GIs. Besides, he had performed his first job for Doc a week before by typing up the final invite list. Lieutenant Virginia Brown's name did not appear.

"Glad you're here, son. I need you." Fenton leaned forward in his chair and touched Hume's knee. "Eddie, this is an important evening. To me. To a lot of good people."

"That's great, Doc, but what can I do that's more important than being back in Normandy clearing bombs?"

"Well, since you asked," Fenton replied and pulled from his vest pocket a sheet of paper on which he had handwritten a lengthy list of very specific instructions. "Mostly just things here at the hotel, checking on the food, the table decorations, while I do what politicians are required to do, shake hands and grin like a crazy man. We're going to be in the same ballroom where the British peace delegation worked after the end of the Great War. You know, 'The War to End All Wars.'"

Edward suspected Doc remained haunted by that experience. He rarely mentioned it when they were back home. Just like Pops.

"You know I'll do what I can, sir."

"The first thing is for you and your driver to go pick up the medallions we'll be awarding our honorees. They're just finishing the engraving at a little shop near Notre-Dame and are supposed to be ready after ten in the morning. You need to be back here with them before eleven thirty or so in order to meet with the caterers and oversee all the details for the dinner tomorrow night. The schedule of events is on the back there. And there's an address and directions for the shop. But be there early. As you've likely noticed, this city is a madhouse. If you don't take charge of the staff from the get-go, they'll do it their way or not at all. Use your command skills, Eddie."

Hume scanned the list. He had seen similar ones before when he worked for Fenton. Long, detailed, and specific. "No problem, Doc."

"I knew I could count on you. You have your own room, which I suspect is something of a luxury compared to where you've been lately. Enjoy it while you can. Check with the front desk for your key, but they don't speak much English around here." Doc Fenton leaned forward and again touched Edward's knee for emphasis. "And, Eddie, thank you. It's wonderful to see you in such good shape and applying all those leadership skills of yours for such a great cause. Enjoy a little bit of your trip if you can. We'll chat later tonight, at dinner, in the restaurant. Promptly at eight. I just saw your folks last week, by the way, but I didn't mention I'd be meeting up with you, or even that I was coming to France." A dark look fell over Fenton's face. "Way things go in war, and considering what I've heard about the kind of work you do, I could not be sure you would still be...well...that you would be able to come to Paris."

Edward smiled. "I'm doing fine. You can tell the folks you saw me, and I still got all my fingers and toes. And I do appreciate your confidence in me, Doc. And your concern about my well-being, too, misguided as it is."

"Humble as ever, Eddie Hume. A true-blue gentleman. The guy who voted for the other guy for class president and lost by one vote. That's you, Edward Thomas Hume, and that's what makes you honorable."

They stood, shook hands, hugged once more, and Edward hustled off to fetch Hank and their bags. If he was going to start taking care of all those things on Doc's extensive list before dinner, he really needed to get to work.

10

Józef Steiner felt a pang of guilt each morning when he was ushered out of his cell by a *kapo*, a prisoner assigned to oversee other prisoners. That's when the Blacksmith of Dachau was typically nudged forward by a Mauser muzzle and forced into a war-torn Mercedes-Benz bus filled with fellow prisoners bound for a day of brutal and often fatal labor. He was herded past the other detainees who stared at him with a mixture of hatred and envy. Most assumed he was aiding the very monsters who kept them herded together within this barbed-wire nightmare, starving, suffering, dying in their own excrement and vomit. They could see he was better fed, clothed, and treated than they were as he was bused away each morning.

"Give me the ability to see the good things in unexpected places and talents in unexpected people."

Józef mentally repeated these words to himself at the start of every day. They had been whispered to him each night by kind Sister Julia, a German Catholic nun, as the orphaned Polish Jewish boy went to sleep. Though difficult, he held hope that not all Germans were bad people, even if many were complicit and twisted by Nazism.

Józef knew he had to become an essential worker if he were to survive each day. But fellow prisoners assumed he had volunteered to help the Nazis. He rationalized that he was not helping the Nazis by doing bomb disposal, defuzing, detonating and clearing Allied-dropped devices. His dangerous duties would save the lives of innocents caught within a blast zone.

On this misty, warm August morning, the bus dropped off Steiner at a spot along the River Isar in Munich, eighteen miles from Dachau. He was to deal with an American thousand-pounder dropped with the intent of destroying a key bridge. A camouflaged Mercedes-Benz L3000S was waiting beneath an ancient field maple tree when the bus let him out. Two fresh-faced graduates of *Hitlerjugend*, Hitler Youth, scarcely old enough to shave, exited the truck to stand guard over Steiner as he worked. He was now in the custody of *SS-Obersturmführer* Helmut Schmeg, a particularly unpleasant officer who was in command of the two adolescent soldiers, and who now sauntered his way from the shade of a tree.

Schmeg did not bother with a *guten morgen.* "Blacksmith! Get to work! Rain is coming!"

The SS officer pointed to a spot near the damaged bridge that spanned the Isar. The Wittelsbacherbrücke was an arched structure connecting two city districts. Traffic had been diverted to fourteen miles downriver due to the damage and imminent danger from the unexploded bomb.

Steiner could see the risk of the swift current and debris in the river. They could easily cause the bomb to move and possibly explode. On earlier missions, Józef had observed children swimming at this very spot in the river. The bomb, with a colorful sentiment painted onto its side by the Americans, stood like an ominous sentinel on the far side of the Isar. It was only a few yards from the bridge, its nose partially in the muddy water, tangled in the roots of a knocked-over sycamore tree.

"Blacksmith, is the bomb American or British?" Schmeg asked impatiently. He knew nothing about the variety of bombs. Józef was already halfway across the chest-deep river, carrying his bag of tools over his head, aware of what he was dealing with.

"American, Lieutenant."

"No wonder they are losing the war," Schmeg pompously proclaimed. "They cannot even make a bomb that explodes!" The lieutenant laughed at his own joke but Józef looked back to see the young soldiers behind him rolling their eyes, shaking their heads.

Steiner knew already that the bomb was time delayed, like so many he was seeing of late. Würzburg, Dessau, Kassel, Mainz, and Hamburg—oh, the fire tornadoes of Hamburg!—had mostly been wiped away by such devastating Allied bombs. Berlin was being pounded day and night now by unchallenged Allied aircraft. Most bombs were exploding. This one had not.

Suddenly removing his pistol from its holster, Schmeg pointed it toward Steiner. "Soldiers, join me in giving Blacksmith encouragement in his mission!"

The boy-soldiers, in their oversized, mismatched uniforms, dutifully lifted their Mausers and pointed them as directed, even though he had already crossed the rapid current with full intentions of quickly disabling this UXB. When he looked back, he could see that a crowd of onlookers had gathered on the bridge and the riverbank, curious but certainly unaware of the potential danger.

As he sometimes did lately, Józef Steiner considered the possibility of deliberately detonating the bomb, to abruptly end his imprisonment. And his life. Though, according to what he was hearing, the war was going badly for Germany. Who knew how much longer it would last? Or would his captors make sure he did not survive so he could never be a witness in the inevitable war crimes hearings? When those thoughts came, it made sense to him to end this troubled life the convenient way so he might transition to *Gan Eden*, the afterlife promised by God to all Jews.

"What size is it?" one of the soldiers called out, feigning interest.

Józef wiped the mud from the side of the bomb to see letters stenciled on its iron skin.

"One thousand pounds," he answered.

Schmeg wrote the information in a small leather-bound book so he could later meticulously add the data to his report.

Now there were more civilians on the riverbank behind the soldiers, others on the roadway approaching the bridge, attracted by the activity, curious about when the bridge might reopen. Józef knew what came next. Schmeg would morph from military commander to performer, posturing for his "audience."

"Ah, that American bomb, it may well explode at any moment," the officer loudly proclaimed as he turned to face the onlookers. "And so close to the bridge, which will surely be destroyed unless the weapon is defuzed." Schmeg typically took credit for Steiner's work. He gestured toward the young soldiers. "And these good servants of the Führer and the Reich will die if the Blacksmith of Dachau here should make even the smallest mistake. I selected this Jew to save us. He is obliged to do so, in the name of the Reich and the people of Germany." The lieutenant strutted dramatically back and forth along the riverbank, pistol in hand, waving it above his head. He suddenly fired a shot into the mud only a few meters from where Józef examined the bomb. The crowd buzzed as Schmeg spouted a command: "Get to work, Blacksmith, before that thing kills us all!"

Steiner did not flinch. He had been an unwilling participant in this kind of skit before. He only looked back and tossed the German commander a casual salute and a head nod.

As he did, he took notice of someone in the crowd. The most beautiful person he had ever seen. A young woman wearing a bright blue scarf. Even from this distance, he was captivated by her lovely face and braided auburn hair. She held in front of her a basket of ripened red apples.

She could have stepped from a Renoir canvas.

Lieutenant Schmeg noticed her, too. He openly leered at her for a long moment before he turned again to shout at Steiner, swaggering even more for her benefit. She took several steps back, her eyes cast downward.

The lieutenant seemed to remember he had a larger audience for whom he needed to perform. "You speak English, Blacksmith. Wording on the bomb, what does it say?"

Clearing away more mud, Steiner pretended to be trying to read the words. But they were clear and, compared to some previous messages on Allied UXB's, innocuous.

"To Herr Hitler, from the Mighty 8th," was what he shouted back to Schmeg, and that was exactly what it said.

"It looks longer."

"Sir, are you sure you want me to fully translate it, because there is profanity? Should everyone here, including women and children, know the message?"

Schmeg had his book opened again, pencil to a page. "Of course, you idiot Jew! The Führer must know!"

In waist-deep water, leaning against the root-bound device, Józef suppressed a laugh as he answered in German, loud enough for everyone gathered along the Isar to hear. "It says, 'Fuck you, Hitler, from the Mighty 8th.'"

Many of the locals burst out laughing. The soldiers nudged each other and snickered. Lieutenant Schmeg scowled as he fired a bullet into the air to silence them all.

The audience pulled back. The soldiers straightened up and re-aimed their rifles at Józef. Their commander could well order them to shoot the Jew for uttering such blasphemy.

"Enough!" Schmeg growled. "Get to work. Now!" He stooped to retrieve a camera from a nearby gear bag and handed it to one of the soldiers. "Go. Take pictures. Get in the water. Find an angle that shows me in the background, supervising, telling the citizens about the horrors of the American death bombs dropped amid innocent civilians."

The soldier obediently stepped quickly down the bank, waded into the water, wedged himself against a rock near Józef and the bomb, and began snapping pictures. "This one is very difficult," Steiner told him. "I will be unable to deal with it as planned. It should be detonated in place, even though it will likely further damage the bridge."

Wide-eyed, the soldier considered the bomb, the bridge, the people watching, and then Lieutenant Schmeg, standing with hands on hips, his weapon thankfully now back in its holster.

"Blacksmith, you will not get out of this situation so easily," the boy said, imitating his CO's sneer. "You have handled hundreds of bombs. This one is special only because it is the next one."

Józef almost laughed at how hard the young man labored to appear threatening. "Believe me, this one is impossible without losing the bridge or part of it."

"You have no choice. Look at my lieutenant. He is not going to be satisfied until this is defuzed."

Józef steadied his breathing and concentrated once more on the detonator at the tip of the bomb. "This will explode at any time. It is armed. No way I can defuze this one. I will attempt to safely detonate it but all these people must move farther away."

Wide-eyed, the young soldier waded back to the far side riverbank, yelling, "Move back! Everyone! Move back!"

Józef watched the crowd pull back as one. Many of them had been close to exploding bombs before. Then he saw the woman again. The one with the blue scarf and braided hair. She stood there, looking at him. She might have been his seraphim, his guardian angel. Just the sight of her brought Steiner immense inner peace despite the armed bomb, the flooded river, the pompous SS officer waving his pistol about.

Schmeg walked to the water's edge, sizing up the situation as the drenched soldier was helped from the river by his partner. The lieutenant approached, scowling. Meanwhile, Steiner pulled a long fuze line from his satchel and began draping it across the bomb's tail.

"Blacksmith! You cannot run a fuze line in the water!"

Steiner ignored him. Once he had set up the line, he stuffed his tools back into his gear bag and waded to the middle of the river. He stopped there, braced himself against the current, and shouted to a group of young boys still standing, watching from the bridge.

"Evacuate! Leave the bridge! Now! Danger!"

They ran away toward safety, as had the others who came to watch. There was one straggler at the river's edge, though. Behind the SS lieutenant, the woman with the blue scarf stood in place, holding her basket of apples, intently watching Józef. Even from that distance, Steiner could see her smile and her slight nod in his direction. Finally, she turned and joined the retreating crowd.

Schmeg was seething. "Do not shout commands at them! Or at me! You do not have that authority. Now, I order you to defuze that bomb, not detonate! Get back over there!"

Józef waded closer to the lieutenant, then stopped, still up to his thighs in muddy water.

"Sir! There is no choice. It must be blown up. I cannot get to the detonator to take it apart. And if I don't blow it up, it may explode on its own or it may sit here for months, clogging traffic. The bridge will remain useless. It is delayed action. We cannot take a chance."

"I have orders! You must defuze this thing so we can study it!"

"Sir! I am telling you, there is no way to get to the detonator. We must blow it up." Józef pulled a wire from his pocket and waved it at the officer. "I need more fuze line! And more nitro!"

Schmeg thought for a moment, then spun around and faced the soldiers. "Go get more line. More nitro. We will make a show if it, then. We are detonating! My orders!"

The officer clearly wanted to impress his audience with a fireworks display. Or maybe, after supervising Józef Steiner on so many of his bomb disposal jobs, about half of them, Lieutenant Schmeg had finally grown to trust the Jew's judgment.

The soldier grabbed what was needed out of the truck, waded out, and handed everything to Józef, then scurried back to dry land, farther away from the ticking bomb. Schmeg remained in place, holding his ground at the water's edge.

"Sir! You also need to move back."

Helmut Schmeg dug in his heels, standing up straight, again all for show. Steiner waded back over to the bomb. He placed a flat rock near it as a platform so he could mix putty and nitroglycerine into a paste. He then stuck the fuze wire into the lethal mixture and forced the glob inside the bomb. Next, he unspooled the line as he waded backward upstream. Emerging from the water, he climbed onto a rock, still on the bomb side of the river, draped the line across a tree limb, and continued to stretch it as far as it would go before the spool was empty. He was about two hundred yards from the weapon.

He held up the empty spool for Schmeg to see and shouted, "Sir, I need more wire! Too short!"

The officer stamped his foot and pointed his pistol at the Blacksmith. "Enough! No more delays! Ignite!"

Józef shook his head as he reluctantly lit the fuze wire and, as it began to sizzle, jumped into the Isar and waded as furiously as he could while shouting, "Clear! Clear!"

The clock in his head was ticking down as he reached the near riverbank, not far from where the lieutenant stood as if hypnotized by the unfolding events. The wire sizzled, sparking and spitting relentlessly, devouring the fuze wire as it moved to the bomb.

"You better run, Lieutenant!" Steiner warned as he scrambled out of the water near the SS officer, aiming for safety behind a tree he had already spotted.

As Józef ran past him, Schmeg purposely stuck out his booted foot, tripping him. Then he removed his pistol from its holster and pointed it at Steiner's head, a broad smile on his face, and looked around to be sure townspeople were watching from behind rocks, trees, and structures.

At that instant, the American thousand-pound Mk 82 bomb, with four hundred pounds of high explosives crammed into its iron hull, reacted to the final spark. It detonated. That unleashed a terrible shock wave, thick smoke, a guttural roar, and a hailstorm of flying metal shards. Splinters, branches, water, mud, and rock flew to all points of the compass. Another section of the bridge collapsed, sending a mini-tsunami downstream.

Józef ignored Schmeg's pistol and covered his head with his arms. He was painfully pelted by flying and falling shrapnel.

When it seemed to be over, Steiner rolled onto his back and looked up at the SS officer.

The man still stood in place, as if mocking the bomb's supremacy. But, despite the lingering smile, there was a problem with his defiant face. A jagged piece of metal had struck him between his eyes. Blood spurted from the wound. Schmeg's knees suddenly buckled, and he collapsed to the muddy ground, his dead weight landing atop Józef.

The two soldiers, looking on from behind their truck, gasped at the sight of their commander, lying still in the muddy river water.

The lieutenant was obviously dead.

Still bleeding from his own wounds, Józef helped load Helmut Schmeg's body into the bed of the truck.

"Blacksmith, you know you will have much to explain to the commandant," one of the soldiers solemnly told him as Steiner pulled bandages from a bag and worked to cover his wounds. "No matter what story you tell, High Command will not like any of it."

The young soldiers promised Steiner they would report truthfully, sharing that the lieutenant was warned and had plenty of time to get to shelter before the blast. That it was nothing more than an unfortunate accident while their commanding officer was bravely overseeing hazardous duty. Again, and despite their promise, Józef knew the witnesses would likely tell the commandant whatever he wanted to hear, whatever kept them from sharing any blame. Once again, the Jew would be on his own.

When Steiner walked around to climb into the covered bed of the Mercedes, he noticed something they had missed while loading the lieutenant's body. There was something lying beneath the bench seat. A blue scarf. Wrapped around a perfectly ripe and succulent apple. Stitched into the scarf was a name: *Birgit Franz*. And he could smell perfume on the cloth.

Józef's eyes brimmed with tears.

For the first time in nearly five years, he smiled. He took a big bite of the succulent apple. Its juice ran down his chin. Its taste, its sweetness, was near overwhelming.

As he chewed and as he studied the scarf, he vowed that if he made it through this war, if none of the bomb disposal missions blew up in his face, if he was not marched away with so many others to never again be seen, and if he was not murdered by his captors to assure he would never be able to testify to all he had witnessed, he would one day come back to Munich—not to Dachau but to this spot on the bank of the Isar River—and he would find his guardian angel and thank her for the gifts.

Birgit Franz. His seraphim.

Unknowingly, that beautiful woman had granted him so much more than a piece of fruit and a fragrant square of fabric. She had provided him with the most powerful reason yet to survive. Survive not simply to remain alive. Survive to truly live.

Like his APG buddy Edward Hume, bomb squad Captain Hedley Bennett enjoys talking while he defuzes bombs. Or while doing anything else. He maintains it helps him relax and concentrate. The obsession scares the hell out of his squad, "The Bomb Merchants." And baffles the women with whom he is making love.

"You know there's a place out in West Texas close to Odessa called Notrees. Really. It's called Notrees, Texas."

His sergeant, Tony Gabler, holds a light so it illuminates the fuze pocket of a US five-hundred-pound UXB as his captain works. And talks.

Gabler responds, "Bet I can guess where the name comes from."

"Damn right! Kind of strange for a kid from Washington, DC, and straight out of high school to be in such a place. But that was me and what I did. Every kid should do that. Better than going to college, I say. Especially when you can't afford it. So, I helped build a bridge there when I was with the CCC. Legend has it they had one tree, but then it got knocked down somehow when they were putting up an oil depot after they found black gold out there. Could you hand me my green-handle pliers if you're not too busy scratchin' your balls?"

"Here you go, Captain."

"Plenty of trees around here for damn sure, if Patton's tanks don't flatten 'em all on their way to Berlin. I hear it's been rough going lately for the Third, though. Now that they're past Paris and hittin' all these hills and valleys around Lorraine. Somebody told me they're having trouble gettin' gasoline brought in fast enough to keep up with Old Blood 'n' Guts. Could be the trees are gettin' their revenge for what happened at Notrees. That and the Nazis maybe decided to make a stand here, buckin' up and holding their own."

As if for confirmation, there are sounds of savage combat, echoing off the hill-sides around them. Much like the nearby borders of Germany, Luxembourg, and Belgium, the lines on a map marking territory controlled by Allies and Germans are difficult to discern in the cockeyed reality of war.

"Captain, I hate to be a nag, but—"

"Since when, Tony?"

"Maybe so, but how sure are you that we're still behind the Third Army? I got that same feeling I had before, you know, when we damn near got captured. Feels like we're on an island out here all by ourselves and there could be a Nazi sharp-shooter behind every tree and rock."

"That feeling you got? Probably just gas. Fart and it'll pass. I'd say from the sound of all that back and forth our boys are pushing the Krauts on toward Nancy by now. What kind of name for a French town is Nancy? Jesus. Notrees has a better ring to it, don't it?"

With a final pull, Bennett extracts the exploder fuze from the American bomb with a flourish. Gabler waves back to the squad—or what remains of it now that it has violently lost three members—to let them know they've neutered the bomb.

They have been seeking shelter underneath the truck, helmets on, just in case. This time, there will be no immediate removal of the bomb's carcass. The engineers are busy elsewhere. There is plenty of live stuff exploding nearby. Very nearby. This one had been a threat to the adjacent roadway while it was still armed, a hindrance to Patton's parade. It will be no problem now. Toxic material falling from the sky is the primary concern. As if to make the point, an especially potent artillery round lands just down the valley from them. Chunks of rocks and northeastern France earth rain down on them.

"Captain, we need to get this stuff buried and detonated before the Krauts detonate and bury us!"

"Okay, okay, Sergeant," Bennett snaps. He knows his squad is of the opinion he is too cavalier at times. That he takes risks he does not have to take just to get a job done quicker. He also knows they still partly blame him for the two incidents that took the lives of their squad mates. He still believes that having their CO show confidence helps them handle the pressure of such hazardous duty. He stands, holds up the exploder for them to see—even as another shell lands a few hundred yards away, and shouts an ironic, "Clear! Clear!"

Before Bennett can take a half dozen steps back toward the hole his men have shoveled out beneath the limbs of a gigantic red oak, not far from the river Meurthe, a loud, gruff voice in a foreign tongue calls out, "Halt! Stoppen!"

Hedley Bennett stops. German soldiers—maybe eight or ten—encircle the clearing, rifles pointed at him, Tony, the men beneath the red-fendered truck.

"You are, how you say? Bomb squad, right?" the apparent leader asks.

Hedley flashes his best smile, hoping to disarm his enemy just the way it has most people he has met over the years. But it seems his charming grin has no effect on the German soldier. He uses the muzzle of his rifle to direct the BD captain to his knees.

Bennett looks up, smiles even bigger, and says, "Hedley Oscar Bennett. Captain. Serial number oh-81333-zero-9. From Washington, DC."

The German frowns, pauses a moment, then steps closer to Hedley and looks hard at the American's dirty face. "You look much like the film actor. The one in the Gone with the Breeze motion picture." Then, satisfied the man he has captured is not anyone famous, he says, "You have luck with you. We have value for what you do. You with your rote kotflügels. Red fenders. We know the thing that such markings signify. You will help us with—"

"Hedley Oscar Bennett. Captain. Serial number oh—"

The German viciously strikes Hedley in the jaw with the butt of his rifle, knocking him to the ground. "Allowed to live. But do not test my patience!"

There is still the roar of battle around them as the Bomb Merchants march eastward single file. Down a scenic vale. Across a clear-water stream. Up a forested mountainside where the high sun is now shadowed by smoke.

Marching toward the nearby but indiscernible German border.

11

When the first bright stab of sunlight hit his face and woke him up, he believed that he was in his bed back in Mahanoy City. He half expected the aroma of eggs and bacon as Mom got breakfast ready for him and Tommy and Pops, the sounds of Glenn Miller on the radio coming in from the big station in Philly. Opening his eyes after the best night of sleep he had had in many months, he took in his surroundings and was startled to find he was in a room in the Hotel Astoria on the Champs-Élysées in Paris. Visiting the City of Lights, a lifelong dream that pre-dated his more recent vivid nightmares.

He, Hank Anderson, Doc Fenton, and several other members of the congressional delegation had enjoyed a sumptuous dinner in the hotel's restaurant the previous night. His system more accustomed to bland mess hall chow and K-rations, the rich food and glasses of wine brought Edward a night of fiery indigestion. The conversation left his mind roiling with thoughts of home and friends and family that Doc mentioned as he shared seemingly endless anecdotes until late into the evening. Some were quite personal, embarrassing Edward with Hank Anderson sitting there, taking them all in. Fenton was well meaning, of course, bringing a bit of home to Edward, but such talk allowed long-suppressed memories to surface once Hume's head hit the surprisingly lumpy pillow.

Once back in his room, Edward sat at the antique desk and tried to write a letter to Mom and Pops on a sheet of fancy hotel stationery, but the words would not come. He took a long-anticipated bath, the first good one he had enjoyed since England. But he kept thinking of his squad, back in Pontorson, still getting cold showers in a makeshift latrine. Then there was the nauseating image of a fat German officer who had likely bathed—or done who knows what else—in this same elegant claw-footed tub where Edward was now mostly submerged beneath bubbles and hot water.

Outside his window, the fireworks sounded like gunfire. Shouts of celebration, too, that could have just as easily been screams of soldiers caught in crossfire. And music. Music from somewhere he could not quite discern, even after he closed his window. He finally noticed a radio in the far corner of the room was switched on, its volume low, and its dial set on a station broadcasting peppy marching band music in observance of the liberation.

He sat up on the side of his bed, checked his watch to find he had slept an hour longer than intended. Then there was a knock on his door.

"Captain, you up?" It was Anderson.

"Give me two more minutes, Corporal."

He hastily pulled on his clothes, ran a comb through his thick hair, put on his cap, and went out to meet Hank, who had been waiting patiently in the hallway, sitting on the floor, thumbing through a French-language newspaper. Toothbrushing would have to wait. So would breakfast, though they managed to grab a couple of buttery croissants from a platter in the lobby. Getting those medals back to Doc Fenton and his big event took priority over personal hygiene and food.

Making the drive along the Seine and to the neighborhood surrounding Notre-Dame Cathedral was problematic. The streets still teemed with pedestrians, finally free to move about. Military vehicles—mostly American and a few French—made their own roads wherever they could, even over sidewalks and across expansive plazas where previous challengers to this or that monarchy had been publicly beheaded. At least according to Hank's running tour-guide-like commentary, delivered as he sawed the jeep's steering wheel side to side and honked his horn to hurry their passage through the jam of humanity.

They made it to the engraving shop right at ten o'clock. The place remained closed despite what the sign on the door said. They watched all the activity along the nearby Rue de Rivoli, around the Hotel de Ville, and on the river just beyond. Motion, noise, frenzied activity all around them.

Eleven o'clock came and went. No sign of life through the tiny shop's front window. Edward checked Doc's list again. They were in the right place, now an hour past the right time.

He finally walked around to the alleyway behind the shop, climbed the stairs to a door one level up directly above the engraver's shop, and knocked. A bleary-eyed man still in his robe finally answered, squinting in the bright sun, shielding his face with his forearm.

"*Oui? Qui est-ce?*"

Yet again, Edward fell back on his high school French. Too much wine the previous evening was the man's excuse for not yet opening his shop below. Hume could sympathize. The man said he would put on clothes, meet Edward downstairs. "*Un moment.*"

The first thing the old man did when he ushered Edward and Hank into his shop was to hug both soldiers and kiss them on both cheeks.

"*Merci! Merci beaucoup! Les Allemands*...Germans...*très mauvais*. Bad!"

Both men smiled but blushed a deep red, looking sideways at each other. Neither was comfortable being kissed by another man.

"Woz would have kissed him back," Anderson whispered. "On the lips." Edward gave his corporal a pointed glare.

With the box filled with engraved medallions in tow, they cranked up to start toward the hotel. Maybe they could cross one of the bridges over the Seine to the West Bank to find a less congested route. Hume's appointment with the hotel's banquet manager was in less than twenty minutes. But after only a few blocks, well before passing the Louvre Museum once again, they heard a female voice yelling. Stridently yelling.

"Red fenders! Please! Help us! *Ailes rouges! S'il vous plaît! Aidez-nous!*"

It was an elderly nun, running their way awkwardly, frantically waving her arms, clearly in distress. Hank pulled to a stop without asking the captain's permission. Edward instinctively kept his hand on his pistol handle.

"Sister, how may we help?" the corporal asked her.

"You are explosive technicians, yes? The red fenders. God has sent you to us!"

The nun explained that she served in a nearby orphanage. One of the children had found a device in the street near where there had been fighting between the Free French and the Germans. He had foolishly brought it to his ward and hid it beneath his bed. When the nun learned of it, she headed toward the Hôtel Le Meurice, the headquarters for General de Gaulle, to see if someone there might help her. She saw Edward and Hank first.

"Baptiste, the boy, he refuses to remove the device," the sister explained. "His father went to war for the Resistance and has not been heard from for more than three years. We do not know what happened to his mother. But Baptiste, he says the device is for his father when he returns from the fighting, a gift, and he will not let it leave from beneath his bed."

Edward frowned, checked his wristwatch, then looked back at her. "But how do you know the red fenders, who we are?"

"My sister, she lives near London. RAF red fenders saved her neighborhood from a Luftwaffe bomb. She has written me the story many times to show that God is powerful, benevolent. My being a bride of Christ is not in vain. You must help us. The orphanage, it is only a block from here. We have evacuated, but Baptiste refuses to leave his bed."

Hume nodded to Hank. To hell with the wristwatch. The banquet. The medallions.

The look on the woman's face was all it took. Hank already knew the decision his captain would make. He had pulled the jeep onto the sidewalk, mostly out of traffic, grabbed Edward's tool bag—yes, he brought it with him to Paris—from beneath the seat, and hopped out.

At least fifty children played in a small park across the street from a building that appeared to have been converted from something else, likely a hotel, into an orphanage. When they saw the American soldiers approaching, many of the children ran to greet them. One little girl gave Hank a small flower. But there was no smile on her face, nor on the faces of those other fatherless and motherless kids. There was heartbreaking dullness in their eyes. They likely had little concept of liberation or what had just happened in their city, or why everyone else seemed so suddenly ecstatic.

A wave of melancholy washed over Edward. He could not imagine what it would have been like not growing up with Mom, Pops, and Tommy. Always there when he needed them.

"C'mon, Hank. Let's see what Baptiste has brought home."

The boy, maybe ten years old, sat, legs crossed, in the middle of a small bed surrounded by several dozen others just like it. There was a defiant look on his young face. He was not about to move or give up his prize.

"*Tu n'auras pas mon souvenir!*" "You will not get my souvenir."

The boy relented only after Edward explained he would be allowed to keep the device, but that they first had to make it safe. Safe so he could remain alive to present it to his father. Of course, Hume had no idea if he would be able to keep that promise.

Once under the bed on his belly and with Hank by his side—assuming there would be no jobs to document, he had left his camera in his hotel room—Edward quickly determined it was a German Wehrmacht M24 "potato masher" grenade. But it was a variant he had never seen in person. There was a white band around the device's wooden handle and markings on its top that confirmed it was not an explosive after all.

It was a smoke grenade.

Hume slid from beneath the bed, rolled over onto his back, and told Baptiste if this had been the standard M24, and had its arming cord been pulled, many people would have been hurt or killed when it exploded. And that blast would have occurred less than five seconds after the cord was yanked. He finally made the boy understand that he and his corporal would carry the grenade outside—or the boy could carry it himself—and then everyone could observe from a distance as they made the device safe. Then, Baptiste could have it back if it was okay with the sisters. He could give it to his father when he returned from the war.

The mob of children, a dozen nuns, and many passersby watched from the park as Edward placed the potato masher on a cement step at the entrance to the orphanage. Hank watched, peeking from behind a nearby tree. With an exaggerated bow to the spectators—several of the nuns had hands to their mouths in disbelief that this crazy American soldier was about to detonate a bomb on the steps of their institution—and a theatrical flourish, Hume pulled the cord from the device. Then he stepped quickly to join his corporal behind the tree.

Some gasped as others cheered when the odd-looking grenade suddenly began emitting thick gray-black smoke. It was wafted away on the breeze, back toward the southwest and the River Seine. The display lasted a surprisingly long time, but when it finally fizzled out, the crowd cheered mightily.

Edward walked back over, bent to examine the grenade, touched it to be sure it was not hot, or that it might have more smoke to spit out, then casually picked it up. He motioned for Baptiste to come over, bowed to him, and solemnly presented the boy the spent smoke grenade.

"For you. Your father. Bring back to your home no more *explosifs, oui*? No boom-boom!"

Now everyone was trying to pat the Americans on their backs, giving hugs, saying "*Merci beau coups!*"

"Captain, we gotta go!" Hank finally reminded his CO.

"Yeah, we gotta make sure they don't put too much salt in the consommé, right?"

As Edward and Hank jogged back to the jeep, the captain said, "Shit, Corporal, except for Doc Fenton, I won't know a solitary soul at that banquet tonight. And as much as I respect the medical personnel, and even though Doc wants me there, I'm thinking about ditching this party and heading back to the squad soon as we get things squared away."

Hank looked sideward at his captain. "Hell, sir, you get a fine meal and another bath in a real tub and a night's sleep in a nice feather bed." Breathing hard from the run, he was still able to add, "Besides, you never know who you might run into. If a US soldier can't get laid in Paris right now, he ain't tryin'!"

Edward laughed as he jumped into his seat in the jeep and pointed up Rue de Rivoli, toward the Eiffel Tower. The iconic structure stood boldly erect on the distant skyline.

"Truth is, our orders came from the colonel, not from Doc Fenton," Edward noted as they blended into traffic. "And we obey orders. I go to the banquet. You wander the City of Lights like a tourist. That make you happy, Corporal?"

Anderson nodded, grinned, but kept his attention on the melee of the narrow street they were transiting.

For the first time in two days, Edward thought of Captain Hedley Bennett and his Bomb Merchants. In the briefing the morning he and Hank left Pontorson, there had been a mention that Bennett's squad was overdue to report in from somewhere in the Lorraine region. Surely, they had shown up by now. And that reminded him that he and Hank needed to find time to get Edward's picture in front of the Eiffel Tower as proof he had won their latest wager.

God, he prayed, as they sped back toward their hotel, *let Hed and his boys be okay.*

That led to thoughts about his own squad. Most likely, everything was fine back in Pontorson. Edward had tried to convince himself on the trip to Paris that the team was having an easy few days without him pushing them. Woz would keep things on an even keel. The guys knew what to do and what not to do.

As the corporal tried to conquer the gridlock and get them back to the hotel and their assigned duty, Hume tried to take in the iconic scenery and the euphoric mood of this storied city, another place he had so long imagined visiting.

He could only hope reality would not intrude on his fantasies as it had so brutally done back at Mont Saint Michel.

12

Gene Wozinski took off his glasses and rubbed his eyes with thumb and forefinger. Myopia had kept him out of the Air Corps. Now the glasses made it difficult to focus on the tiny etchings on the dud bomb he was struggling to identify. He knew he was only supposed to look at the thing, make notes, and place white flags next to it, then warn those who lived nearby not to get near it until the BD captain returned and made it safe. But Woz was amped. He had just swallowed one of the little pills, chased with lukewarm water from his canteen. It already had him rationalizing mightily.

Hell, he had undergone much of the same training as Captain Hume had, back in Maryland and with the RAF in England, even if he never qualified to enter the program for squad captain. Since then, he had plenty of opportunities to observe as the captain and Brit bomb disposal guys worked on devices, many very similar to this one. He had a background in science as a high school science teacher before the war in Chicago and that fed his confidence. Dammit, he knew precisely how to handle it, make it safe, right there and then.

Why not? Why couldn't he—despite being "only a digger"—go ahead, do this simple job, and maybe save some lives and property?

Wozinski had already been dubbed "the Clark Kent of bomb disposal" by the squad members. That was based on his black-rimmed spectacles and well-built physique. Actually, he did resemble the character in the new *Superman* comic books.

I'd just be solving a problem, he told himself. Like he had asked his students to do back in the classroom in Chicago.

A hundred yards away, the other Kaboom Boys—Morty, Pete, and Carl—rested in the grass trying to absorb what little warmth the dim sunlight offered, smoking, arguing, laughing, doing what Private Morty Schwartz called "kibbitzing." It was Morty who noticed Wozinski was getting mighty intimate with the bomb he was examining and still had not planted any flags.

"Shit! Captain's only been gone a day and Woz is about to defuze a fifty-pounder!"

"I better go over there and stop him," Carl offered, but by the time he was up on his feet, they saw Gene pull out several white flags and start planting them into the ground around the UXB. The watching villagers did not seem pleased as Gene jogged over to where the squad waited. Neither did he.

"Damn waste of time!" Woz muttered.

"Man! I thought you was gonna shitcan that bomb on your own, Superman!" Pete called out.

"I was close. Then I heard Captain inside my head, yelling at me and saying, 'Got that?'"

"Good call, Gene," said Morty. The men seemed relieved. Not Wozinski.

"Maybe we get a drink in town. Blow off some steam," Carl suggested and started for the truck.

But Wozinski was looking back at the white flags flapping in the wind, at the villagers gathered in irritated knots, pointing at the still-lethal bomb, and at the Americans who were supposed to fix it.

"I was close." Gene climbed into the truck. "Damn close."

"Yeah, we noticed."

"Guys, go get your drinks," Woz told them. "Drop me off at the barracks. I got somebody I wanna go see."

Like their captain, both Gene and Carl had made interesting local friends since arriving in Pontorson. Hank stuck mostly to reading and Morty spent any spare time wandering about, looking for local Jews, trying to learn about people that folks back home were asking him about.

Carl had met his new *ami* as they were busy inventorying equipment for the truck while setting up shop on their first day there. That new acquaintance was a handsome but obviously underfed jet-black standard French poodle that trotted up to Kostas. The critter was begging for food and a belly rub. Carl had seen the animal from a distance before, playing with those he called "free-range kids," youngsters who liked to tag along with the BD boys, soaking up excitement by watching the squad work. From a distance, of course. He could only assume the young poodle had been separated from his owners during the latest fighting. Now, at least for the time being, the pup began living beneath the squad's truck. Though he was quickly adopted and spoiled by the entire group, everyone knew it was Carl's dog. Captain Hume was all for it. A "squad dog" was good to have for morale. Truth was, Edward missed Sarge, his own best-friend boxer back home.

Carl named the poodle Whitey. He thought it was perfect for a midnight-black animal. And Whitey seemed to like the K-ration canned meat far better than the soldiers. That made the pup even more loyal to the squad members, and soon Whitey appeared to understand commands in English as well as American-accented French. So far, nobody had broached the subject of what they might do with Whitey when the squad inevitably transitioned eastward. Hank Anderson pointed out that General Patton usually had Willie, his English bull terrier, in the jeep with him as he shoved his Third Army toward Germany. Edward told them he would be fine with the poodle riding with them in the truck so long as he did not get in the way of their work or somebody higher up the command chain did not object.

The attachment to Whitey led the men to form a closer relationship with the orphaned kids, too. The youngsters loved that dog, and anyone who loved the poodle was all right by both kids and soldiers. Before long, a trust developed, and whenever they had free time, Carl and Pete started teaching the war-scarred kids of Pontorson the basics of baseball.

After the men cleared a field of landmines, the children were safe there playing America's pastime. The game was actually stickball, Pete's preferred variant. They used techniques and rules from his days playing in the streets of Bay Ridge, Brooklyn, dodging taxis and lorries. The kids delighted in learning the game. It also took their minds off the nightmare that was their daily lives.

They used for their bat the handle Ronzini sawed off an Army-issued broom. They relied on his personal supply of Spaldeen Hi-Bounce rubber balls. Pete had hauled them from home all the way to France, just in case a game broke out at a base somewhere. The youngsters quickly became serious about the competition, spending most days in the mine-cleared field near the barracks, playing endless games, well beyond nine innings. Whitey enthusiastically chased hitters around the base paths and retrieved foul balls. Carl and Pete coached when they could, in between missions, but not nearly as much as they would have liked. These kids surely craved male attention, mentors, father figures.

A couple of the kids had gotten quite good at hitting and fielding, including one eleven-year-old named Theo Toussaint. He seemed intent on taking revenge against the Nazis by murdering Spaldeens. Theo told Carl and Pete that the Germans had taken his father away to a labor camp. Equally tragic, they had ignored his mother's tuberculosis, barring her from the crowded medical facilities to make room for wounded German soldiers. Theo blamed the Nazis for allowing her to die. His propensity for smashing home runs caused him to launch one too many rubber balls into the outfield bocage. Only about half were recovered, even with Whitey's help. The unsupervised games were costing the team their meager equipment supply.

"Hey, guys! Too many balls in the hedgerows!" Pete pointed at Theo. "You're ready for the major leagues and that means we need to clear another diamond with a bigger outfield and move the games down there." Pete pointed the kids toward a larger pasture down near the river with Mont Saint Michel and an ancient windmill in the distance. It would be an idyllic place for a game with bleating sheep in a nearby salt marsh as their fans, even if the animals were more interested in grazing than watching hour after hour of stickball.

Gene Wozinski's new friend and his relationship with her were considerably more complicated than Carl's and Whitey's. A barmaid in her early thirties—a full decade older than Woz—Agathe Dumoulin approached Woz one night at the newly opened "No Name Bar." The place had become a regular stop during the squad's infrequent off-duty time, primarily due to the ample supply of calvados and local wines.

When she walked up to the table, Woz assumed the barmaid would be interested in Carl. Most women were. And Woz was also aware some women had intuition that informed them his version of Clark Kent might not be interested in females. But she confidently looked directly at Gene, effectively ignoring the others.

He saw at once that Agathe was not like other girls who enjoyed chatting and giggling with soldiers, and who sometimes wanted much more. That suited the romantically starved Allied soldiers. She was more direct. More self-assured.

"This one, it is on me," Agathe announced in passable English as she poured Gene another shot of calvados—Normandy's traditional apple brandy—from the bottle on her tray. She had nothing for the others at the table.

Carl's eyes widened as he punched Gene's shoulder. "It's your lucky night, buddy!"

Wozinski's face was flushed already from the two glasses of calvados he had consumed. Now it turned a deeper hue of scarlet as a result of the barmaid's forwardness.

"You like?" she asked him with a dazzling smile.

"I do."

"More?"

He could not be sure if her last question was about the drink or something else. It suddenly occurred to Gene this attractive woman might be offering him a new opportunity, a chance for something he had never built up the nerve on his own to attempt. Sex with a female. His few prior physical relationships had been with men, fleeting, clandestine. He had kept his homosexuality a secret except for the few men with whom he had a brief relationship. The Army could never know, of course. That would certainly lead to a dishonorable discharge. Some of his squad members had their suspicions, he knew.

But maybe he had been wrong all along about his inclinations. Maybe a willing woman would help him confirm it.

The alcohol may have played a role in his initial decision to submit to Agathe Dumoulin's bold advances. Regardless of how it started, the relationship quickly became very complicated.

Agathe's husband had disappeared in the early days of German occupation. Later, she entered into a heated tryst with a German soldier but kept it secret. Such collaboration resulted in public humiliation, especially after the liberation by the Allies. She hoped the SS sergeant could help her learn the fate of her husband. He did not. But he did provide food, money, and companionship, all scarce commodities.

And along the way, her German soldier had introduced her to the amphetamines so many of Hitler's soldiers had been issued by the bagful. The pills were soon doing much more to get her through the dismal days than food, money, or disdained companionship ever could.

Now, Wozinski expressed his doubts to Agathe that he would ever be able to fully make love to her, no matter how much she tried to help him. Eventually, she offered him some of the SS "battle fatigue" pills to see if they might do some good.

"And maybe they will also make you the braver when you cause the bombs to not go boom," she said.

"Oh, I am not allowed to work on the bombs," he explained. "Protocol."

"But maybe the pills, they will make you defy your protocol, your commander, make you brave enough to fix the bombs. I saw you today putting out those flags. You must stop the bombs."

"I'll try for the...for the lovemaking. Not for the bombs."

They did nothing for the lovemaking. But they did make him feel brighter, more alert, more positive about himself, about going out there every day and doing what he did, about his future after this war ended and he pursued his plans to become an engineer. Agathe had plenty of the pills left, was happy to share, and he began caching them in his shaving kit back in the barracks, starting each day with a couple of them to get him going.

Soon he felt invincible. Maybe even ready to defy the captain and tackle one of those bombs if it posed a particular hazard. Prove himself a strong BD man, like he always thought he should be.

The pills, he finally admitted to himself, actually did make him feel like Superman.

Dr. Ernst Alwin has no guilt whatsoever over the number of people who have died as the result of his work. Death is inevitable in both war and life. And the cause of Germany is a righteous one. He is convinced the Führer—the leader for life of the German Reich—and the National Socialist Party—the Nazi Party—are correct on all points, that the war is the proper response to the harsh, vindictive treatment of Germany by the Treaty of Versailles at the conclusion of the Great War. That there is a conspiracy among the world's governments against Germany, determined to keep the once great nation in submission. That the anti-Deutschland movement is led in part by inferior races, such as the Jews—especially the Jews—and the land-hungry empire builders, the Russians. And then there is the intellectual class: academics, professors, teachers, economists, lawyers, journalists, writers, artists, and other professionals whose rabid opinions contribute to the decline of society. He is convinced an Aryan-led empire could and should return all of Europe to its previous glory. To how it was before the world's democracies condemned Germans to die from cold and hunger, in a place where formerly wealthy and aristocratic citizens burned money in the winter to provide heat because wood was more valuable than Reichsmarks. No, they should do whatever is required to assure victory. That includes the systematic elimination of the impure, the mongrels, the homosexuals, the socialists, the egghead intellectuals whose theories override common sense and logic.

Ernst Alwin has also heard whispers that his country—in consultation with the Empire of Japan—is on the verge of a scientific development that will once again turn the course of this war back to Germany's favor. He is not supposed to be privy to such knowledge, but he has curious, loyal informants in many high places within the Reich mostly due to his wife's connections—a cadre of smart men who understand Alwin will be a powerful ally in a victorious post-war Germany—and they report to him that work continues on the "super bomb."

However, finding a source for the nuclear materials the lead scientists believe necessary to complete and test this weapon prevents its deployment. Ernst believes Werner Heisenberg and others have grossly miscalculated how much uranium would be necessary to create an effective atomic bomb. Additionally, they refuse to consult with Jewish physicists, the top minds in the world regardless of what the Nazis believe are their ethnic defects. That area of expertise could be utilized, voluntarily or otherwise, before those scientists would become subject to the Reich's Final Solution to the Jewish Question. Alwin knows from his own work—and that of Albert Einstein and other Jews—that a much smaller and more achievable amount of U-235 could be used to construct a fearsome "dirty" bomb. He also has scientist friends with whom he attended university who claim to have access to sources for U-235 that he hoped to arrange for his own experimental use. He would now be able to tap them should he be called upon to do so. Plus, and even more important, his training and dedicated work right here in his Dachau laboratory has led him to conclude that he can design a bomb that requires far less such material than some claim will be necessary. Yet it will create much the same results and adequately demonstrate the awesome power of such a weapon. And Ernst is convinced that once his country and the Japanese have shown the power of this super bomb, they will never actually have to ignite another one. It will be the deterrent effect that will immediately end hostilities. The so-called Allies will rush to seek peace before another "demonstration" proved it could instantly end the lives of millions of people. And then, just when the Allies believe they have won the war, they will be more than willing to reverse the advance of their attacking forces. Germany could truly reunite the continent of Europe under one government, overseen by the visionary Hitler.

He just needs the opportunity to present his plan.

Ernst is a trained physicist. He has not exactly been wasting his time so far with switches, fuzes, trick circuits, exotic biological schemes, or ever more powerful traditional explosions and the means to create them. Those efforts are serving their purpose, even if the Allies still push across France from the west toward Berlin. Even as Russia threatens from the east. He, of all scientists working on behalf of the Führer, understands how such a catastrophic device as this super bomb can work.

Not even Helga, his politically astute and savvy wife, comprehends the power Ernst has within his reach. No, she is more interested in parties and coffee klatches with the wives of high political figures than she is in his vital work, but she is her father's daughter, raised by one of the oligarchs, a former aristocrat and businessman who also serves Hitler.

Soon, though, they will all know. Helga, Herr Albert Speer, and Herr Kanzler Hitler himself.

This is why Ernst Alwin whistles quietly, happily, and ignores the screams from the laboratory buildings along his route on this chilly morning. It is only a short hike from his quarters to his laboratory. And it is there where he will continue to work on the final details of his ultimate death engine.

13

The Kaboom Boys had their first job even before the dust from Hume and Anderson's jeep had settled as they departed Pontorson. Grenades. Booby traps. An ammo dump. Dangerous souvenirs. But no bombs.

However, the very next day, they got the call to take a look at the UXB Gene Wozinski had come so close to working on. Then, that evening, the squad was summoned from the No Name—and had to track down Woz at his girlfriend's place—to go take a look at a potentially deadly device just discovered by a couple of goldbricking soldiers in a bug-infested bunker adjacent to the Pontorson airfield. Wozinski led them into the concrete underground structure, maybe a machine gun nest or a bomb shelter for the airfield's previous occupants. Kostas and Schwartz looked over Wozinski's shoulder as he determined what the device was.

"Well, it's a bomb," Carl said, stating the obvious, as he slapped away a spider's web. "Looks American. Guess we call somebody with a captain to come fix it, huh?"

"Yeah, and it's been here for more than a couple of months already and still ain't popped," Pete added. "No emergency."

"If it was gonna blow on its own, it probably would have gone off already, right?" Morty commented, hoping Wozinski would not take this one farther than he had the previous device.

Both men had already come to the conclusion that an abnormally hyped-up Wozinski might soon decide to ignore the captain's orders and established procedure.

Gene looked back at both men. His eyes were startlingly wide and wild in their flashlight beams. "The hell if we call anybody else, guys! This is barely a bomb. But if this thing detonates, it could put the airstrip out of commission for a while." A plane on takeoff roared past outside as if to confirm Wozinski's point. "I know this device. It's German. It's a butterfly bomb."

Luftwaffe butterfly bombs were so named because of the thin cylindrical metal outer shell which opened when the bomb dropped giving it wings like a butterfly.

"So let's back out of here and plant some flags, what say?" Carl suggested.

"And get the hell out of these damned fire ants!" Morty was dancing around, slapping the stinging insects off his arms.

"Lookit, boys, I saw plenty of these with the RAF back in England," Gene said, his voice growing louder, his words coming more rapidly. "No, no, no. Not in the field, no, but in the training room, you know. Plenty of 'em. They look just like a butterfly when they drop. You guys heard of 'em, right? It's a snap to fix these things. I'm a bomb demolition man. Any real man can do it. Nothing special. Captain, he'll understand. Just this one, just this once..."

Morty gave Carl and Pete a serious side-eye. Gene was acting off-the-scale odd.

But before they could argue with him, Gene spun around, back to the small bomb, screwdriver in hand, and was already removing the cover over the fuze pocket.

"You work on that bastard, you do it on your own, pal," Morty declared. Carl nodded in agreement. "You can have the bomb, the butterfly, and the fire ants all to yourself."

As they exited the bunker, Carl stopped and turned back to ask, "You okay, Woz? You're sure acting all fidgety."

"I'm doin' good," Wozinski answered, but he was talking to the bomb, armed with a screwdriver.

Kostas, Schwartz, and Ronzini got busy digging the disposal pit in a nearby pasture, then found shade to have a smoke and wait for Woz to emerge with the lethal innards. And hoped they would not hear a blast instead. They pointedly did not discuss Gene's strange behavior of late, or his choice of romantic partners.

A long half hour later, Woz emerged from the bunker, canvas sack held high like some kind of trophy, grinning broadly as he double-timed it their way.

"Defective fuze. Never would have detonated. I guess they were having trouble getting good help back in Deutschland when they were building these things," Gene reported. No mention was made of the other two men abandoning him in the bunker with what could just as easily have been a lethal device.

Gene would go on to defuze four more bombs before Edward and Hank returned from Paris, performing each forbidden job solo and over the pointed objections of the rest of the squad.

The following day after the bomb at the airfield, the squad was returning from a full ten hours of mostly grunt work. As usual, Whitey ran to greet them and beg for more canned meat.

It was growing dark. Everyone was bushed. Everyone but Gene Wozinski.

"Guys, if you don't mind, I have a date with a girl." Oddly of late, Gene felt the need to specify the gender of his partner for the evening though none of them especially cared. "Can you guys get the tools cleaned up and back in the truck? Give Whitey a bite to eat before he gnaws a hole in my boot again? The supply sergeant gave me some shit for that one."

"Sure, Woz. Since you have a date with a girl," Pete teased.

Before Gene could leave, though, a man came running their way from down the street. He waved his arms, yelling, clearly in distress. Carl retrieved his rifle from the truck, just in case.

"*Officier! Venez! Vite! Un bombe. Un garçon est blessé!*"

"What's he screaming about?" Morty asked.

"Something about a bomb, a boy hurt," Gene replied.

Then they were back in the truck, Whitey watching curiously as they left him behind, unfed. The man rode along in the cab, directing them to a spot not that far away, on Rue des Moulins—Road of the Windmills—the main route from Beauvoir and Mont Saint Michel to Pontorson. He guided them to where a sizeable crowd had gathered, milling about along a walking path next to the River Couesnon, adjacent to the new field where the kids now played their marathon stickball games.

"They don't look none too happy to see us," Carl noted.

It was true. Those gathered there pointed to the Americans and shouted indecipherable but obviously angry words.

"Whatever happened here I betcha they think it's our fault," Gene said as they hopped from the truck and followed their guide past the shouting townspeople, across the walking path, and into thick brush along the riverbank. There was a sizeable hole down there, vegetation ripped away by a powerful blast of some type. There was still smoke in the air and still more drifted up from scorched earth. And remnants of red cloth were snagged on the few remaining nearby bushes.

Another man stepped up, a clearly distressed man, his face pale. "I speak little English. But I see what happened here minutes before."

"Please," Gene urged.

"The *garçon*...the boy...he walks toward where he and the others play the games, looking for the spheres...the balls they throw and hit. He sees a Nazi flag down the *colline*, near the river, in *des buissons*...the bushes. I was believing he goes for to get the flag for a souvenir. No. He hits and kicks at *le drapeau*...the flag. Angry, he is. Very much angry. The Germans, they took his father away. His mother, she dies. So, he is angry at the flag with the swastika from the Nazis. He kicks it. Hard. Then, *boom*!"

"Jesus," Morty muttered from behind the eyewitness. "Booby trap. But the thing had to have been here for months."

Gene nodded to the man to confirm that he now understood what happened. "There is no longer danger." He pointed to the seething crowd. "But why are they so angry with us?"

The man struggled for the right English words. "They believe you...the Allies...do not do enough to make safe the people of Pontorson." He raised his hands, palms up, signifying he does not necessarily agree, but there is nothing he can do about the prevailing sentiment. Gene and the others have seen it before. Yes, plenty of appreciation. But resentment, centered now on the only ones on whom they can focus their frustrations. Regardless of what the Allies may have done and sacrificed to liberate the people, to bring them peace.

Admittedly, standing there on the riverbank amid the smoke from this latest violent explosion, peace is not necessarily a tangible reality.

"The boy? Was he badly hurt?" Gene asked.

With a sorrowful shadow on his face, the man responded, "No. He is... how you say? Torn apart. *Mort*. Dead."

"So sorry. So very sorry," Gene said, but with a very bad feeling in his gut. The boost from his morning pills was wearing off. "We have taken care of so many of these devices already. But it will be years before they are all gone. Many of our soldiers have died, too. Please, tell everyone to be careful. We will do all we can to make them safe as we locate them."

Pete and Carl had been walking briskly up and down the path, looking for any other potential deathtraps. They saw nothing. Now, they stepped up just in time to hear what the man was reporting about the boy's death.

"You say a young man was killed in the blast?" Carl asked.

"*Oui*. A boy from Pontorson with a sad story, like so many."

"You know his name?"

"*Oui*. Everybody, we know Theo Toussaint. As I say, his story..."

They all looked at one another, tears already in their eyes, shock on their faces. Theo. The boy who had been taking his revenge on the Nazis with a broomstick and a Spaldeen Hi-Bounce ball. The kid who reminded Gene Wozinski of so many of his students back home.

It would be a somber ride back to the barracks now with the passing of an honorary Kaboom Boy.

Sitting in the truck's passenger seat beside him, Morty noticed how Gene was fidgeting even more than usual. His hands moved around the perimeter of the steering wheel like it was hot to the touch. He tapped the wheel as if he was playing some odd musical instrument, bounced in his seat, worked the clutch pedal up and down unnecessarily, maybe just to cause the engine to whine and complain. Meanwhile, Pete and Carl sat in back, studying their own hands and boots, not saying a word.

When they came to a stop in their assigned parking spot at the row of tents, Morty and Gene spotted a soldier, sitting on the steps on his duffel bag. He was petting Whitey, who noticed the squad's truck pulling up. The soldier stood and tossed them a friendly wave when he saw the Kaboom Boys sign in the truck windshield. He and the poodle headed their direction as the squad members climbed out of the vehicle.

"You the guys they call the Kaboom Boys, I reckon," the soldier said, pleasantly enough. He offered his hand to Woz. The stripes on the waiting soldier's sleeve indicated he was a sergeant. And BD. He had left his helmet atop the duffel bag, revealing a head full of mahogany-brown hair, neatly parted and combed back but longer than the typical GI haircut. And both BD boys immediately noticed the sergeant's unusual eyes. Catlike, copper-colored and expressive. Noticed his slightly crooked nose, too. They would soon learn that facial feature was the result of a playground fight years before. "I'm Sergeant Jack Morrison from Hebron, Nebraska, just finished up BD training at APG and with the RAF, learned all the latest stuff, and I'm your replacement guy reporting for duty. Where's the CO?"

Gene Wozinski stepped back and looked the newcomer up and down. "Well, not sure anybody could replace Ace Taft," he pointedly remarked. "But we're sure as shit glad to get some help. We've been damn busy around here lately. You say you know the latest, huh?"

"Indeed, I do," Morrison proudly stated.

"Captain Hume's off in Paris for something or the other," Morty explained. "And so is his acting number two, but Captain will put your ass right to work if you can dig a hole and take pictures and drive a jeep."

Still in a funk, the other two men offered weak welcomes to Morrison. "Sorry, Jack," Woz finally said. "We're glad to see you, but we just got some tough news about one of the local kids we been helping get through all this shit."

Morrison accepted the apology with an understanding nod, but he did not ask for details about the bad news or the local kid. Instead, he took one big step back, looked for a long moment at the face of each man in the new squad of which he was now a crucial member, and, with an odd look in those distinctively colored eyes of his, announced, "I just have one question for you boys."

"Mess hall's a block up the way, there," Morty said, anticipating the newcomer's query. "And the powdered eggs ain't for shit. Stick with the pastries and biscuits if you don't want a terminal case of the shit-squirts."

"The coldest beer within walking distance is at Hotel Dupont but even that's warm as piss," Carl added. "Even so, don't touch their liquor, no matter the label on the bottle they're pouring from. It's mostly H2O. You got to drink most of the bottle to even get a goddam buzz."

"Don't bother asking for ice either," Pete offered. "They ain't heard of the damn stuff around here."

"And the girls that hang around at the Dupont will go out back with you and screw like rabbits if you buy 'em enough drinks and feed 'em enough chocolate and talk sweet to 'em," Morty continued, eager to speak about something, anything other than Theo Toussaint.

"So welcome to lovely goddam Normandy, Sarge," Gene said. "It sure as hell ain't Nebraska or Brooklyn or Colorado, but it's sure as shit home for all us BD bastards for the next little bit."

Jack Morrison took another step backward, as if shoved away by the nature of the comments from his new teammates. He lost his smile for a moment as he again considered the men's faces. "No, I appreciate it. The thought, anyway. But that's not at all what I wanted to ask you boys." He broke into another broad smile, his eyes glowing. It was as if a switch had been thrown somewhere beneath that mane of mahogany-hued hair. "My question is, do you all know Jesus Christ as your one and perfect Lord and savior?"

Morty was the only one to respond, and that was under his breath, more a growl than an answer.

"Jeez," he said. "What the fuck?"

Captain Hedley Bennett tries to concentrate on better days, growing up in Washington, DC, but the memories that make him crack a smile are of his time in Texas. Those wild endless plains stretching into the distance like a moonscape, the full moon shining on distant dark-lavender mountains as he and his fellow

Conservation Corps workers sit around a campfire and tell lies until the beer runs out and even the coyotes give up for the night. But as powerful and pleasant as those recollections are, they do not erase the pain, fear, and misery of this hellish place in which he now finds himself.

After being marched miles across fields and through villages for most of two days, allowed to stop limited times to nap and eat a few bites of what could only loosely be defined as food, Bennett and his men ended up at what appears to be a huge prison camp. The squad is divided into a couple of adjacent cramped, filthy cells inside a long, low barracks building, one of at least two dozen like it that they could see, lined up row after row, in tight formation. Fellow inmates confirm it is a prison camp, one in the village of Dachau near the city of Munich. There are thousands of other people being held there, too. POWs. Political prisoners. Jews. Russians. Poles. Brits. Americans. Many have cryptic numbers tattooed on their forearms. Most wear prison uniforms with vertical stripes. Many are taken outside each day to work, only to return at night hungry, exhausted. Still more are herded out and do not come back. Others seem to never leave their cells and die right there, or simply drop dead in the cramped, fenced open spaces around the barracks. Fellow prisoners are detailed to carry them away on small wagons, the bodies to be burned in a large on-site crematorium or buried in mass graves nearby, the Americans learn.

It is a nightmare.

Beginning that first night, with no chance to recover from the long, forced trek, Captain Hedley Bennett is required to suffer through an hours-long session in a windowless room. That night, there is only Bennett and a German SS-Standartenführer*—equivalent to a US Army colonel—named Werner Schubert. It is merely the first of the daily interrogations and torture sessions he will endure.*

The officer, Schubert, is a walking, breathing cliché of a German interrogator, a harsh man with a nasty disposition. After a friendly enough greeting to begin their first few minutes together and the offer to Bennett of a cigarette and a bottle of chilled water, Schubert abruptly pivots in anger when his prisoner rejects the gifts but continues to recite his name, rank, serial number, and hometown. That show of disrespect earns the American BD man the second savage blow to his handsome face since their capture, this time not with a rifle butt but a closed fist in a leather glove. The blow opens a nasty cut on his cheekbone that bleeds profusely. His hands are now bracketed to the chair arms. He cannot even press the wound to stop the bleeding.

"Captain Bennett, I understand you are a cowboy, so let's play nice. Geneva Convention nice," Schubert tells him, but not very nicely at all. "Simply order your men to be cooperative and you do likewise to set an example. Do you understand me, my English, is it good, Captain? I practiced it by watching your western motion pictures. John Wayne. Gary Cooper. Errol Flynn. Clark Gable. Anyone ever tell you that you resemble Mr. Gable somewhat? I especially enjoyed the German girl, Marlene Dietrich, with Mr. James Stewart in Destry. *That, of course, was before we forbade her films when she renounced the party and turned her back on her mother country."*

"Hedley Oscar Bennett. Captain. Oh-81333-zero-9. Washington, DC."

Schubert touches the fire at the lit end of his cigarette to the back of Hedley's trapped hand and then drops the butt into the prisoner's lap. The American gasps, wriggles to shake the cigarette from his lap, then grinds it out on the cement floor with the heel of his bare foot.

"But please understand, Captain Bennett, we know that you and your men are bomb demolition technicians. If you and they cooperate, you can still save the lives of many noncombatants, women and children, by making safe the unexploded bombs your aircraft have so viciously dropped on the innocent people of Deutschland instead of onto military targets."

From there, with no signal of capitulation from Bennett, the torture gets worse. The sessions usually end with the captain being brutally beaten with a canvas bag filled with gravel, sometimes by Schubert, sometimes by other guards. At times, the captain believes he cannot survive, but another prisoner, a Brit, is a medic. He does what he can—with medicine and the few bandages swiped from the camp guards' sickbay where he works—to tend to the captain's injuries.

His squad members arrive at a conclusion on their own. The German colonel makes a valid point when he says the squad can help save innocent lives by doing their captors' bidding, by defuzing dud bombs. And Tony Gabler, without even consulting with his suffering CO, agrees to begin doing that work, but only when the UXBs they are assigned threaten civilians or non-military structures. There seems, then, to be a bit less torture and cruelty against the captain. He is only carried away and beaten every third day or so. And, at least in the beginning, the missions do meet Gabler's criteria.

On an especially chilly morning, Hedley Bennett is led away from his cell by the guards as usual. But on this day, they take a different turn on the path at the end of a long row of buildings. Not to the left, toward the interrogation cell, but in the opposite direction. It is a much longer walk to wherever they are going. He limps along, struggling to keep pace with the guards, but his legs are wobbly, bruised and sore from the beatings. Still, the guards drag him as if they have a schedule they must maintain.

Finally, they tug him through the door of a nondescript building beneath a grove of trees at the far reaches of the camp. Once inside, the place looks much like the structure where his cell is. It has a long, dark, drafty, dirt-floored hallway, but there are no bars or cells. Instead, there are only closed doors on each side. It occurs to Hedley this may be where the medical experiments on prisoners he has heard about take place.

His escorts open a door at the end of the corridor and roughly shove him into an office. He staggers but refuses to fall.

It is a surprisingly well-appointed office and in stark contrast to everything he has seen so far at this place. A large photograph of Adolf Hitler commands most of an entire wall. The guards hold guns to his back as he is told to stand there and not move. A good eight or nine minutes pass. Every contusion and bruise hurts. His damaged leg muscles throb. He becomes dizzy, shaky, afraid he is about to collapse, but he does not want to give the Germans the satisfaction of seeing such surrender.

When Bennett believes he can stand no longer, a door at the other side of the office abruptly opens and an impeccably dressed man in street clothes—not an obvious interrogation officer in uniform—steps into the room.

Hedley forces himself to remain alert, to remember all he sees and hears. Someday, when the war ends, should he and his men survive, they will almost certainly be called upon to report what they have witnessed, what they have experienced at the hands of these unbelievably cruel men.

So, is this man a new and different kind of interrogator? Or an executioner? He certainly does not look as threatening as Schubert or the others. He has an air of intelligence. Almost antiseptic. But there is something disturbing in the man's eyes. Something even more ominous than an SS uniform or a leather-gloved fist or a bloody bag of gravel.

"Please, have a seat, Captain Hedley Bennett of Washington, DC, the home of

the free and the brave." He speaks German-accented English, but with more of a British lilt. "Make yourself comfortable. You and I, Captain, we have much in common. I am convinced that we will soon be fast friends."

That last statement is more fearsome to Bennett than anything Schubert or the others have said to him so far. But he is grateful for the chance to sit. He moans involuntarily as he eases down into a chair in front of the desk. He flinches, half expecting a punch from one of the guards or the slap of the burlap bag that so often follows any admission of pain, involuntary or not. But there is no punch or slap.

"Hedley Oscar Bennett. Captain. Oh-81333-zero-9. Washington, DC," the captain volunteers, smiles broadly despite his cracked, swollen lips, then again braces for a blow. But nothing happens. No retribution.

The man in the suit takes time to remove an expensive-looking pipe from his pocket, tamp in some tobacco, and light it. He puffs away contentedly for a moment, the sweet aroma of the smoke so powerful it causes Hedley's stomach to turn. "Please, I am sorry for being so rude, Captain. My name is—" The head guard, still standing there with his pistol pointed at Bennett, interrupts, clearing his throat pointedly, nodding a firm-jawed, No. No names.

"Ja, ja. Of course. Where was I? Oh, yes. We...you and I...we have important matters to discuss."

The man bends and lifts something from the floor. A leather briefcase. He places it on the desktop, sits down in the office chair, and deliberately pulls some papers from inside the bag.

And then Hedley realizes he can see one of those many details he has vowed to remember.

On the briefcase's handle, embossed in gold, are the initials "E. A."

14

Somewhere, in the middle of another sleepless night, it occurred to Edward that his obsession for Virginia Brown might be a sign of weakness. Maybe even a dangerous distraction, not only while dealing with UXOs but while performing this different kind of duty for Doc Fenton. He felt guilty for how much he was consumed by his longing for the Army nurse. The one he had so briefly met some six weeks before smack-dab in the middle of all the confusion and chaos of medical personnel desperately trying to save lives while he defuzed a live bomb. He had no real reason to believe such an isolated chance encounter had meant nearly so much to her. A meeting brought about by a German bomb, a deadly instrument of war, which was certainly not a positive omen for a fruitful relationship.

However, Lieutenant Virginia Brown was different from his one other serious romantic bond, Rachel Levine, back home in Mahanoy City, Pennsylvania. First off, Captain Hume was not really sure he was in a relationship with Virginia Brown. One based on a fleeting conversation in the crush of war, a sudden, unexpected kiss at the entrance to a field hospital tent, and her impulsively giving him her stateside phone number. For later, after the war ended.

But Rachel had been his fiancé and represented his past. She and his past were now over. Edward saw Virginia as his future. That exciting life he craved through his teen years as he gazed at photos of European sights in magazines and flickering images on the screen during travelogues at the Brill Theater back home. Usually with Rachel at his side.

He knew he needed to stop looking at the face of every female he saw these days, hoping it might be her. He had already determined she was not on the list of invited US Army medical personnel coming to the banquet. Besides, his first full day in Paris had already been hectic enough without such diversion. The Hotel Astoria personnel were stubbornly uncooperative. Maybe it was their nature. Or possibly they were simply hungover after days of celebrating their city's liberation. Edward and Hank Anderson heard much talk about what had happened shortly before their arrival, about General Charles de Gaulle triumphantly marching along the Champs-Élysées preceded by four tanks as most of the city cheered. But with the task at hand, Hume knew there was still much to get done in the next few hours before the event was scheduled to begin.

Once back from retrieving the medals at the engraver's shop, he found that the large, round wooden tables and gold rattan chairs had yet to be pulled out of the storage area. Food preparation in the hotel kitchen seemed to him to be hopelessly behind schedule as well. And the requested bunting and other decorations lay all about the ballroom floor with no one tasked to get it all hung.

As the two of them pitched in and helped staff unstack chairs and arrange tables, Hank made a point to thank his commanding officer. "Sir, thank you for bringing me along. Just being here, I feel like I'm a part of history, the euphoria, of what the French must be feeling."

"Nah! It wasn't me. It was 'Lady Luck.' You drew the ace of spades."

Hank grinned sheepishly and put a shoulder to the next table.

"Sir, what else needs to get done?" Hank was not invited to the event, so once his work was done, he could explore the city and maybe find a romantic partner, even if it was only for a night.

"Don't worry, Corporal. We'll be finished so you can go take in some local culture."

Edward and Hank, with the help of some late-arriving hotel employees, had things in hand by late afternoon. As Edward surveyed the room, he imagined it full of Nazi officers and their girlfriends, enjoying a night at this historic hotel, even as their counterparts inflicted so much misery, pain and death on the rest of the world.

As Astoria staff set the tables with simple white plates, utensils, wine and water glasses, the entire ballroom came to life. Even more so as candles were lit on each table next to vases filled with fresh flowers ordered from a shop recommended by Hélène LeRiche, one owned by a relative of hers. Edward was pleased he could include a bit of Hélène in the room. And his best French friend had been so pleased to be able to contribute. *Bleuet de France*, a late summer wild cornflower, pale peach roses, and miniature sunflowers all added to brighten the plain tables covered in white linen.

"Sir, this place looks like a wedding could bust out any minute," Hank said as he wiped sweat from his face with a sleeve.

"Okay, Hank, you can go experience Paris!" Edward told him, patting him on the back. "If we make it through the war, we're now qualified to be caterers or wedding planners!"

"Weddings end up in war too often, based on my own experience."

Edward nodded. "Look, just meet me in the hotel lobby at 1200 hours tomorrow and we'll drive on back to the real world. Have some good stories to tell me, okay?"

Hank did not hesitate. He ran from the ballroom, past uniformed guests, dignitaries and fashionably attired French civilians who were already gathering in the foyer outside.

Confident the hors d'oeuvres were finally coming out from the kitchen, Edward hurried to his hotel room to change into his dress uniform. His former boss, Doctor Ivor Fenton, was holding court in the hotel lounge and bar area, entertaining a group of French and American government officials. He had confidently left all final preparations to Hume, not unlike the years Eddie handled the congressman's election campaign, which he handily won, a seat in Congress in November of 1939. Rushing back into the ballroom, he took one last opportunity to survey the setup as guests were already finding their seats, and so he could report to Doc Fenton, if asked, that all was well.

Then, impossibly, he saw her.

It was Virginia Brown. But she seemed to be in distress.

He could not make out the rank of the man seated next to her, but the guy was all over her, trying to pull her closer, to kiss her. She was resisting as forcefully as she could without causing a scene. The others at the table—maybe reluctant to risk sullying such a prestigious event or maybe because the gold oak leaf on the officer's epaulet indicated he was a major—tried to ignore the situation. Hume headed that way without even considering what he would do when he got there. Doc Fenton and the key guests were now taking their seats at the head table.

"How nice you could be here," Edward blurted out, maybe in the direction of Virginia.

Virginia looked up. Her eyes widened when she recognized him. Her green eyes, as dazzling as ever. "Captain Hume! Why are you...? I am so glad to see you again."

She nodded in the direction of her tormentor. Major Paul Richardson, her superior officer, the chief surgeon Edward had previously met the same day he did Virginia. And thoroughly disliked. The major was clearly drunk as a skunk.

Edward leaned down, his face inches from the Army doctor's. "Sir, I see that you are now a major. Congratulations on the field promotion. But, sir, you are not on the invitation list. How did you get here?"

"I got here in a goddam convoy is how—" he started, then, even in his inebriated state, recognized Edward. He held his glass of burgundy high. "Captain 'What's His Name,' the stubbornest bomb disposal man in the US Army! So, what the hell are you doing here, my man? We got a bomb somewhere before the soup course?"

"I worked for your host back home when I was his congressional aide." Edward nodded at Congressman Fenton, who was deep in conversation with a French dignitary. But Richardson paid no attention. He was now distracted by a server passing by with a bottle of wine on a tray. "Boy! Boy! *Vino!* Here!" But the server was not obligated to follow orders from the slurring American. He hurried on toward the head table.

"Now, may I borrow your seatmate for a moment, Major?" Edward nodded to Virginia. "I'd like to introduce her to Congressman Ivor—"

"No!" Richardson snapped, instantly furious, and unsteadily stood, ready to fight, throwing what might have been a weak punch in Hume's general direction. "Lieutenant Brown is my date for the evening."

"I most certainly am not," Virginia stated quietly but with finality. She stood and stepped next to Edward. "I'd be honored to meet the congressman, Captain Hume."

"Oh, yeah! Captain Hume." Richardson laughed, wobbling noticeably. "Last time I saw you, you were wearing that ridiculous canvas balloon suit!"

"You mean my protective gear I wore as I saved the lives of you, your staff, your patients."

Without warning, the doctor lost his balance. Edward caught him before he fell and eased him back down into his chair. Only those at their table seemed to have so far noticed the disturbance. And continued to try to ignore it.

"Second time this war I've saved you, Dr. Richardson," Hume told him. "Enjoy your meal. Fresh lamb from the salt grass pastures around Mont Saint Michel, I understand."

With that, Edward took Virginia's arm and escorted her across the room to the head table.

"Thank you," she told him.

"You're welcome, in so many more ways than you could ever imagine."

Edward introduced the nurse to the congressman, who graciously thanked her for all she and other nurses were doing. Then Fenton introduced Virginia to everyone else at the table, describing her as Clara Barton, Florence Blanchfield—the famous Army nurse who sat at a table only a few feet away—and Florence Nightingale all rolled into one.

Edward smiled, winked at her and gestured to her to take the seat reserved for him at the head table, inviting her to dine there. "Lt. Brown, I hope you don't mind, but I think you would enjoy the company at this table far better than at your previous one."

Edward waved to a waiter to pour her a glass of wine, then pulled over an empty chair from another table and placed it next to hers. Not too close. Not presuming anything.

"Thank you," she said in a whisper. Then there was a hint of anger in those green eyes Edward had so often dreamed of. "The major was drunk before we even got here. Then he tried to tell me there was a mix-up with the rooms, but I could stay with him, that he would sleep on the divan. He's a major all right. Major bastard."

Hume glanced toward the major's table. He was face down on the tablecloth, passed out.

"We'll make sure you have a room," Edward said with a smile and placed his hand reassuringly on hers. She did not pull away, nor did she seem offput by the offer of the room. "I'm just glad you're here." Then, for some reason, he looked into her eyes and asked her, "You *are* here, right?"

She glanced around the room. Smiling servers moved about beneath breathtakingly beautiful crystal chandeliers, offering plates filled with fine food and endless replenishment of drink from fancy-labeled bottles. There was laughter, joy, all the signs of dispirited folks freed for an evening from unimaginable wartime experiences. Many of the guests were only hours and miles away from battlefields, bloody field hospitals, makeshift morgues and cemeteries. But for this brief time, they seemed to have temporarily forgotten that ugliness amid the elegance of a historic hotel in the heart of the world's most glamorous city so recently liberated from its evil occupiers. There was optimistic talk at their table of a realistic possibility for an early end to the war. And hopefully for lessons learned about how to avoid yet another one.

"I'm not sure," Virginia told Edward, finally answering his question. She took a sip of her wine, put her hand on his, looked back into his eyes, and asked, "*Am* I?"

15

Hank had carnal intentions from the moment his CO released him to "go experience Paris." He did not give Captain Hume a moment to come up with another chore ahead of the soirée. Hank saluted and hurried back to his assigned room at a nearby hostel shared with other enlisted men. There he enjoyed the rare luxury of his second bath of the day. He lifted the aromatic toilet water off the basin and doused himself generously. There was not much he could do to improve either of the two uniforms he had brought with him, though. He figured any potential companion for the evening would understand given the circumstances and overlook the wrinkles. As he started to exit, Hank checked to make sure he had his Army-issue condom, glanced at his image in the little mirror, then grabbed his camera, hoping to capture on film a few of the city's sights.

Once he stepped out onto the Champs-Élysées, Hank turned east on a whim, toward the noise of a bar. He figured he would start his evening with a drink and then go looking for friendly local females eager to show him their appreciation for what he and his fellow Allies had done on their behalf. It was so crowded and frenetic near the river, he strolled down a quiet side street that led him to the Place Vendôme, a big neoclassical square. From the guidebooks that he had swiped from various places, Hank knew to look for the massive Vendôme Column with the statue of

Napoleon Bonaparte in Roman robes at the top. And there it was. For Hank, all the history he had read about now became real. He looked about, ran to a different vista, stopped, looked some more, trying to see everything he could before the evening light waned, all while snapping photos like a common tourist.

Hank knew the Hotel Ritz—Ernest Hemingway's favorite haunt—was just up ahead, past the column and to the left. He started that way at double-time. It would be worth postponing a possible roll in the hay if he could somehow catch a glimpse—maybe even shake the hand—of the literary legend.

Then something caught his eye, stopping him in his tracks: a bistro, its small streetside tables mostly empty. Beneath one of the tables, an open book, spine up, likely dropped or forgotten, left behind by someone. Hemingway's *For Whom the Bell Tolls*. Papa's latest, though it had been published four years earlier.

Hank had read somewhere that it was a story of love and death during the Spanish Civil War. It seemed especially appealing to him because it told how a saboteur, a dynamiter with much in common with the Kaboom Boys, devised a dangerous alternative method to blow up a bridge. Hank felt akin to the author in another way, too. Both of them had an addiction to confronting then outwitting death.

Anderson knew he had to have that book.

He hopped over the low wicker fence and row of boxwoods, stepped quickly to the table, and took a seat. As subtly as he could, he retrieved the book from the ground, placed it in front of him, and opened it, giving the appearance he had been there for hours, reading. He was thrilled it was an English-language edition.

A shadow fell across the table. "*Qu'est-ce que tu voudrais?*"

A waiter, looking with disdain at Hank's crumpled uniform.

"Sorry. I speak *non Français*. Coffee, *cafe*, please. *Merci*. With milk and sugar."

The waiter paused, formed his lips into something of a sneer, and dismissively uttered, "*Oui*. Coffeeeee weeth meelk an shoo-gar," before turning on his heels and disappearing inside.

After delivering the coffee, the waiter pointedly ignored Hank for the next hour, which was fine with him. He was already on chapter four, his coffee untouched and cold, when another shadow darkened the table and the page of his salvaged book. His first thought: *The book's owner, back to retrieve his property.*

"Pardon, soldier, but that patch, the one there, on your sleeve," she said.

It was a strikingly lovely woman. A short-cropped blonde-haired woman with an intoxicating smile. She was touching—no, she was caressing—the red felt bomb BD patch, stitched in gold thread, centered on his right jacket sleeve.

Hank shook his head, confused. Once he began reading the book, he had completely forgotten his original mission, to get himself magnificently laid. Now this beautiful lady, at least ten years his senior—one with an American accent, not some erotically grateful French girl—had singled him out and approached him with the weakest pickup line he could imagine.

He smiled back at her. Any port in a storm.

"Bomb demolition. Ordnance disposal. Booby trap removal. An explosives garbage man, basically."

"Do you mind?" She nodded to the chair across the little table from him.

"Please," he told her. "A cup of coffee or something?"

She shook her head. "I see you're a fan of Hemingway," she said, nodding toward his book.

"Yes. Yes, I am. Especially this one, based on what I know about its main protagonist. We both deal with things that go *boom* and we both have a thing for beautiful women. You?"

"I can see how you would be a fan," the woman told him, then lost her fetching smile as she sat back in the chair. "A fan of Ernest's, that is. And I am, too. But isn't the whole world?"

"Guess not everybody likes his style, though. Too manly for some."

"Oh, that's one of the things I love most about him."

"Whaddya mean? You know the guy?" asked Hank, hopeful he would be given an introduction, if he should be so lucky. Then a thought struck him. "Wait. You're not Martha Gellhorn, are you?"

"No. Oh, no. He and Martha are estranged. Divorcing, I hear. They just haven't gotten around to the paperwork, as they say. But he's staying right over there at the Ritz. Since the day of liberation." She pointed at the ornate structure. "That corner room with the big bay window on the second floor. Yeah, that's where he pulled out Martha's picture, dropped it in the toilet, and blew that poor shitter to bits with his pistol."

Hank's mouth fell wide open. "How do you know all this? You're not a friend of hers?"

"No, I'm Mary Welsh. We both happen to be war correspondents and close to Papa, but please don't get us confused."

"But why're you out here talking to me and not in there with him?"

"I'm doing my job. There's an event for wartime medical personnel at the Astoria tonight, but when I got there I didn't see much of a story so I left after a fine meal. I was headed back to the Ritz when I saw you reading the book." She gazed at the hotel window for a moment, then looked back at Anderson. "I was there when he murdered the toilet. He does have a certain *je ne sais quoi*, especially when it comes to attracting women journalists. Martha might legally be his for a bit longer, but this damn war sure has a way of dissolving matrimonial bonds."

"Yeah, I think I read one of your pieces somewhere. You interviewed Churchill, right?"

"I was at a press conference, that's all."

"Still impressive. I wish I could do that."

"I guess it's hard for you soldiers to keep up with all the action we write about when you're in the middle of it," she said.

"I'd like to be a writer someday," Hank told her. "But, you know, I oughta graduate high school first, I guess." Hank blushed. Why had he told her that?

She laughed. "Don't worry about that. I know many fine journalists who never finished school. You have to read. That's the way to learn to write. Listen, too. Listen and you'll never run out of good stories to tell."

"Convince my dad, the dentist."

He hushed for a moment. He was well aware he talked a hell of a lot more than he listened. Mary reached over and again touched his BD patch.

"I like it." Mary smiled. "You can't miss it. I suspect it represents plenty of interesting stories. Why would somebody do such a job?"

Hank grinned and sat back. "Because somebody has to."

Mary Welsh apparently liked his answer. She pulled a steno pad from her jacket pocket and wrote it down. She asked him more questions. The right questions, in Hank's opinion. And he was more than willing to answer them.

"You think this 'BD,' this bomb demolition, is a story?" she finally asked.

"I sure as hell do! One tick away from death, the handsome, young soldiers of BD are convinced such imminent death makes them even more alive..." He trailed off, grinned, and blushed again. She nodded seriously.

The cafe owner eventually shooed them out so he could shutter the place. But before they left, Hank was able to buy a nice bottle of Cabernet Sauvignon and stealthily snag a couple of glasses. They moved to a bench in the square. There they talked for a few more hours, mostly about Hank's experiences, the recent mission defuzing the Allied bombs in the bay around Mont Saint Michel, the tragic death of squad sergeant Ace Taft, and how that affected Hank and the others. He even opened up to her about how he initially blamed his CO, Captain Edward Hume, for that tragedy.

"Why blame him? Soldiers die in war."

"I know. Now I know. But you have to blame somebody, or you might end up blaming God."

The two sat quietly for a few moments, the city around them even in the wee hours still very much alive with the clamor of excitement and hope, no one sure about how much longer the war might continue. But Paris was now free from Hitler's tyranny. Surely the end was near. At least for the war in Europe.

The wine bottle was empty. Hank realized it was getting late, and he and his captain had a long ride ahead of them tomorrow. "So, Miss Welsh, you think *Time* or *Life* would be interested in a story about us Kaboom Boys?"

"But isn't everything you do top secret? Won't you get in trouble if I write a story?"

"I'll ask Captain Hume what you can write about. He's here. He helped arrange that soiree you were at."

"That's not typically how journalism works but I don't want you to get thrown into the stockade. Look, you will learn that if you decide to become a reporter, you never allow authority to tell you what to write."

"Might be worth some time in the slammer to let folks know what we do over here."

Mary laughed heartily. This was certainly not what Hank had expected when he set out from the Hotel Astoria for the evening. But the corporal was satisfied it had been worth the investment of his time and effort. And the cost of a bottle of wine and a couple of glasses.

Hank stretched and smiled and pointed to his Leica. "I take all the pictures and help write reports, so for the most part, I'm telling the story of BD."

"Hank, keep at it," she told him. "In the end, it's all about the story, right? Just like somebody's got to clean up all that unexploded ordnance, somebody's got to tell these stories. Otherwise, they're lost to history."

The air had grown cool and carried a heavy mist off the Seine when they finally shook hands and parted. They made a promise to catch up somewhere down the way, maybe once the Third Army had pushed into Germany, so she could interview him further, and perhaps his CO as well.

She hurried away as if she had an important middle-of-the-night appointment. "It's been a pleasure, Corporal Anderson," she called back over her shoulder.

"Pleasure's all mine, Mary."

She was headed in the direction of the Ritz when she stopped, looked back, and waved to him through the mist. He could see that look on her face, though. The melancholy expression so many people had when they left a BD man. Knowing the odds—and Hank had played up the ten-week life expectancy statistic—they knew they could be saying farewell to a dead man.

"Be careful. For God's sake, be careful!" Mary Welsh called back to him.

Hank waved and started back to the hostel, content with the evening's conversation and the Hemingway book under his arm. He passed thriving parties in bars and bistros along the way. Exactly the kind of places he had originally planned to hit on his one free night in Paris. It was now predawn Sunday morning. He and the captain would be heading back to the squad in only a few hours. For some reason, he now felt more exhausted than randy. He went straight to his room, stripped down, left his uniform in a heap on the floor, and took what he knew would likely be his final tub bath for a long, long time.

He immediately fell asleep in the warm water amid suds and the heavy aroma of the fragranced bath salts he had decided at the last minute to add to the bathwater recipe.

♠

He assumed she was asleep. Even in the dim light through the hotel room curtains, he could still see a slow pulsebeat at her throat. Only a few minutes before, that heartbeat would have been pounding in racing rhythm with his own.

Her eyes were now closed. They had been wide, staring hard into his eyes as they spectacularly climaxed together.

Edward was sad that the moment had passed. The moment he had visualized in sporadic dreams since the day they met. Now, she appeared to be asleep, her exhaustion acute, as was his. But he could not fall asleep. He had never felt so free as he had when he was lost so deeply inside the perfect woman. The one who had unexpectedly stepped from his dreams and into his bed in a fancy hotel room in Paris.

But the sharing had started earlier. After they left the banquet, they sat on the balcony of his room, overlooking the night's festive post-liberation activity below, talking, sharing details of their personal stories, thoughts, wishes, visions, and regrets that neither had ever felt comfortable telling anyone else before.

"This is awkward, but I need to tell you," Edward said. "I've been looking for you for most of my life."

"Nothing to be awkward about," Virginia responded. "I'm glad to hear you say that, Edward, because I feel the same way. You're unlike any man I've ever met."

"And how odd is it that it took a damned war to bring us together?"

"One that's going to pull us apart again soon, too," she said, a pained look in her eyes.

"Then let's not waste another minute watching drunk Parisians throw firecrackers at each other," he told her.

They stepped inside to open a bottle of Bordeaux but, instead of pouring it, they embraced, kissed, and ended up in bed, learning still more important things about each other.

Now, here they lay, Edward on his side, facing her, wishing she would wake up so they could talk more. Virginia on her back next to him, apparently sleeping.

"Do you believe in love at first sight?" she huskily asked him, firing away without warning.

Her sudden words startled him. Stunned to the point he jumped, shocked she was as wide awake as he was. And having the exact same thoughts.

She rolled to face him, smiled and kissed him. She touched his cheek. Those sparkling green eyes now looked into his bright, steel-blue ones. "Sorry. I tend to say whatever's on my mind before it gets stale and forgotten."

"No."

"No?"

"Not until now. Believe in love at first sight, that is." He kissed her in return, slid his hand to the small of her back, and gently pulled her as close as he could without hurting her. "But to be honest, as a measure of full disclosure, I fell for you that day at the hospital tent. If that's love at first sight, guilty as charged. When you kissed me that day—"

"I thought *you* kissed *me*," she interrupted, laughing, putting her leg over his hip, the arch of her foot on the back of his thigh, edging him even nearer to her.

"Virginia Brown, all I know is that I've thought of you every single day since, so..."

"So?"

This time their lovemaking was slower, more loving, no less lustful, but even more satisfying.

"I have an idea," Virginia announced once she again regained her breath.

"If it involves making love to you again, you're going to have to give me a few minutes," Edward admitted with a grin.

The sun was just beginning to watercolor the eastern sky as they dressed. Virginia led him outside, down the street, over a bridge across the Seine to a Catholic church she had picked out the previous day in anticipation of mass this morning. The sign at the outer gate said it was Saint-Joseph-des-Carmes, constructed circa 1620. Sunday Mass would be at 8:00 a.m. But Virginia opened the gate, walked through the courtyard, right up to the big, heavy door, and gave it a tug. It opened. She waved for Edward to come on, to follow her inside.

"Did I mention that I'm Lutheran, not Catholic?" he asked. That was only one of the personal details he had not yet shared with her. But he followed her as she requested.

Even without people, and despite being cavernous, the place was warm, welcoming, inspiring. They sat at a pew near the back of the nave, surrounded by Doric columns and beneath a cupola decorated with beautiful artwork.

She took his hand and held it in her lap. "I want you to know I do not do what we just did with just anybody I meet wearing a strange canvas outfit on a battlefield," she said, her expression earnest. "But I'm not a damn bit sorry, either. Look, seriously, I don't know what happened that day at Saint-Lô, you in those silly-looking bomb squad coveralls, me covered in blood and guts. But something tells me we might have a future together if we can only make it through this war alive and reasonably sane." She turned to him, eyes wide, misty, something in them that implied that what she was about to say would be very nearly a plea. "Edward, I'm not presuming anything. Tell me if I'm reading this all wrong. But if you agree, I need us to make some promises to each other right here before God. And I *am* Catholic, so whatever we say sticks, okay?"

She pointed to the front of the church, the massive altar, the painting of the Last Supper. Edward nodded. Right now, he knew, he would promise this woman anything, anywhere, in front of any flavor of deity. And he knew if she was about to make similar vows to him, it could well be the very thing it would take to get him through this war and on to a life without bombs and booby traps and soldiers blown asunder.

Before they left Saint Joseph and went looking for breakfast, they had vowed to remain true to each other, to keep in touch, to reunite as soon as the vagaries of the US Army and the demands of this war permitted. And, if they both still felt as they did at this very moment on a back pew in the nave of Saint-Joseph-des-Carmes tucked away on Rue de Vaugirard in Paris, they would move on to the next phase of a life together, whatever they decided that might be. And that meant maintaining their aim for healing, helping, being a positive force, and experiencing without hesitation the colorful, adventurous life they both craved. But it would all be magnified a hundredfold because they would be doing it together. Then they sealed the deal on their knees in prayer.

As they were about to exit the church, Edward dropped a franc into a box and lit a candle.

"For us."

Virginia smiled, her eyes brimming with tears.

Once they were back outside, the first rays of sunlight mottled by the breeze through the trees along the river, Edward did not break the mood at all when he said, "I'm so hungry I could eat an omelet the size of the Arc de Triomphe."

Virginia laughed. "I was thinking more a stack of crepes as tall as the Eiffel Tower!"

They embraced right there on the street, kissed long and hard, then walked briskly along the River Seine, toward the Champs-Élysées, mutually convinced that no matter what fears, doubts, and awful obstacles might be thrown in their way, they were now and would always remain together.

Even when they were apart.

She is not at all surprised to see him holding court in the Ritz bar when she arrives, even at this hour, after her long chat with the BD soldier. But Papa's audience, French Resistance fighters he considers to be his personal anti-fascist squad and he their commanding officer, are all asleep or passed out, heads down on the table.

"Mary! Been out on the town, I see!" he shouts as he waves a greeting. "How about a nightcap? Francois, a dram of her favorite gin for the lady."

"No, thanks," interrupts Mary. "It's well past bedtime for us serious and sober working journalists," she jokingly responds, but she walks his way anyhow. "I do need my beauty sleep, you see."

"In my opinion, you are dangerously beautiful already," Ernest says with a raised eyebrow.

Mary Welsh in many ways reminds Ernest Hemingway of his current wife, Martha Gellhorn. He does stick to type in that regard. But he has plans for this woman to become his next wife after the now inevitable divorce from Martha is final.

"Got any cigarettes?" she asks. "I've been out for a couple hours."

"How'd you survive?" Hemingway laughs as he hands her his almost empty pack of Camels.

She cocks her head and asks him, "Whaddya drinking, my kitten?"

"You know I only drink water when I work." They are both aware that is not true. "And I am working."

"So am I but I've been out 'n' about looking for actual stories."

"Remember what I told you? Don't bother with churches, government buildings, or city squares. If you want to know about a culture, spend a night in its bars."

"Thanks for the advice. But I have been working tonight." She is tired. She sits in the only empty chair at the table, the one next to him, and takes a sip of her drink. "I stumbled upon a fascinating story. One I've not seen or heard of anyone writing."

Ernest, always interested in a good story, leans forward. Even if it was a scoop upon which his new girl had dibs. Even if claim-jumping story ideas had been one of the problems between him and Martha.

"Tell me."

So, she does. Including how the corporal with whom she spent the evening had found a copy of Papa's novel beneath the table at the café.

"Likely some damn critic tossed it there," Ernest says with a snort.

"At any rate, I just spent three hours with that kid from Denver who's in one of the new bomb demolition squads the Army Air Forces have in the field now. He trained with the RAF and they've been defuzing bombs and mines and ammo dumps and booby traps between here and the Channel since D-Day. These guys are amazing, drama and death a constant part of their day. Every minute of every

day. People will love their story. Young guys who have a thing for explosives and tempting fate." Her eyes are shining. She has grown even more excited about the possibilities as she tells Hemingway about it. "And, Ernest, here's the best part. He says when they were deployed, the life expectancy of a BD man was only ten weeks, and—"

"Mary," Ernest says, holding up a hand, interrupting, then abruptly erupting in laughter. He drains the last of the liquid from his glass before going on. "Aw, Mary. I betcha that boy from Denver was mighty handsome. Part of his charisma, no doubt. You didn't ask me, but I think you're wasting your time on a story like that. This bomb demolition thing, those guys are serious and important, but really, they're little more than garbage men, cleaning up the trash of war. People want to read about infantrymen—real soldiers—and fighter pilots and paratroopers and Rangers and Adolf Hitler. The people left homeless and overcome by war. Go find those stories, dear. That's what readers and editors want."

"Well, thank you for your wise counsel, Mr. Hemingway, sir," Mary says sarcastically. She stands, spins on her heel, and briskly walks away. He has planted a seed of doubt about her story. Maybe he's right. Maybe nobody wants to read about such things. So maybe she will table it for the time being, keep the notes, learn more should she later meet the kid from Denver. The kid who steals reading matter, who wants to be a journalist, who took her picture with his Army-issue Leica as she signed his copy of Ernest's book. Or until she runs into his CO, a man who craves an exciting existence and likes to talk while he risks his life fiddling with death packages.

But that means she needs to find some other compelling account to share with readers, another tale to weave. One even better than whatever Ernest or Martha might come up with.

She will. She knows she will.

16

Private Pete Ronzini finally gave up on finding meaningful sleep. The death of the French kid was weighing heavily on him, like a concrete slab on his chest. The constant bickering with his fellow New Yorker, Morty Schwartz, was starting to bother him, too. The missions. The jobs. The war. Rubble and ruin everywhere he looked. The air so thick with dust it seemed he could chew it. It was beginning to be too much.

Also bothering him was the new man. He had turned out to be an annoying Bible thumper, not a regular guy like Ace Taft. The captain would be coming back in the morning to learn about Gene and what he had been doing with the UXBs—against specific orders—and that would likely further upset the already volatile chemistry of the squad at a really bad time for such distraction.

He rolled over to check his watch. "0137." The other guys snored. No sleep issues for them. Even the new guy, Jack. Pete had heard him mumbling in his sleep earlier, and swear to God, he was quoting a Bible verse. Something from Hebrews about God's word being like a two-edged sword dividing soul and spirit, joints and marrow.

One Kaboom Boy was missing: Gene Wozinski was not in his bunk. Probably still out with that woman he'd been seeing. More bad chemistry. Woz had not been the same since he hooked up with her. Each of his squad mates had a theory about what was going on there, what her angle might be.

With the intention of taking a walk, maybe hiking off some of what was eating at him, Pete quietly dressed and went outside. Before he knew it, he was in front of one of Pontorson's livelier bars, one he and the squad had abruptly ducked out of several hours prior, when the threat of a tussle with some locals appeared likely. They had never run from a fight, but it was late, and they were temporarily captain-less. Nobody to get them out of a scrape if the MPs showed up.

Pete was suddenly about as thirsty as he had ever been. He stepped inside for a quick, lukewarm beer.

The place was still packed at that late hour with an eclectic mix of US soldiers—infantry, engineers, clerks, pilots, medics—and mostly young locals. Pete recognized some of the Frenchmen, still there from the earlier visit. The same ones who had been angling for a brawl with Americans. They claimed to be former Resistance Fighters and were irritated for some reason that the US soldiers dared occupy "their" bar. Ronzini hoped the mood had cooled just a bit as he stepped through the door and plowed through the smoke and noise to the bar.

He decided not to tempt fate with a leisurely brew. He would only get a couple of shots of whiskey, down them, and then go back to the barracks. Maybe the liquor would work some magic on his sleep-deprived brain.

Then someone—one of the Americans—yelled something profane about Germans in general and the SS specifically. Several soldiers shouted back, "You got that right!" and "Fuckin' Krauts!" and there was a unanimous toast to the bloody demise of all the "Nazi bastards of Deutschland." One of the resistance guys piped up, yelling, "*Tête de caboche!*" "Cabbage heads," the favorite derisive nickname the French had for Hitler's minions. Another round of mostly good-natured cheers and jeers followed.

Maybe the friction in the bar was subsiding as the target became the Nazis, not each other. Men who purported to be aligned on the same side against the evil Germans. Pete tossed back his first shot.

But then, a drunk US infantryman stood up, wobbled, then pounded the table with his heavy beer glass. "Long as you Frogs can find a hiding place, you can call 'em whatever you want to. But who the hell would you call to come rescue your asses if the goddam Krauts come stormin' back'?"

"Who do they call, Smitty?" one of his buddies shouted, laughing, nudging.

"US. Us. The good, ole US fuckin' Army infantry! That's who!"

"And what do the French do if the cabbage heads even fart in their direction?" the buddy asked, giggling, urging on his friend.

"Wave a white flag!" yelled someone else.

"Yeah!" A combat engineer, drinking alone at a nearby table, responded loudly. "They surrender! They're French, after all, born with their arms in the air when they come out their mommies' twats!"

That set off another round of jeers. Some of the locals stood, fists clenched. Not a good sign. The mood had abruptly spun back in an ugly direction. Pete swallowed his second shot, grimaced as it burned all the way down, chased it with a glass of water, and then turned to quickly make his way for the door before things turned really nasty.

Someone stepped in front of Ronzini, stopping him with a firm hand on his chest. "Looks like this American hero is...how you say? Making a run to it...before the real fighting begins." It was one of the self-identified Resistance Fighters. One of the ill-tempered ones from earlier in the evening. "So, who is surrendering *this* time? Is it *Shor-tee*?"

Pete's temper flared. Hank Anderson always told him he had a "Napoleon complex" because of his lack of height. Maybe so, but he could see the odds were against him here.

"Look, I got no beef with you, *ami*." Ronzini had been in plenty of bar fights and, despite his short stature—often the cause of those brawls in the first place when somebody goaded him about his shortness—he usually held his own. But on this night, he was simply too drained to fool with such. The two quick shots of whiskey were already doing their job, too. He was a tad dizzy. "Friend, I gotta be ready to go to work in the morning."

"Well, *Short-ee*, I got for me much trouble *weeth* you and your *freins*," the Frenchman spat back, slurring his words, stepping closer to Pete, still blocking his way. "You come here to our bar, making *zee* claims about your bravery and how you resist against the Germans. But you do nothing. Why are you not be chasing the SS now, brave *Americaine*? You remain here, drinking our drinks, doing *le sexe* to our women. Not fighting. Why do you not fight, then, brave, bragging *Americaine*?" The Frenchman clumsily flicked with his finger the red BD patch on Pete's sleeve.

It was not the first time Ronzini had encountered angry French citizens, either. Men and women resentful of the "we're saving your asses" attitude of some Allied soldiers. Things usually settled down and they all became drinking buddies by evening's end. But now, everyone in the joint was watching him. Something snapped inside Ronzini. He had to respond and because he quickly reverted to Pete from Bay Ridge, Brooklyn, it would be in a less-than-diplomatic style.

"Look, Frenchie, I never said a word about you or nobody else. But I'm BD. Bomb disposal. I risk my life and do more to save French lives every day than your ass likely does in a month anymore. Least not since we came and liberated your asses. Now you're out there raising turnips and butchering hogs and hiding in a hole from Nazis that ain't even here no more, thanks to us." Pete rudely shoved the man's hand away to the loud approval of the other Americans in the bar. "Now, kindly move your ass and let me pass so I can do some more French ass-saving in the mornin'. Got that?"

The man's nostrils flared, his eyes widened, and his face reddened. From experience, and even as tired and tipsy as he was, Pete recognized all the signs. This was not going to be easy. The guy had to show out for his friends. An angry, drunken, and likely poorly aimed punch was about to be thrown his way. And since Pete was easily five inches shorter than this guy, all he had to do was step back, duck the fist, then do whatever he needed to do to slip past the bastard.

But instead of that expected roundhouse punch, the man reached behind his back and in one swift, sweeping motion, retrieved a long, evil-looking knife. And before Ronzini could dodge, the Frenchman plunged the blade deep into Pete's chest, between the second and third ribs on his right side, just missing his heart.

The place went quiet. So quiet those nearby could hear the sound of air rushing from Pete's lung. Blood spurted. Ronzini's knees buckled.

By the time the drunken Frenchman was subdued, Pete was on the floor, clutching his chest where the knife remained, its handle moving in rhythm with Ronzini's heartbeat. He looked up at all the faces swirling around—French and American—all staring down at him, stunned.

"Hey, I gotta go to work, guys," he managed to say, gasping, reaching up with a hand for assistance. "Help me up. We got a job...We gotta...damn. Damn..."

Then everything in Private Pete Ronzini's world went misty black.

♠

"Hell of a waste, if you ask me," Captain Edward Hume was saying, primarily to himself. "Mostly a show for the politicians and Army brass, but it took you and me and all those medical folks away from our real jobs for a couple of valuable days. But I've got to admit there were a couple of unexpectedly magical hours—"

"Tell me more, sir!" Corporal Hank Anderson was all ears as he steered around a long line of troop carriers parked on the roadside, all pointed east, while the convoy's human cargo took a meal-and-latrine break. The war was close again, not a million miles away as it had been back in Paris. The frequent roadblocks, document checks, troops on the move, fighter planes flying air cover, and even smoke and fire and the distant sound of artillery, confirmed it.

"Sorry, Corporal, top secret."

"Gotcha, sir!" Anderson maneuvered his way through a particularly narrow slice of the roadway and changed the subject back to the woman he had met. "Dunno, Captain. Maybe that lady journalist will give us a little publicity for what us BD men do when she files her next story. I'm gonna keep my eyes peeled for *Time* and *Life* just to see if she writes about us," Hank noted as he came to a stop, half blocking the road while a truck ahead idled. "But we got a couple of good meals out of the trip. Real beds and bathtubs with sweet-smelling soap. Not a bad break for us at all. And now we can get back to the guys—"

"Okay, what's this?" Edward interrupted. An MP was running their way, angrily waving at them.

"You gotta move your ass off this road right damn now, Corporal," the soldier told Hank.

"And you gotta move your ass out of our way so we can get back to our unit, Sergeant," Captain Hume punched back. "Third Army don't own this thoroughfare."

"Matter of fact, it does, sir." The MP pointedly put his hand on the butt of a holstered pistol at his side. "At least for the next few minutes. General Eisenhower is coming through here directly, and you better be parked way the hell over there in that orchard when he does."

Sure enough, a jeep surrounded by four others—one in front, one behind, and one on each side—topped a hill and came rapidly rolling in their direction. General Dwight Eisenhower sat in the passenger seat, head down, studying papers in his lap. But when he looked up and in the direction of where Edward and Hank were now trying to move, the general motioned for his driver to stop. Then Ike hopped out and stepped over to the BD jeep.

The most important Allied officer was coming their way. Edward and Hank looked at each other, hopped out, stood tall, and saluted.

"At ease, men. Captain, it's good to see you again," Eisenhower said and grabbed and shook Edward's hand. "Good to see you alive!"

"Thank you, sir," was all Edward could manage in response.

"It's been a good long while! Captain Hume? Right?"

"Yessir!"

"You know, when I saw all that red, especially those red fenders on your jeep, I thought there might be a slight chance it was you. But even if you were another BD man, I still wanted to say thanks for what you and all the BD squads are doing here. But since it's you, Hume, let me thank you for your earlier help. You're saving lives, reclaiming land and helping us to be able to keep pushing the way we must if we're going to defeat Hitler."

"Yessir! It's been a long six weeks," Edward responded. "That's why we're trying to get back to our squad at Pontorson. We got lots of work to do and I got called to Paris to help impress a bunch of congressmen."

Ike flashed his famous grin. "Politics plays a part in war. If we don't have Congress on our side, we simply can't get it done." He lowered his voice and added, "Captain, sometimes I think politics is dirtier than anything that happens on the battlefield."

"That's what I hear, General."

"All right then, I won't hold you up any longer." Eisenhower again shook Edward's hand. Hank's, too. "But dear God, boys, be careful out there. We need you. All you BD men. Every man jack of you."

With that, Eisenhower tapped the red fender nearest him with his knuckles, then hustled back to his jeep, climbed in, and the entourage was gone in a dust cloud.

The MP had witnessed the entire exchange. His wide eyes confirmed that he was stunned by what he had seen.

"Sorry, Captain. I had no idea you and the general..."

"No problem, Sergeant. You were doing your job and doing it well. You got us out of Ike's way quite effectively."

They exchanged salutes and Edward pointed toward Normandy.

"Let's go, Hank."

The MP called after them, "Just be careful. As you well know, we got mines everywhere. And a few Krauts what got separated from their units when they were running like scalded dogs."

They had traveled a good ten miles before Hank's curiosity ultimately got the better of him. "Well, Captain, I am impressed as hell. Ike? You're buddies with the Supreme Allied Commander in Europe who just happens to wear four stars?"

Edward smiled. "I never told anybody about it. Especially you guys. But now you know. I met him back in England, just before 'Overlord' launched. I got called to the general's HQ. He wanted an update on exactly what BD did. A status report on the state of BD. And he wanted details on what we would be doing once we followed the invasion forces. I just happened to be the only BD officer available to give an update, I guess. He never mentioned France. We talked for over an hour. I guess I made some sort of impression since he still remembers my name and made a point to stop and say hello."

"You sure as shit made an impression, sir."

Edward stared ahead through the bug-spattered windshield. There was smoke on the horizon, a long line of tanks approaching, soldiers camped in a copse, other men crawling on their bellies poking bayonets into the dirt of a nearby field, looking for mines.

They had left the fantasy world behind. Reality was dead ahead.

"We all have our jobs to do, Captain Bennett."

Doctor Ernst Alwin offered the American a cigarette. Bennett desperately craved a smoke, but he shook his head. "Thanks, pardner, but no thanks."

"And mine is to create cruelty that will hasten the end of this war. Surely you understand we of the Third Reich are only trying to return our country to its rightful place of strength on the European continent. What else should we do?" The scientist lit his own cigarette and took in a long drag. "I do not understand why you will not speak. Is it that you actually enjoy the interrogations?"

Bennett lifted his head and looked directly into Alwin's wide-set, dark-brown eyes.

"How can you Germans be so smart when it comes to science and industry and waging war and creating weaponry, but so damn stupid about everything else that matters? About what people really want and need?"

"What do people really want, Herr Bennett? You Americans, so sure of yourselves and your means of governing?"

"Peace. Freedom. Democracy. The ability to follow your own course and have a say in who your government is and how they run the country. That's all." Hedley was exhausted, his voice strained.

"Since you brought up the subject of weaponry, I want you to tell me about your *super bomb*," Alwin said, heavily emphasizing the last two ominous words. The scientist had convinced his superiors that he could learn about the long-rumored nuclear bomb the Americans were supposed to be developing if he could capture a bomb demolition expert. Like Captain Bennett here. That was the only reason he and his squad were allowed to remain alive. "All I need is your confirmation such a project exists. I am aware a mere captain would know few details. But give me that confirmation and your interrogations will cease immediately."

"You know what I know. You use the same ingredients. Amatol. TNT.

Fertilizer. We've dropped enough of 'em down your stovepipes by now you oughta be pretty familiar with what goes into our weapons. Just like we know the kind of cruelty you create in your labs, there, Doc."

Alwin frowned and held up his hand. "Do not insult me, Herr Bennett. I will allow our skilled interrogators like *Standartenführer* Schubert, here, to obtain the information in their own very effective way. And as I have explained to you, your help will only serve to shorten the war. And that, after all, will bring a quick end to this dying that so much disturbs you. Surely you see your lack of assistance only causes more death and suffering."

"Seems like your damn homicidal Führer is pretty damn good at doing that shit." Bennett closed his eyes. "All I know is how to make bombs safe. Yours. Ours. Theirs. And you are the sons of bitches who are—"

"But certainly," interrupted Alwin, "an officer and bomb demolition expert, such as yourself, Captain, has heard something about the super bomb your country is developing. A bomb based on an atomic reaction is what we know. Your military would already have you training to defuze such a powerful weapon. Yes, no, maybe?"

"Amatol. Sodium nitrate. TNT. Fuzes. Fuze lines. Detonators. Fuze pockets. Those things I know, just as you do. 'Atomic?' I have no idea what the hell you're talking about." Bennett opened his eyes and looked up at the German. "I've never heard a word about such a weapon. And even if I had—"

Alwin nodded solemnly, took the cigarette from his lips, and ground it out in a nearby ashtray. That was Schubert's cue to pull the canvas bag out of a drawer and, in one move, slam it down with force on Bennett's thigh. The captain yelped in pain.

"If you insist on remaining quiet, you are simply condemning more people to death, Herr Bennett. You cooperate, the war ends sooner and so does the killing. With such a weapon, we will not even have to deploy it. Merely the threat of its killing and destructive power will bring a quick, negotiated end. You must know that. Otherwise, I am afraid, those millions of deaths will forever be on your conscience, sir. Forever."

Another swing of the canvas bag, this time to Bennett's left shoulder. He tensed but could do nothing more but gasp and sob. And weakly repeat, "Hedley Oscar Bennett. Captain. Oh-81333-zero-9. Washington, DC—"

Another swoop of the canvas bag badly bruised the back of Hedley Bennett's left hand.

"Nein. Nein. Nein. Not the hands," Alwin told Schubert as the scientist idly touched his finger to his tongue and then used the spit to wipe a new drop of blood from his lab coat sleeve. "I told you that before, you idiot. Those hands will be of great service to the Reich when the handsome captain ultimately comes to his senses." A ponderous pause, then, "If the captain comes to his senses."

Schubert nodded solemnly, raised the bag once again, and resumed his brutal "interrogation" of BD Captain Hedley Bennett.

On the back of a white napkin she carefully copies an American address. One in Brooklyn, New York City. Hélène LeRiche is writing a letter to Rose Berg, introducing herself as a friend to her husband, the American Military Policeman Michael "Mickey" Berg. He has no idea Hélène is sending this letter. One in which she expresses how she would like to become friends with Rose because she is friends with her husband. The father of their sweet baby, David.

But the real reason for the correspondence is because she wants to reassure Rose that her husband is alive, healthy, safe, and eager to return to her. In her naïve, nineteen-year-old way, Hélène believes this is her duty. A reassuring note to the worried wife of a dear friend. A way to help another woman suffering the pain of this war. a letter Hélène would want to receive if she were in the same situation as Rose.

It takes Hélène LeRiche's letter six weeks to arrive in Brooklyn. It catches Rose Berg by surprise. She is suspicious of a letter from some female with a French name, from Pontorson, where she knows her husband is stationed. It is clearly not an official Army letter.

She decides it is likely something Mickey will need to explain to her, if he can, and that explanation should be delivered in person. When he gets leave. When the war is over. When he finally comes home to her and their son.

Why is a French woman she does not know sending her a letter?

The envelope, innocent or not, remains unopened on the kitchen table in their apartment, propped up against the salt-and-pepper shaker set Mickey sent to her as a first wedding anniversary gift when he arrived in England.

And there it will remain.

17

He could not stop thinking about her. The varying tableau as their jeep passed from war-torn towns to beautiful vistas and back to more rubble offered no distraction. He had been with her twice. The first time hardly counted since they were surrounded by injury and death and lethal unexploded ordnance on the brink of blowing them all sky high. But it was there, at the field hospital at Saint-Lô, that he immediately fell hopelessly in love with Virginia Brown. Then, the magical second encounter in Paris. Rescuing her from the drunk surgeon at the banquet. Spending a dreamlike romantic night in a historic hotel. Wandering the predawn streets together. Professing their dedication to each other in a picturesque four-hundred-year-old chapel.

Could Edward be in over his head? Captivated by love, lust, loneliness, or plain old infatuation? But Virginia had every characteristic he had always hoped to find in a future partner. The total antithesis of Rachel. Nothing like Lois, the one-night stand back in Baltimore just before shipping off to England. Amazingly, Virginia seemed to love him back, just as quickly and deeply and eternally. Impossible as it all sounded, they were now committed to a future with each other. Only the war stood in their way. Only the war. No other woman had ever had this effect on him. To the point that if he was not careful, it could affect his BD work. His life and the lives of others depended on him keeping his head. Lack of concentration was the top enemy of a BD man. And Virginia Brown, if he allowed her to be, was one hell of a diversion.

All these thoughts swirled through his mind as he and Corporal Anderson bounced and bumped their way back to Pontorson.

"You know, Hank, that gala was a royal waste of time," Edward blurted out at one point. This time they were waiting in line to once more show their credentials and get waved through a checkpoint. He snapped up his head, surprised to hear his own harsh words spoken out loud.

"Well, Captain, they did honor some deserving medical teams. Good for morale, don't you think?" Hank countered. "And you got to see your girl. Take some good with all this bad, sir."

Earlier Hume had casually mentioned to Anderson that he had visited with Lt. Virginia Brown but volunteered no further details, though he knew Hank was dying to hear them. "There is that. But you know what really chaps my ass?" Edward held his tongue for a moment but then went on and said what was on his mind. "All those damn officers, living the good life in Paris since the liberation, while our boys get by without proper overshoes and winter gear. It's not gonna let up 'til late spring, even into May in some spots. If I was running this show, the attention and moolah would go to soldiers in the field, not some damn party to hand out medals."

Hank was quiet for a moment, then asked, "So, Captain, don't you think Patton and Eisenhower will have this thing wrapped up before the snow flies?"

"No, I don't. That's what's bugging me." Edward had always tried to be optimistic when it came to discussing the end of the war, but he had recently read troubling reports expressing concerns about the approaching winter.

"What you hearing?"

"Hitler won't go down without committing everything he has. Put yourself in his boots. He'll concentrate on us, not the Russians on the Eastern front. He'll just try to hold his own there and not try to take them on in the snow again. He'll figure us American boys have lost our will to fight, that we're dog tired from moving so fast, that we're running out of supplies and gas because we're advancing at Patton's crazy pace. That makes us ripe for a counterattack."

"Then why don't you take this on up the command chain, sir? You being on a first-name basis with General Eisenhower 'n' all. Ya got some pull. After all, you did it once before."

That was true. While still gaining on-the-job training back in Britain, in an especially tense situation, Edward and Ace Taft were forced to take care of a full load of bombs on a blazing B-17 stalled on a critical airbase runway. The airplane had just come back from a mission without dropping a single bomb. Hume, at the urging of his squad, had written up a complaint urging the Army Air Forces to no longer return to bases carrying unreleased, "hot" bombs. Instead, they could jettison their loads in a safe place. Whether it was based on his recommendation or not, that practice did become policy soon after. And the reason for their adventure in the bay around Mont Saint Michel, too.

"I may just do that," Edward said, already composing in his head the wording and the routing of his suggestions.

As they passed the last checkpoint and rounded the final corner at the barracks building in Pontorson, Edward glanced over at Hank. The corporal was bleary-eyed, bushed, uncharacteristically quiet as they neared the end of the eight-hour obstacle course from Paris to Pontorson. The sun had long since fallen into the sea out beyond the temporary air base by the time they got back.

Breaking the silence of the last fifty miles, Hume sighed. "Look, I know you're tired. Me too. But we ought to get the squad together right away to make sure everyone's still on point."

"Even if we didn't bring 'em back any souvenirs?" Anderson smiled crookedly. "I had a feeling I wasn't going to bed just yet. But I agree, Captain."

"Tonight, before we kick off a new week. We all need to be on the same page."

"I understand, sir." Anderson nodded. "Way I see it, our being gone broke the routine. Ace's replacement will be here any day now, too, and that changes things. We need to keep our edge, not get bored and sloppy. And any day now, we might get moved to the front."

"Yep. All that. I see you've been thinking about all this, too." Edward's voice trailed off as they pulled to a stop. It was just after midnight. Something seemed odd.

"Truck's not here," Hank pointed out. "Must be something big or scary if they're working this late." They would've walked to a bar.

The captain had the same thoughts, but there was no point in trying to track them down. He and Anderson had unpacked and stowed their clothes and were about to head for the mess hall when they heard the squeak of the truck's brakes, its engine dying as it coasted to a stop. Edward stepped to the doorway.

"The corporal and I expected welcome-home banners and confetti, but you guys—" The looks on their faces stopped him mid-sentence. He also noticed a new face among them. But a familiar one was missing.

Gene Wozinski was the first to speak, his voice quavering. "Captain, we need to talk."

Edward sensed bad vibes. "Good! My plan, too. Youse guys hungry? Eat 'n' talk?"

"No, sir, I don't think anybody has an appetite right now."

It was a warm night, lit by fireflies and stars, a soundtrack provided by a chorus of crickets. The men settled in the grass beneath a tree in the little park across from the barracks.

Hume quickly welcomed Sergeant Morrison to the squad. Then Woz updated the captain on what had happened to Private Pete Ronzini the previous night.

"They took him to the town hospital first," Wozinski reported, his voice shaky. "But he's getting treated by Army docs at a field hospital now. He's holding his own but...well...Pete's kinda in bad shape. Surgeons patched up his lung but there's a high risk of infection."

"That's where we've been, sir, trying to learn what we could," Morrison added. "The Resistance fighter that stabbed him, that guy, he was really drunk. The French police arrested him, but the MPs told us they let him go. He's some kind of local hero, a reputation for making life miserable for the Krauts, but also known for his bad temper. We're all praying for Pete, sir."

Self-defense, the local *Gendarmerie Nationale* had determined, though most of the bar's patrons testified the guy challenged an unarmed Ronzini and initiated the fight.

"I'll look into it," the captain said. "That doesn't sound right. And we'll be sure Pete's getting what he needs."

Jesus. Pete, stabbed, just holding on. But Edward sensed there was more.

Wozinski shared the news about the kid that they all—including Hume and Anderson—had taken under their wing, grown close to, getting himself killed by a booby trap. Theo Toussaint. "TT." The boy who had turned fourteen on July 14th, Bastille Day. The kid who had boldly explained to Edward that the 14th might be France's party for the people, but it was really the national celebration of his birth now. That he had big plans for his life. That he expected to grow up and do great things despite being an orphan.

Edward had an even bigger lump in his throat. He held back tears, put on a brave front for the squad, but his heart was breaking.

There would be no funeral for the boy. The family—at least the ones who could be located—insisted that he be buried with a simple white cross in the part of the pasture where centerfield was, where he so enjoyed learning from the American soldiers to play stickball. Edward and the squad would help dig the grave.

"Something else, sir," Gene continued quietly.

"Spill it," Hume said, but only after a deep sigh.

"We got word this morning that Captain Bennett and the Bomb Merchants are MIA over in the Ardennes Forest, close to the border. Nobody's saying what they were doing up there, and nobody's heard from them for several weeks now."

Gene handed Edward the dispatch. The cold words on the thin paper sent a chill up the captain's spine. Gene looked away, waiting. Edward finally responded.

"They're a bunch of tough, gritty bastards, those guys." Edward hoped his doubts were not obvious. "Captain Bennett is the strongest BD man I know. So's Sergeant Gabler and the rest of his guys."

"Yeah! Yeah, they are!" several of the men agreed.

"BD men. We're all brothers, you know," Edward added, but his eyes were moist. He hoped it was dark enough his guys wouldn't notice. "Besides, Anderson and I, we got photographic proof that we won our first-BD-captain-to-the-Eiffel-Tower bet, so Hedley and them boys better show up to fork over that bottle of Jägermeister!"

Hume assumed there was no more bad news, so he nodded toward the new man, ready to more properly acknowledge him. Their first moment face-to-face. "And you, Sergeant? We are glad to have you in the squad."

"Sir, thank you," Jack responded, and offered a sharp salute. "I'm Technical Sergeant Fifth Grade Jack Morrison. My personnel file and orders are in my duffel bag. I'll get them to you right away."

"We'll get to know you better, no doubt. And you us. But now it looks like the squad's back down one man again," Hume said, clearing his throat. "You've had good training. You've impressed the RAF. And Captain Duncan Smythe gave you a good report in a personal message to me, so we'll be throwing you right into the breach first thing in the morning, first light, first mission."

"I appreciate Captain Smythe's confidence. I'm ready, Captain. And I'll be praying for Private Ronzini," Morrison responded. "And for all of us. God, in all His glory, will bless."

The men looked at one another, rolling their eyes. Hume noticed, even in the darkness.

"I suspect we'll all be praying." Then Edward turned back to Wozinski. "I know we're all upset about Pete, boys. Any word on what they'll do with him if he makes it?"

"I heard that he might be on his way back to England or something like that," Morty reported.

"Back to England? Huh." Edward knew that meant only one thing: Pete was in bad shape but there was reasonable hope he might survive. "Look, I'll go to the hospital tonight and find out more about what's going on and give you guys a full update. He's our brother and always will be."

Hank gave Edward a nod, acknowledging his driving duties for the night were not yet finished. And Hume cleared his throat once more. The mention of "brother" had almost caused him to lose his struggle to remain cool and composed.

"We got plenty more work to do. And our lives depend on us staying focused." Edward could only guess at his men's reactions as a cloud covered the half-moon. "Okay, now, give me a quick rundown of what youse guys been up to while Hank and I were AWOL."

The captain sometimes lapsed back into his northeastern Pennsylvania accent when tired or under pressure. "Youse guys" was a tell. Events were piling up, weighing heavily on the boss.

Wozinski took out his cigarette lighter, flicked it to life and used it to give him light as he quickly read from a sheet of paper a list of the jobs they had done since the previous Friday. When he finished, there was only the cricket choir for a full half minute.

"I heard mention of bombs, Corporal," Hume finally said. "Four bombs, if I counted right."

"Yes, sir. None of the four was armed. Defective fuzes or they were just dropped unarmed with no cotter pins pulled. I followed procedure and took care of 'em." Wozinski extinguished the lighter, putting the men back into inky darkness.

"But you're telling me you accessed and removed the fuze pocket covers of four UXBs?"

"Yes, sir. I thought we should make sure they were not armed and on the verge of detonating."

"Then you absolutely did not follow procedure," Edward said, loud enough to silence the crickets. "Or follow my specific orders or US Army BD protocol. Come see me in my quarters after we break up here. Got that?"

Every man stared at Gene.

"Yes, sir."

"Everyone else, dismissed. Anderson, wait for me at the jeep. Corporal, follow me."

Beginning with the morning he signed US Army enlistment papers back at Fort Indiantown Gap, Pennsylvania, Edward Hume had harbored one big doubt about becoming a bomb demolition squad captain. It was not leaving home, family, jobs, or his fiancé, undergoing intense training, or laying bare hands on deadly explosives.

What worried Hume was becoming a commander of men, giving orders which would put them at risk or get them killed. Making decisions for a motley crew, a bunch of headstrong guys barely out of high school but facing death every day, ordering them to willingly perform tasks they may or may not understand or agree with.

Since then, there had been times when Edward wondered if he possessed that crucial talent necessary for leading men. The worst moment he had faced so far after Ace Taft's shocking death at the ammo dump explosion had been when Corporal Anderson brazenly accused him of being the primary cause of the sergeant's horrific death. There had been danger of that belief spreading to the other squad members. Hopefully by now Edward had proven his worth as a leader, but he knew he would always be tested.

Edward strategized every military decision, calculating the consequences, bad or good. What was the objective? What were the prospects of success? The chances men could be hurt? All considerations Colonel Thomas Kane drilled into prospective BD officers from the get-go back at Aberdeen Proving Ground, Maryland. Teaching in near-equal portions both bomb disposal and leadership. There were inevitable skirmishes among his men. Especially men under such intense pressure. The vitriol between Privates Schwartz and Ronzini, two guys from competing New York City neighborhoods, compelled other squad members to pick sides. Distraction! Edward had decided to defuze that situation as soon as he got back from Paris. A bar fight had, in a backhanded way, temporarily taken care of that for him.

Now his primary command challenge had just become Corporal Gene Wozinski. The young Chicagoan—maybe, in Hume's opinion, the smartest guy in the squad—now sat on Edward's cot, eyes unnaturally wide behind his black-framed eyeglasses, right foot rhythmically tapping the floor, sweating profusely in the cool room. He looked at his captain, his expression hinting he was braced for his reprimand.

"So, tell me, Corporal. What made you ignore my orders and violate the most important protocol we have?" Edward started. He had sat in the only chair in the tiny room, his knees almost touching Wozinski's, and he could feel nervous energy radiating from the corporal.

"I just needed to make sure they weren't about to blow up and kill a bunch of people like that device did to Theo. And they were all duds anyway."

Edward studied the list of jobs, then looked up. "The first bomb, the one at the airfield, came before the kid got killed."

Wozinski shook his head, as if to clear it. Sweat flew from his brow. "Maybe. But that one could have done damage to a vital runway. The Air Forces are still supporting the advance out of Pontorson, you know. Even if they are closing the airbase next month, they still got lots of Thunderbolts coming and going. It needed to be fixed quick."

Edward consulted the list again. "Well, says here the UXB had been there a couple of months at least. You could have waited two days 'til I got back. Or called in one of the other squads. You did not have to directly disobey—"

"Sorry, Captain. So damn sorry. Please." The young soldier had abruptly segued from stubborn defensiveness to begging forgiveness. And appeared ready to burst into tears. Edward took note of the dramatic mood swing.

"Wozinski, are you okay? Physically okay? You taking any kind of medicine?"

There was a guy, back in Pennsylvania, who started taking pills to go back to the mines after close calls in a couple of ceiling collapses. Nobody trusted him anymore. Nobody wanted to pull a shift with him. Wozinski reminded him of that guy.

"Well, sir. I want to be honest."

"That's always a good idea, Gene."

"Can we talk about this just between you and me?"

"What do you mean?"

"Off the record? I don't want to get in trouble."

Edward wanted to get this settled, to learn what was going on, to take action to try to fix it, but he was hesitant to give Wozinski a pass on such a serious disobedience of orders. "Have you done something that could put the men in jeopardy?"

"No, sir! No! I'd never do that!"

"Then why 'off the record' then?"

"Sir, please. Just this once."

Edward shook his head and inhaled deeply. For some reason he still trusted this boy. If what he was about to say turned out to be incredibly bad, he would deal with the fallout. But as tired and disappointed as Hume was at the moment, he wanted to find out what was happening and get it repaired. Before it blew up like a "dud" UXB.

"Okay. Off the record. Just this once."

"These, sir," Wozinski said. He took two white pills from his pocket and opened his hand to show them to the captain. "They keep me alert. Ready to go, go, go. They make me stronger, more confident, Captain. They're called 'Pervitin.' Amphetamines. Pep pills."

Hume took the pills from Gene. "Army docs give you these?"

"No. Agathe does," Gene said. "My girlfriend."

"A Nazi collaborator? How else would she get 'Hitler pills'? These damn things are 'Hitler pills,' Woz."

"No, sir. She was not. Is not. She was just trying to get food and be protected. She says the SS took the pills all the time and you got to agree they functioned pretty damn well. These are the last of them. She gave them to me to help me...you know...because she likes me and wants me to be strong. Like a real man ought to be."

"You say this Agathe, she's your girlfriend?" Hume did not want to go down this path, but he had to understand what was going on. He needed Wozinski, and especially now that Ronzini was gone. They were likely to be heading eastward very soon, deeper into France, and then into Germany. Their new orders were coming soon, any hour. But was the kid a drug addict hanging out with a Nazi spy?

"You gotta know by now, sir—" Gene started, then stopped, composed himself, and went on, tears on his cheeks. "I mean, you...you surely figured out by now that I...I'm not heterosexual."

Colonel Kane had warned there would be moments like this one. Edward did not allow his face to show any reaction. But off the record or not, by his oath as a United States Army officer, he would be required to report what Gene had just told him. That would have serious ramifications:

a less-than-honorable discharge for Wozinski, loss of veterans' benefits, a public record of what the Army considered to be a mental illness. And even a prison sentence if it was determined he was a security risk. Taking drugs from and having a relationship with a Nazi collaborator would be powerful evidence of just that.

Edward had pretty much known all along that Gene was homosexual, but it never interfered with his work. The rest of the squad had to know as well, and it had caused no issues. It was war and Woz was needed. Trust was the currency of leadership. Character was at the core of that trust. Gene had character. He had earned the trust of his squad and his CO. At least up to this bitch of a bad-news night.

"Look, sir, I do a good job. I'd never give away any secrets. I've sure as hell kept this homo thing a secret all my life. From my folks. My brother and sister. The nuns at the convent where I went to school. The other teachers and administrators. Nobody knew. Or if they did, they never said anything. I was afraid the squad would notice. I thought a girlfriend might change their minds. Might keep you and the rest of the Army from catching on and kicking me out. Agathe, she's my insurance."

"She lives here?"

"Yessir. Born and raised in Pontorson."

"Last name?"

"Dumoulin."

Edward jotted down her name. "I'll need to check her out, Gene. For your safety. For the integrity of the squad."

"Yessir. And, sir, she's gorgeous. I thought maybe she could, you know, change me." The soldier had begun pounding on his thigh with a clenched fist.

"Gene, have you shared any information with her that would be considered secret, confidential?"

"No! And she never asked me for anything. She just wanted to be safe. The war, it can be brutal for a woman. The pills, they don't work for what I really wanted them for. For sex with a woman." Wozinski's foot continued tapping madly on the floor and there were tears streaming down his face.

Hume had somehow managed to keep that noncommittal expression on his face and his voice even and unemotional when he asked his questions. But Gene Wozinski appeared to be on the edge of hysterics.

"Calm down, soldier. It's the pills that cause you to do things you would never do otherwise. Like disobeying your CO's direct orders. I'm no doctor but I don't think they'll help with...you know...that other problem youse got there. And they may give you a boost when you first take them but they sure as shit will drop you to rock bottom when they wear off. The Nazis didn't care if they made their commanders do crazy shit. That was part of the plan." Hume leaned in closer to Wozinski as the kid fought to overcome his emotions. "Promise me, you're not gonna take another one of those 'Hitler pills,' right?"

The corporal nodded ever so slightly, and his voice quaked as he responded, "I won't, sir."

"It's an order, and I hope you obey it better than the last one I gave you."

"I will, Captain. I will."

"And listen to me, okay?" Edward knew the message he wanted to impart but he had no idea how to phrase it. Still, he knew he was right, so he charged on, hoping he was not actually making things worse. "Look, I don't care how you spend your private time, as long as it doesn't affect the squad or how you do your job. I don't give a good goddam whether you're homosexual or whatever. You're a good man. A good squad mate. A good soldier. A good BD man. I've got confidence in you, Woz. You're way, way stronger than you think you are."

Wozinski was much calmer now, as if a weight had been lifted, a switch thrown. "Sir, I appreciate it. There's one more thing."

Oh, Lord, Edward thought. *What else?*

"Please don't let anything happen to Agathe. They drag these women out into the street and do awful things to them. Please, don't let them do that to her."

"I'll do all I can to protect an innocent person. That includes her. But I still have to see what I can find out about her. Understand?"

"Yes, sir." But Wozinski did not look or sound all that convinced.

"Look at me, Corporal. And listen to what I am saying. Do not expect my understanding in this matter to be an indication that I will be lenient or anything besides by-the-book in the future. If you ever again disobey an order of mine, I'll see that you are removed from duty, punished appropriately, and that you do not ever have the opportunity to put anybody else's life in danger, including your own. Got that?" Edward dropped the pair of pills onto the floor and crushed them with his boot heel. "Dismissed!"

With Gene gone, Edward sat back in the chair and studied the olive-green blanket, the few articles of clothing hanging on a tent pole, his helmet on the floor in the corner, a clipboard full of paperwork beneath the chair, a copy of the *Army Regulations* book on his duffel bag. All trappings of a US Army commanding officer.

He was once again in doubt that he had demonstrated proper command leadership.

But he had done the best he could. He had kept the squad intact. He hoped he had also put what he felt was a good man back onto a better path.

That, he decided, was all he could do. He slid over onto the cot, exhausted. He would postpone his hospital visit to Ronzini.

Captain Edward Hume decided what he most needed was a few hours of deep, recuperative sleep.

♠

"Sorry we couldn't give you a bigger welcome to the Sixth Ordnance BD Squadron, Morrison, but as you likely noticed, things have sort of gone off the tracks the last few days."

Captain Hume had invited the new man to sit with him at an early breakfast in the mess hall, away from the rest of the squad and the bitter mood hanging over their heads. Carl Kostas, Whitey at his heels, had jogged to the field hospital well before sunrise to check on Pete Ronzini only to find his captain already there. The nurse assured both of them that he was alive, holding his own, but still critical and unavailable for visitors.

Now, Edward was about to give Morrison a quick rundown when the sergeant abruptly dropped his chin to his chest, put his hands together in prayer mode, and said grace in a raspy whisper over his powdered eggs, overcooked bacon, and stone-hard biscuit.

"...and amen," he closed and looked up. "Sorry, Captain. Now, as you were saying."

"You've met the rest of the squad. And let's hope you get to know Corporal Ronzini soon, too."

Morrison chewed, swallowed, and responded, "I'm praying for his quick recovery. And I've asked the others to get on their knees and do some serious conversing with God."

"Yeah, about that, Sergeant," Edward said. "I'm all for speaking to God and praying and all that, but there was one other thing Captain Smythe mentioned in his evaluation of your work. I'm gonna tell you this straight. All that evangelizing can get on people's nerves. I'm going to ask you to ease up. We got guys of all religious persuasion over here, too. Roman Catholic, Lutheran, Methodist, Episcopalian. Even one Jew, and what we've been seeing and hearing about the way the Nazis have been treating Jews has weighed heavily on all of us, especially Private Schwartz."

"I'll try not to get on people's nerves, Captain," Morrison promised, looking hard across the table at his CO. He touched his nose with his finger. "My snout didn't get bent like this when I was born. It got broke in a playground fight when I told a guy he wasn't acting very Christ-like, and he proved my point by punching me. But Second Timothy tells me I am to do the work of an evangelist and make full use of my ministry. And like Paul says in Romans One, 'There will be anguish and distress for everyone who does evil, to the Jew first and also to the Greek; but glory and honor and peace for everyone who does good.'" The sergeant took a big bite of his biscuit, grinned broadly, and nodded across the mess hall to where Morty Schwartz and Carl Kostas sat together, eating in silence.

Edward cocked his head. "Well, no preaching if it threatens the chemistry and the concentration of my squad. We have to focus on what we're doing here. Not necessarily in the afterlife, close as it may seem sometimes. Got that?"

Morrison lost his grin. "I see what you're saying, sir. Teamwork. I played eight-man football back in Nebraska. Team that small, we had to work together or we'd for sure get our hind ends beat."

"Perfect analogy, Jack. I'll use that sometime when I'm doing some of my own kind of preaching."

"God bless you, sir," Morrison said, beaming now.

"I do not believe I sneezed, Sergeant Morrison. Zip it. Got that?"

"Got that, sir."

Yet again, the captain was unsure if he had passed this latest test of leadership. The captain motioned Hank over to his table and quickly laid out the new hierarchy. Morrison would be Hume's number two as ordered by BD higher command. That put him in the hole with the captain and all UXBs. He would also drive the jeep. Hank would continue as photographer and documentarian and Gene as the truck driver. Gene was relieved to know that Captain had checked out Agathe Dumoulin and she got the all clear. That meant Gene was also in the clear.

Hank would ride in the jeep with the captain and Sergeant Morrison, always ready to jump into the hole to take pictures of anything new or unusual, rare as it was to find new stuff anymore. Most UXBs now were Allied. At the morning brief at the Hotel Montgomery, he would request a replacement for Ronzini. Nobody could be sure Pete would ever be able to rejoin the Kaboom Boys.

"Sergeant, fill in the rest of the squad on the changes and get loaded up while I'm at the briefing at HQ learning what pretty messes we get to play with today. And maybe I can get some word on when we're moving. If we're moving."

But in his mind, as he turned and trotted away, Captain Hume was thinking, *God help us. God help us all.*

18

There had been no bombs to handle for a few days, so Józef Steiner was sitting on his cot quietly practicing his English. He had begun learning the language better with the help of another prisoner, an unusual detainee. Sergeant Evan Llewellyn Edwards was one of the rare Brits to be held at Dachau. He was a thirty-three-year-old career soldier with Britain's Welsh Regiment and was more than willing to help his fellow prisoner when Steiner shared the primary reason for becoming more proficient in the language. Someday, he hoped to testify to officials or maybe even some kind of tribunal about the unbelievable cruelty he had seen at Dachau. He believed Brit-accented English would be more effective than German or Polish. Wyn Edwards thought it was a capital idea and hoped he might one day have such an opportunity, so Józef returned the favor and began tutoring him in German.

But after only a few months, Sergeant Edwards, like so many others, disappeared. Word was that guards had taken him away. No one knew his fate. Józef Steiner could only pray.

This day, as Steiner worked on present tense phrases, he was harshly interrupted by guards and dragged out of his cell even more urgently than usual. They shoved him into the back of an Opel Blitz truck—not the usual bus—and hauled him to a location in the village of Aying, a quaint spot in the district of Munich. As they pulled to a stop, he caught a glimpse of his rush job. He felt a cold hand on his heart. This would be his 247th bomb, but it was different. It was held upright, clutched in the limbs and leaning against the trunk of a big, bare chestnut tree, yet its nose had been impaled several feet into the earth, burying its fuze pocket. The grip on his heart tightened as Józef approached the device and the pit around it, dug by the fellow Dachau One Hundred BD workers who now rested in the grass nearby.

By the time he placed his ladder against the tree and climbed to where he could inspect the bomb's identification plate, his hands were shaking and his knees threatened to buckle. Where was this sudden fear coming from? He had defuzed 246 bombs and had never had such a visceral reaction to a job. Not even the first one, when he knew nothing of what he was doing. But this one was different. He could not determine how, though. Even the sweet music of songbirds in the trees around him did not lessen this sudden, absurd fear that had taken hold of him.

Steiner had no doubt about this being unexploded bomb number 247. Each night he had meticulously updated a secret log with details of each device he touched. He wanted a knowledge base to share with other members of the Dachau One Hundred, though he suspected such a thing was forbidden.

Then, several nights before, as he sat on his bunk, documenting a fuze removal from number 246—a British ten-thousand-kilogram "Tallboy," an "earthquake bomb"—he failed to notice when one of the friendlier SS guards came in with an armful of firewood for the smoky wood heater in the cellblock. That was a luxury only the *kapos* received, and it was only an effort to keep them healthier so they could work harder for the Germans. The guard saw Steiner writing something. Despite Józef's protests, the guard snatched up the notebook, quickly determined what it was, and ripped it apart. Then he stuffed the pieces in among the hot fire the guard had kindled in the heater.

"Herr Steiner, I am saving your life!" the guard told him emphatically. "Some of the other guards or one of the *kapos*, they see what you do, you will immediately be on the way to the crematorium with your Jew brothers and sisters. If they do not shoot you on the spot and throw your body on the pile."

It was true, of course. And the guard, who had known Steiner for more than four years, was risking his own life to save Józef's.

Steiner decided he would not touch this massive, dangling device caught in the tree limbs. It would be dangerous—even without his screaming instincts warning him—to probe the fuze pocket or poke at the detonator. He could see there was a typical American message on the bomb's casing: "Up Hitler's Keister Sideways!" And the plate identified the weapon's model and serial number. There was even something frightening about that common set of numbers, but he could not quite decide what it was. Just that he should absolutely not defuze this device, regardless of the consequences.

No one should.

Józef shouted to his handler, "We must blow it up in place! It cannot be opened and defuzed!"

"*Nein!* The orders are to deactivate. We must not cause damage. Now do it!" the young guard shouted back. There were no seasoned Nazi officers available for this job. The German Army had become too thinly spread, so many sent to the front to fight the Russians or moved north for a rumored counterattack against the invading Allies. "And our scientists require the bomb parts to study! Now get to work, Blacksmith!"

The bomb began to sway slightly in the breeze. It was an American-made Mark 65 one-thousand-pounder, likely dropped from high altitude, yet it had somehow gotten snagged by the chestnut's limbs. Too unstable to be worked on. But that still was not it.

His instincts continued to scream for caution. It even occurred to Steiner that the confiscation and destruction of his notebook might have been an omen, a warning to not handle any more bombs. Certainly not number 247.

Decision made, he lingered on the ladder until his hands stopped shaking. From there, he could see over a nearby hedgerow and stone wall, into the peaceful, shaded garden of a lovely home. It felt as if it was on a different planet than Dachau, especially with the songbirds of Aying providing a tranquil concert. This could be a place where the kind young woman who left him the apple and the bright blue scarf might live. But he knew it was the home of the daughter of a high Nazi Party official. And that was the reason his orders were to neutralize the UXB, not blow it up in place.

The lone guard stared hard at Steiner when he came back down the ladder, then walked toward him with no canvas bag full of fuze and detonator parts.

"Steiner? Finished? Already?" he asked hopefully.

The other three men in Józef's POW squad stood as well. They were ready to dispose of the materials Józef was to have removed from the American bomb and then go handle the next device.

"Blacksmith! Answer me!"

"No. I will not be working on this one," Steiner said forcefully as he walked past the guard. "This one cannot be deactivated. Nobody else can safely do the job either. It can only be blown up, *Korporal.* I must do that right now. There is danger it will suddenly drop, explode, and kill us all. You, me, everyone close by. We must detonate it now."

The guard was flummoxed. Without a superior officer on site, it was his decision. The young soldier—only recently a member of Hitler Youth—raised his rifle and pointed it at Steiner. The Blacksmith kept walking deliberately toward where the Opel Blitz truck was parked, just over five hundred meters from the bomb. The guard was aware that Steiner was too valuable a piece of property, a rare bomb demolition man, to simply shoot him for the least provocation. But what if the Jew defied orders and refused to do his job? If he showed such disrespect for the young guard in front of the other prisoners?

"But why, Blacksmith? I need bomb parts for Doctor Ernst Alwin! And to protect the home on the other side of that wall over..."

But Józef kept walking. He did not hurry. He had made his decision. Either way, he might die. By bullet or by bomb. The songbirds provided him with marching music. He kept up that same pace all the way to the truck.

"Whenever you are ready for me to detonate, I will," he called back. He knew he was the only one there who could safely set off a bomb, and perhaps even "accidentally" blow up the home of the daughter of a Nazi officer. The three other detainees watched with interest as the drama played out.

The guard lowered the rifle barrel. He did not chase after Blacksmith. Steiner would be appropriately punished later. There was still a job to do. An urgent job. He eyed the others, the men in the striped uniforms, staring back at him. He turned his rifle on the trio.

"Zimmerman! You're a doctor, yes?"

"Yes, *Korporal*." The doctor knew if Steiner had deemed this weapon of war as unfixable, it should only be detonated, not disarmed.

"Then you must be the smartest one left. Into the hole. Open up that bomb and deactivate it! Now!"

The doctor hesitated.

The corporal shook his rifle threateningly. "Go!"

Zimmerman shrugged and climbed down into the hole. He had actually defuzed Mark 65s before, but none as problematic as this one appeared to be. But with the rifle of a nervous, unsure, teenaged boy aimed at him, what choice did he have? He would take his chances with the thousand-pounder.

Meanwhile, Steiner sat down on the running board of the Opel, confident the young guard would ultimately allow him to do this job the safer way. Just then, as if the revelation had wafted in on the breeze like the music of the songbirds, he realized what it was that had ultimately caused him to walk away from number 247. It was not intuition or an omen at all. It was a minor thing he should have noticed immediately. The serial number and model number were stamped on the plate screwed to the bomb's metal skin. "AN MK65," as usual. But now, in his mind's eye, he recalled a difference. Something he had not noticed initially.

There were two additional characters that had not been present on other bombs like this one. "A1." A simple block "A" and the number "1."

That meant this was a modified design, highly volatile and unstable. The kind of device that would blow just by someone looking at it. Only a few days before, a *Bombensuchkommando* captain had casually mentioned it to Steiner. They rarely informed The Hundred about such minor details. Someone gets blown up, other prisoners are put to work in his place. And there is one less mouth to feed.

"Nothing important, Blacksmith," the captain had irritably told him. "Something to do with the exploder. Just do your job and enjoy the benefits you receive for your service to the Reich."

Józef noticed Zimmerman walking over and kneeling in the hole around the device, looking for the fuze pocket. Steiner jumped up and started to run back toward the UXB, to stop the work.

He had taken only a few steps and was about to yell a warning when a vicious blast knocked Józef backward, off his feet. He landed on his back in the middle of the roadway. His head slammed into the cobblestones. His breath was knocked from his chest. Shards of tree bark, leaves, rocks, and clumps of dark earth pummeled him like sullied snow.

There were bloody human body parts scattered about.

Steiner lay there, unable at first to move, but he willed himself to do so. Gasping for air, he instinctively reached skyward, coughing and gagging.

The songbirds of Aying had gone silent.

19

As September morphed into October, and inevitably November, the Kaboom Boys carried on in the deepening winter cold, handling booby traps, munition dumps, bombs and more. There seemed to be no end to unexploded ordnance. Nowadays they were ranging farther and farther to the east through France, working in the wake of the invasion forces. This meant long rides, late night returns to Pontorson, occasional nights spent on the roadside in tents or sleeping beneath the vehicles, and very little downtime for rest or recuperation. It seemed there was never a time when they were warm. But thankfully, that made for even less time for intersquad tensions to uncoil, rise up, and bite.

"Thank God for small favors," Edward told his reflection in his tiny shaving mirror each morning. He knew his mom would have corrected him: "Thank God for *all* favors, Eddie."

Even so, he kept close watch for any signs of trouble among the strong personalities of the Kaboom Boys. He made it a point to periodically pull each man aside, probe and suss out any simmering intersquad issues. He also had those long rides with Jack in the jeep next to him, driving, humming church music. Those could be challenging at times, as the sergeant continued as well to subtly quote brief passages of scripture. But at the same time Edward found the man to be intelligent, articulate, and well meaning. As it was with each guy in the squad, the newcomer was complicated, and he came equipped with his own quirks like the hair trigger of an anti-tamper fuze, requiring special attention. It remained the captain's main mission to keep the team focused.

Pete, still in grave condition, was moved back across the Channel to a military hospital near London. That made it far more difficult to get updates on his condition, but his buddies knew he would be getting much better care. Edward was crushed by the fact that he might never again see Pete, never hear him proudly claim to be an "Italian meatball from Bayside, Brooklyn." No one heard what ultimately happened to the French Resistance fighter who had stabbed him. The locals had simply wiped away the incident like so many other bad memories.

Until recently, Edward managed to take advantage of those wonderful home-cooked French meals with Hélène LeRiche, her mother, and an expanding, eclectic group of French friends at the Devereaux home. Those visits offered a touch of civilization at which they could all forget the war for a few hours. He was always accompanied by Military Police Captain Mickey Berg, who was still hopelessly enamored with the just-turned-twenty-year-old French woman, despite his marital status. Mickey held on even after Hélène made it clear their relationship would be no more than a friendship. Chaplain Russell Lowe, who served with Edward as Mickey's wingman during these heavily chaperoned gatherings, was usually there, too. Hélène continued to hold court as she had during the late summer and could not stop talking about her plans to begin school at the University of Rennes in January 1945.

Then, on a chilly evening in mid-November, things changed.

Over fresh fish and *salade niçoise*, Hélène tearfully announced that she and her mother would soon be relocating to Rennes, in Brittany, seventy-five kilometers away, to live with friends while in school. Hélène would finally be able to attend law school. This night would be their last meal together.

Mickey Berg was near tears. His feelings for Hélène, for his family back home, the stress of being a Jew in a war he saw taking such an especially harsh toll on Jews, and the day-to-day pressures of his military duties had him reeling. But Berg also had news to share before dessert that evening.

He and his MP squad were being transferred to parts unknown—location classified—but somewhere distant from Pontorson.

Hélène vowed to write to him every day. She also promised to work even harder learning English if he agreed to do the same with his French.

"But your English is already superb, Hélène. So much better than you think it is," Mickey told her sincerely, and all the Americans at the table nodded agreement. "But my French, *c'est horrible.*" And again, the Americans nodded in agreement.

As Marcelline LeRiche stepped to the kitchen to bring in the next course, Edward used his spoon to click his glass. He, too, had an announcement.

"We Kaboom Boys got our marching orders as well," he shared. "We're being sent east, and that is all I can say." Edward could not say they were being moved toward the Ardennes Forest in Belgium. "But it's a place where they need BD help."

The group glumly gave a collective sigh as they picked at the last of their food. No doubt, all this news had brought an abrupt end to these most pleasant gatherings.

Chaplain Lowe was the first to break the awkward lull. "I love and respect everyone here. May we bow our heads to ask for divine guidance as we now walk separate paths."

After a moment of bowed heads and silent prayer, the Chaplain whispered "Amen." Marcelline had just reentered the dining room.

"*Merveilles?*" she asked.

"'*Miracles!*'" Hélène shouted.

Marcelline set down on the sideboard a delicate ceramic blue-and-white bowl with gold engraved fleur-de-lis. It was filled with twisted sweet pastry, delicately flavored with orange zest and brandy, and dusted with powdered sugar and a touch of cinnamon.

"A special-*tee* for a final soirée togeth-*air*," she said in her halting English, with a broad smile but a big tear on each of her red cheeks.

Details about the squad's move came at the 0600 briefing the next morning. There was also updated word on Hedley and his squad, news equally as chilling as the November wind off the Channel. Their burned-out truck and jeep carcasses were discovered in the Ardennes Forest, near the German border. There were no signs of bodies or burials. The prevailing opinion was that they had been captured and were being held by the SS.

"Hed Bennett and his Bomb Merchants will pull through," Edward assured the assembled officers at Hotel Montgomery. "They're tough as a woodpecker's beak. Son of a bitch'll be doing rope tricks for the guards when we roll in and liberate 'em."

The Kaboom Boys were to pack up immediately and move to temporary quarters near the Toul-Ochey Airfield (A-96), an ALG—advanced landing grounds—near the towns of Metz and Nancy. That would put them on the eastern border of France, at least seventy-five miles from the German frontier, south of Luxembourg and Belgium. Also, just west of where Hedley Bennett had been doing his last job when he disappeared. That put an ominous spin on things.

That airfield had served the Allies during World War I, then was captured early in this war by German forces. The Luftwaffe made little use of it until early 1944. Then they moved a squadron of Messerschmitt Bf 109 fighters to hinder the continuous swarm of British and American bombers going to and from the German Fatherland. By then, the Allies were pounding major cities in Germany night and day. Then the US Third Army took back Toul-Ochey in late August 1944, and in November, it became the home of the 50th Fighter Group of the Ninth Air Force.

Engineers spent several weeks digging up German landmines and retrieving ordnance from abandoned German planes and weapons, then piled all that dangerous junk into a huge pit, a supposedly safe distance from the newly renovated landing strip and refurbished base buildings. Fearful local residents did not consider it far enough away from their villages, though.

"That's the plaintive cry of the Army calling your name, Edward," joked Hume's CO. "Take your bunch of clowns and deal with that dump before that shit blows up and kills a bunch of people and causes me a pile of paperwork."

"Part of the job, Colonel."

Edward had composed and submitted his share of recommendations for how the Army was risking men's lives by not adequately addressing the threat of overflowing ordnance dumps. He considered it ironic that he had worked so hard to avoid the hazards of coal mines only to find himself dealing with cooking junk piles of lethal explosives, poised to vaporize anyone in range.

But now, they had to get to where the problems were. They loaded everything they had—and all they could requisition or steal—into the truck and jeep. They could not count on finding BD supplies at the airfield.

The Allies had declared the Ardennes region a "quiet area," with little enemy activity of late. But there had been strong rumors of a possible German counteroffensive, attacking what Hitler's generals knew to be the weakly defended Ardennes Forest. Their aim would likely be to split the US and British lines and recapture the Port of Antwerp.

At least the Kaboom Boys were getting their wish, heading east, closer to Berlin, closer to the end of the war. Many of the US Army troops in the area were recent arrivals, green reinforcements, still undergoing training. The more seasoned troops in the Ardennes Forest were there primarily to rest up before a final push into Germany when winter weather waned.

As they drove away from the town, Edward took one last look at Pontorson. He vowed to return one day, and to stay in touch with Russell, Mickey and Hélène. He petted their adopted mascot, Whitey, who had happily claimed his usual place in the back of the jeep next to Hank. The assumption had been that the black standard poodle would remain behind and find a new home far from bomb blasts, but Edward had a last-minute change of heart.

"Holy shit!" Carl said with a laugh when he saw the dog in the back of the jeep.

"I guess that answers that," said Gene.

"Oh, my stars," exclaimed Jack as he was about to climb beneath the steering wheel of the vehicle. "Sir, I think this is a sign. Ecclesiastes says, 'To all the living there is hope. A live dog is better than a dead lion.'"

Hank was climbing into the jeep when he saw Whitey there. "Sir, you want me to ride in the truck now that Whitey's claiming a seat in the jeep?"

"Nope, Corporal. You might start smelling like poodle, but I think there's room for you and Whitey back there."

Heading east, the trip from Pontorson via Le Mans allowed them to skirt the congestion of Paris, passing through Troyes to Toul. The route was long and slow and physically wearing but offered little sign of recent battle or enemy presence. But then, only a few miles short of their initial destination, all traffic on the main supply route came to an abrupt and frustrating stop.

"School crossing," Sergeant Morrison deadpanned. Edward grinned. The new guy did have a bit of a sense of humor at times, unlike how Duncan Smythe had so bleakly painted him in his letter. At least when his comments did not originate from the King James Bible.

"Dammit, supper's gonna be cold when we get there," growled Edward. An MP sauntered over their way from where his vehicle blocked traffic on the main road. He stopped, reached over, and tapped the top of the red fender with his billy club.

"Ordnance demolition, right?"

"That we are," Edward replied. "Why're you asking?" Hume suspected what the answer would be. It was commonplace for them to be stopped and directed to some lingering UXO problem. Sometimes the devices were truly a danger. Often not. Regardless, Edward felt obligated to have a look-see if they were not rushing to a more lethal puzzle that needed solving.

"We got a mess up there and I suspect you're just the ones we need to clear it."

Hume and Morrison looked at each other and grinned. "We don't usually make house calls, Lieutenant, and we'll have to charge you extra. But whatcha got?"

An Allied aircraft, almost certainly a P-47 Thunderbolt fighter bomber suffering some mechanical issue—though no one had admitted to committing the sin—had jettisoned two five-hundred-pound bombs before landing at Toul-Ochey. In the process, the pilot perfectly bracketed the main highway with the pair of deadly explosives. The danger had immediately brought to a halt the massive import of supplies along this vital route into the area. The MPs had redirected what traffic they could to alternate routes, but the narrow rural roads made that a slow go. BD help had been requested through the normal channels but there had not been a response. Engineers from the base had been told about the problem but declined to try to move the bombs. That, they reminded, was a job for explosive ordnance demolition guys.

"God must've sent you boys," the MP in his Cajun drawl told them as he walked along beside the jeep, leading them toward the problem. Morrison nodded vigorously. Then the MP added, "Or maybe it was 'Old Blood and Guts' what did it. You know, the two of 'em, God and Patton, they about equal in rank, I reckon."

Morrison ducked and frowned, as if he thought they might be struck by stray lightning in retribution for the MP's blasphemous observation. Edward gave it more of a laugh than it deserved, then offered, "I'd say we should award that P-47 pilot the Nazi Iron Cross, but I'd really rather enjoy a week's rest on a beach with a cold beer and a girl in a hula skirt."

The men laughed as they were guided around an MP barricade. Hume split the squad to dig out each of the two bombs. He stood in the middle of the roadway, watching them work, before he went into the fuze pockets to determine if they were armed. Regardless of the state of the fuzes and detonators, they were a danger if passing traffic disturbed them.

He had just begun accessing the first bomb when he felt a rumbling and noticed clods of dirt tumbling down the sides of the muddy hole. Now what? Surely not Patton again. He looked up to see a column of aviation engineer vehicles coming his way around the barricade. All were loaded with bulldozers, backhoes, and other heavy equipment, apparently on their way to a major construction project.

A lieutenant colonel jumped from the cab of one of the trucks and made his way over to peer down, hands on hips, at a mud-encrusted Captain Hume. There was a smirk on the colonel's face as he asked, with a haughty attitude, "You the CO here? Hard to tell with all that clay you're wearing."

"That I am. Captain Edward Hume. Alrighty now, I really need you guys to quit causing a damn earthquake while I have my head buried inside a five-hundred-pound bomb."

"I'm in command here now," shouted the newcomer. "We've decided to go ahead and build a bypass around this ordnance so we can keep things moving. The boss is getting pressure from above to keep supplies flowing. Now just get along to wherever you're supposed to be, then, and let us get to moving dirt. Somebody can come back later and fix 'em."

Edward slowly climbed from the hole. It was beginning to feel like his Patton incident. He stooped down so he could be eye level with the engineer. But the guy was so short in stature that Hume had to bend his knees and stoop over to get face-to-face.

"With all due respect, sir, you try to operate heavy equipment anywhere near those two bombs, with unknown fuze conditions, you're risking the lives of everybody involved and causing craters that'll shut down this highway for a good long while. Not to mention the time it'll take to collect body parts and put 'em in pillowcases for their mommas. Got that?"

Edward knew his squad was watching, judging him as he challenged the feisty lieutenant colonel, who was now doing a slow burn.

"Okay, I get it. But really, what are the chances they'd explode?" he asked in an exasperated voice. "And don't give me any exaggerated bullshit, Captain, just to win the moment."

"Won't know until I get into them. And that shouldn't take but a few minutes each if you'd quit pulling rank and let me do my job. Providing they don't decide to blow up on their own anyway after all that shaking and rattling you and your guys just caused. And then, Colonel, if you and your boys still want to play in the dirt around here, have at it. But we'll be out of here by then, after making France just a little bit safer," Edward said. He turned and started back toward the hole, then spun, looked at the colonel and added, "And I'm not trying to win the moment, by the way. I'm just trying to save your ass and all that pretty equipment the taxpayers provided for you."

But Hume had won the moment. The engineers carefully and slowly pulled their trucks out of harm's way and waited while Edward did his job. When he was finished and both bombs were defuzed, the Corps of Engineers CO decided they had more important work elsewhere and drove away without even a "Thank you," an "Attaboy," or a "Bless your heart."

The BD squad, without the help of any of the now-departed heavy equipment, had to winch the bomb carcasses from the boarded-up blast wall holes, roll them down a hill into a field where another larger hole had been dug, and then safely blow them sky high without an audience, creating debris, dust and a cacophony of noise. At least, as they climbed back up the hill, they could see traffic flowing once more, including a convoy of vehicles and tanks with a long column of troops walking alongside, once more bound for battle.

♠

Captain Hume and his squad continued eastward to their new base. But as soon as they arrived, they experienced the sting of repercussions from their roadside penis-measuring contest that afternoon. When they arrived at their new HQ, a complaint by the engineer lieutenant colonel awaited Hume. The document cited a poor attitude by a mere ordnance captain while discussing an ongoing issue in the field. Hume countered with his own statement of dissatisfaction, rebutting the complaint and explaining that the two bombs could have killed almost everyone involved. There was no immediate response.

As a result of the incident and the follow-up exchanges, the Kaboom Boys were rewarded with a denial of the superior mess privileges afforded the aviation engineer battalion at Toul-Ochey. The exclusion was a major disappointment. Engineers were purported to enjoy the finest food across the entire US Army because of the difficult, painstaking, dirty and dangerous jobs they were constantly called upon to do. They often performed miracles while under enemy fire and facing oversight by an intense military bureaucracy. Word had it that their cooks would go out into the woods and shoot wild boar and deer and round up fresh produce to prepare. It was extra tough to handle the sleight when the Kaboom Boys' Thanksgiving meal turned out to be exceptionally bland. Still, Jack said grace—three minutes and forty-six seconds' worth, timed by Carl—and they pretended to savor the simple meal. As Hank pointed out, it was much more akin to the primitive pilgrim's meal than what the engineer colonel's guys were likely enjoying.

As he tried to chew a rubbery bite, Edward thought of all those Thanksgiving dinners he had enjoyed back home with Mom, Pops, Tommy, other relatives and friends. A meal his mom spent a week preparing. He could not help but wonder what his chances were of being back at that familiar family "groaning board" for Thanksgiving 1945.

About the same chances, he decided, as his beloved Phillies winning the '45 World Series after finishing dead last, forty-three games out of first place in the just completed season. Even if Bill Veeck did manage to buy the club, as he had vowed to do, and stock it with the top players from the Negro leagues. And the likelihood of being home by next year grew slimmer as Herr Hitler stubbornly continued to prolong the war when everybody with a lick of sense knew Adolf and the Reich were done for.

Hours after Captain Mickey Berg said goodbye to Hélène LeRiche, her mother, Pierre and the rest of the Devereaux family, and the others who had so graciously accepted this Jewish American into their midst, he was off to his new assignment. The Army and the war did not allow for lingering goodbyes.

Two days later, Hélène packed up her few belongings and she and her mother made their way to the Pontorson train station, jostled and surrounded by hundreds of eager fellow passengers, all searching for a new way, a peaceful life. But for her, and despite parting with such dear friends, this move was joyous, different from her previous dramatic escapes to safety ahead of bombs and artillery shells. Her dream of becoming a lawyer had grown stronger every day even as the war doggedly dragged on.

Hélène and her mother boarded a train for the fifty-mile journey to Rennes, where they would stay in the home of a family friend, one who provided the young woman something she had been deprived of for four years, the luxury of a bedroom all to herself. But it was a room in which the elderly head of the household had died of tuberculosis. She was assured everything had been cleaned and disinfected, most of the bed linens burned. A few weeks later, she began to feel ill and was diagnosed with TB. That put an end to her plans for school. At least for a while, should she even survive the dreaded disease.

One day when she felt especially ill, her mother brought her a letter from Captain Edward Hume. The envelope also contained two sepia-toned photographs. One was handsome Edward, an image snapped by Corporal Hank Anderson. He had his foot on the running board of his bomb disposal jeep, hands in the pockets of his field jacket, wearing his garrison cap, facing west—she imagined—toward Rennes and Hélène. A message in Edward's neat handwriting was on the back: "Do you remember the B.D.S. jeep? —Edward, Hiver (Winter) 1944–45. Somewhere in France." The other image was likely from a photo booth, a head shot of Hume with his officer's hat slightly askew and a big toothy smile. Just the way she always pictured him in her fondest memories. On the back were the words, "I look more happy in this picture because I was thinking of you. Love. Edward."

She cried, then coughed violently for a bit before reading the enclosed letter.

"I thought you might enjoy these photos and be reminded of our good times. You helped me see France in a completely different way. When all you see is war, you forget about the times of peace."

Hélène willed herself to stop crying, to not aggravate her tortured lungs. She had received a letter from Mickey only a few days before, and it had left her in a much different mood. Berg wrote at length about his wife and children back in New York, then revealed that he was now somewhere near the German border. "The Jews are vanishing," he penned. That only caused her to worry more about him, about how that whole other aspect of the war must be affecting her dear friend.

But now, Edward's letter and photos had a far more uplifting effect on her, and just at a time she needed it most. She vowed to get better for both of them, to one day travel to the United States to visit with her American friends. When the war ended, of course. And it would. Soon.

If nothing else, Hélène LeRiche was forever optimistic.

20

Every step he took caused fire to shoot straight up his legs like hot electricity. The canvas bag full of rocks that had been used to beat Hedley Bennett's face and neck was sometimes replaced by a metal rod to the soles of his feet. Dr. Ernst Alwin felt that was okay since they still wanted their prisoner to do the Nazi's BD work. The American needed his hands to do so. Not his feet. The pain was so great that in his bunk at night, he gnawed on a folded rag to muffle his cries. He did not want his men to hear.

It was not the beatings that had caused Bennett to start thinking about rendering UXBs safe for the enemy. He had decided from the beginning of their capture that the SS interrogators would beat him to death before he would willingly do anything to help those bastards. It was, of all people, Ernst Alwin who had Hedley thinking about giving in.

The scientist had been especially persuasive at one of his visits, just before Schubert once again began beating the bejesus out of Bennett.

"Why do you do this, resist me, when you know I am right?"

"You are the enemy."

"But you would be saving lives."

"I was already saving lives when you sons of bitches stopped me," snapped Hedley.

"Why not for the German people, Captain? Do they not deserve to live?

Be safe? The mothers? The babies? The old people? My wife, my children, my parents?"

"Not for you Nazis. For the Allies. I am all for saving democracy one bomb at a time," Hedley answered with a snarl. And he knew what the response would likely be. "Democracy. Freedom. That is what I work for."

"Democracy. How quaint," Alwin said. "Schubert, show him what we think of his democracy." Schubert lifted a rod and whacked Bennett hard on the back of his shoulder. "That is what we think of democracy."

The thought had been planted, though. Bennett could still do some good by saving innocent lives. Then there was another motivating factor: One of his guys had been badly hurt defuzing devices, forced to do so at gunpoint. It was a tricky British device the American had never been trained to handle. Though he survived, he was not getting the proper medical care and Hedley felt tremendous guilt over his plight. Since only captains defuzed for the US Army Air Forces—a concept the Nazis were unable to fathom—his remaining squad members were in even more real danger. In the German view, if a soldier wore a BD patch on his sleeve, he was a bomb demolition man and capable of doing the work. Another of Bennett's men decided that running from the guards would be a better option than having a 250-pounder explode in his face. He was shot in the back, died instantly, and his body left for hours for prisoners to eventually remove and bury in an unmarked pit.

"Sir, what you thinking?" Sergeant Tony Gabler, Hedley's number two Bomb Merchant, whispered from the next cell.

"That I'm going to do what I got myself trained to do, BD," Hedley told him. "Then they'll leave the rest of you boys alone and let us work the way we were trained to do."

Bennett was told by a Jewish *kapo*, one who played a pivotal role as a servant to one of the medical doctors who did sinister experiments at Dachau, about the tall, skinny man called "The Blacksmith." Bennett already knew about The Hundred, the prisoners who were forced to neuter bombs with no training. And how this Polish Jew had somehow survived hundreds of those bastard bombs. But Hedley had no idea if their paths would ever cross.

It had been an unusually warm day for that time of year, so most of the inmates were turned out of their concrete cells to wander about in the fenced-in area. It was also an opportunity for other prisoners to douse everything inside with powerful insecticide—the same compound used in a more concentrated form to gas Jews and other prisoners—to kill lice, bed bugs and fleas. The effects of bug bites killed many and greatly diminished the captives' work output.

The Blacksmith was sitting against a fence when Gabler pointed him out to his captain. The man's face was turned to the sun as he savored the welcome warmth of its rays. He was emaciated, his skin a sickly gray, his head shaven, revealing crusty patches of skin on his skull. But he still looked better off than most of his fellow Dachau prisoners.

Bennett had so many questions for Steiner, but he hesitated to approach the man about whom he had heard so much. He did not want to disturb the prisoner's precious bit of peace, but the captain's professional curiosity finally won out.

"Do you speak English?" Bennett asked him.

"A little," Józef responded with a slight smile, looking up at the American who now blocked his precious sunlight.

"I didn't want to bother you, but I just wanted to meet you and ask—"

"You are one of the American *bombentechnikers, ja*?" Steiner interrupted.

"I am. Well, I was. I am not sure right now. I was a US Army BD man. But since I ended up here, no more bombs unless it's for my side." The man nodded. Bennett assumed he understood. "I cannot decide what to do now. I do not want to do bombs for these bastards, but they keep pushing my men to do work they've never been trained for and tell me I will save innocent lives if I do the work. But I took an oath. I cannot do jobs for the enemy."

"I do not, either. No more bombs."

"But you did a great job surviving all those UXBs."

"*Ja*, I defuzed 246 bombs for the Nazis. No more."

Bennett felt wobbly, so he sat down next to Steiner uninvited. The Blacksmith did not seem to mind.

"So why did you stop doing something you were so good at?" Hedley asked.

Steiner abruptly put his hand on Bennett's shoulder. He was shocked at the strength of the man's grip, at the power in his tranquil eyes and calm face. Traits he never saw in any of the other prisoners in this hellish place.

"For once, they speak the truth, my friend. You would indeed save the lives of children, women, old men, many who do not know a Nazi from a nail. The bombs the Allies drop, they do not know, how you say? The difference between the monsters and the innocent ones." Steiner slowly shook his head. "From what I hear, the Allied bombers want to destroy everything to demoralize the German people, hoping they will turn on Hitler. Consumed by massive fires, piles of rubble everywhere from Munich to Hamburg. But you, with your hands, you can still save lives of those with no power over the Führer and his cast of devils."

Hedley gave him a hard look. "Whoa, hoss! You just told me you don't do BD anymore but you're telling me I oughta?"

Steiner shook his head. "I will tell you why I stopped. You must do what you feel is right. Your duty to your country, your men. That is what democracy is, no? At first, I had no choice. They pointed guns at me, at my head and my heart. I knew they would shoot and not even think about it. I had to survive because God gives us the will to survive. Then, after so much pain, I lost the will. But now, I have a new reason for—" He stopped short, thought a moment, and went on. "I have reasons now to live. But now, after doing it for so long, my hands..." He let go of Hedley's shoulder and held his hands up for the American to see. They shook. "I can, with much effort, repair the commandant's clocks and shoe the general's horses or work on the radios in the officers' quarters so they may hear Hitler speak his madness, but if I should be compelled to touch a bomb fuze again, I will, without intending to, blast away myself and anyone around me. That helps no one. I have told them this and, for some reason, they finally believe me. At first, no. Then, after the 247th bomb, when four men died because I did not at first take notice of a valuable bit of information. But now, they see my...tremors. The shaking hands."

"I understand. But I took a vow to never do anything to help the enemy," Hedley said, his voice breaking. "I could go to prison after the war." A pause, then a big grin. "But hellfire, I reckon I'm already in prison!"

Steiner smiled. Despite discolored teeth and cracked lips, it was as if someone had turned on a bright light somewhere inside the man. "I must be truthful. I mentioned I now have a reason to live, to survive this war. Otherwise, if I were certain no one else would be harmed, I would consider allowing one of the bombs to take me to the next life." Steiner leaned in closer to whisper in Bennett's ear. "I have told no one else this. My reason for staying alive has the name Birgit Franz. I have seen her once. I will see her again. For that moment, I must remain alive. When we are liberated—and I believe this will not be much longer in coming—I will go find her in Munich. I believe that. I will marry her and that, sir, is my reason to continue to live."

The explanation seemed to have robbed Józef Steiner of all the strength he had available. He closed his eyes and let the sun again touch his stubbled face.

"I understand," was all Hedley Bennett managed to say.

"And perhaps you will consider that if you begin to make the unexploded bombs safe, you will not only be saving lives of the innocent, but of yours and your men's. And one day, you will be able to tell the world of the awfulness that has taken place here. At first, they will not believe, but you will help them see." Then a sad look overtook his face. "I believe there will also come a day in the future when people will once again doubt this level of evil could have been. Then your testimony may be the only thing that keeps it a part of the lore of war. That, Captain, should be a powerful reason for you to remain alive as well."

The next day, as the guards walked Hedley to Dr. Alwin's office and before suffering the first blow from the iron bar or the sack of gravel in the interrogation room, Bennett informed Schubert he had decided he would begin assisting in defuzing ordnance that threatened the lives of innocent people. And that the guard could inform Dr. Alwin of his decision but assure him yet again that he knew nothing of any "super bomb."

When Bennett told Schubert of his decision, the look on the brutal interrogator's face was not one of disappointment at all. Instead, it was that of undisguised resignation. Maybe the war had truly turned, as Schubert had heard from whispered updates. Maybe all the German troops and artillery had headed to the west, toward the Ardennes, Luxembourg, and Belgium, attempting a last-stand fight to the death, not to launch a bold counteroffensive.

"Do you know something I do not know?" Schubert asked, his worried face gone gray. The war and all the demands by superiors had finally started to take a toll on the lowly guard. "Are the rumors true? Are Allied troops nearing the border?"

"What you thinkin', Schu? Maybe you about to get payback for all this meanness you been dishin' out? There will be war crimes commissions, and your name will be at the top of the list." Bennett settled back and allowed himself a pleased smile. "What made you do what you've done? When did you become an animal?"

For a moment, Hedley thought the torturer might grab one of his tools and start warping him again. But instead, the SS man sat down hard in the chair Dr. Ernst Alwin had often occupied during all those interrogations about some super bomb Bennett was supposed to know all about.

"For my country. But first, my wife. My two boys. End the war before they get conscripted. I still believe the Jew, the Negro, the homosexual pollutes the superior Aryan bloodline. Germany suffered so much after the Great War." Schubert was laying out his grievances as if he had rehearsed it. "My family was once wealthy and powerful. We lost everything. My father took his own life. My mother took in boarders to our manor house. And ultimately sold her body to help feed us. I joined the Party and the SS to rebuild Germany." The interrogator stopped and studied the ceiling in the little room. "Eventually, I came to know that I enjoyed torturing people like you, Captain Bennett. People who were a threat to the Reich. I do not consider you to be human. You are the enemy and stand for everything we Germans are against."

The guard was ranting the way Hedley imagined Hitler would if they were in the same room facing one another. Bennett thought the bastard was about to jump up, grab a whip or metal bar, and maybe try to kill him this time. But he felt it was his duty to continue goading Schubert, to resist.

"Can I tell you, you're damn good at what you do, Schu. Damn good. And soon, this shithole will be covered up with soldiers who will happily hurt you back aplenty. That includes Doc Alwin and the whole lotta ya."

Schubert suddenly stood and stepped toward the door. "*Danke*, Captain. I will tell my commanding officer that you have relented and will help with defuzing the bombs."

Schubert was gone. The first time Bennett had been left unscathed by the sadist. It would be twenty minutes later before one of Schubert's underlings came to usher Hedley back to his cold, filthy cell.

The next day, Hedley Bennett became the latest prisoner at Dachau to be forced at gunpoint to defuze a UXB. He would deal later with the possibility of going to prison for consorting with the enemy. Maybe he could explain it to the US Army as well as The Blacksmith had explained it to him.

♠

It was difficult to get a good night's sleep at their new billet. The Kaboom Boys were lodged in a drafty old building directly beneath the usual approach for all the air traffic landing at the ALG at Toul-Ochey. All night, one after the other, the planes loaded with supplies and reinforcements roared in. The fighters, leaving or coming back from bomber escort duty, were bad enough. Worse, though, were the C-47 Skytrains with their twin Pratt & Whitney Wasp engines. The men swore they could feel the hurricane off those propellors.

"One of 'em rattled a couple of fillings out of my teeth last night," Carl groused at breakfast one morning. "Captain, you want to complain to Command? Maybe make 'em cut their engines and glide in real quiet-like?"

"Not an option," Edward answered. "They're usually hauling gasoline. You want one of 'em to come in too low and set your whole world afire?"

"Probably your teeth chattering's what loosened up those fillings, Carl," Gene suggested. "I ain't been warm since we left Normandy."

"Agreed on that point," Hume said.

"We shouldn't complain, boys," Morty Schwartz offered, then dropped his fork onto his metal plate with a clang for emphasis. His voice grew louder, angry, and several other soldiers in the mess hall stopped eating and looked his way. "Imagine what those poor folks in the Nazi camps are going through. My people, especially. The Jews."

"Easy, Private," Edward said. "We're on the way to help them."

"Besides," Hank said, "maybe Herr Hitler has learned his lesson about cold weather warfare out there on the Eastern Front and won't try anything funny over here. By spring, we'll have taken Berlin and shaved off that funny mustache of his and..."

His voice trailed off. Nobody seemed interested in speculation after such a rocky night.

The next evening, as evidence that Germany was not done yet, a lone Luftwaffe night intruder dropped a single SD-1 Splitterbombe cluster bomb near the airbase. The device consisted of a cannister that contained as many as two dozen small bomblets. The cannister had a charge designed to blow it open at a set distance aboveground and allow the smaller devices to cover a wide territory and explode on impact. They were primarily used on the battlefield as anti-personnel weapons or to damage larger targets like warehouses or airfields. This time, the bomber aircraft's aim was bad. No damage was done to the runway, but the cannister filled with bomblets came down on a nearby farm. The cannister's detonator worked but none of the small bombs exploded. They did shred a truck and, in the process, killed a young American soldier and a French girl who occupied the vehicle's cab at the time.

That left a messy job for Hume and his squad. First, they needed to find all the UXBs and then determine if the bomblets were equipped with timed fuzes or anti-tamper detonators. For some reason—maybe conscripted laborers had deliberately sabotaged this load so they would not blow up—none turned out to be armed. Still, each contained enough explosive power to maim or kill anyone else within a hundred feet or so with flying shrapnel. That was what made them such effective anti-personnel weapons.

They also had to move enough of the small UXBs a safe distance away from the truck to allow medics to retrieve the two bloodied bodies. Then they had to find all the others and confirm that they, too, were not primed to explode. But even if they were not armed, jostling or dropping one might still cause it to go off. They would need to be handled carefully and taken to a deep pit for detonation, all in one big boom.

"Jesus. Look over there," Jack Morrison said, almost in a whisper. They all looked to where the sergeant pointed.

"Jesus, indeed," Edward exclaimed.

One of the young medics was quickly walking their way with a bomblet loosely held in his arms, cradled like a baby. He had a broad grin on his face.

"This one of yours?" he asked. "I was gonna ask if I could keep it for a souvenir and—"

"Stop!" Hume angrily shouted. "Put that thing down! Carefully! Very carefully!"

The kid came to a halt, a frown replacing the smile. "Shit, y'all got no call to yell at me."

Then, defiantly, he tossed the bomblet into the air. It fell to the ground a few feet in front of him. Maybe thirty feet from the squad. If the thing had gone off, hundreds of small shards of its metal case would go spinning in all directions, each bit of it potentially deadly.

Other than a feed trough and a small pile of hay, there was nothing behind which to hide. The men still dove for whatever cover they could find while the medic stood there, mouth open, obviously wondering what the hell had caused them to scatter like that.

The device did not explode.

"I suggest you get on your horse and ride out of here before I kick your ass all the way to the North Sea," Hume told him, climbing to his feet, seething. Edward had landed in a pile of fresh, pungent cow manure.

As the men stood, dusting themselves off, Carl Kostas said, "I don't think we'll ever get through to these damn souvenir hunters. What they thinkin'?"

Morty Schwartz looked up at a darkening sky, threatening snow. There were tears in his eyes. "You guys, you remember all the times I told Pete not to touch a flag or a Kraut helmet or that pistol he found at that chateau that time? Never could get through to that son of a bitch."

"They told us a million times back at APG, too," Carl reminded.

"Captain Bennett's squad, too. Dumbasses!" Hank added.

"Zini. He takes all of them risks and nothing happens, then he goes and gets his damn self stabbed in a bar by what's supposed to be one of the good guys," Morty went on. "Damn ironic. Damn ironic, ain't it?"

The men began gathering their equipment while Hank snapped a few pictures of the neat pile of bomblets, of Carl gently placing the last one on top. He abruptly stopped clicking and turned to Schwartz.

"Morty, credit where credit is due. I want you to know I'm impressed."

"What the hell you talkin' about, Hank?"

"How Pete got hurt? That actually is a good example of irony. Most people don't know what the definition of irony is and—"

Morty grabbed a nearby shovel and began chasing Hank around the barnyard until Edward finally had to order them to stop it. To get the bomblets loaded, transported, buried, and exploded, so they could get onto the next mission without anybody else getting hurt, whether by booby trap, bomblet, or knife.

Or BD squad shovel.

Lieutenant Virginia Brown has deepened her resolve to never allow herself to become accustomed to blood, broken bones, and young dead bodies. Especially those that expire on the table in front of her as she does all she knows how to do to pull them through. However, it is becoming more difficult for her to accept the disorientation brought on by renewed fighting, of not knowing for sure where she is geographically, what day of the week it is, whether it is daytime or night, and what is happening beyond the surgical tent, where she works, and the rickety cot in the nurse's bivouac on which she collapses for brief sleep whenever she can.

Now, a Luftwaffe plane buzzes overhead as she makes a dash from the supply building, through the shade-tree smoking area, across open ground, and back toward the medical tent. None of it offers much shelter from strafing or cluster bombs, but it is all she has. The surgical tent is where she has worked all night. Where she belongs. And now, after a quick smoke break, she carries crucial cargo. Tucked in her arms against her breasts is a load of precious, urgent medical supplies.

Low and directly overhead, in the predawn-lightened sky, the German fighter plane dodges black smudges of ack-ack, dipping threateningly, wings wobbling as if it might crash. Virginia throws herself down in the mud and leans against a limbless tree, denuded by earlier ordnance. She waits for a bomb to drop or bullets to spew from the warplane's guns or even for it to crash close by, flinging parts and fire all about. She is not concerned about dying, ending her twenty-four years on this planet right here and now. She is more concerned about ruining the sterile supplies she totes.

Virginia is accustomed to things falling out of the sky, even during most of autumn when the threat of the Luftwaffe has diminished. There has been an ominous increase lately, though, since Thanksgiving. Since it got cold and there's snow. More enemy planes. More icy wind. More mangled young men. Colds, flu, trench foot, frostbite. Since they moved to this place of tree-covered mountains. Where the bombed-out forest provides the only open ground suitable for setting up the field hospital.

What is this place called? The Ardennes? Someone said they were in Belgium. Someone else said France. Virginia does not care. Men bleed and die the same regardless of the borders that encircle them.

Now, as she lies there in the sludge waiting for whatever is going to happen with the airplane, she remembers how one object that fell from the sky months before may have altered her path in life. Altered it in a deliriously happy way. It was a hissing fifty-pound bomb that landed without detonating in the middle of their cluster of field hospital tents near what was left of Saint-Lô. That deadly chunk of hardware brought her Captain Edward Hume from Pennsylvania. He showed up with his squad to try to make the deadly device safe. Since then, and since their brief tryst in Paris, her thoughts so often turn to him when she needs hope, strength, resolve. Thoughts of his deep, serious eyes, his strong body next to hers, his auburn hair askew after their passionate lovemaking at the hotel in Paris, his calm way of dealing with the most terrorizing problems as if they were no more than a leaky pipe or a flat tire.

She knows she should stop thinking of Edward now. Her patients need what she brings. The surgical supplies. Her practiced hands putting pressure hard against a blood-spurting wound. Need her to present the surgeon the right tool to try to correct the hurt that has altered the future of the latest kid on whom he works.

Edward cannot help her now. Thankfully, Captain Richardson has mostly let her be since Paris. But the thought of Edward's strength, determination, and courageous calm does aid her in doing what she has to do.

She sets her jaw, stands, looks up, just the way Captain Hume would have. The plane still banks on the horizon, but there has been no bomb, no bullets, not even one of the blood-red distress flares. She turns and hurries on toward the tent. What did the obnoxious surgeon, Dr. Richardson, always tell her? "A dead nurse does me no good. Take care of yourself." That is usually followed by an invitation to come sleep with him in his tent so he could hold and protect her throughout the night.

Just before she ducks back into the surgical tent, to the groans, cries, and smells she knows so well, she sees the plane is now flying away, its engine sputtering as the noise fades. When Virginia stands across the operating table from Richardson, he notices her shaking hands. He says nothing. He has his own hands deep in the chest of a soldier. He might still be mad about what happened in Paris. At least what he remembers of it. They nod at one another as he pulls a nasty mass of sharp metal from the boy's bloody lung.

She works by muscle memory as her thoughts inevitably wander. The woman journalist—the one married to the writer Hemingway—had embedded with her unit early on. She asked Virginia if she was accustomed to the carnage. "Accustomed to" as in "comfortable with."

"I can't be," Virginia answered, without even thinking about it. "I have to be horrified by what I see, or I might stop caring. If I stop caring, boys die, and it would be my fault. If I get adjusted to it, I couldn't do my job."

The journalist had nodded knowingly, the slightest smile on her face, then she made a powerful point.

"Yes, Lieutenant Brown. And you know what? I feel exactly the same way about the stories I'm called upon to tell."

21

0600. Morning Briefing.

Edward struggled to keep his eyes open. That cup of coffee was not doing the job. He had not slept well. It was not the constant discordant sounds of landing aircraft. Not the chilly draft of a north wind seeping through uncaulked cracks in the ancient stone barn that had been converted into temporary sleeping quarters either. He tossed and flopped inside his down-filled, olive-green sleeping bag. Christmas was only a week away and, as with Thanksgiving, it was an emotional time so far away from his family. Of course, he missed Mom and Pops and especially his late brother, Tommy, but it was worse now, around this particular holiday. Worse to the point of being physically painful. All three family members and Virginia Brown had made appearances in his all-night nightmares.

Hume finally gave up trying to sleep, got up and dressed, and ate a K-ration chocolate bar as he completed a report on the Splitterbombe incident. He noted that the brightly painted yellow devices were typically deployed in battlefield situations by being dropped by low-flying aircraft. Edward started to connect the dots, deducing that the Germans were in a desperate state, likely low on bombs, using whatever they had while the creative Nazi scientists devised something bigger. Were the rumors that there would soon be a German "super weapon" true?

Now, exhaustion showed up late. Once at his new HQ awaiting the start of the morning brief, it was all Edward could do to keep his eyes open. But the gossip circulating around him rudely tugged him awake.

"Other shoe's droppin' as we speak," an engineer announced importantly. "Hitler's gone even crazier. He just launched some kind of big-ass assault through Luxembourg and Belgium."

"You're full of shit, man," a supply unit captain countered. "Adolf couldn't muster enough troops to take down a hotdog stand, much less the 12th Army. His own generals are trying to kill him and Stalin has half of Russia marching toward Berlin."

Hume shook his head. His squad had mentioned hearing scuttlebutt a couple of nights before at a newly discovered drinking spot in Toul. News of German troop movements headed in their general direction. As many as half a million soldiers and thousands of tanks and artillery pieces. Edward had pointedly dismissed such nonsense. There had been no such news from any of his superiors. But he also knew that sometimes boozy scuttlebutt picked up in a bar was truer than whatever Army intelligence was saying. Or anything the brass was revealing.

"No, it's happening," the engineer insisted. "A hundred miles north of our happy asses, too. You'll see when the colonel—"

The door burst open right on cue and the colonel trotted in with his two aides. The look on his face and the urgency in his step confirmed something was going on. Everyone, including Edward, was instantly wide awake as their commander unscrolled a map hanging on the wall, grabbed a pointer, and started the briefing without benefit of his usual "Good morning, Ike's garbage men!"

The Allied command, headed by General Eisenhower, had remained convinced the Germans would not launch any kind of counterattack, and especially through northern France or Belgium. Word was the enemy soldiers just across the border, all the way from Hamburg south to Stuttgart and Munich, were only there to rest up, dig in, and prepare to defend the Rhine border and the Fatherland from the Americans, Brits, and Canadians barreling in from the west.

The limited number of Allied troops on the French and Belgian side were also there for rest as well as training the newly arrived reinforcements.

There were logistical issues, too. The Ardennes region was heavily forested, mountainous, and lacked wide roads. Transporting supplies, troops and artillery or deploying tanks would be a problem for both sides if serious fighting occurred. The Allies had moved so rapidly across France toward the German border that keeping the advancing troops supplied had already become a major problem.

"The Krauts don't have so much of a supply problem," the colonel said, tapping Germany on the map with his pointer. "They're defending their home soil now, not troops spread out all over Europe and North Africa. But they need fuel as bad as we do. The thinking is they're going to try to split our troops north of here and make a push for the ports at Antwerp. They still hold the Netherlands after Market Garden went bust and the 82nd and 101st got chopped up pretty good. So much for the war being over by Christmas. And looks like they somehow found the firepower and cannon fodder to try to pull off this next stunt of theirs, the 'bastids.'"

"How's that possible, Colonel?" the supply captain asked. "We heard they're on the run."

"Who the hell knows? But even with all this cloud cover the last few days, our aircraft have seen what they think is between a quarter and a half million troops on the move. Lots of tanks and artillery, too, and they're already using that. The guess is they're going blitzkrieg-style, like they did in '40. But back then they were all the way through the Ardennes before they encountered any resistance worth a shit. And we know how that turned out. We got some troops up here, so maybe they can slow 'em down. And they've already started repositioning about anybody else they can spare to try to stop what they're sayin' will be Hitler's last hurrah. We can't count on much air support until this weather clears, though. God knows when that'll be." The colonel spun around and looked hard, first at Edward and then to the representative from the Army Air Forces Engineers. "And be aware the Luftwaffe is making a comeback of sorts, too. What few planes and pilots they got have been dropping bombs already. Dropping them through the clouds since they know about where our guys are and don't give a good goddam who or what else they hit. Between what they're shittin' on our boys, all the usual unexploded artillery shells, and their insistence on burying a ton of landmines as they go, you boys are about to be busier than you've been since D-Day. You up to it?"

Both men nodded, but with little enthusiasm. They could still be back on the Normandy coast and be plenty busy handling UXOs. Plenty busy for the next several centuries.

"All right, then," the colonel went on. "Orders are being drafted as I speak. We'll issue ASAP but go ahead and get ready to be mobile. All of you. You just thought this damn war was about to be over. Dismissed!"

"We're ready, sir." "Our guys are set." "We'll send 'em back across the Rhine with their tails smokin'!" It was as if the coach had just delivered a rousing pre-game speech.

The colonel stood there nodding, a slight smile on his face. Then he had a final thought.

"Oh. And Merry Christmas, men. Merry Christmas!"

The mess hall for non-engineers at Toul consisted of a big, patched tent loosely arrayed over rows of rough, wobbly tables and chairs. The canvas was fixed to a permanent building where the kitchens and food storage areas were. It was clear nobody expected it to be a long-term facility. The squad noticed the wind through gaps in the tent walls quickly cooled their coffee in the tin cups as well as the scrambled eggs on metal plates. They began wearing their jackets and gloves to stay warm while quickly and silently eating, saving conversation for when they were in their vehicles on the way to the day's missions.

The sudden arrival of their CO and the news he brought them this morning had everyone talking, though. Their war for the past few months had certainly continued to offer its share of drama and danger, but now there was the likelihood that their list of risks once again included having enemy soldiers shooting at them. Distant artillery pounding them. Even the occasional fighter/bomber strafing them or blindly dropping bombs on them. That would result in UXBs possibly equipped with newer and even more clever types of lethal anti-tamper fuzes, specifically designed to blow up in their faces and cut off their heads.

"We gotta get busy, guys," the captain told them as he gulped down his own chilled eggs and tepid coffee. "Pack all the clothes you got, clean or dirty, and stow your duffels on the truck. We'll need to load every tool we got, too. And they're holding tents, field rations, fuze wire, gunpowder, and detonators for us at supply. We'll be loaded down."

"We just got settled in, sir," Carl noted. "How long you expect we'll be out there?"

"Only God knows, and He ain't sharing," Edward replied, drained the last drop from the cup, and spit out coffee grounds.

"It's not how we oughta be celebrating the birth of our Lord 'n' Savior," Jack said quietly.

Edward looked sideways at the new squad member. "I'd say it's a perfect way. Making safe all those bombs and mines and dud artillery shells. Saving lives. That's a better gift, I say, than gold, frankincense or myrrh."

"Sorry, sir. I didn't mean to go too..." Morrison's voice trailed off.

"No, no. It's okay, Sarge. Besides, it's our job and we gotta do it no matter if the date on the calendar is red or black. Now, let's get our asses in gear and do that very thing!" Edward stood, another fiery football coach ready to lead his team onto the field and to victory.

Hank Anderson raised his hand, a player wanting to ask a question first. "Captain, you know what it'll be if we make it 'til Thursday?"

"Thursday," Hume answered, his face blank. "Thursday, December 21st if I remember correctly. First day of winter, too, I believe."

"Thirty weeks since we officially became a squad, sir. We blew that ten-week survival rate for BD squads right out of the water, didn't we?"

The captain leaned over to rap the wooden tabletop with his knuckles. "Don't jinx us, Corporal. I plan on extending that statistic to infinity. But remember, not all of us made it, either. I don't know if Ronzini counts against us, but Ace Taft sure does. Now, let's go and do some good for somebody."

As they filed out, Morty Schwartz muttered, "Hank and I tried to tell you bastards that ace card would bring bad luck." He pulled his Star of David on its chain from inside his shirt, removed a glove, and vigorously rubbed the symbol.

Gene made the sign of the cross and gave the tabletop another sharp knock in the same spot his captain just had. But more than favorable luck, at the moment he most longed for a couple of those powerful pick-me-up pills Agathe Dumoulin once had available for him.

"Probably eighty degrees right now at Malibu," Carl observed to no one in particular. "Knees bent, boys. Knees bent."

No matter how bent their knees were, they could never be fully prepared for the horror that awaited them.

22

Captain Hedley Bennett was surprised to see it was SS-*Standartenführer* Werner Schubert who was making all the racket at his cell door, calling Bennett's name, waking him up two hours before the sun had appeared above the neatly aligned but cursed buildings of the Dachau prison camp. He had not seen his assigned torturer for more than two weeks.

"Werner? That you?" Bennett asked, sitting up in his bunk, ignoring the fleas that scrambled with his movement, rubbing his eyes with his aching, scarred fists. The rest of his squad were stirring now, too. It was about their usual rise-and-shine time these days. "*Guten morgen*. And *heil* goddamn Hitler!"

"Come with me, Captain. Only you. Not your squad," was all Schubert said until they had walked all the way over to the torture room, past rows of buildings, adjacent fenced areas already filled with living human skeletons who preferred the frigid but clean air to the night's accumulation of dead bodies and the moans of the near-dead inside. Inside, where it was only a couple of degrees warmer anyway until they were allowed to build fires in the stoves.

Once the two men arrived at the painfully familiar site and stepped into the tiny room, the German finally spoke. "*Sitzen*," he ordered, motioning

Bennett to the same chair where he had suffered so much agony. "Sorry. Sit. Please sit."

Damn! How polite! What the hell?

"How's the wife and kids?" Bennett asked. No response. Maybe a quick unintended blink of the torturer's dull, emotionally vacant eyes. "You miss all our happy times together, Werner, my old *compadre*?" Hedley went on, spurring him. He knew that nothing he might say would have any effect on what the Nazi was probably about to do to him. But there was some satisfaction to be derived from goading the son of a bitch. "You wanna beat the shit out of me once more, for old time's sake? That it?"

Schubert eased down in Dr. Alwin's chair. "I want you to tell me what you know about the course of the war. I know the incoming prisoners of war inform you of what is happening. I need you to confirm that what I am learning through my sources is true. Not for the SS. Not for the Gestapo. Not for the generals or the Führer. For me. For my family."

Hedley felt no remorse for the man sitting across from him. But the look on Schubert's face had become downright pitiful.

"Hell, you boys are hauling or marching away a lot more POWs than you're bringing in lately. Gotta be a reason. Tell me what you know, Werner. Then I'll maybe tell you what I'm hearing. If you give me a cigarette, that is."

Schubert tugged a pack of smokes from his jacket pocket. Hedley was surprised to see they were Chesterfields, one of the brands included in American soldiers' rations. Bennett also noticed the man's hands were shaking when he struck a match and lit the cigarette for him.

Schubert lit his own Chesterfield, took a deep draw. Somehow his mood seemed different, like he was just a normal man, no longer a vicious animal. A bully, maybe attempting to make amends with his victim because his fate has been abruptly altered.

"The things I am hearing, the quick advance of your forces across France was finally halted at the Rhine. Hitler ordered the Panzers and the 7th Army to join up and move back westward, to divide the Allies in northern France and Belgium and try to recapture the port at Antwerp that the British had claimed. They were making good progress so long as the clouds prevented Allied air strikes. But now, since Christmas, everything has changed. With the return of the sun came the bombs and the strafing. We had no air power to counter the Allies. Then things turned in your favor and the battle was lost." The German swallowed hard, the worried expression on his usually expressionless face deepening. Then he went on, being unusually forthcoming. "Many died on both sides. But now I hear your armies will soon be on German soil. That the Russians are pushing us out of Leningrad, and we are in retreat. That Hitler himself is preoccupied with dodging assassins from every quarter and those who do not want to murder him want to depose him and arrange a surrender to end this war with better terms than how they managed after the last one."

The man slumped, out of breath and hope. But his news finally gave Hedley some hope. And if the room in which they sat did not hold so many horrible memories of bloody pain, Hedley might have even felt sorry for Schubert. Especially when the man regained his breath and shared his reason for this morning's honest assessment of the war.

"It is my family, my wife and boys, Captain Bennett. I have come to terms with this. I know, if I live, I will possibly be brought to trial for what I have done for my country. Brought to trial in front of those who can never possibly understand. But I still have no regrets. I did what I did and I helped in what we have done here at Dachau for what I consider to be all the right reasons. To some, it seems barbaric, I know. They will paint us as animals for our actions in the camps and in rooms like this. But I remain convinced I did what was best for the Reich. To preserve the Aryan race. For the future of the world. But I do not want my family to suffer at the hands of those who will never agree. War trials and testimony and the disdain that will certainly come for centuries from those who cannot comprehend the righteousness of and necessity for our methods."

Jesus. This bastard still thought he was justified. But he feared humiliation like that suffered by the German people after WWI. There were plenty of others like him who Bennett knew were loading Jews on boxcars and taking them to be gassed and incinerated every damn day. He heard. He saw.

Hedley was startled when Schubert quickly stood, took one step to the desk, opened the middle drawer, and withdrew a Walther P-38 pistol. Captain Bennett's initial thought was that the SS guard had decided to eliminate witnesses, starting with him. Instead, Schubert deliberately handed the side-arm to Hedley, handle first.

"I want you to kill me," Schubert said. "I have left a note explaining what I am doing so you will not be punished. I want to die, and by your hand," Schubert told him.

Hedley sat stone-faced. What kind of sick trick was this one?

"Yes, you heard me, Captain Bennett. I want to die. Die before I am captured and before I am tortured, and I am executed like a common deserter. I cannot live with dishonor, knowing I can no longer help to ensure the survival of the Reich and the Aryan race with my actions. And even though you will never understand, I want you, Cowboy, to be the one who ends my much suffering."

Bennett's eyes narrowed as he tried to get a read on what his captor was really doing. He was confused by Schubert's rant, but he was sure of one thing. This would not end well for him no matter what the guard promised. Hedley decided the only thing he could do now was listen, not shoot the man in the head, even if he wanted so very badly to do just that.

"On behalf of all the many others, you will go back to the US Army and continue saving lives, doing your demolition jobs on bombs and mines, clearing lands so the German people can live without fear once more." Schubert breathed in deeply. "My family, my little girl and my two young boys. My wife. Her mother. All those who still believe I am their hero. I want them to believe that I was killed defending the Fatherland. That you grabbed my gun and killed me. Maybe they will never learn the things I have done on behalf of the German people. Do you understand, Captain Bennett? I am a hero to my family. And I must die a hero."

No, Hedley certainly did not understand. It was such a convoluted explanation that it made no sense whatsoever.

Hedley considered the offer for a half second as he instinctively took the pistol from Schubert's hand. But then he leaned over and gently placed it down on the desktop.

"No. I will not give you such an easy way out, Schubert. Not my problem that you're too gutless to even kill yourself. If you don't have the balls to do it, then—" Hedley closed his eyes. He knew he might well have just assured his own immediate death.

Suddenly the door opened. Dr. Ernst Alwin stepped into the room, a quizzical frown on his face. How long had he been listening?

"What is going on here, Schubert?" He pointed to the pistol on the desk, easily within Hedley Bennett's reach. "Why do we have our bomb man in here? The sun is up. Why is he not out in the field defuzing dangerous ordnance by now?"

Schubert stood frozen for an agonizing moment before he abruptly snapped to attention, thrust his right arm upward in the usual Nazi salute, and shouted, "Heil Hitler!"

Alwin returned a half-hearted wave. "I am confused. The pistol?"

Schubert relaxed, but his face was ominously blank. "Dr. Alwin, I am doing what I feel is best for the Reich and for my family. And for my Führer and all he stands for."

Then, before either Bennett or Alwin could react, Schubert grabbed the Walther, waved it in turn in the general direction of each man, then placed its barrel to his right temple, and pulled the trigger.

The SS interrogator's blood and brains splattered, mingling with the other ugly stains of human misery on the wall.

He collapsed with a thud to the cement floor, twitched once, and then was still. Alwin and Bennett looked on, open-mouthed, wide-eyed.

A wisp of smoke drifted upward from the pistol where it had fallen to the floor. Werner Schubert had become just another casualty of this vile world war.

And the gun smoke from the Walther could just as well have been a freed spirit, climbing heavenward, seeking bliss.

She regrets not making it to Paris. She hears it is magical now that the city is liberated from the Germans. She reads some of her estranged husband's many dispatches, but Ernest writes little of the atmosphere in the city, of the ethos of the people who have been freed from four years of Nazi occupation. Martha Gellhorn knows he prefers stories of infantrymen and tank brigades and bold, intrepid fighter pilots. And he longs to keep pace with Patton in his reverse blitzkrieg toward the Rhine and beyond. To be in combat, not now-peaceful Paris, after he and his "brigade" have liberated the bar at Hotel Ritz. To brandish a rifle and oversee his ragtag bunch of mercenaries as they live out their warrior fantasies on Collier's expense account. His writing reflects a less intimate view of the human condition, she believes.

She still has no official press credentials since he possesses hers and she must move stealthily about on her own. No jeep like his with a mounted machine gun or "PRESS" in bold letters across its grill or stenciled on the front of her helmet. She still must rely on her unique ability to find amity with the average soldier. The guys driving trucks and jeeps or trains that go here and there and where she needs to go to find stories. Her kind of stories. She is astute at finding men who accept bribes of cigarettes and chocolate bars if they allow her to hitch a ride to wherever the bullets are flying or to pass through a checkpoint unchallenged.

But she never quite finds her way to Paris. Instead, she happens upon the brutal battle to the north—Luxembourg, Belgium, France's Ardennes region—on which the outcome of the war now surprisingly seems to turn. A smile, a smoke, a dirty joke eliciting a description from a junior officer that ends up front and center in one of her articles for Collier's. *The officer tells her that this area has now, with the return of the sun, become "wonderful Kraut-killing country." She loves the alliteration and suspects her editor and readers will as well.*

But she also writes of a stark juxtaposition, of the "scenery for a Christmas card and the snow that makes everything serene" from a distance, but up close there are "all the usual vehicles of war, and the artillery," and the bombs from the Thunderbolts on the horizon causing so much clamor. Indeed, there are plenty of dead Germans, their red blood stark in the white snow. When she looks deeper, she finds rubble and destruction masked by the peaceful, white blanket. The battle lines remain fluid, she learns from official communiques she obtains in barter for a bottle of wine. There are actually no "lines" in the Battle of the Bulge. Another missive from command says, though, that the Germans have been shoved back, that the "bulge" has been ironed out. The "bulge" that gave this battle its peculiar name.

Martha spends New Year's Day 1945 in Luxembourg. With nothing to drink, she tells readers, it is just another day. Since a "beautiful fat-flaked snowstorm had started"—oh, the alliteration again—Martha and others decide to ignore the rumble of artillery and the P-47s pounding the enemy only a few miles away. They find a makeshift sled and go "coasting." The hill is filled with Luxembourg's children, bravely venturing out, joyfully sledding.

One of the soldiers wisely observes, "Children are smart. People oughta just go coasting." Forget war, killing Krauts, and bulging battle lines. Just go "coasting."

Yet her alienated husband would never consider a moment or a comment such as this to be a passage worth printing. But Martha remembers that profound observation by a homesick soldier and includes it in her next dispatch.

"On the night of New Year's Day, I thought of a wonderful New Year's resolution for the men who run the world: Get to know the people who only live in it," she would write.

Wonderful sentiment, she thinks as she types away. Patently impossible, of course. Men who run the world are as flawed as the rest of us.

Only a few weeks later, Martha Gellhorn will hear the news of a staggering Russian discovery in formerly German-occupied Poland. A discovery at a place called Auschwitz that will eventually drag her into covering an even more disturbing aspect of this waning war. A discovery that proves how horribly flawed men who deem themselves fit to run the world can become.

A powerful war story that will burnish her journalistic legacy and shock the world.

♠

Dr. Ernst Alwin has never considered himself to be a "mad scientist," though he has overheard some of his staff describe him as such on the hidden listening devices he has had installed throughout his Dachau lab. But in a way, he perversely considers such a pejorative to be a compliment. His creative work with biological agents and tricky bomb fuzes has helped mightily the efforts of the Fatherland and Herr Hitler. And he knows that if he can get an audience with Werner Heisenberg—one of the greatest physicists of the twentieth century and the controversial leader of Germany's nuclear fission research—and some of the other key physicists he knows are working on a super bomb, he can convince them that his ideas can make such a weapon possible. And do so in time to still win this war.

But Heisenberg has been locked away, hiding the genius from the Allied bombing and an impending invasion. More rumors swirl, though, that Heisenberg's loyalty to the Reich is in question. Although he considers himself a German nationalist who works as a leading scientist in the Nazi nuclear weapons program,

Heisenberg has never become an official member of the Nazi Party. Some claim he may have deliberately sabotaged the German atomic bomb project to prevent its full development. And that his being a Jew is a reason Hitler never fully backed any nuclear weapon option.

Paranoid bastards! After all, the man received the Nobel Prize, an award endowed by Alfred Nobel, the inventor of dynamite. (That irony is most appreciated by a man such as Ernst Alwin.) Alwin does believe other rumblings that Heisenberg is at an impasse in his work. And Ernst believes he has the solution, even if he has gotten none of the expected help from the American bomb demolition captain he has interrogated at Dachau.

Alwin's contribution may be the Reich's only hope to quickly and effectively create such a weapon, demonstrate its powers on some worthy target, and salvage a victory. The answer he holds, the notes locked in his safe in his laboratory, could save the Fatherland from another debilitating and humiliating Treaty of Versailles.

Still, no one listens. Do they not understand that a single detonation of the bomb over Stalingrad or Warsaw or London would stop the Allies dead in their tracks? In the wake of only a million or so instantaneous deaths—and even if it is the only workable version of the bomb the Reich possesses—the device would immediately end the Allied advance and have them pleading to negotiate for peace.

How many lives could such a demonstrative deployment ultimately save?

Ernst Alwin has been thinking much of late about life and death. Witnessing the SS officer, Schubert, blow out his brains might be a reason. Other than his father succumbing to tuberculosis, he has never before witnessed the death of another human. Also, in his mind, the pathetic men, women and children put to death at Dachau are not truly human.

There is no way for Alwin to know how many lives to this point have been lost to his own various lethal creations. Or how many Allied soldiers decided not to become bomb demolition men because of his ingenious anti-tamper fuzes. Now he must convince his direct superior, Albert Speer, or Heisenberg himself of the feasibility of his schematics, that they can still bring a victory for the Third Reich.

He must keep trying.

♠

Lieutenant Virginia Brown carves out enough time away from gore and mayhem at the operating table to write two or three short letters per week, a brief daily respite from the unmitigated hell of nonstop surgeries. Quick notes to her family in Miami Beach or to her newfound love, Edward, somewhere in France or Germany. She has no idea how many missives will find him but scrupulously writes a couple of lines anyway. Maybe merely trying to keep the magic alive.

She has also taken to penning letters to someone else. Someone important to Edward and whose address in Pennsylvania he gave her. Mrs. Hume, Edward's mother. Virginia wants the woman she has never met to get to know her.

Virginia has now received two replies from Mom. Both are long, rambling, frenetic letters, but warm, too, even if she does not necessarily understand who Virginia is or her relationship with her boy. They are filled with delightful stories of her "Eddie" growing up and updates on people Virginia has no way of knowing. But Mom seems to think she does. She also cannot get straight that the nurse and her boy are not in the same place. She insists Virginia tell Eddie about some person who passed away or how his dad's sciatica has gotten better since he started stretching in the morning and how the fall vegetables and the rose bushes she and Eddie planted together were more beautiful than ever this year. They thrive in the little garden behind the row house despite early frost and a dusting of snow before Thanksgiving.

Virginia was careful in her correspondence with Edward's mother. She truly was, as Edward described her, a "Nervous Ninny." But a very sweet and loving one.

The responses from Mom remind Virginia of those she receives from her own mother. Those come in twice a month, like clockwork, and run to five or six pages of tiny, tight cursive. Though Virginia has assured her as well that Hitler's days are numbered and that she should be home soon, Mellie Brown does not seem to comprehend. She tells of chatter in the neighborhood of German U-boats allegedly still being seen from the South Florida beaches and fishing piers. Even in Biscayne Bay. Of ships being attacked by the submarines a few miles offshore from Miami Beach. Of her fear that SS troops will come storming ashore at Bal Harbour or Key Biscayne some balmy night.

However, one thing in her mother's replies is different from those of Mrs. Hume: She never acknowledges Virginia's many mentions of her new friend,

Captain Edward Hume, the handsome and wonderful bomb disposal expert with whom she has fallen in love.

Maybe those parts of her letters home are redacted, blacked out by the censors. The parts about how quickly the Allies are moving toward the Rhine, too, and that the war's end appears to be nigh. Mellie Brown ignores news of the fellow in Virginia's life, avoiding any talk of the future, preoccupied with the upcoming German invasion on Florida's beaches.

So, Virginia figures, she and Eddie will just have to one day show up holding hands and walk right up the pebble path beneath the two cabbage palms and through the front door of the little cottage on Carlyle Avenue.

That's all she can think about as she stands there at the operating table, dizzy from exhaustion, void of emotion, overlooking another struggling soldier, passing sterile instruments to the surgeon who has become even more painfully bold in his advances since they returned from Paris.

The pebble path, cabbage palms, cottage on Carlyle Avenue, Captain Edward Hume next to her, her mother in her yard swing in the tiny, lantana-laced backyard, enjoying the coolness of the early morning, turning, looking up, spotting her and Edward.

Maybe then Mellie Brown will realize a U-boat won't launch a torpedo into the pool at the new National Hotel, that the Nazis are not going to come marching down A1A, and that her hard-to-please baby girl has somehow found someone who meets her impossibly high expectations.

23

What Edward had heard about the fighting in Ardennes sickened him. He and his squad remained at a constant state of heightened alert and insanely busy, returning to their assigned barracks at Toul-Ochey only every week or so for resupply and maybe a day or half day's rest. Now, with the New Year imminent, the air base under American control and major repairs completed, it had been turned over to the Ninth Air Force and the 50th Fighter Group. Three squadrons of Republic P-47 Thunderbolts now flew regular combat missions from there.

Squad members heard plenty of reports of brutal battle, tanks firing at each other at point-blank range, SS troops lining up Allied POWs and executing them—as had happened at Malmedy where more than a hundred unarmed Americans were lined up and most of them murdered by machinegun—and German artillery raining down shells into snow-filled foxholes where soldiers desperately sought shelter from ordnance as well as the cold. Some of the brutality they witnessed themselves, sometimes picking up rifles instead of picks and shovels and firing at an invisible enemy out beyond the tree line until help arrived or artillery was redirected and they could safely take on their next job.

"I thought hell was supposed to be hot," Carl blurted out one bitterly cold day. They were digging into frozen ground where a five-hundred-pounder required their attention.

Jack Morrison perked up. "Jesus says in James that hell's hot enough to set your tongue on fire if—"

Carl shut off the Bible lesson by hurling a frozen clod in Jack's direction.

"Cut it out, guys," Edward ordered. "Get this thing dug out before the SS rains hell on us." But Kostas was right. This particular part of hell was bitterly cold.

About a month into the campaign now, Edward would get smatterings of details about the ongoing fighting at the early-morning briefings with his direct commanding officer. And they all shared news from the only other BD captain working in the region. The Germans figured the Allies would be tricked into thinking that the massive enemy troop movement they could easily see would be defensive in nature, a final cannon-fodder wall near the border to deflect and stymie the invasion. Yet on December 16, 1944, the Germans began their aggressive assault with a massive, predawn, ninety-minute artillery barrage, followed by an unmistakably offensive push. It was the reporters who dubbed the resulting showdown "The Battle of the Bulge" because of the protrusion on maps where the Germans had so quickly launched their surprise invasion and shoved battle lines westward. The assault was being waged in harsh, wintry conditions with eight inches of snow on the ground in some spots and an average daily high temperature of twenty degrees.

"This is it," the CO told the briefing attendees, wringing his hands. "Like Custer, it's Hitler's last stand. And, like the injuns did, Hitler caught the US Army with our pants down. At least the skies finally cleared over Christmas and we have air power working for us. Any of you hear about General McAuliffe at Bastogne?"

"No, sir," they responded in unison.

"The Krauts had him, elements of the 101st Airborne, a bunch of those colored guys from the 969th Artillery, and some of the 10th Armored surrounded there, and demanded surrender." The CO poured himself another cup of hot coffee. There was a grin on his face. "The general sent back a one-word response. 'Nuts!' Even though our guys were in deep shit, he told 'em what he thought of their demands and held out over Christmas until Patton's 4th Armored cut a path through the bastards and got 'em some relief." He paused to blow on the coffee and then took a sip. "I know it's been dirty work so far. Ammo dumps, stacks of landmines, an Allied bomb here and there, and you've all helped keep things moving out there. This is probably the Luftwaffe's last big play in the Low Countries. Thanks to our fighters and those flak guns, damn Krauts lost close to three hundred aircraft. But here's where you guys come in. Some of the crashes still got live bombs on 'em. Some of the bastards jettisoned bombs up there, trying to limp home empty. Others got rid of loads all along the Rhine. Some blew up. A bunch didn't. We got plenty of reports of unexploded ordnance endangering airfields, roads, and even troop shelters. You can bet that whole area from Dusseldorf to Munich is about to see a bunch of Americans and Canadians and all that UXO could cause one hell of a traffic jam." Putting down his cup abruptly, he smiled broadly and chuckled. "So, guess who gets to go make sure they can drive right on into the Fatherland and say a 'good day' in person to old Adolf?"

"That's what we do," Edward responded quietly. "Any help coming, Colonel?"

"You two are all we got here," the CO admitted. "The engineers are blowing up on site what they can without killing folks or knocking down villages. We lost a captain and his squad at Malmedy. 'The Malmedy Massacre,' the papers are calling it now that the survivors testified to what happened. And we still haven't heard from Captain Bennett and his squad, so we assume they met a similar fate. Or that they're in a POW camp somewhere on the other side of the river, and if so, the Krauts will likely be forcing them to defuze bombs on behalf of the Third Reich."

"Not the Hedley Bennett I know," Edward responded, this time much louder.

"Well, we'll see," the colonel said. "Now, get your boys fed and watered and back out there doing their job. We'll get more BD guys here when we can, but for some damn reason, not many people want to volunteer for the duty you nut cases perform. Keep up your spirits, men."

When he got back to the barracks, Edward was not the least surprised that the squad already knew more about the German counteroffensive than he did. They also knew they no longer needed to scurry when they heard any aircraft approaching, fearing the deadly Luftwaffe. At least, not necessarily. Heavy, lethal fighting still raged on nearby as they headed into the new year.

Indeed, on the first day of 1945, while on a routine run to destroy stacks of dug-up landmines, they looked up to see German fighter-bombers on the way to carry out a desperate coordinated daylight air offensive—in a thick fog—against Allied airfields on the western front.

"Thought the Luftwaffe was done for," Morty Schwartz observed.

"Evil never dies," Hank Anderson responded.

"Their feet run to evil and make haste to shed blood. Proverbs," Jack Morrison added.

"Does the guy never have an original thought of his own?" groused Hank, but under his breath.

The enemy fighter-bombers went on to hit RAF airfields in the Netherlands and Belgium. Edward would later hear that the 358th Fighter Group launched a dozen fighter planes and shot down sixteen of the enemy warplanes and sent many more limping back home. And Army intelligence maintained these were the very last planes the decimated Luftwaffe had to put into the sky.

Even letters to Edward from Mom made reference to the Battle of the Bulge, expressing her hope he was far away from the mayhem she read about in the papers. And asking him if he was keeping warm. So far, Edward considered himself and his men lucky that they were only suffering sniffles, and he told her so.

And somehow missives from Virginia Brown found their way to him, too, with cryptic hints that indicated she was farther south now, working in a field hospital set up to support the inevitable mayhem once the Allies moved across the Rhine and into Germany. And she also expressed her hope that Edward was nowhere near the brutal Ardennes fighting. And that he was keeping warm.

When he returned from the CO's briefing that morning, Hume was met at the door by an angry Private Morty Schwartz, waving a newspaper, the *New York Times*. His folks made certain he got a copy, even if it was typically weeks late.

"See, Captain! They're finding concentration camps in France! Bad places. Forced laborers. Pits full of dead people. Almost all Jews! And they say it will be a hell of a lot worse in Germany and Poland. Maybe thousands. Hundreds of thousands. Maybe my relatives over here we ain't heard from."

Edward held up both hands in a nonthreatening way, then clasped them as if saying a prayer, urging Morty to keep it together. "Schwartz, I've told you. What we can do is help keep the Army and the Air Forces moving. The sooner we get over there, and have Hitler and his staff in the hoosegow, the sooner we can see and deal with whatever ugly shit they've been doing."

Hank stepped closer, ready to lighten the mood. "Captain's right, Morty. Now, sir, what's the word? A month's leave on the French Riviera?"

"Or Greece, please," Carl beseeched. "Best food on earth. They'll wrap a cow turd in grape leaves, and you'd agree it was delicious."

"I got that gal back in England," Morty offered. "We get a week over there, I know she'd be willing to let me dip my wick in her—"

Hume held up a hand to cut off the banter, dusted the snow off his jacket, and grinned. "Not exactly. Looks like we're going to be defeating the Hun by doing exactly what we've been doing for the past seven months. Doing surgery on two-thousand-pound firecrackers."

There was one fact the squad had not been aware of that hoary morning. They found out when the captain informed them that they were about to be on the move yet again. And Hume was only mildly surprised that they seemed happy about it.

Then he remembered what several of the Kaboom Boys had told him. Fast-tracking to Germany meant moving closer to the end of this damned war.

The squad had hardly gotten underway, heading for a temporary billet tucked deeply into a forest in the Vosges Mountains, when Edward received an urgent message ordering them to divert to a more southerly track. They and the other BD team had been urgently summoned to deal with three heavily booby-trapped German fighter planes resting in the middle of a forward landing strip near the town of Lunéville, not far from the western flank of the Vosges Mountains. They knew—and Hank compulsively reminded them just in case they didn't—that they were now the closest they had ever been to the German border, ninety minutes from Strasbourg, the Rhine River, and the sovereign soil of the Third Reich. Army Air Forces urgently needed access to the airstrip, so Hume and his team rushed to the spot. The Advanced Landing Ground Y-2, Lunéville Airfield, had been a Christmas present of sorts to the 324th Fighter Group when, on December 25, 1944, the airstrip was deemed operational by the Twelfth Air Force.

After a night of temperatures in the single digits and with light snow falling, Edward was working with ripped and tattered gloves, trying to neuter the frighteningly rigged live ordnance on board one of the trio of German aircraft. The going was tricky and dangerous. Numb fingers could easily lead to a mistake causing an instant and life-altering detonation. He was also under pressure from one of the lead engineers. The major had made it clear that he should disarm the booby traps instead of blowing them up. Somebody wanted the German planes intact so they could study them. Why? The Luftwaffe was kaput. And God knows they had plenty more hulks to look at all over Europe.

Then, a welcome reprieve. Word came that they had a far more critical job, one that involved possible loss of life if it was not addressed. Another battle of wills was avoided. They safely detonated all three aircraft so the engineers could haul their remains away to a scrap heap somewhere. Then the engineers could get busy repairing the runway damage.

Soon, they spotted the Grand-Ballon. At almost a mile tall it was the highest point in the Vosges. There was also smoke rising between their current position and the big mountain. Not thick, black smoke, like a structure ablaze. White smoke, like a forest fire. It was likely a beacon showing them the way to their next job. Edward had seen plenty of white smoke back home when a careless hunter or indiscriminate lightning bolt set ablaze the thick woods along Broad Mountain, overlooking the Mahanoy Valley.

It took them an hour to reach the spot. The fire had mostly burned itself out by then. A couple of bored soldiers leaned against their jeep, a warming campfire in front of them, smoking, waiting.

"What we got here, guys?" Edward asked, returning their salutes, his eyes searching the scene for the five-hundred-pound bombs that had reportedly been dropped somewhere in the dense forest.

"One of our P-47s went down over there, sir," the older-looking one—maybe twenty-one, maybe not—explained, pointing at the smoke and ash. "That started the fire. Dang thing carried a couple of '*fivers*,' they tell us, but we can't see where. Seems like nothing's left."

"Anybody heard any loud booms?" Hume asked.

"No, sir. Reckon not. Not a soul around. Pretty desolate here. Just rocks and trees."

"Then we'll assume we've got a pilot wandering around the woods, or stuck hanging from a tree, and a couple of 'fives' still intact somewhere and ready to blow despite the crash and fire. Or maybe the pilot jettisoned his load before bailing out. Have you guys looked for him?"

"Yeah, for the last two hours. We just got back. Nothing but squirrels and the odd deer."

"No body?"

"Not that we can see."

"You didn't look in the cockpit of the P-47, right?"

"No, sir. In case he didn't get rid of the bombs before he augured in."

"Good thinking, Corporal. Okay then, I need you two to stay clear. Back over there next to where my guys are parking the truck. Two five-hundred-pounders, if you didn't know, cause one hell of a ruckus."

Captain Hume and Sergeant Morrison, carrying tool bags, waded into the hot ash. It was an eerie, quiet world of wispy smoke, the skeletons of scorched beech trees, and smoldering brush. An underlying carpet of melting snow made for a muddy mixture to slog through. As they walked, the warmth from the embers felt good through their wet leather boots, though.

"Holy shit," Edward said. Through the smoky haze and mist, he could see the ghostly form of the Thunderbolt fighter/bomber resting on its side less than a hundred yards ahead, its belly facing them. The remaining intact wing pointed straight up, reaching skyward. Hume warily eyed a bomb still attached to the underside of the P-47's wing.

"M-64, all right. Yep. Five-hundred-pounder. No idea what the impact of the crash and then the fire might've done to its guts. Especially the wiring." Edward looked warily around them. "And where in hell did that other bomb—?"

BOOOOM!

Though they were still sixty yards from the airplane and bomb, the sudden blast blew both men off their feet, setting them down well behind where they had been standing. Stunned, they were mostly unaware of the whirling shrapnel and debris flying all around. Tree limbs and branches cracked and crashed down, cut loose by the blast and flying metal shards. When he could, and when the whizzing debris had stopped, Edward raised his head and tried to focus on Jack. The sergeant stared back blankly, wide-eyed.

After a few moments, bells still chiming in his ears, Edward was finally able to speak. "You okay?"

"I think so." But Morrison had cuts on his face and was bleeding. "Not hearing too well. You, Captain?"

"I think I still have my balls."

Another fifty feet closer or with less trees between them and the plane, they would likely have been badly injured. Or killed. Edward noticed cuts to his hands and could feel stings on his face and forehead. When he wiped his brow, his hand came back bloody.

With their hearing stunted by the way-too-close blast, Edward yelled when he told Jack, "Guess we don't gotta defuze that one, Sarge!"

Through the continual ringing in his ears, Edward made out muffled words. "You okay, Captain?" It was Hank, underwater, a hundred miles away.

"Still breathing!" shouted Edward, climbing unsteadily to his feet. Jack did the same.

They still saw no sign of that other five-hundred-pounder. Or the pilot. They theorized the wing under which the egg hung had been shot away in whatever air-to-air combat caused the Thunderbolt to go down. Maybe that second bomb detonated in midair or hit the ground elsewhere, several miles away. It could still be intact, ready to explode at any time. All the squad knew was that it was nowhere near the P-47's debris trail. The two bored soldiers would now be tasked with approaching what was left of the plane's wreckage to see if they could determine if its pilot had managed, by the grace of God, to have bailed out. Or to recover what was left of the unfortunate soul after the crash, fire, and most recent bang.

Edward knew they had to shake off the effects of this really close call, physical and mental. Though he and his sergeant had bloody cuts on exposed skin, near-deaf ears, and pounding headaches—and almost certainly concussions—there were more jobs to do. Indeed, because of these couple of detours, they were already overdue reporting to their next staging area. It would be within spitting distance of the Rhine and what was left of the German army, retreating but still viciously fighting.

But the captain also knew the pressure was taking a toll on the squad, on their concentration, on their interaction with each other. He and his men really needed a break. Or some hope they might even be going home soon.

But, like that missing five-hundred-pounder, such relief was nowhere in sight.

Captain Edward Hume was again caught up in a nightly ritual. Once more bivouacked in tents in cold weather and not in makeshift but more substantial barracks structures made it bad enough. But in their present camp, the ground beneath his cot was rough and uneven. That left the door open for the recurring nightmares. Lately, it was the same vivid dream that had him falling from the sky with no parachute, unleashed bombs plummeting downward all around him, whistling shrilly, but with neither he nor the bombs ever quite hitting earth. When he inevitably awoke, he usually was about to fall off the narrow, flimsy cot onto the cold, hard ground. His green fatigue blanket was too short, leaving his feet exposed to the cold, requiring three layers of socks. But it was the faces haunting his foggy head, mostly as shadowy phantoms, while he was descending earthward, that ultimately drove away truly restful sleep.

His brother, Tommy, killed not in war or a coal mine collapse but in a wreck on a mountain road when he tried to dodge a deer.

The kid, Theo Toussaint, who had fallen in love with stickball and thrived on the father figures happily provided by Hume's Kaboom Boys.

Ace Taft, serious but with glimmers of dark humor, dedicated, compassionate, complicated. A man who may have cared too much. Blown to smithereens in Normandy when that damned ammo dump went up, leaving Edward forever unsure if it was a tragic accident or a suicide due to his melancholy over the loss of Taft's fiancé in a factory fire.

Pete Ronzini. Short in stature but tall in bravado, the son of a Brooklyn Navy Yard dockworker, always ready for a fight to prove himself worthy—and that a man's height did not determine his manhood—but then stabbed by someone who should have been friendly to him.

Edward's "Clark Gable" look-alike friend, Hedley Bennett, leader of the Bomb Merchants, now likely buried in a shallow grave somewhere in the Ardennes. Maybe not far from where the cold wind buffeted Captain Hume's tent as he tried to find rest.

He was also puzzled about why Virginia Brown never made an appearance in that recurring dream. Then he decided this was a good omen, even if he had little faith in omens. That it possibly verified that she, unlike all the others, was okay.

And now, here he was, suffering insomnia on slanted soil in the mountains of far-eastern France, unsure what the future held, other than more UXBs to kiss, caress and make safe. More live-and-ticking UXOs to keep out of the hands of local radicals like those Nazi guerilla fighters they kept hearing about. The lunatics who called themselves "The Werewolves" and vowed to kill Allies any way they could for as long as they could in the name of their Führer.

As he usually did when sleep would not come, Hume surrendered and tried to find something useful to do. With his flashlight, he studied the map of the Vosges region. But as he did, he made a vow to himself. He would carry on, avoid dangerous distractions, keep up his normally positive attitude for the sake of the squad. He would just have to overcome frustration made worse by a lack of sleep, proper nourishment, and details concerning their future. Not to mention his wavering self-confidence when it came to commanding a diverse and rowdy squad of men. That was the only way he knew to try to avoid some kind of bad outcome.

The Kaboom Boys were to remain at this spot, doing what they did, until told at some future time to follow most everyone else eastward, into Germany. Word was the Russians had crossed most of Poland already and would be in the German capital by the end of April, roughly three weeks away, but that hundreds of thousands would die on each side in the process. Scuttlebutt was that top generals—including Patton—had tried to persuade Eisenhower to race ahead, to beat the Russians there, to allow Americans to be the ones who accepted Hitler's surrender and placed the bastard under arrest. But Eisenhower decided, at General Omar Bradley's urging, not to risk American troops in the destructive house-to-house fighting, a vainglorious charge that most believed would be inevitable. By standing down, the Allies would be able to fight another day. Let the Russians get chewed up taking Berlin.

Before Edward knew it, dawn was near. He decided to go to the officers' latrine for a morning constitutional. But when he looked up, he was startled to see a young soldier standing just outside his tent flap.

"Mornin', sir," the kid said as he saluted. "I wasn't going to bother you 'til the sun came up, but I saw your light. Got a dispatch for you."

"No problem, Private. Where's home?" It was a question he often asked lately of soldiers he met. It surprised him how often he found common ground with strangers.

"Amarillo, Texas, sir."

"You know Captain Hedley Bennett? He spent some time in Texas."

"Can't say I do, sir," the blue-eyed youngster said as he handed Edward the envelope.

"You know where Notrees, Texas, is?"

The kid scrunched up his face, thinking. "Can't say as I do, sir."

"Thanks. Go on, now, and be sure to dodge bullets and don't touch anything that can go kaboom, okay?"

"Yes, sir." He had Hume sign a sheet of paper on his clipboard. Then, another salute and the young soldier disappeared. Another person Edward would meet on this crusade of his, but another one whose fate he would likely never know. The kid could be back in Amarillo in a few months courtin' and sparkin' and doing whatever else people in Amarillo did. Or he might step on a landmine before the sun set on this day.

He slid the single page from its envelope and read it by the dim light of the rising sun. It was hardly a dispatch. It was only simple directions like so many others he and his men had received over the past ten months or so. Simple orders to go to a nearby village to set up their tents, then clean up an ordnance dump made up mostly of ammunition, landmines and left-behind German "potato-masher" grenades, especially prized by souvenir hunters. Then to concentrate on a Nazi military camp in another small town nearby once it was liberated by approaching Allied troops. It had been reported to be a training facility of some sort, possibly riddled with booby traps, and would require sweeping by a BD squad.

He looked at the name of the first town. It was unpronounceable. But the document indicated the name of the other small village nearby. One Edward had heard of.

"Well, I'll be damned," he said, to himself, to the newly arrived sun, and to the fading ghosts of Tommy, Ace, Theo, Pete, Hedley, and all the others who haunted his dreams on these sleepless nights.

Dachau.

24

Now came a time for firsts. Captain Hume and his Kaboom Boys crossed the Rhine River for the first time the first week of April 1945, about two weeks after the first major Allied incursion into Germany and just after Easter, which fell on April 1 this year, and was the fourth day of Passover. Along with the 324th Group Advance Party, they were deployed through the Vosges Mountains and across a recently erected bridge, thanks to the quick work of the Army Corps of Engineers, replacing a bombed-out structure that allowed them to drive right across and into Germany. Not quite like tourists on a lark, but close.

"Does this make us April Fools?" Hank asked as he urinated on German soil, in plain sight of and just across the river from Strasbourg.

"Some Kraut sniper shoots your pecker off, you gonna feel pretty damn foolish," Morty observed.

"You guys notice how the gingerbread houses on this side of the river look just like the ones over on the French side?" Anderson asked, ignoring his squad mate's jibe.

It was true, though. Coming down into the Rhine Rift Valley, the men were surprised to see that the German houses on the right bank—the east side—looked the same as the Alsatian houses on the left bank. The people, too. All the same. French or German.

"Same except for all the white sheets hanging off of them on this side of the river," Carl noted. "Good to see all of 'em so willing to surrender."

It was true. Most homes had white sheets blowing from windows or tied to their roofs.

"They just want to be sure we know they're no threat," Hank said. "Anyway, you guys notice how friendly these regular German folks we've met are. If you didn't know, you'd think they're just regular—"

"Shut the hell up!" Schwartz angrily interrupted. "Ain't nothing good about these sons of bitches. They're all in on it! Don't you ever forget it. You hear what the Russians found? My Uncle Ezra wrote me about places like Madjanek and Auschwitz. Your fine, friendly Krauts did all they could to hide what was happening, but they found suits of clothes and dresses and shoes for hundreds of thousands of people. Just nobody left to wear them. Hell, guys, they found sacks full of human hair! Gold teeth in jars on shelves! Ditches filled with skeletons!"

Schwartz was weeping by the end of his rant. Stamping his foot. Fists clenched as if he was ready to punch somebody. Anybody. Captain Hume put his arm around the private's shoulder.

"Easy, Morty. We've heard those rumors, too, but there's—"

"Hell if they're just rumors! My people back home know about it. They hear. Even some news reports showing up now in the papers and magazines, even if they are way in the back. But nobody believes them either. Mostly the Hebrew papers, though, they put it on the front page. Uncle Ezra tells me. But most nobody in New York believes them either, 'cept those Jews who've lost touch with family and friends. No humans could be that cruel, they figure. Just the Jews complainin' like we always do. You'll see. Everybody will see. Uncle Ezra keeps telling me to find out more."

Schwartz jerked away from his captain, stomped around behind the truck and lit up a cigarette. The men quietly finished their business, climbed back into the vehicles, and pulled out, now aiming south toward their next assigned billet.

It took them a couple of weeks doing odd jobs along the way to work their way over to the town in the Bavarian region with the odd-sounding name of Oberpfaffenhoffen. There they were to camp while handling a tricky "situation." It had been described as looking like an archaeological dig adjacent to an airfield. It was called a "bomb cemetery" and was bigger than a football field. There they would be tasked with blowing up tons of bombs and other ordnance so those munitions would not fall into the wrong hands. There were fears based on reliable evidence that some SS officers might try to seize what they could and mount their own resistance against the Allies. That included those ominous-sounding "Werewolves."

"What was that town again?" Jack asked as he guided the jeep along the artillery-potholed dirt road.

Edward was already studying his map. "Oberpfaffenhoffen, I guess is the way to say it."

"Sounds like the noise a Ford Model 48 with a stuck piston would make," Hank offered from the jeep's back seat.

"Close to anything else we might've heard of?" Morrison questioned.

"Dachau," Hank offered.

"Dachau I've heard of," Edward said. "They got a Nazi ordnance lab there. We've seen some of their work up close."

"Supposed to have good beer there, though, like Munich and every other burgh in Bavaria," Hank noted. "Nice little town according to the guidebooks. At least the ones from before the war. I doubt much has changed there, though. Pretty little Bavarian town and far enough out of Munich to dodge all the bombing. They probably never saw a Nazi or an SS soldier there. Except for those weird bomb scientists, that is."

"I doubt we'll have much time for sightseeing if we ever get there," Captain Hume told him. "But I'd sure like to see those labs if they're still there."

♠

Carl had set up his shaving mirror and helmet full of cold water in a bush behind their tent, adjacent to the landing strip at Oberpfaffenhoffen. Morty and Gene flanked him, prepared to take care of what they considered to be a totally unnecessary bit of personal hygiene.

"Somebody remind me again why we gotta shave," Carl said, dragging the dull razor painfully across three days' worth of stubble.

"Some chapped-ass colonel back in England where they got plenty hot water and sharp razors said so," Morty answered. "That's why."

"Ain't been long since summer and they was telling us to shave with cold water, so we don't get razor burn in the heat," Carl reminded. "Man, what I'd give for some hot water right about now."

It was going to be another exhausting day, almost two weeks into the bomb cemetery job. Most of the construction guys, the engineers, had moved on, working on bridges and critical roadways that had been blown up or land-mined by the fleeing Germans. That meant the Kaboom Boys had to dig all their holes the old-fashioned way, with picks and shovels. Then they moved all that abandoned UXO—some of it very heavy and unwieldy—as efficiently as they could, usually carefully hoisted or rolled up on timbers into the back of the truck so they could take it to a safe place to detonate it. Planes came and went day and night from the suddenly crucial airfield, dusting them with grit and debris, whether they were working clearing the bomb cemetery or snagging some sleep in their tents. The captain's prediction had been correct. They had not had time for any sightseeing. And the Germans still held Munich in a tentative grip.

"Same asshole that denied us our medals, too, I betcha," Morty groused. Both the 358th and the 324th Group had, with much fanfare, just been awarded the Presidential Unit Citation, an award for "extraordinary heroism" against the enemy. But the bomb disposal squads had been declared "attached units" and therefore not eligible.

"Same son of a bitch that declared they don't have enough transportation to send us home so we gotta stay over here handling hot ordnance even if we're slotted to leave," Hank Anderson added, joining the others with his own helmet full of water and shaving mirror.

Gene laughed and said, "You know you'd miss us and all the good times we've—"

"Son of a bitch!" Carl suddenly yelped.

"Calm down, Surfer Boy," Hank urged.

"Naw! I just cut the shit out of my chin shaving with cold water and a dull-as-a-froe razor in the damn freezing dark!" The sun had just raised its head out beyond the airstrip, contributing little light and, so far, no warmth. "Tell the captain I had to go to the hospital tent for a blood transfusion."

"Worst thing is, Carl," Hank said, "they hear you got a scar on that pretty face of yours, all the women in Europe are gonna go into mourning and—"

Suddenly, another interruption. An aircraft buzzed low overhead, seemingly just yards above them. So low the wind off its single propellor shook loose their mirrors from where they hung in the bushes. The four soldiers instinctively hit the ground.

"Jesus! That's a Stuka," Hank shouted. "Where'd he come from?"

The German pilot was already banking hard, working to get lined up on the end of the runway.

"He's coming back to shoot our asses is what he's doing," Morty yelled as he tried to crawl beneath the bushes.

"No. No he's not. See how he's waggling his wings. That means he wants to surrender," Hank explained, pointing at the Junkers Ju 87 dive bomber.

"The French guys ain't gettin' the message, though," Carl said, pointing.

Sure enough, the French Army anti-aircraft gun crew just down the way, likely awakened by the plane's low-altitude noise, were sprinting to their positions on the other side of the runway. Hank ran out into the clear, waving, shouting, but the gun crew apparently saw this as an opportunity to deal out a bit of vengeance. They promptly opened fire on the Stuka with their .50-caliber guns. They kept it up until the German plane's wheels touched the runway. They only stopped shooting when they realized they might hit people, tents, Allied aircraft, and buildings on the Kaboom Boys' side of the landing strip.

Morty, Carl, Gene, and Hank had already hit the ground again, this time ducking the French fire. When the shooting stopped, they raised their heads and watched the pilot purposefully taxi his plane over to the flight control van, two hundred feet from them, switch off his engine, coast to a stop, pull back his canopy, and step out onto the wing while ecstatically pumping his fists in the air. By then, dozens of armed soldiers had arrived on the scene, rifles pointed toward the pilot. But the German was grinning broadly, dancing happily, pointing to bullet holes in the canopy. Then he turned to the gathering crowd and performed a deep, exaggerated bow from the waist.

Everyone laughed, including the Kaboom Boys, who had now joined the group around the Stuka. But just then, the aircraft's other passenger, the forward observer, pulled back his own canopy, stuck his head out, and vomited all down the side of the proud warbird's fuselage.

They later learned the two men had been stationed in Czechoslovakia. There was only enough gasoline left at the base to allow one plane to try to flee Allied invaders. Or, if they chose, to surrender. They drew straws. This pilot got the short one and was allowed, with his observer, to fly away.

The Stuka was Swiss-cheesed with .50-caliber bullet holes. It was a miracle they had not been killed. And they would be prisoners of war of the Americans, not the Russians. The pilot had chosen wisely, as it turned out.

"Luck of the draw," Hank noted.

"All that waggling and wiggling," Carl guessed.

"I know what it was," Morty said. "Look at the nose."

Sure enough, just behind the propellor, there was a small bit of artwork. It depicted a playing card.

The ace of spades.

"Tried to tell you all along it was good luck," Morty said, wiping a lingering dollop of shaving cream off his face with the back of his hand.

"No, you didn't!" Carl started. "You were the one..." But with a wave, he dismissed the discussion entirely. As usual, Morty was just giving him some shit.

Kostas still had a more pressing job to finish: shave the other side of his face without cutting off his head.

25

Józef Steiner was once more just a simple, incarcerated blacksmith. His refusal to detonate his 247th bomb had gotten him tossed cruelly back into his old cell block at Dachau. Except for those times when he was taken outside to fix broken gizmos or care for the camp commandant's horses, Steiner was nothing more than another miserable, hungry, sick prisoner—but luckily still alive—wondering when it would be his turn to be hauled out and executed. Or be used in the horrifyingly inhumane "medical experiments" he was hearing about. There were stories of prisoners strapped down naked in the cold until they passed out, then "researchers" trying various methods to revive them, such as dousing them with scalding water. Or testing limits of hypothermia, supposedly to determine how much and for how long Luftwaffe pilots could withstand being shot down over the frigid waters of the North Sea or soldiers on the Eastern Front could survive bitter temperatures on the battlefield. Prisoners who lived through such torture told of being immersed in vats of ice-cold salt water and left for hours. Hundreds of prisoners died in these experiments. Nobody seemed to care.

But Józef refused to give up hope.

The reason was the same and simple: Birgit Franz. He kept in a corner, beneath his bug-infested sleeping pad, her carefully folded but frayed blue scarf, now faded to a grayish hue. The one she had left for him at the Isar months before. Every night he caressed her embroidered name on the scarf, even though he had lost most of the feeling in his fingertips from the cold weather, the harsh working conditions, the chemicals, and the rough, sharp metal of the bomb casings. The scent of her perfume on the cloth had long since faded, overtaken by the stench in the cell. He ached to recall it.

There was something else, too. He sensed a new level of apprehension among the SS who oversaw this hellish prison camp. When he was out on a job, he watched how they scrambled to try to cover up their criminal deeds, taking extra effort to keep even inmates from witnessing incriminating sights. Others who worked outside the fences noticed it, too. Stacks of bodies bulldozed into mass graves, then covered over with dirt. Shrubbery planted in the freshly turned soil. Railroad cars filled with more cadavers rolling away to some other place for disposal and concealment. Some of the *kapos* had now begun to offer smiles and extra portions of gruel to the prisoners, clearly to curry a bit of favor should they soon have to answer for their collaboration.

Only a few days before, he had witnessed another event portending an imminent change in their situation. Thousands of skeletal prisoners were being marched away from the camp, urged on by shouting, threatening troops. The inmates dubbed them "Death Marches." One of Józef's guards revealed that many were headed for Tegernsee, fifty miles south, near the Austrian border, though it was obvious to many of them—and most were yellow-star-wearing Jews—that they would never survive such a trudge.

So Józef, searching for any reason to hope, vowed to live. Willing himself. He found strength by singing with other prisoners "Dachau Song," an anthem composed by a pair of fellow inmates.

"We became hard as steel. Stay human, comrade. Be a man, comrade. Do a good job, get to it, comrade, for work will set you free."

And they sang with extra exuberance the last few words of the chorus, mocking the prominent "Work will set you free" sign hanging above the camp's entrance. The cruel, false promise that those prisoners who behaved and worked hard for the Fatherland would be freed.

Other prisoners warehoused nearby took inspiration from Józef. They knew he was among the longest sufferers of this place, a true survivor. Most knew it was only his special touch with the unexploded bombs that had prevented him from joining so many of his contemporaries in the box cars, crematoria, and mass graves. Some took issue with his aiding the Nazis, even when he tried to explain his justification for doing what he and the other members of the Dachau One Hundred did. But despite that, he remained a gentle soul, suffering quietly, not only from the hardships everyone else had to endure but from survivor's guilt, the overwhelming feeling that he should have long since died alongside his fellow prisoners.

It helped, too, that he occasionally saw and was now able to talk briefly with the American Army bomb demolition technician, Captain Hedley Bennett. Thankfully in English. They compared notes. Told tales. Commiserated. But mostly what the American brought to Józef was more reasons to hope. Bennett was convinced that their liberation was near. He convinced the Blacksmith, as well.

"When's the last time you saw a Junkers or a Messerschmitt fly over?" he asked. "Adolf's done lost his airpower and the troops and tanks are hustling on back toward Berlin. You can hear our bombers still pounding Munich now that there's no ack-ack or fighter planes to chase them away. Just a matter of time, my BD friend. Just a matter of time."

"From your lips to God's ear," Steiner always told him, first in English, then in German. But always in a hopeful tone, silently praying God might finally be hearing.

April flowers—tulips, crocuses, daffodils—brought optimism. They were just visible near the officers' quarters at the far side of the compound. Józef was standing on tiptoes one chilly morning, as he so often did, gazing out the only window on that side of the building, looking at the narrow soul-buoying sliver of color from the flowers, when he heard considerable commotion.

For a while, there were only people shouting. Terrified shouting. Then more yelling. Yelling in English? And gunshots. Explosions he knew from his experiences to be grenades and light artillery shells. Sounds of a full-blown skirmish. Even after it quieted down some, there were still occasional volleys. *Firing squads?* Józef wondered. They certainly sounded like the firing squad executions he had heard so many times over the years. The open area behind his building was a favorite place for such mass murders.

The other prisoners were agitated, pounding on the walls, shouting at what they hoped might be their long-awaited liberators. Afraid they might die in the crossfire after waiting so long for and being so close to blessed freedom.

The Blacksmith merely settled down on his cot, pulled on his boots, and patiently waited, the scarf in his hands like a prayer cloth.

He had waited so long, after all. He could wait a few more minutes to learn if the long, long nightmare was now ending. After all the death he had dodged, the possibility of a stray bullet did not concern him.

Soon, he would learn if all that hope he had maintained—the hope that had kept him alive—had been worth it. If he could find Birgit Franz. If she had survived the Allied bombings. If she was unmarried.

If she still had any interest whatsoever in a simple, broken, but hopeful blacksmith.

♠

Martha Gellhorn would later write that she was in Dachau when she learned World War II—at least in Europe—had come to an end. And that this happenstance was a bit of perfection since this was the place that for years had conducted a systematic policy of prisoner abuse and torture.

"Dachau seemed to me the most suitable place in Europe to hear the news of victory. For surely this war was made to abolish Dachau, and all the other places like Dachau, and everything that Dachau stood for, and to abolish it forever," she wrote.

But she was also angry.

"We are not entirely guiltless, we the Allies," she went on to write, "because it took us twelve years to open the gates of Dachau. We were blind and unbelieving and slow, and that we can never be again. We must know that there can never be peace if there is cruelty like this in the world."

Private Morty Schwartz would have agreed completely.

Now, as the Kaboom Boys' vehicles approached the high fences and low buildings of the Dachau prison camp, he pounded the dash of the truck in rage. Skeletons—hollow-eyed, living ones—stood many rows deep along the inside fencing, calmly watching all that was happening on the outside. There were many bodies piled up on the ground. The soldiers would later learn that many of those were prisoners who rushed to greet their rescuers only to be electrocuted when they touched the fence. For others, the joy and excitement of their impending release was simply too much for their weakened systems. They collapsed and died where they had stood.

Captain Hume and his squad had been pulled off the bomb cemetery job to race over to Dachau. Even before the first Allied soldiers liberated the camp, they feared there might be booby traps and landmines aplenty and called for help. By the time the liberators arrived, the prisoners assured them that the frantic SS had not had time to set up such deterrents. But the squad was told to stand by, to do what they could to help. In the chaos, nobody seemed to know what that might be.

A soldier leaning nonchalantly on a pile of ration boxes caught Morty's attention. Schwartz immediately pointed to the wasted women and men at the fences and yelled. "Give them something to eat, goddammit!"

"We try to feed them, they eat too much, and they die in front of us, so shut the fuck up!" the soldier responded without even turning to look at Schwartz.

"Guys! Look at this," Schwartz went on. "Just look at this. My God, I told you. I told you."

Carl, Gene and Hank had no comeback. They, too, were dumbfounded at what they were seeing. Overcome by the stench, astounded by the sights, they were not sure what they should do. They had already passed piles of emaciated corpses, train cars on a siding track packed with badly decomposed human remains, and thousands more walking skeletons wandering about, dazed.

Just ahead of them, Jack pulled the jeep to a stop and began coughing, overcome by the unimaginable odor. Edward put his hand to his mouth and nose as he stared in disbelief at the horror before him. He looked around for someone to direct them to their assigned mission, to where they might speak with whoever was in charge. But everyone seemed stunned by this awful montage. There was an unnerving silence, only haunting whispers hanging in the cold air.

Jack swung out of the jeep and stood motionless for a moment, stunned. He closed his eyes, stretched out his arms, raised his hands, palms up, and did the only thing he knew to do. He prayed aloud: "Lord, be with those who grieve, who suffer, who have died. Give us peace in the midst of this storm. We must trust in your plan even though we cannot understand. Amen."

The 42nd Infantry had first entered the camp earlier that morning. They expected to find a training camp for Hitler's elite SS forces, but there had been little resistance. The enemy gave up surprisingly quickly for SS, throwing down their rifles and surrendering. Many ran away. Others changed clothes and cowardly blended in with the prisoners. The 42nd guys assumed most of the hardcore top SS had long since fled. There was no sign of Ernst Alwin or the other ordnance scientists.

"Jesus Christ, who could have had any idea about any of this?" Edward exclaimed, also to no one in particular.

"Sir, Jesus Christ had nothing to do with any of this," Morty cried. "People knew, sir. I've been telling you. My family knew, and they're four thousand miles from this shit. Nobody wanted to listen! No one wanted to believe this was possible."

Suddenly feeling nauseous, Edward climbed out of the jeep and leaned across the hood, covering his nose with his forearm. Several soldiers around them were physically ill, vomiting. Edward tried to hold back but he also threw up.

"I'm sorry, Morty," whispered Edward, wiping his mouth on his jacket sleeve. "But I've heard you all along. I've reported what you've been telling me. I passed it up the chain of command. Beyond that, I had no idea what to do. And now, here we are. And I still have no idea what to do. But we will do something."

"Look, guys," Hank suddenly told them, pointing. "Over there!" Something was going on across a small unplowed field. A couple of US soldiers had four SS troopers lined up, standing beneath a tall beech, their hands in the air. And suddenly, without warning, the Americans raised their M1 rifles and fired point blank at the captured Germans, emptying their .30-06 clips, ripping apart the unarmed prisoners.

Morty spun around and headed back toward the truck. He grabbed an

M1 and began looking for a German—any German soldier—on whom he could wreak some of his long-gestating revenge. His squad mates watched, wide-eyed, but made no move to stop him.

But a firm hand on his shoulder did. It was the captain.

"Whatcha doing with the rifle, Private?"

"If it's open season on SS—"

"No. That's not what we do. That puts us at their level, Morty," Hume quietly told him.

"I don't care, sir." Morty's face was flushed. There were tears on his cheeks.

"Yes, you do. See? The 42nd is taking those shooters into custody already and I bet their CO is going to make sure this kind of thing stops. But think about it. Execute them here, they don't really pay the price. You just put 'em out of their misery. We want to make them pay. Make them face the world and testify to what they've done. Make them spend the rest of their lives thinking about what they did in this place. Some won't care, some will. But it's what we do in a democracy. We do not summarily execute people like the Nazis do."

"Innocent until proven guilty, huh? Look around, Captain. Tell me those bastards are innocent."

With tears still on his face, Morty grudgingly returned his rifle to the truck while the captain went looking for somebody who could tell him specifically what he and his squad were supposed to be doing.

That ammo dump they were supposed to be making safe had just become a much lower priority.

Instead of digging holes and detonating UXOs, the Kaboom Boys became stretcher bearers and sincere empathizers. And they were proud to do it. With bandannas on their faces and their hands gloved, they had been assigned to work their way through the filthy buildings, helping those who could not walk from their cells out to the broad parade grounds beyond the main gate. That was where those in the worst shape would lie in the warm sun, take cautiously offered food and water, and wait for medical attention.

At one point, Captain Hume saw a couple of US Army chaplains praying over a group of sick prisoners. He walked closer, hoping to see the face of his friend, Captain Russell Lowe. It would have been a long shot. He could be anywhere in Europe by now. But he was not there, giving spiritual comfort to the poor prisoners of Dachau.

When Hank and Carl stepped into one of the buildings, it looked to be empty already. They were half blinded by improbably bright sunlight shining into this morbid, dark place through a long, high window. But in the shadows in a far corner, they were surprised to see a man sitting stoically on a cot, his haggard face expressionless. He wore the familiar striped uniform and yellow star.

"*Brauchst du hilfe?*" Hank asked, using what little German he knew. "Need help?"

The man looked up and smiled through the stubble on his face, his few remaining teeth yellowed and stained. He clutched in his hands some kind of rag. Maybe a memento of his life before Dachau.

"The patch on your sleeve," the prisoner said in a whisper.

"Bomb demolition," Hank told him.

"We are brothers, then," Józef Steiner proclaimed, his grin now impossibly, improbably broad. "We are 'brothers of the boom.' God is good, sending you to take me out."

They slowly led the frail man from the decrepit barracks building, past the thirty-one other structures just like it, through the gate in the now-deactivated electric fence, through the shadows of a couple of the seven guard towers, past a broad bed of beautifully flowering plants, and to the parade ground. There the Kaboom Boys took their first break of the long, disturbing day and got to know this man with whom they had so much in common.

"You say 246 bombs? No training?" Edward could not believe it. "How'd you pull that off?"

"One at a time. I knew that I would someday encounter a device that I would not attempt to defuze, even if the SS threatened to shoot me. I would be able to sense that it would kill me. And when I found it, I walked away without hesitation. Unfortunately, the man they forced to work on it..." He closed his eyes as his voice trailed off.

"Tell me, how did you make it through all that abuse you saw and took for so long in this place? You had to have doubts about ever being liberated, right?" the captain asked, settling down on the ground next to him.

Józef smiled and there was a sparkle in his eyes when he again opened them. "I had reasons to live. I defuzed the bombs so more innocents would not die. That became a reason. I taught others so they could help prevent such senseless death." He showed Edward the scarf. "And there is someone who was kind to me one dark day. I want to try to find her, remind her of the gifts she gave to me that day, and tell her how that generous bit of kindness was another thing that kept me alive until this glorious day of freedom. Then, we will see what happens from there. Regardless, I have survived because of her. That allows me to thank Birgit Franz for what she did for me."

"That's a staggering story, Józef," Edward told him. "You should tell some of the journalists when they get here."

Steiner did not seem at all interested in doing that. He continued slowly chewing the K-ration biscuits they had given him, heeding the warning not to eat too much or too fast. Then, a sudden moment of clarity struck him.

"Captain, there were other soldiers here at Dachau who speak English. Americans."

"Americans? I'm looking specifically for ordnance disposal men who might have been prisoners."

Steiner stopped eating and allowed himself a smile. "Yes. Yes. Also bomb demolition. I am talking about a good-looking man. Raven-black hair." Steiner nodded. "A Captain Bennett. Hedley Bennett. His men, they called themselves Bomb Merchants."

Edward was astonished. What were the odds? The other Kaboom Boys now leaning over Edward's shoulder were equally as shocked. Hume jumped to his feet. "They're here? Where?"

"They were. I have not seen any of them in the past week or so. They could be out, working on bombs."

"Hedley and them, they worked on bombs for the Nazis?" Hume asked, disbelieving. He knew Hedley could be charged with assisting the enemy if it was found that he was handling bombs for the Nazis. He hoped Blacksmith had his facts wrong.

"For the same reason I did for so long," Steiner answered. "To save innocent lives. Not to help Herr Hitler in any way."

Hume studied the man's face for a moment, then nodded. "Józef, I must find Captain Bennett with your help. Tell me where to look if you can. And, another thing, I have no idea how this is going to work, but you are welcome to stay with us in our tents and eat all the mess-tent food you want. Join us. You can even go with us to whatever job we've got if you want. Maybe even help us. We're going to be around Munich for a while, I'm thinking. Then, when you're ready and strong enough, we'll be glad to drop you off wherever you want to go so you can look for your friend. Or you can stay with us, help us, make the world safer one bomb at a time. Whatever is right. It would be our honor to make you a Kaboom Boy."

"They called me 'The Blacksmith' here, a name from my previous life." Steiner allowed the afternoon sun to warm his face. "Captain Hume, I have no other place to go for the night. I will accept your kind offer since you will have me."

"Of course. We got blankets. Food. A cot and a pillow."

Steiner's face changed. "I appreciate your kind offer to join your excellent squad, Captain. I do not believe I would make a very good 'kaboom boy.' See, my hands shake. I never want to see another grenade or landmine or bomb, if you will understand. I just want peace. I want to get back to living, not just surviving."

Edward nodded and smiled. "Understood, Józef. Now, stay right here and we'll come get you when we know where we'll be pitching our tents." Edward helped him stand. "Now, I got to go find a friend of mine and let him know there's a bet he still needs to pay off on!"

The last time Edward looked back, Steiner once again had a big, genuine smile on his face.

26

Corporal Hank Anderson was exhausted, more from what he had witnessed this day than from the physical effort expended helping scores of pitiful people make their way out of the prison barracks. There were many victims of Dachau—men, women, and children—who spontaneously formed lines, with great dignity and no confusion, to greet him and other soldiers. The raw emotion, the undisguised gratitude, was palpable. Also bushed was Whitey, the squad dog, who had settled into his favorite spot, beneath the truck and behind a tire, to catch a nap, ignoring all the activity around him.

Finally, as night fell and the temperatures did likewise, Hank and the rest of the squad went back to where the jeep and truck were parked in a field near the unfathomable place where they had spent most of the day—hopefully far enough away so they could avoid the odor from the prison—built a campfire and grabbed themselves some food. But they felt guilty knowing how many starving people there were all around them. The captain, still off trying to get word about Captain Bennett and his boys, had not yet returned, so they had no specific orders or word on where they would spend the night. It could well be right there in that field.

Anderson found it difficult to eat. To talk, as well, which was most unusual. Certainly no one was in the mood for the typical good-natured back-and-forth that took place when the squad ate together. The carryings-on that distracted from the stress of a typical day digging out UXBs and disposing of other dangerous scrap. No, what they had seen this day while offering not bomb demolition but humanitarian aid had silenced all of them, sapping their spirit to the point such cajoling had no chance to elevate the mood.

Hank went around to the darker shadows behind the truck to take a leak and was just buttoning up when he felt a touch on his shoulder.

"What?" he growled, startled. First thought was that it was one of the prisoners, emerging from months and years of captivity, emaciated and emotionally scarred, seeking food, a cigarette, whatever it was that symbolized freedom.

"Sorry, Corporal, I didn't mean to scare you."

A female voice. It surprised him. He turned to look at her. Even in the semidarkness, he could tell she was a tall, attractive blonde with a dazzling smile. She wore a GI's herringbone twill cap. He could just make out letters scrawled on its bill with a marker, spelling out the word "PRESS."

"You almost got yourself pissed on," Hank admitted. "Sorry. There being a war going on and all, you can't blame a guy for being a bit skittish."

"Anyway, I do apologize. I'm a journalist and wonder if you'd take a minute and tell me who you guys are and about what you've been doing and what you've seen and heard around here today."

"Who we are?" Hank was most curious about how a woman journalist had gotten here.

"Red fenders on your vehicles and 'BDS' on your windshields say you're bomb disposal, right?" The woman nodded toward the truck and jeep. "But you're not disarming bombs around this place, I don't think."

"No, ma'am. None we've been made aware of anyway. This place is a prison camp."

"So, if you're not here to disarm bombs, what is it you're doing here, if I may ask?"

"We were sent here to help deal with a clean-up of what they told us was an SS training camp. No bombs or mines or booby traps, but we always look anyways. But as you can see, this was no training camp, and whoever said so was dead wrong."

Hank motioned for her to follow him back to the fire and invited her to have a seat on a pile of gear. The others had all left, likely to also answer nature's call or to try to scare up something better to eat than K-rations.

"That fire feels nice." The journalist lady stretched out her legs until her combat-booted feet were near the fire. She leaned back against the truck tire. "I heard there may be snow in a day or so."

"I come from Denver, so I'm fine if I never see another snowflake in my life." Hank did not want to consider the possibility of more cold weather. He promptly changed the subject. "Okay, so it looks like I'm destined to meet every female journalist in all of Europe," he told her, offering her a cigarette. She took it and leaned over to light it on an ember from the campfire.

"What do you mean, Corporal?"

"Anderson. Henry Anderson. My friends call me Hank. There can't be many of you gals covering the war. But I spent most of a nice evening in Paris a while back talking with another gal reporter. Ernest Hemingway's wife."

The woman laughed hard. Was it a moment of hysteria after all she had seen this day? "Hmmm. You did, then? Hemingway's wife, you say?"

"Well, not his current one. I thought at first she was that Gellhorn lady. But I found out they may be splittin' up. She's supposed to be the next one, though. His fourth. Her name is Mary Welsh. She works for *Time* and *Life*. You probably know her, right? Since there's not that many lady reporters over here."

"I know of her." She took a draw or two on her cigarette. "Hank, I'm Martha Gellhorn and I'm covering the war for *Collier's* magazine." There was no hint of irritation or offense in her tone. But it was not the fire that turned Hank's face crimson, so brilliant it was obvious even in the limited light. "Don't worry about it. Folks get his wives and mistresses and concubines and whatever mixed up all the time. I think even he does."

"I am so sorry, Miss Gellhorn. Mrs. Hemingway."

"My byline is 'Martha Gellhorn,' so just call me Martha, okay?"

"Sure...uh...Martha. I read your stories all the time and you are such a great writer. I never in a million years thought that I'd meet you." Hank wanted most to redirect the subject again. "I've been thinking about being a journalist myself once all this shit...this war...is over. Or a news photographer. Or both. Maybe you could do our BD story. Maybe beat that Mary Welsh to the punch."

"Maybe. Maybe I will," she said, flipping the cigarette butt into the hissing fire. "But I've got a lot on my plate right now with some other stories. The one here I have to tell first. All about the bondage and suffering of these people you've been rescuing. What have you seen and heard today?"

"Ma'am, I apologize. You're exactly right. It's awful. I'm still trying to get my head around it."

But Gellhorn was not finished. "There are hundreds of thousands of people like these in other camps all over Europe, I'm hearing. Maybe more." She took another offered cigarette from Anderson from his pack of Army-issued brands. "So many who didn't survive, Hank-from-Denver. Count yourself lucky you were born in the United States and not here. Jesus Christ! It's almost too big a god-awful, insanely wicked story. I've got to tell it. But who will believe me? How can I make anyone, the world, understand and believe what went on here? What we've seen? How can I string together the right words to assure the world never forgets? How do you describe the cells and how bad they are? The stench of death? Did you see the dead? Emaciated, starved to death. And behind them, healthy German bodies. The guards. Nauseating."

"I know I will never understand what happened here." Hank was numbed by what he had witnessed.

"No one will believe us." Her voice had grown louder, more strident. At the end, out of breath, she leaned forward again, coughed, and angrily spat into the fire.

"I know, ma'am. I know." Hank could think of nothing else to say to her.

"I know one thing," she finally said. "If we ever again tolerate such horror as this, we don't deserve peace."

"And that is exactly how you ought to write it, then," Hank told her. "Paint 'em a picture, ugly as it is. You have that gift. The ability to use words and the platform of the magazine where it can be shared and that will be around for others to read for the rest of history. You can go a long way toward letting people know, and in a way they won't ever forget. And nobody can ever deny it happened."

Martha turned and smiled at the corporal. "And since you told me to, that is exactly what I'll do, Hank." A pause. "Say, you don't have maybe a bite to eat. I lost my appetite a while ago, but I think I may have just found it."

"Nothing but K-rations until the field kitchen catches up. All I got is a can of diced ham, and I think that's what gave me a bad case of the squirts the other...oh...sorry, ma'am."

Gellhorn laughed again. A laugh like pleasant musical chimes. How in hell could that Hemingway guy let somebody like this get away?

The rest of the squad was now coming their way out of the darkness. They were unusually quiet.

"I'll take my chances, soldier. I'd eat a dead buzzard off a dung wagon right about now." She glanced up at the returning BD boys.

They stopped, looked curiously at this attractive woman with the fetching laugh. Not at all what they expected to see at their campfire.

She waved at them. "Welcome back, you crazy sons of bitches. Why don't you sit down here with Hank and me and tell me all about this bomb demolition business? And what you've seen here today. Somebody somewhere might want to know."

It may have been Edward's East Pennsylvania–slewed German accent. Or the simple fact that most of the people he encountered—soldier, prisoner, whoever—were near-hopelessly disoriented, confounded, knocked from their orbit by all that had been happening in this place all day. But no one he asked seemed to know anything about Hedley Bennett or any of his squad. That is, until just before nightfall when he approached one dull-eyed inmate, sitting, leaning back against a scraggly tree in a courtyard between two administrative buildings, likely still awaiting a stretcher. He was cocooned in a fatigue-green Army blanket, but his brown-stained teeth still chattered from the chill.

"American soldier prisoners? Have you seen any of them?" He resorted to English. Then to a bit of desperate description that came to him from out of nowhere. "One of them looks like the American actor. Clark Gable."

It was impossible to guess the age of the haggard man. His mental state. To discern if he understood any of what Hume was saying. But when the prisoner looked up, there was an improbable hint of brightness in his eyes. The slightest smile on his cracked lips. His voice was raspy, hardly a whisper, when he spoke.

"Yes. Clark Gable. *It Happened One Night*. Claudette Colbert. I was once a journalist. Like Clark Gable in the motion picture. But I was guilty of writing the wrong truths." The man pulled a skinny arm from the blanket and shakily motioned for something to drink. Edward handed him his canteen. He swallowed all the water in a few gulps, coughed a bit, spat, wiped his mouth with a filthy sleeve, and then went on. "Your American soldier. He and his bomb squad were the last to be sent away with the others on the march toward Austria, to a place called Tegernsee."

"A march? You don't mean like..."

"Yes. The SS. They march so many of us away to other labor camps to do work. Some only recently got here after surviving a march from Buchenwald. And they send them off again so soon with thousands of others so the Allies...you...when you come, you do not see how many were here and how they have been abused. Few will survive such a journey on foot, I fear. There may be snow, even in April. This long after Passover, for us. Easter for you."

"When did they leave? The Americans?"

The man thought for a moment. Time was surely fuzzy for him. "This morning. Yes, it was this morning at first light. They could not have traveled far. So many tired and sick."

"Thank you. Thank you very much." Edward started away, then turned back to the man. "Can I get you anything else, sir?"

That long-unpracticed smile once more. "A night in my bed in Hamburg with Claudette Colbert to keep me warm. If you could arrange such a liaison..."

Edward grinned. "I'm afraid that's beyond the reach of a simple bomb demolition captain, my friend."

"It is okay," the man said. "Beyond the reach of a simple newspaperman from Hamburg as well, I suppose. But the mere thought of such a thing has kept me alive for three years, two months, and…" A pause, then, "…twenty-six days."

This recent prisoner had a much better concept of time than Edward had imagined. The captain gave him a sharp salute and made his way into the descending darkness of a Bavarian evening.

There were times he simply could not believe what he was seeing. Or that he was a miserable part of it. No nightmare had ever been as vivid. A year and a half of war had forced him to view much hurt, danger, suffering, cruelty, inhumanity. But now, on this march from Dachau, skirting Munich, and on to wherever it was they were being herded, the normally optimistic Captain Hedley Bennett quickly became so demoralized, he most wanted to lie down and die peacefully.

Many of the thousands of others trudging along with them did just that, just not voluntarily. They were so sick, weakened, half-dead even before they were herded out the gates at Dachau and ordered not to stop walking until told to do so. Many soon collapsed. Some were left to die where they fell. Others were shot dead. Sometimes their fellow marchers were told to drag the bodies off the roadway and into ditches so military vehicles would not have to run over or steer around them.

At first, Captain Bennett and his squad—now down to three men—would quickly pull fallen but living marchers off the road and into the bushes, hoping someone would find them and have mercy on them. Then a guard saw what they were doing and fired a shot at them, deliberately missing but hitting home with his harsh message.

Bennett obediently waved his men back into line. He knew he needed to stay strong, not lose control now, even if he most wanted to defy the heartless young guard's bullets and charge at him, rip out his throat with his bare hands, and stomp on his body as he once did timber rattlesnakes in East Texas.

But the Allies were getting closer. He sensed it just as surely as he did the scent of evergreens now riding in on the chill breeze. They would be freed soon, even if they were moving still deeper into territory controlled by the Germans. All they had to do was stay alive. Stay alive and not react when an SS soldier stood over a fallen woman in the middle of the roadway and fired several rounds into the patch of scabs on her bald head.

It was almost dark at the end of the first long, soul-sucking day, and they had made it to a point south of Munich, near a town the signs proclaimed to be Sauerlach. The waning sun continued to paint the snow atop the distant high mountains to the south in pastel pinks and yellows. That was when they were abruptly shepherded off the roadway and into a dense stand of trees. Guards moved among them and told them to lie on the ground and sleep for a few hours before it got any colder. And anyone who so much as raised his or her head would be shot dead.

When he was convinced that their herders had moved on, Bennett defied the order, lifted his head, and confirmed no SS were nearby. "Soon as it's dark, we're gonna march our happy asses right back to Dachau," Hedley whispered to his men. "Stick to the woods, stay low, and be quiet as a church mouse."

"Quiet as a what?" Sergeant Tony Gabler asked.

"Never mind. You got my point, Gab."

"No. You must not try to run," someone on the ground nearby offered. "They will shoot you."

"A chance I'm willing to take," the captain responded, far more confidently than he felt.

"Then I guess we are, too," Gabler added.

The four men crawled on their bellies a few feet farther into the woods, until they were behind a thick hedge of hawthorn. They lay there for a moment, fully expecting shouts and shots. There were none.

Slowly, they slithered along the muddy ground, back in the direction from which they had just come. There was plenty of vegetation, so they soon crawled on their hands and knees, then rose to a crouch and made much better progress. After about ten minutes, Hedley motioned for them to stop while he slowly rose up to look around.

There were no prisoners to be seen. But there was an SS soldier ten feet to their right, near the roadway, his back to them, leaning against a signpost, trying to light a cigarette in the breeze.

"*Verdammte Französische treichhölzer!*" the man cursed out loud. "Damn French matches!"

Tony Gabler tapped Bennett on the leg. The sergeant had already taken a string from his boot and showed it to his captain. Bennett gave him a solemn nod.

With only a few silent steps on the thick groundcover, Gabler was close enough to the German trooper to slip the bootstring garotte over the man's M-35 helmet and pull it brutally tight around his neck before he could make a sound. He struggled briefly, tried to pry himself loose with his fingers, but soon collapsed, maybe dead. Gabler continued for another full minute to tauten the string as hard as he could, even when it cut into his own numb fingers, his blood mingling with that from the German's throat. He kept throttling the SS trooper until he felt a hand on his shoulder.

"He's gone, Gab," Bennett quietly told him. "Let's drag him out of sight and go on, okay?"

Then they covered the body with leaves. Even in the darkness, the captain could see tears on his sergeant's face. "It's all right. You did what you had to do, Tony."

"But I ain't never killed a man before."

"That wasn't no man. That was a rattlesnake. A varmint. You think he wouldn't-a happily shot and killed you if you broke out of these woods running away?"

"I know. I know. But still, I could feel his heart beatin' against my chest. And then I couldn't."

They stayed off the roadway itself, keeping to woods on either side, waiting for clouds to cover the half-moon before crossing pastures or other open ground. Bennett figured that with no map they should follow the route they had come down and get back to the camp at Dachau. And pray every step the place would be in Allied hands by now. There was more traffic passing than they expected, too, even after what they estimated to be midnight. Mostly German military vehicles scurrying south, away from what the Bomb Merchants hoped was the Allied advance. But they had no way of knowing. There were no sounds of artillery or bombing. No battle.

Twice they had to dive into the brush when they met another group of camp prisoners being driven their way, even this late and in moonlight. It took a while for the clots of poor, struggling people and their trigger-happy guards to amble past them. The urgency for the Bomb Merchants was to try to get through the northern suburbs of Munich before daylight. That city may or may not be in Allied hands by now. Even the mostly uninformed citizens who lived along the remaining stretch of road to Dachau would immediately know Bennett and his men were American soldiers. Would they remain loyal to Hitler, shoot them or capture them, or turn them in?

Worst case, the Germans were still militarily in charge in Munich and Dachau. They would shoot any Allied soldier on sight. Maybe the rumors the last few days were not true and neither place was even close to being taken by the Allies. The SS sons of bitches could be an obstinate bunch when it came to surrendering. If so, Hedley and his guys would just hide out during the day, then try to get closer to the border, closer to advancing Allies, at night. But they needed to find such a spot before daylight.

The very first bright rays of dawn suddenly fell upon a slight rise in the road only a hundred feet ahead of them. It was as if someone had switched on the lights in a darkened room. A German Panzer tank or a "mule" half-track might abruptly appear there. Or a platoon of enemy soldiers. Or the first of another pitiful pack of marching prisoners being herded along. There was little covering brush, so the captain decided they should quickly find some, then backtrack to find a hole to crawl into.

"Night's over. Hit the ditch, dogies!" Bennett quietly ordered.

But before he could follow his own command, he noticed something odd. Something that made him freeze in place, on his knees beside a hayfield, and watch. The shaft of sunlight illuminated a lone person, a man, just coming over the hill, walking nonchalantly down the damn road as if out on a leisurely morning stroll. Improbably, the guy appeared to be wearing the combat uniform of an American soldier but carried no rifle. No landmine detector. No radio. Nothing.

And as the walker drew closer, Bennett could see the fellow was glancing left and right, actually crisscrossing the roadway in a winding trail from one side to the other.

The sun-anointed soldier appeared to be searching for some lost critter.

. . .

Dr. Ernst Alwin is a very intelligent man. Certainly not delusional, at least in his own estimate. Now, despite his unwavering loyalty to his country and the Nazi Party, to the Führer and all he represents, the scientist has deduced that the war is lost—through no fault of his—and the cause stifled, at least for now. That means he must segue to survival mode.

Many of Hitler's higher-ups have already done so. But some have taken their own lives to avoid imprisonment, torture, guilty verdicts, executions or, worse, lifetime sentences doled out by their vengeful conquerors. Others have left the country, mostly to South America, but Alwin sees that place as the underside of the planet, where one goes to hide, not to prepare to one day once again revive the dream of a German empire that unites Europe, controls the inferior races, and assures a racially pure Aryan society.

No, he will survive this setback by taking steps to convince the Allies that he is willing to cooperate, to share his discoveries in the field of ordnance use and disposal to be deployed against Japan, to be a good boy in exchange for his freedom. After all, the Allies have not won it all. The Japanese continue to fight. The Russians, preoccupied with their own desires to unite Europe under their control, have so far refused to go to war against Japan. Ernst is convinced he can persuade the Allies that his unique expertise can help conclude the war in the Pacific as well.

Again, if he can get before the right people, he can show how his own plans for a "super bomb" could quickly help America bring hostilities with Japan to a fiery conclusion. That should assure that Alwin will remain free and alive, able to unite with other survivors of the Reich's loss and continue the cause. Just look at how they rebuilt the Fatherland after the Great War! And without a few miscues, this outcome would have been much different. The next one will be.

He has abandoned his office at Dachau, sneaking away in the dark of night. There is word that the Allies are negotiating through the Red Cross for surrender of the prison camp there. He knows they will surely take the camp, one way or the other, by the end of April. He has thrown every note and document he can find into the trunk of his car and taken them—along with his family—to his summer home in Tegernsee, overlooking the lovely lake there and with a view of the Bavarian Alps. And now that he is in Tegernsee, the scientist vows to continue in his attic lab as many of his experiments as he can. For the cause. For Father Germany.

Now, he watches out the rear window of his chateau as his children inno-

cently play in the garden below, catching late spring snowflakes on their tongues. The sun is almost down, and he worries the children will become chilled and get sick. But before he can call them inside—Helga is in her room, sulking—he realizes the calendar on the wall still shows April.

It is now May 1.

Such inaccuracy bothers him greatly. He snatches down the calendar, flips the page to the new month, and hangs it back up.

May. May 1945. Much better.

The scientist takes a sip of coffee without tasting it and considers the pile of papers on the desk before him. Having the wrong month displayed on his office wall distracts him. So do the innocent giggles of his children down there in the darkening garden. And the sullenness of his wife, who prefers to be back at their home in Berlin drinking wine with the wives of high Party officials. She does not understand that the Russians will be coming soon, that they are reasonably safe here.

He switches on the radio for the news. It is tuned to the Hamburg station for some reason. He usually prefers the Berlin outlet for its better signal this far to the south.

The first words he hears cause him to immediately go numb. Grand Admiral Karl Dönitz is speaking, making an earthshaking announcement.

Hitler is dead. Killed in battle, a hero, bravely defending Berlin.

Ernst Alwin is an intelligent man. He knows to doubt the reports of how Herr Hitler died. Now, more than ever, he knows he must find a way to be a friend to the enemies—and soon to be conquerors—of the Fatherland.

He far too often suffers the guilt of the blessedly redeemed. The unwarranted but brutally real remorse of a soldier who kneels to tie the string of his combat boot only to have a sniper's bullet intended for him whiz past and cut down the unfortunate man standing behind him instead. The it-should-have-been-me conscience of a sailor, late to meet his assigned submarine, watching from the pier as the boat disappears in the sea mist, only to later learn it has been lost with all hands, sunk by the enemy. The feeling of a fighter pilot, limping back from a

dogfight, the only one from his squad somehow blessed to be able to do so, struggling to rationalize why he survived and they did not.

Private Pete Ronzini knows such emotions are irrational. But life's irrational, too, goddammit!

From his bed on the second floor of the house in which he grew up, he can watch the neighborhood kids play stickball on Senator Street. That only reminds him of Theo, the French kid who took so quickly to the game and died when a vicious UXO reared up and chewed him to death. Now, the Army doc over at Fort Hamilton tells Ronzini a stray germ could—and one day likely would, if he did not keep the wound clean and dressed—find its way into what remained of his scarred and wrecked right lung, make itself at home as surely as the French Resistance fighter's knife blade had, and finish him off, too.

Ronzini's fiancé and his mother took the prognosis to heart at first, fussing over him, not allowing him to stand at the window where a single draft of cold night air might strike him down as surely as a Nazi bomb. Now, not so much. They're busy. Mom's tired and it's hard anymore for her to go up and down the stairs with his meal tray and clean clothes. He even suspects Gina—who no longer talks of marriage or house or family when she stops by—is seeing someone else. Someone who can draw in a deep breath without setting off a coughing spasm and an explosion of sputum. He dares not ask her. She might tell him he's guessed correctly.

Pete gets occasional letters from his fellow Kaboom Boys, though it takes them most of two months to make the trek. Reading between the lines, he knows they could well be in Germany by now and the whole shitstorm is nearing its end. Or not. Hitler has new weapons, like the rockets he continues to rain down on poor Britain. Ronzini knows his buddies cannot say much about what they're doing. Or about his replacement. Morty Schwartz mostly worries about the fate of the missing Jews. Hank Anderson rambles on and on about his trip to Paris and the interesting people he met along the way and his elaborate plans for life after hell. He wonders how Gene and Carl are doing, who won the bet to the Eiffel Tower, and especially about his captain, Edward Hume. Would anyone even know to tell Pete if something happened to any of his brothers back there? Don't they know about the four-walled hell in which he exists?

There are a few old guys from the VFW over on Prospect Avenue who put on their garrison hats and stop by to keep him company sometimes. They mean well but all they want to talk about is their hijinks in the Great War, Yankees versus Dodgers, or whenever the hell FDR is going to quit being president when anybody with peepers can see the man is sick.

So, Pete Ronzini lies here in the same bed in which he slept as a kid, looking at but rarely listening to the same Philco 80C radio on which he had once hung on every word of Red Barber's play-by-play of the first "Subway Series." The 1941 World Series in which his beloved Dodgers fell hard to the hated Yankees after first taking a two-game lead.

He was depressed for weeks. That was one of the reasons Ronzini had ultimately joined the parade of young men his age, went down to the recruiting station, and signed up for the Army. Why he volunteered for bomb demolition duty because it sounded exciting. It even helped that the hated Yankees were sometimes called "the Bronx Bombers." The Japs bombing Pearl Harbor provided the final impetus should any have been required.

Now, instead of once again counting the leak spots on the ceiling or listening to the kids in the street screaming curse words to make themselves feel more grown up, something makes him decide it might be time for him to rejoin the world. And do it before the urge to leave it overwhelms him.

Pete painfully reaches over and switches on the Philco. It's on 1010, WHN. The very first words he hears are that Adolf Hitler is dead. Cause of death unknown, though the Nazis are claiming he died a hero, defending Berlin from charging brigades of invading Russians.

Simultaneously with the staggering news, a bright shaft of sunlight coincidentally illuminates that window that looks out on his tiny slice of Bay Side, Brooklyn. Surely, with Mussolini and Hitler gone, Japan won't try to fight the world alone.

The war is over. Or it soon will be.

Leo Durocher has the Dodgers playing better ball. Some say they might even get to the Series again.

Since she still comes around often and even brings him draft beers from Farrell's Bar, Gina obviously still cares for him. Still wears the cheap engagement ring he gave her before shipping out to basic training.

And just to be sure things are getting better, he sucks in a deep breath of air, holds it half a minute, then exhales. There is no cough.

It's not too late.

For the first time in weeks, he eases off the bed, shuffles over to the window, watches as a kid clubs a Spaldeen down Senator Street, almost all the way to 6th Avenue. Then as an ill-timed lorry makes its way down the roadway, right through the kids' stickball diamond, the youngster who is taking his homerun trot grabs hold of the rear bumper of the truck, pulls himself up, and rides it from second to third, fist in the air, celebrating.

It's not too late to try to live after all.

♠

Royal Air Force Captain Duncan Smythe feels the need to wax philosophically to the minions gathered around the small mustard-yellow cluster bomb darted nose down in the bog. They are near Burgh Castle, west of Great Yarmouth and along the coast. The wind still blows cold off the North Sea, even if it is the first week of May. Smythe has warmed himself with several slugs of single-malt Scotch whisky from the flask he keeps in his jacket, next to his heart. That is another reason he is even more talkative than usual this morning.

This bunch of newcomers to the fray is half Yanks, half Brits, all moist behind the earflaps and scared to constipation now that they realize what they have signed up to do. But it is his task to train them so they can have a better chance of doing the job without becoming bomb fodder.

"Wise ye are to be just as frightened by this here little tyke as ye would be by a two-thousand-pounder, me lads," Smythe tells them. "You'll be just as dead by the bite of an asp as by getting gnawed upon by a sabretooth, got that?"

This is just another of the ten or so of the bomblets they've located so far, likely jettisoned by some Luftwaffe Kraut bombardier years before. Flotsam of war. Evidence of evil that everyone has now come to realize will linger for centuries, to be claimed and neutered by those that are willing and properly educated on such endeavors. Unless somebody who has no idea happens upon one of them in the meantime and pays the price.

"Captain Smythe, why the fuck do you do this?" One of the Yanks. Pink-cheeked kid, sweet breath fogging in the chill. Likely climbed off his hobby horse to dash off and enlist to seek adventure and have himself some war fun. Employing vulgar language now to make himself feel more aged and worldly.

"Cause if I don't, who will? Wonderful way for a chap to do good for his fellow

man." Smythe sniffed, idly scratched his scraggly beard, and turned serious. "Truth is, we do this because the closer to death we are, the more alive we feel."

"Heard that plenty from you old hands, but if you do the job right, you're not close to death at all."

"Beg to differ. You'll encounter fuzes and detonators you're totally convinced you know how to handle, only to discover one way or another that you really don't. They got blokes over yonder where they fly flags adorned with the swastika what spend all day every day figuring ways to fool the likes of you, just so your mother gets you back home like she prays for each night, but in bits and pieces to be buried in a gunny sack."

The kid grins smugly. "I finished first in Major Kane's class at APG. I think I can handle my shit."

Smythe looks hard at the kid. "Overconfidence has killed plenty BD boys already and will kill plenty more long past this war being over. Don't forget to remember that fact, me lad. Even a tiny little yeller device like this one here..."

The RAF bomb disposal man nudges the little rusty, pocked cluster bomb with the scuffed toe of his boot.

It explodes.

27

Carl was first to rise on their second day in Dachau. Born in Greece, raised in Alabama and then California, he maintained he stayed perpetually confused about what time it was. He was stiff and groggy from the cold night spent in the sleeping bag on hard ground beneath the truck. They had decided not to break out the tents for what originally was supposed to be a one-night bivouac.

First thing, Kostas checked to see if Captain Hume had come back sometime during the night. He was nowhere to be seen. Morty was gone, too, but Kostas knew where he was. He was already back inside the camp, trying to help do whatever he could. He told Carl when he left to come get him if they needed him.

But the CO being gone was disorienting. It left the private as momentarily panicked as he had sometimes been when he got raked off his surfboard by a big wave, lost in the roiling water with no in or out, up or down. It reminded him somewhat of what it had been like when Captain was off to Paris. Without their anchor, he had no idea where they were supposed to be or what they were supposed to be doing. Then, standing there in mostly darkness, shivering as he pissed into a bush, he remembered where he was, what wickedness surrounded them in this place, and he had another mild attack of vertigo.

"God bless you for watering the foliage." It was Hank Anderson.

Kostas jumped. "Jesus, Hank. Sneak up on a guy, good way to get your boots pissed on."

"Captain ain't here," the corporal said, joining Kostas in his irrigation project. "Ain't been here all night."

"Guess that puts Morrison in charge."

"In charge of what?" came another voice. Sergeant Jack Morrison, making it a three-way pee party.

"Us, of course. Captain's still off looking for Captain Bennett, I guess," Hank explained. "We don't know where to eat or shit or what to do without orders. And I don't know about you guys, but I need to find a place to eat and shit pretty quick now."

Morrison buttoned up, walked back to the truck, got down on his knees near the front tire, and began to silently pray. Carl and Hank lit cigarettes and stood there, watching him, watching the promise of a blessedly warming sun on the eastern horizon.

"I hope he's asking the good Lord for some sausage and eggs and strong, hot coffee," Hank finally said. "And a close-by latrine or I'm gonna fertilize this foliage while I'm at it."

Morrison stood, dusted off his knees, and turned toward Hank and Carl. "Colonel Sparks and the Third Battalion's supposed to have set up an HQ in one of the SS camp administrative buildings," he said. "I'm to check on what they want us to do today if the captain's not back. Mess tent's going up close to there. It'll have hot grub by now. They should have some latrines set up in that field we passed yesterday near the main gate."

Carl looked sideways at the sergeant. "Did God tell you all that just now?"

Morrison grinned. "Naw, captain told me last night before he left." He paused. He sure hoped the captain had not gone AWOL. The guys had assured him that would never happen, but Morrison did not know him that well yet. "God just told me we're going to have to work hard and be His arms and legs helping His poor creatures here in this god-awful place. So, we oughta get to work, right?"

Anderson looked up at a cloudless sky and gave an enthusiastic salute, followed by a strong, "Yes, sir!" Maybe Morrison was made for this moment, perfect for this job. Maybe there was about to be ample opportunity for him to show it.

Captain Edward Hume was beyond exhausted and weakened. Even to the point of hallucinating. Just out of Munich proper, he mistook a herd of goats in a moonlit pasture for a field full of soldiers, on their bellies, ready to open fire on him. The animals bleated mockingly when Hume dove for the bushes, resulting in painful scratches and thorn wounds. Now, he was no longer sure he was still on the right roadway. The one that led south in the direction the SS were reportedly marching their prisoners, including Hed and his boys. It had been easy early on to confirm. Pitiful bodies of prisoners—most with bullet wounds—had left trails of blood to where they had been dragged off the roadway into ditches or underbrush. They made macabre but effective signposts. Now, he had to keep oscillating from one side of the road to the other, looking for signs he was still going the right way.

The previous day, the squad involved in emotionally taxing rescue efforts at the hellish camp, would have been enough to drain anyone. But then, when he heard that his buddy, Hedley Bennett, and his squad were still alive, that they had been incarcerated there at Dachau, and had been marched off that very day, the captain experienced a powerful injection of energy. He decided not to take the jeep. That would have meant dragging Sergeant Morrison along as his driver, and that would have taken the default leader of the squad away. No, Hume figured, marching away on foot a thousand weak and sick men and women would necessitate moving slowly. They would have to rest and even stop to sleep at night, wouldn't they? He should be able to quickly catch up on foot. At least, he hoped so.

Now, though, with the sunrise impending and with the cold, the fatigue, the horror of the dead people along the roadway, and the raw concern sapping what remained of his emotional momentum, he was about to give up his crusade and head on back. There was more to do back there, including the UXO jobs they were to do in the first place.

Besides, what if he did catch up with the marchers? There would be armed guards, of course. And the only weapons Edward had were his pistol and his pulse-pounding rage.

He would take his chances, he told himself. But only for a few more miles through no-man's-land, well ahead of the Allied advance, putting him still very much in German-controlled territory.

Suddenly, he was blinded by a brilliant blast of sunlight. He stopped, shaded his eyes. And, in the process, saw movement on the roadside. Movement amid a short stand of bramble bushes.

A man, ten feet off the roadway. On his knees. One of the poor prisoners, resurrected? A Wehrmacht soldier, drawing a bead?

"A BD boy worth his salt oughtn't be wandering around in enemy territory!"

Bennett! Jesus! Hume was hallucinating again for sure. But this bleating goat was talking to him about BD boys.

"Hed? That you? I thought I was seeing a ghost!"

"Damn near it."

They embraced, right there in the middle of the main highway that ran from Munich to Tegernsee. Then he had to hug the other men from Bennett's squad. For the moment, there was no war, no enemy, no kinetic threat of death. Just a bright, hopeful sun and the possibility for rescue from hell.

"You owe me a bottle of Jägermeister," Hume abruptly announced. "Even though it is a German beverage."

"No matter. It's still good stuff. Seventy proof, right?" Hedley smiled. "Betcha we can grab a bottle somewhere near the front lines." Hedley could still come up with a quick joke. "So, you show me and my boys the way back to wherever the US Army is and we'll discuss settlin' up, right?" Bennett grinned. "But you know, I mostly just want some K-rations, a chocolate bar and a pack of Lucky Strikes."

Hume just happened to have a standard pack of smokes—four cigarettes—in his jacket pocket. He gave each man one and lit them up.

"Sorry to say I finished off two chocolate bars while I was walking around looking for your sorry asses. Follow me," Edward told him, and struck off, retracing his path back toward Munich and Dachau. He glanced back to be sure they were able to follow. Bushed as they were, they appeared rejuvenated by the cigarettes and such a far-fetched, coincidental encounter in the middle of Bavaria, Germany.

Their only stop for rest was at an apple orchard near a little village called Taufkirchen. There was no fruit, of course. Just the early buds promising a good crop. But as they rested beneath one of the trees, an elderly woman suddenly emerged from the tree line and walked their way. Hume pulled his pistol from its scabbard and placed it between his leg and the ground. She carried a basket they would soon learn was filled with bread, cheese and fresh milk.

With their limited German, Edward and Hedley gleaned enough to determine she had seen from her house the soldiers enter the orchard and settle down to rest. She had no idea at the time if they were German, Canadian, American, French, or what. She just knew they would be hungry, and she was bound to feed them from what little she had to offer. Her son had been conscripted to fight for Hitler, and she had not heard from him in three years, she told them. She only hoped someone would feed him should he be hungry.

When they made her understand they were trying to get back to Dachau, she closed her eyes, frowned and shook her head. "*Böse*," she said. Evil. Somehow, she knew. But she also gave them a route to follow on mostly deserted country roads west of Munich, likely free of any German soldiers, and one that would easily cut five miles off their hike.

Then, with their renewed energy, they were again on the move. But they had only traversed a couple of miles when a sharp voice from the shadows of the thick woods brutally challenged them.

"Halt! *Stoppen!*"

They did just as they were told but braced for incoming bullets. They knew the German troops fleeing from the invasion had little patience for the people doing the invading.

But it was American soldiers who came out of the woods, rifles trained on Hume, Bennett, and the squad.

"The Cards beat the Browns in the World Series," Hedley sang out. "All-St. Louis series this year."

"Roosevelt's wife's name's Eleanor," Edward added. "His middle name's Delano."

"The football Giants play at the Polo Grounds," Sergeant Gabler offered.

There appeared to only be three or four soldiers, still cautiously edging their way from behind their gun barrels. But there could be a whole platoon back in the undergrowth.

"Okay, smart guys," one of the men said. One with sergeant stripes. "Who was the fourteenth president of the US of A?"

Bennett and Hume looked at each other. At the other squad members, who simply shook their heads. "How the fuck we supposed to know that?" Hedley asked. "We're down-and-dirty bomb demolition guys, not historians! Who was it?"

"Hell if I know!" the sergeant answered. "But if you guys hadda come up with an answer, we'd have shot you right damn now!" And that settled that.

Edward and Hedley could now see the Rangers patches on their fatigues. These guys were the elite. They could have just as easily shot them dead and taken stock later.

"So, here's the real question. What the hell you doing stumbling around way out here ahead of the lines. Trying to get shot?" the sergeant queried.

"It's a real long damn story," Bennett responded. "Why don't we tell it to you while you guys escort us back to behind the lines and some hot grub?"

The Ranger leader shrugged his shoulders and agreed, so off they went, with Captain Bennett providing the detailed version of his story. But they had only gone a couple of miles before the sergeant looked back at Hedley and told him, "Captain, with all due respect, sir, if you don't shut the hell up, I'm still gonna shoot your ass."

Hedley glanced over at Sergeant Gabler. "Gab, you taking notes on this man's insubordination? I'd be all for bringing him up on charges had he not just rescued our asses!"

But Bennett did as asked, saving the rest of his story for later as they walked on through a cold but spring day, all the way back to Dachau.

A light snow had just begun to fall as they finally, thankfully approached their destination. Once cleared through the checkpoint—where they eventually left behind some totally confused sentries—Hume,

Bennett, and his squad were taken to a hastily assembled field hospital inside one of the camp's outbuildings. There, they had to sit and wait—and, thankfully, sip hot coffee and eat chocolate bars "like ducks on a june bug," as Hedley described it.

"You didn't get your feelings hurt when that sergeant told you to hush, did you?" Edward asked Bennett.

"Naw, I get it. And I also know it's hard for others to hear about what we've been through. It's just that now that I'm free to talk, I got to or bust."

"Hedley Bennett," Edward said with a grin. "I'm glad you're still able to be you. Look, I've got something for you, and I've been carrying it for months. It's about time you got it. Step in here."

Edward motioned Hedley into a side room just off the bigger room, the triage area for the hospital. He flicked on a light and Hedley immediately started to choke.

"Holy shit, Hed, are you okay?"

"No, man," Bennett managed to say.

There was a pitcher of water and some glasses on a nearby desk. Edward sniffed the water, then stuck his fingertip into it and tasted it. It was fine. Even fresh and cold. Maybe there for staff and patients. He carried a glass to his friend.

Hedley took a swallow. It seemed to help. But he refused to sit in a chair when Edward slid it over to him.

"You okay, Cowboy?"

"I was until we stepped into this room." His voice was still high and tight, shaky, as if he was on the edge of tears. "Then it hit me. I couldn't breathe." Hedley closed his eyes. "Eddie, I'm pretty sure this is one of the rooms where they beat the shit out of me. More than once."

"Sit here. On the desk. I've got something for you that might help you feel better."

Bennett nodded and sat. Edward pulled out of his breast pocket a gold medallion on a chain. "It's from Mont Saint Michel. A nun slipped me an extra one for my mother or a girlfriend when they presented them to the squad. I decided it needed to be yours. Especially now, since it is a recreation of the statue atop the spire, with Archangel Michel, and he's 'the protector of all warriors.' You, my friend, are the fiercest warrior I've ever known. It's yours."

Edward draped the necklace around Hedley's neck. He clasped the medallion in his fist.

"Eddie, I'll wear it proudly."

Then, despite Hedley Bennett's best efforts, the tears came.

EPILOGUE

Edward Hume required medical treatment for the thorn wounds on his face and hands and the huge blisters on both feet from all the walking he did, first in the search for his friend and then the long hike back to Dachau. On the other hand, Hedley Bennett and his surviving squad members were malnourished, dehydrated, and dog tired, but otherwise in surprisingly good health.

"Clean living and happy thoughts," Bennett told the medic examining him. "That's the secret."

"Being made up of ninety percent bullshit helps, too." It was Edward, who had silently stepped into the medical tent to check on his buddy. "We got another bomb cemetery on the other side of Munich we got to go deal with. Real juicy one. I just wanted to drop by and see how you're doing before we take off to once again cheat death."

"Appreciate your concern, sweetheart," Hedley said. "But you from coalmining country. You wouldn't know bullshit if you stepped in the middle of a pile of it. Now us Texans—"

"You're as much a Texan as I am Japanese, don't forget."

"Once you been baptized in the waters of the Brazos River at Waco, you are a true son of the Lone Star State." Hedley was determined to maintain his typical bravado to look good for his CO and his squad despite his battered body. The two men shook hands. "The colonel told us to take it easy for a few days and they'd get us some more guys to round out the squad, get us back full strength. Ordnance disposal has done lost a captain or two lately, mostly due to some more of those trick fuzes. That means there's some BD boys on the loose that could come in and reinforce those of us who've cheated the Grim Reaper so far." Then a thought occurred to Bennett. "Look, they found a pulse on me and I'm peeing piss and not blood, so why don't I go along with you on this mission? You look like you could use some help. I'm not dead yet, so I'm not done yet."

Hume had long, deep scratches on his face from the thorn bush encounter. And he was limping noticeably on his raw, blistered feet. He appeared almost as tortured as Hedley. But it was obvious his buddy wanted to be back in the saddle.

"I'd never turn down help, even from the likes of you," Edward responded. "Let your guys rest, though. We're only one short of a full squad now. Clear it with the CO and I'll swing by and get you when we're loaded and ready. Hey, this'll give us a chance to talk about the next wager for you and your squad to lose, too. Don't forget you owe us a bottle of that nut wine."

"Don't imagine you'll allow us the opportunity to forget it, regardless of our recent experiences. I figured the new bet might involve the Brandenburg Gate, though. In Berlin. First BD squad there with photographic proof. This time for something that don't taste like kerosene and burn a man's tonsils going down. Maybe a cask of good German lager."

Edward grinned and nodded. "You're on, Cowboy. Now, we got UXOs to dismantle and UXBs to defuze before they blow up half of what's left of continental Europe. With the exception of this particular garden spot, I kind of like the place. Reminds me of home even if we're lacking the Alps in our backyard back in PA."

"'Saving democracy one bomb at a time.' Ain't that what you always say, Captain Hume?" Bennett responded.

The medic had been standing there, syringe in hand, mouth open, listening to the conversation in disbelief. The young man finally shook his head and said, "You guys are crazy."

"Doc, you ain't the first to make that medically accurate observation," Bennett told him.

"Nor will you be the last," Hume added.

An hour later, as Edward and the squad pulled up at the main gate to pick up Hedley Bennett, they found him standing there amid all the disorder talking with a familiar figure.

"I think you guys know my friend here," Bennett said. "Józef Steiner, 'The Blacksmith of Dachau.'"

Steiner stood there, a duffel bag at his feet, wearing new, clean clothes, but looking only slightly healthier than he had when the Kaboom Boys found him sitting on his filthy bed in a squalid cell coddling that piece of cloth. Everyone greeted him. He smiled and nodded.

"Where you headed?" Edward asked him.

"I could stay here. The Red Cross offers a place where it is warm, with food and clean beds. And the Allies want to talk with me about the conditions here, my work with the bombs. But..."

"You're leaving, aren't you?"

"Yes. I am leaving this place."

"But where will you go?" It was difficult for Edward to imagine this frail man being up to traveling any distance. Or having anything left to return to.

"If I wait, they promise me a train ticket to my hometown in Poland once the war ends. But the Russians, they tell me, are there now, and I am not convinced they are much better than the Nazis. I will go to Munich. I can find work. I have smithed for some people there before. And besides —" He had to catch his breath. Just that much talk seemed to have taken all the air Steiner had to devote. He paused. The engines of the BD vehicles idled. There was frenzied activity all around them. A crow cawed enthusiastically across the nearby parade field, at the edge of the dark woods, near the spot where the Kaboom Boys had so recently watched American troops execute SS soldiers.

Edward finally spoke. "How can we help you, Józef? We are, as you put it, 'brothers of the boom,' after all."

Steiner nodded. "There is someone there in Munich that I must find."

"Climb into the back of the jeep, next to Anderson there. We're going right through Munich. We'll be happy...proud...to drop you off."

At his nod, Schwartz and Kostas grabbed Steiner's duffel and tossed it into the jeep. It was surprisingly light even though it likely held all the man's possessions. Then they helped him into the back seat. Hedley Bennett rode in the truck.

Munich had suffered mightily from Allied carpet bombing—saturation attacks designed to accomplish maximum destruction in a designated area —and especially in the past year. Edward had once asked a bomber pilot during a poker game why this particular city was being so hard hit. There was no major manufacturing going on there. No big military targets either.

"Think about it, Captain," the pilot had told him. "Where did the Nazi Party originally get its start back in 1918? The same place that bastard Hitler kicked off all this madness. Propaganda, that's why we hit it so damn hard. Same reason we dropped all those incendiary bombs on Hamburg. And hit Berlin day and night when we got to where we could. By then, we were mostly bombing rubble. We were trying to get the people to rise up against the Nazis. The high-ranking officers, too. Of course, we caused plenty of 'em to rise up, all right. Rise right on up to heaven."

"All I know is you guys are leaving plenty of duds over there," Edward told him. "Guess who draws the short straw and gets to go neutralize the damn things."

"Better you than I, Captain. I just drop 'em like a chicken laying an egg. You can have 'em after that."

Edward glanced back to look at Józef as they rode through the old part of the city, now mostly ruins. There were tears on his cheeks. It had certainly occurred to the man that the person he sought here might be among the thousands killed in the bombing. Or, more likely, had fled the city long before.

Just then, they approached what appeared to be a temporary bridge across a river. A sign indicated it was the Isar. Steiner leaned forward and gently put his hand on Edward's shoulder. Edward noticed it trembling even more than before.

"Here! I will stop and get out here!" he said. His voice quaked just as noticeably.

At Edward's direction, Jack pulled to the side of the mostly deserted street. Men in both vehicles picked up their rifles and looked about nervously. There could still be German snipers or other stragglers here.

Meanwhile, Steiner jumped from the jeep before they had even come to a dead stop.

"Józef? Are you sure? This person you're looking for, she—" Edward again started, hesitated, then continued as delicately as he could. "She may be—" Edward stopped himself again from saying that the woman might be dead. "Well, you know, she may be hard to find," Edward finally said.

"There are close to a million living souls in Munich," Hank offered from the back seat. "At least there were before we..." His voice trailed off.

Steiner did not appear to be listening anyway. There was the slightest smile on his dry, cracked lips now as he looked down to the river below, to a small park, to a stand of trees on the far bank. His eyes remained bright. It was as if he saw something that was not there. Or something only he could see. And that he had been in this place and had seen it before.

"I will start here. I will find her," he said.

"If you don't?" asked Morty.

"And if I don't, I will have done something I often doubted would ever happen. I will have survived long enough to look for her." He pulled something from the pocket of his new, clean Red Cross–issued trousers. It was the dingy, tattered, blue scarf. The one with the name stitched on it. The one they had seen Józef clutching as he waited for rescue inside the camp. "But she is here. God tells me she is here, and He has told me that I will find Birgit Franz."

Edward hopped from the jeep and shook Steiner's hand. The Blacksmith's grip was now surprisingly strong and steady.

"I certainly hope so," Hume said. "Good luck, my friend."

"*Shalom*, Captain Hume," Steiner told him. "And remember, *shalom* in Hebrew means not only 'goodbye' but also 'hello.' And it means 'peace,' too."

"Then *shalom*, Józef Steiner, and I say it in every meaning of the word." Edward was saddened to see Steiner go but knew it was the only thing he could or should do.

Hedley joined Hank in the back seat of the bomb squad jeep as they drove on toward the day's perilous mission. No one spoke until they were a mile or two from where they had dropped off Steiner, not far from the latest bomb cemetery.

"You guys really think he'll find her?" Bennett asked.

"Not a chance," Hank offered at once. "A million people?"

"I hope he does," Edward said, after thinking about it for a short moment. "But it's such a long shot. Anyway, just the thought of her kept him going all this time. We should all be so lucky to have someone like that in our lives."

"With all due respect, Captain," Hank Anderson offered, "you do. That nurse lieutenant of yours."

Hume smiled. "I guess you're right, Corporal. Thanks for the reminder. We all need a reminder sometimes that we got plenty to live and fight for."

They rode on for a bit, past more bombed-out ruins, shell-pocked roads, dangling, interrupted bridges, and hollow-eyed townspeople who looked with only mild interest and no apparent emotion at the conquering Americans as they zipped past.

"He *will* find her!" Jack Morrison suddenly, forcefully opined.

"And how can you be so sure, Sarge?" Hank asked, honestly curious.

"Didn't you hear what he said?"

"What was that?"

Morrison took his eyes off the narrow roadway just long enough to look back at Anderson. "God told him he would."

The Blacksmith of Dachau had provided all of them—but especially Hume—with an inspiring example of resolve rewarded. One Edward would often employ when things seemed too daunting to overcome, and he needed a reason to persevere.

And it occurred to Edward as they neared the next cache of people-killing ordnance that this was an outlook from which the bulk of Europe might now benefit as it finally emerged from hope-stifling, brutal war. Maybe soon, too, in the Pacific.

The image: the long-suffering Józef Steiner, freed in both body and spirit, a man who had once pondered ending his earthly misery by purposely crossing wires inside a death device, now disappearing into the mist and trees along the singing river, marching off into the heart of Munich to the music of songbirds, a broad smile on his face and happy tears on his cheeks, unbroken, unbowed, moving on to a new life—yes, an uncertain life—but one that, despite all he had been through, now promised him abundant purpose and hope.

Toiling, rejoicing, sorrowing,
Onward through life he goes;
Each morning sees some task begin,
Each evening sees it close;
Something attempted, something done,
Has earned a night's repose.

Thanks, thanks to thee, my worthy friend,
For the lesson thou hast taught!
Thus at the flaming forge of life
Our fortunes must be wrought;
Thus on its sounding anvil shaped
Each burning deed and thought.

From "The Village Blacksmith" by Henry Wadsworth Longfellow.

Goodnight from Berlin
A Call to War Book 3

A gripping tale of moral courage in the shadow of victory—where the end of war begins history's most perilous reckoning.

With Hitler's suicide marking the end of the Third Reich and chaos consuming a shattered Germany, Captain Edward Hume continues to lead his bomb disposal squad—The Kaboom Boys—through the deadly aftermath of victory. What began as a coal miner's son seeking adventure far from Pennsylvania has become a mission to save lives in a world still bristling with unexploded ordnance and Nazi "werewolf" fighters who refuse to surrender.

Their work grows deadlier each day—while other soldiers celebrate, Hume's men face booby traps and ticking bombs left behind by a crumbling Reich.

Then comes the mission that will define them all: Hume is ordered to escort Dr. Ernst Alwin, an evil but brilliant Nazi scientist, now a prisoner, who spent the war designing weapons specifically to kill Allied bomb disposal experts, across war-torn Europe to America.

Racing through a landscape of devastation with the very man who tried to kill soldiers like him, Hume confronts impossible choices. His best friend faces accusations of treason at Dachau. The Nuremberg Trials demand his testimony about the horrors he's witnessed. And somewhere in the chaos, an Army nurse from Normandy waits for his return—if he survives the gauntlet ahead.

ABOUT ELAINE HUME PEAKE

Elaine Hume Peake was born on Aberdeen Proving Ground in Aberdeen, Maryland, the site of the first United States Army Bomb Disposal testing and training base. Here her father, Captain Edward Hume learned the fundamentals of BD and became part of the first American army ordnance squads of World War II, setting the stage for the origins of the historical drama series, "The Kaboom Boys".

Elaine studied journalism/mass communications at Towson State University leading her to a multi-year career in television news. She received multiple journalism awards including Emmys and the George Foster Peabody Award for her 9/11 coverage.

Elaine lives in Leiper's Fork, Tennessee with her husband Christopher where she writes and has been enjoying life with their precious golden retriever Lucia.

Sign up for the reader list at

severnriverbooks.com

ABOUT DON KEITH

Don Keith is a native Alabamian and attended the University of Alabama where he received his degree in broadcast and film. He has received awards from the Associated Press and United Press International for newswriting and reporting. He is also the only person to be named Billboard Magazine "Radio Personality of the Year" in two formats, country and contemporary. Keith was a broadcast personality for over twenty years, owned his own consultancy, co-owned a Mobile, Alabama, radio station, and hosted and produced several nationally syndicated radio shows.

His first novel, "The Forever Season." received the Alabama Library Association's "Fiction of the Year" award. Keith has written extensively on historical subjects including World War II, submarine warfare, and fiction, biographies, and non-fiction works on a variety of subjects. He has published more than forty books, two of which—HUNTER KILLER and COLORS OF CHARACTER—have been adapted for the screen.

Mr. Keith lives with his wife, Charlene, in Indian Springs Village, Alabama.

Sign up for the reader list at
severnriverbooks.com

Printed in the United States
by Baker & Taylor Publisher Services